Flowers Wilt, Weeds Thrive

Book 1 of The Scorned World

Brian Wood-Koiwa

FLOWERS WILT, WEEDS THRIVE

For information contact :

http://www.urbanweird.com

Book cover design by Alexander von Ness

ISBN: 979-8-9928137-2-2

First Edition: June 2025

10 9 8 7 6 5 4 3 2 1

This novel is dedicated to my husband and our four-legged children who put up with the morning disappearances to the café and to The City and Its creators It created

I *The City muse in infinite chaos haunted by tangled sinew of wire, glass, and cement in wrathful battle, plunging with excruciating electric ecstasy into the benthos of shadow-drowned alleys up through the decadent firmament ruled over by demigods cloaked in clouded penthouses. I The City behemoth feed—no, thrive—on the surfeit of delirious sacrificial offerings from my parasitic dwellers. I The City, limitless, am the parental creature of all things, observing with ambivalent interest and unblinking un-intent. But ... do I The City dream?*

I The City hoard memories with hushed paranoia, looming with a god's disdain over the eagerly distraught—sightless, wordless but never not hearing. My impervious meshwork of walls—hegemonic, parsimonious, panoptic—vault the rationale of scorn and recluse denial deep within the fossilized innards while voicelessly, eyelessly weeping thin torments of forgetting that pool into obsidian lagoons slick with forfeited selves looking back hopeless.

one

MIMI HAD TO KEEP running. Her quick, shallow breaths from exertion of fleeing the scene of her crime and the occasional bursts of laughter, deadened her to the thunka-thinka and melancholic groans of the viscerdenn racing parallel to her toward Pinku Station and her home turf of Deko-cho. The beast-machine mass transport klickity-klacked sighed from its late rush-hour load of commuters futilely attempting to forget their chronic disease of corporate drudgery. She had to keep running or get caught and killed. She stole a glance behind her. *Those goons are not slowing down.*

Mimi's peripheral vision registered streaks of buzzing neon litter forming her own private tunnel of melted city as she continued running. The only break in the electric tunnel was a Wamono cloister in the distance devouring light for 40 blocks. She would be safe at home but only long enough to say bye to her bestie, co-worker, and roommate. A hit order on her would soon go out to her Dekora sisters once they learned what she had done. She didn't care. It was the smartest thing she had done in a long time, probably ever.

She finally went rogue and very public killed a prized Tsudii Storyliner inside a grimy, greasy ramen shop reeking of an unsanctioned abattoir. The smell of putrefying murdered innocence had made her puke a little into her mouth before she set her eyes on her target. The killing of a person—no matter how far a Storyliner was from one—was part of a normal workday for her. But this was different. She had not only broke the current kill-for contract between the Dekora and Tsudii but worse killed a Storyliner, which until about 30 minutes ago, had been strictly forbidden. She would have both organizations after her head.

The cutting city wind crusted the blood splatter that speckled her cheeks and forehead. She hoped there weren't Storyliner bits on any of her teddy kill totems; they were a bitch to clean. She made a sharp turn down a familiar, narrow alley of ramshackle cubicles of tiny gei-boi chat bars stacked on top one another and held together by cracking concrete, blackened from generations of urban slime. Most wouldn't fit more than six patrons, catering to every body type and fetish one could think of.

She crouched behind a dumpster, took a few deep breaths, and leaned her head back to gaze up at the façade dripping over her. She wished she was up there gossiping about who was sleeping with whom. She tried not to breathe in too much of the back alley stench. The orange and purple neon sign manically dying her jet-black hair let passersby know that gachimuchi—chubby muscular men with a fondness of facial and body hair—were welcome at "Gachirakudo". Despite having none of these characteristics and obviously the wrong sex, the Dekora and the bois of Ni-cho have always embraced a vigorous cross-pollinating nightlife.

She peeked around the corner, her eyes following an emaciated man coming up behind his much larger companions struggling to catch their breaths. His face glowed a chemical orange from a flat device he was frantically scribbling onto.

"Of course, an Illustrator." She tucked her head back behind the dumpster.

"She wath jutht in front of uth," one of the goons said to the Illustrator.

Mimi giggled and took another peek. The lisping giant wasn't too mixi-matchied like most of his kind, just the usual over-pumped muscle. *Hope I don't have to kill Lispy. He sounds cuddly.*

A couple years ago, it would have been an adrenaline rush to see Tsudii (or their rival Suriidii) blood splattered by her newly skilled hands. But she had found herself becoming one of those commuter drones on the viscerdenn. The only difference was that she was considerably more bloodstained. This terrified her more than those oafs around the corner on a mission to rip her apart.

She watched the Illustrator frantically scribble on his glowing device, ignoring the two bodyguards. He was probably a few steps ahead, figuring out what he should have them do next.

That's messed up. She didn't know much about how the whole Tsudii system of terror worked, but she knew that Illustrators somehow controlled their mentally stunted Character bodyguard/henchmen charges. She had to believe those slow-witted boulders of muscle had to have some remaining thread of their previous humanity.

"She disappeared," said the other Character without any endearing speech impediment.

Spiked protrusions ran down this one's back and arms. *Would be popular with those mixi-matchi fetish fucks down on Joy Street.*

The three pursuers looked north toward the electric pink aura spewing out of Deko-cho into the perpetual grey of everywhere else. The Illustrator finally spoke as he glowered toward the dirty pink static, his voice matching his death-shroud stature. "If it were up to me, I'd have every one of those whores exterminated."

"Yea? Well lucky for us, that ain't gonna happen." She reached into an inside pocket of her faux-fur bolero and grabbed her custom-made mini decapitator sheathed in ultra-strong white ceramic and decorated with pastel peach, pink, and blue dancing kittens. The sudden movement scattered the horde of cockroaches that had gathered around her just outside the neon glow. She had paid a lot for the one-of-a-kind weapon, so she had to give it a name; Lucky Kitty Decapitator, eventually shortened to Kitty D.

She snapped her head around the corner, pigtails whipping her face. She pressed the hidden button to unsheathe Kitty D's deadly blade, making the weapon nearly three times the size of its unready state. She gave the blade a good-luck peck before flinging it into the Tsudii posse. The uber-thin blade whispered past Lispy before finding the Illustrator's barely-there neck. Kitty D made a 'fwwa' as it sliced through his grey skin, sinew, and twig of a spine.

The Illustrator collapsed instantly, his papery head landing seconds later between Lispy's massive feet, its face frozen in the same hateful expression as when it was looking toward Deko-cho.

The two Characters looked down at their dead handler then each other. Without uttering a word or even a grunt, they turned and walked back toward the ramen shop, as if sleepwalking.

Mimi made a pouty face. *Shit!* I *wanted to hear Lispy say something again.* She looked down at her prized teddies hanging around her waist. "Have to get two more of you little bears after tonight's fun-ness. She walked over to the decapitated Illustrator to retrieve Kitty D, which was submerging in the widening slick of the freaks' coagulating, inky blood. She stood mesmerized by the schizophrenic reflections cast from the city's neon onto the bodily fluids. Glops clung to the blade. She picked it up with only her thumb and forefinger, not wanting any of the blackish blood and grey bits of flesh to stain her clothes. She kicked the headless corpse. She grabbed a corner of the dead Illustrator's blazer and wiped the gore from Kitty D. "Ech! Disgusting!" Her face contorted like a precious child forced to touch a slimy fish. "Cheap-ass synthetic material. Figures."

She looked up to Gatchirakudo. She imagined sipping on her favorite drink and getting a good dose of the day's gossip. But she felt gross. She decided to head home instead to scrub and scrape off the stubborn bits of kill. Her steps were light, almost in a skip. "I very well may die tomorrow. But on now on my terms."

The chill felt like it could summon invisible needles up from underneath Yuuki's skin. Each one ready to pierce his flesh and even into his kimono. His body heat spirited away into vaporous puffs, casualties in the incessant war with the cloister dank. The trickster steam trails led him to an all too familiar door, the other side of which resided judgment and disappointment.

Yuuki's memory had lost the exact number of summons he'd received from the Master of the Cloister. He was the only novitiate regularly summoned by the Master. Most others when they transgressed were sent directly to the permanently foul-mood Disciplinarian. Everyone knew why Master Kugai provided his favorite novitiate this fatherly buffer. Yuuki was pure in the Master's worry-reddened eyes.

The door was ajar. The shard of anemic light escaping the cell sliced up through Yuuki without warmth. The frayed hem and drooping sleeves of his novitiate kimono whispered along the rough stone floor as he entered the Master's unimpressive cell. He knew the reason behind this latest summons. He had learned the most tangible morsel of knowledge of the outside yet, its real name, and it was worth whatever punishment Master Kugai and old Disciplinarian Hégo could concoct for him.

Master Daiso Kugai stood behind his desk. The persistent dim allowed only a silhouette of his presence. "For all of Gou's Retributions, Yuuki, where is your head?! What did you ask Ren Danshu-sensei, exactly? Do not shrug off your offense like you often do ... or lie". The flush of Kugai's face, scarred by responsibility, almost matched the rough maroon streaks through his long, thick dreadlocks. The hair engulfed that face like tentacles of a soul-thieving kraken. "I know when you are lying," he dropped off into a mumble, "which is most of the time." Kugai placed his palm onto the desk, putting all the weight of his sigh onto it.

Yuuki sucked in a large gulp of the heavy air, inflating his barrel chest. The contrast with the deflated form of the Master was evident to both. Yuuki's arms remained crossed with hands exposed in rude defiance, instead of respectfully tucked into their opposite sleeves. He also refused to humbly glance down and to the left. He was the only monk, novitiate or senior, who dared take such a casual stance in the presence of the Master of the Cloister. Being considered unsullied by the Scorned World outside the cloister had its advantages. All others had experienced violence and chaos before joining—escaping to—the Wamono Order.

"Tell me. Now!"

Yuuki had never seen the Master so angry. *I have the right to be just as angry.* His hands balled into fists so tightly the blood was forced up into his arms.

Kugai locked his arms in a knot, which moving up and down in cadence with his struggling chest. "You are too smart for your own good. Now sit!" He unknotted his arms and stretched one out toward the only chair in the cell.

Yuuki hesitated before obeying. Picking one's battles had become second nature over his entire cloistered life; his entire life. He kept his eyes locked on the Master's and decided to finally answer Kugai's question. "I asked Ren Danshu-sensei what the real name of Keibu-yo was. It is Hi-"

"Do not even form your brain matter around that damnable name!" Kugai thrust his hand to within a fingernail's length of Yuuki's face.

Yuuki fought the urge to snap a bite of the skeletal digit. A more lasting wound would be to heretically weaponize the true name of the taboo outside instead of the whispered 'Keibu-yo'. He let a short stream of air exhale though his nose. *'Scorned World'. Stupid name.*

He was the only one in the cloister, and possibly the entire Order, who needed to ask such questions. This latest transgressive acquisition of knowledge seemed different. Could he be finally banished from this stone world for good? Was that even possible?

Kugai swooped his bird-of-prey face down to meet Yuuki's. He uncannily yelled without shouting, "Nothing of that diseased world should be discussed. How many times do we have to go through this?" Kugai straightened, his face slacking, consumed by fatherly fatigue.

Kugai had effectively been his father ever since he had been found at the cloister's only entrance as an newborn. The community of monks thought it a miracle the baby hadn't ended up as fleshy detritus between the fangs of the Shisa Reincarnate guardians. The newly appointed Master had known immediately that this infant was destined to become one of them, a Wamono.

"I have to reprimand Ren Danshu-sensei for breaking his vow of never discussing the outside abomination. I'll have sentence him to judgment by the Shisa.

He could very well have his current cycle of existence cut short because of your selfish quest for useless information." It was the instructor's first transgression. He could keep it between him and Danshu instead of the drastic punishment. He strained back up and walked to the other side of his desk, his back to Yuuki. "Only Gou-Tairei knows what unfortunate form he would be assigned in his next cycle if he were to fail the judgment. You want that on your conscience!"

Yuuki didn't want gentle absent-minded Danshu to go on trial for his forbidden probing. *Old Danshu is loved by everyone. The Shisa have to take that into consideration.* His intense defiant stare faded.

Kugai exhaled a cloud of resignation and turned around to face Yuuki, his beaded dreadlocks tumbling over his face. The weight of the massive mound of hair forced his head to bow. Yuuki imagined how warm his head would be if not forced to keep the novitiate buzz cut.

Yuuki could barely see the face of his accuser, only a slumped silhouette. The light from the only window high above the desk avoided the still figure. He stopped twisting his binding ribbons for a second when he thought he heard the tired shadow forming words. Nothing. Only the whispered breathing of an exhausted elderly man.

Kugai's hands strayed into the small shard of meager late-afternoon sunlight slicing across the desk. The jittery hand was not severed by the light but by the sharp shadow that cut into everything, and everyone. "I know you are curious, and I understand." Kugai's anger died away as he put all his weight back onto that bodiless hand. "You are fortunately not like the rest of us; tainted by what stalks life out there. The first week or so of your life you spent out there is far less than any of us have suffered. You should appreciate not having had the experience."

Yuuki pictured the Master's rheumy eyes looking decades back to a painful time. *Is he finally going to give up and tell me of the world outside?* Yuuki straightened his torso and tightened his haunches in anticipation. He decided to take a chance and push the old monk closer to a precipice below which the entire forbidden world would unfurl. He had to do it with care. He was more than old enough to know what he needed protection from or at least decide if protection was needed.

Kugai re-emerged from his past and stiffened into the present, adjusting his ice-blue silk cravat and tucking it back into his immaculate kimono. "We have been through this many times." The hem of his kimono trailed behind brushing against the floor as he moved away from the desk. His hidden bare feet slapped against the damp stone, a hushed conversation amongst floor, cloth, and feet.

"And I have never received a logical response." Yuuki was out of line, made audible from the Master's grumbly sigh.

Kugai scraped the lichen skin from the wall and stared at the residue trapped under his long fingernail. "Who gifted you to us is *still* yet a mystery, Yuuki." Kugai released a humored grunt. "Apparently, those few days were long enough for you to constantly complain of the cloister chill. How do you know it is no less cold out ...." He lifted a shaking hand, pointing a scathing finger. "There?"

"Gifted me," Yuuki mumbled. He had heard it many times before, but the dulled edges of that word still wounded. He slapped his foot down on the floor. "I was thrown away!" The childish outburst embarrassed him.

Kugai placed each hand inside the billowing laced maw of its partner's sleeve without as much as a draft disturbing the velvety cloth. "You are correct. I am sorry for treating you as if you are still a child running around the corridors pestering everyone you encounter."

Yuuki didn't trust his perception of a nostalgia-softened voice.

"But this is no excuse." Kugai returned to the stern role of Master of the Cloister. "It does not matter what is out there or even what happened to you or your family. As difficult as that is to hear. You are a Wamono. You have always been one. None of us, not even me or the oldest of our Reincarnates can say that."

Yuuki refused to look at the Master, instead focused on his metal charm bracelet. It was the only proof of his micro-life on the other side. The smooth metal flower charm began to warm from the friction of his thumb and fingers. The older monks told him the bracelet was most likely from his parents who had carefully placed it over his chest after placing him in the simple wooden box he was found in; hence, the archaic Wamono word for 'flower', *Hana*, was attached to his name. The cloister exorcists performed their rituals to cleanse the potentially dangerous object instead of destroying it as they would any other artifact a fresh recruit came in with, including clothing. It was a rare instance of sentimentality overcoming caution.

He continued staring down at the charm waiting for Kugai, hardly listening to the story that never changed. He didn't know what kind of flower the charm represented. He didn't want to know anything real about it. He needed the fantasy.

Kugai's expression returned to empathetic. "You must have faith, Yuuki-Hana, that your mother, father, or whoever had good reason to leave you at our entrance twenty years ago."

Left to be devoured by those ravenous Shisa. He thought of the hundreds—maybe thousands—of more unfortunate, tasty infants that might have been left at the entrances of all the cloisters. It stabbed at his guts. "I deserve to know what I am being saved from. I am not asking to go outside the walls. I am simply curious."

"You deserve nothing!" Kugai slammed his foot on the wet floor. Empathy gone. "Stop fiddling with that bracelet. I do not want to hear one more thing about how miserable you are here. You have no idea what misery is!" He bent down and stared at Yuuki again, forcing him to look up from his wrist. "You are here. You must live by the Wamono rules, your rules, and be grateful you are in this sanctuary—alive. You are almost an adult, act like one."

I am an adult. Yuuki's eyes narrowed into a hard, hateful stare, his hands tightened back into fists.

"Go see Daiso Hégo-sensei for your punishment. We are done here." Kugai waved his boney hand as if shooing a pesky fly.

"Yes, Sama." Yuuki bowed with head slightly left and downwards toward the floor and turn around without taking a step, as prescribed when leaving the presence of the Master of the Cloister or any other high superior.

He walked out of the glacial cold of the cell into the simply frigid of the corridor, fists still clenched and vision blurred with the fertile seeds of tears. "Knowledge is no loner enough. I have to get out."

He had dragged himself several meters along the abrasive wall. He wanted wounds to justify his tears, but his kimono was too much of a defense. He had the urge to untie his binding ribbons and strip off his kimono, to be naked not Wamono. But who would he be?

He let his head feel the wall. "Why do these stones not feel the way it should … normal?" He craned his neck to stare up the wall. He waited, hoping, for an edifying response, but stone doesn't have the burden of explanation. *There is no choice in what we are born into, and I had that un-choice, twice.* The cloister walls were as much his parents—his family—as Kugai and more so than whoever his real parents were. But like all parental figures, they often disappointed. "What is choice when I never had the choice of me?"

A faint vocal gurgling bubbled from the wall near Yuuki's ear. "Please, do not fret not-so-little Yuuki-Hana. This entity we call Yuuki-Hana is who you are. He is who you are no matter what you are."

"Engyo Ibura-sama? Were you listening in the whole time I was in there?" He didn't hesitate to use the formal honorific, "sama" with his ancient friend. It felt deserved.

"Yes, I am sorry to say, I have." The bile-hued fungal slime Reincarnate's amoebic protrusions crept nearer to Yuuki's ear, measuring the minute changes in the atmosphere and, more importantly, the mood of the young novitiate. "Ears are rather inefficient listening devices. Fortunately, I have none."

Yuuki almost hugged the seeping wall to catch the tiny words bursting forth from the hundreds of micro bubbles forming and quickly dying on the Reincarnate's semi-transparent formlessness. "Are you going to lecture me too?" The breeze of his pheromonal frustration whooshed over the gentle slime, signaling the wise Reincarnate the emotional state of the young monk.

"I believe you have had a sufficient amount from Dogen Kugai-sama and am certain more will come from Daiso Hégo-sensei." Yuuki imagined his friend with a tiny smile.

"Master-sama does have a point, Yuuki," the Reincarnate bubble-spoke. "The world exterior has no place interior. You despise the barrier walls, I know, but they protect you and of course provide me, along with our other diminutive residents, with a means of movement and nourishment."

"Protect me from what? None of my questions are ever answered. Even questions about you and the other Reincarnates." He blew a teasing breath making the sentient goo retract. He didn't expect an answer.

"My past lives are of no matter. However, I will privy you a little secret."

A tiny annoying voice in the back of Yuuki's mind told him not to get too excited. He ignored it as always. He leaned in even closer to his friend. He could taste the salty stone tears that magnetized to his lips.

"I do not remember my past lives," the Reincarnate bubbled. "Just as you have not yet remembered who or what you were in your past lives. If you had any, that is. It will only come—"

"With time and wisdom." Yuuki sighed, letting his temple thud against the stone after finishing the favorite Reincarnate phrase.

"Yes, time and wisdom, which requires patience above all," the Reincarnate repeated. "I may never have the privilege of the knowledge of myselves past. I would not want to. There is a psyche-maiming danger in that. We have thousands of degrees between knowing nothing and everything of ourselves. We have no need—no life-sustaining need—to comprehend all that had happened to us to understand who we are at this stage in our cycles. You learn more through patience, in having the will of knowing what you can know, and in living your best current life than futilely attempting to obtain answers to every query about your worlds."

"But I would sometimes like at least one or two questions answered."

"You need to know what questions to ask: a future-orientated endeavor. Knowing about the outside, of your very brief uncloistered past, will not guide you to these ends. Knowledge is not in receiving answers alone." Yuuki nodded and started picking at the black moss clinging to life between the cracks in the wall. "Start asking questions about the inside, and I do not mean within this physical stone structure. Seek answers that you have the power to answer. Now go along before you incur yet another punishment for being late."

Yuuki clasped his cold-numbed hands and bowed to the mustard-colored slime, "The thousand lives you lived are for only you to remember. The thousand more are for you to live." With the traditional parting phrase for Reincarnates, Yuuki turned away without stepping. "Ibura-sama, are there any Reincarnates out there?" He stayed facing down the myopic corridor expecting no answer or a refusal to answer.

"Almost everything, even you, is or will be a Reincarnate. We Wamono are privileged. We continue cycling within the cloister, always safe. A self-contained universe of going and coming."

I cannot be stuck here cycle after cycle: infinity. He turned his head back to the wall. "Keep well, Sensei." Not satisfied with the usual cryptic response, he began the walk down the long corridor thick with chilled humidity. The only sounds other than his large bare feet slapping the floor, and the tiny echoes they produced, were the constant tears dripping from the walls and ceiling. He stopped, remembering to re-adjust his cravat for his meeting with the cloister's disciplinarian, then took a deep breath before continuing his barefoot soliloquy for the always-there walls never listening or speaking but strangely aware.

"I have been waiting!" Daiso Hégo stood hunched, supported by a gnarled stick of wood.

Yuuki stood in the doorway, not wanting to fully enter. "Apologies sensei, I ..."

"Never mind. I do not have all day."

Yuuki lifted his head from the polite bow, his feet involuntarily choreographing a mini back-and-forth interlude with the invisible barrier separating him from inevitable punishment. The disciplinarian's living quarters were even starker than Kugai's. Instead of a desk, there was a small round table notched with damp rot and decades if not centuries of disciplinarian rage. The table and its companions, a simple wooden chair and spindly cot, haunted the barren room. Noticeably less light fought its way through the sole window.

Yuuki couldn't clearly see the ancient man's face but knew there would be a scowl clinging to it with misery wrinkles like claws. "Do you know the old root cellar below the southwest wing?" Not a strand of sinew that once formed muscle on the old monk moved.

"No, sensei, I do not." Daiso Hégo was the one person who frightened Yuuki. He looked frail, but he knew how to use that twisted, sinister-looking cane as more than a walking aide. The ironic flower motif carved into it made it that more insidious.

Hégo mumbled, "No. Of course not. Why would you?" He shuffled a little closer, his features becoming uncomfortably more visible. His stormy grey eyebrows were the first to creep into view, each studded with a half dozen gold and silver captive-ball piercings. He raised one life-heavy eyelid and slid his bloody-egg-yolk eye up to stare at Yuuki. "It has not been used in centuries but still requires cleaning. We cannot allow anywhere in this blessed sanctuary to become derelict nor do we want such neglect to be an invitation to Retributions."

Yuuki immediately registered where this was heading.

"You will toil down there until it is clean enough for a Master of the Cloister to reside. Do you understand?"

"Yes, Hégo-sensei, I understand." He couldn't resist an addendum behind his tight lips. *Your next cycle should be as an Inanimate you deserve to be.*

Hégo moved in even closer, his cane clip-clopping with his barely steps. His breath reeked of the afternoon's meal of fish and fermented bean paste. "You can find it on your own, I am sure."

Yuuki fought the urge to back away from the man's stale stench, keeping his head down and to the left.

Hégo slowly turned away. His long, coarse grey dreads almost touched the floor behind him. "Think of it as an extra lesson in a person's innate bearings and intuition. Now get out of here before I give you another filthier cell to clean."

Yuuki's fists ached with rigid anger.

The rickety monk hobbled toward the sole chair and struggled to sit down, making sure his ashen hair was safely out of the way. He let out the typical old man's "issho" to signal the struggle involved in any physical exertion then exhaled a guttural sigh, announcing successful completion. "I do not understand why Dogen puts up with such insolence." He changed his gaze to the dim light unlucky enough to fall into the gloom, losing himself in a past. "Out there is dead to us. We have been long dead to it. Unfortunate."

Yuuki stood frozen, not knowing what to do. He was sure the surly monk thought he'd already left. There was regret in the elder's voice, an emotion Yuuki never witnessed from him.

Hégo, sensing a lingering presence, snapped his head toward Yuuki. The sudden twist of his papery concertina'd neck startled Yuuki. "I told you to go!"

Yuuki rammed his fists into his sleeves, bowed left and down, swiveled around, then shuffled out the cell. He couldn't move quick enough. Beads of sweat burst through then smeared their way down his cheeks and back, the cooler, fresher air of the corridor sending electrifying pulses throughout his body. The shock vivified a resolve. "I do not care what these frightened fools tell me, I will find my Hinodé." It was the first time he spoke the precious true name of the taboo world aloud.

In his cell, Hégo leaned back into his chair and almost lost his balance. A spasm ran through Hégo's hand resting on the ball head of his cane, helping him regain his balance. "Thank you, old friend."

two

MIMI COLLAPSED EXHAUSTED INTO the fake-candy-red swivel chair, the only real piece of furniture in her and Jojo's flat besides a couple futons and tiny kitchen table with no chairs to keep it company. She didn't even bother taking off her Mary-Janes. Bits of dried blood flaked off her hip-length pig tails onto the chair.

She was about to float into fatigue-induced unconsciousness when the jingling of her roommate's keys brought her reluctantly back into the moment. She opened her eyes just enough to roll them. "Here we go," she mumbled. She pretended to be passed out, which she desperately wanted to be.

"Heya Mi-chan!" her roommate shouted from the cubicle-sized foyer. The only quick-glance difference between the two was Jojo's amber pigtails opposed to Mimi's jet-black ones and puppy instead of teddy bear kill totems. "Mi-chan? You here?"

There's only one room for fuck's sake. Just look around the damn corner.

Jojo set her constant companion, Pucchi, down. The odd dog, both cute and ugly, jumped out from his custom-made carrier and started prancing around, excited to be out of his black and pink mobile prison and not sure what to do first. "Miiiii-cha ... oh, there you are. How was your ..." She finally noticed that Mimi was not acknowledging her. "Another night out with the bois I see." Her smile transformed into tight puckered anger. She scuffle-ran over to Mimi and grabbed both her pig tails, yanking as hard as she could in opposite directions.

"Aoowwwa! What the fuck, Jo! Psycho bitch."

"What are *those* doing in here?" Jojo pointed as if scolding a cat for bringing a half-dead rat into the house.

"Oh, they refused to come off. You know how shoes are. Stubborn bastards."

"Don't be a sarcastic bitch." Jojo pouted.

"Don't be like my mom. I pay half the re ..." She stopped, realizing she stuck her shoed foot in her mouth.

"Yea, about that." Jojo folded her arms, not letting go of the mom role. "When are you going to pay up? You owe your half of the rent for the past two months."

"I know, I know." Mimi's faced brightened with a smile. "I just did a kill. I've earned a nice deposit of kané for it."

Jojo maneuvered her way around the hillocks of dirty laundry and other detritus toward the kitchenette, arms still folded. "By the time you get paid for it, you'll be three months behind." She changed her mind and walked back, more in a huff. "If you didn't spend every night in Ni-cho with your boozehound 'boifriends', maybe you would be able to pay for this apartment, which—"

"I had to off five Suriidii golems in three nights," Mimi finished Jojo's often used words of self-sacrifice before Jojo could voice them.

Jojo stopped and gave her friend the evils then continued solo, "Yea, exactly. To pay the four month's rent in advance and the rip-off thank-you gift to the perv owner downstairs just to move in."

Mimi didn't want to tell her best friend that she had already been paid for the job. She would know something wasn't right. A Dekora would not be paid for her month's hits until the next monthly payout party at the Pink Palace.

Jojo walked the few steps back to the kitchenette and opened a packet of instant noodles. Pucchi jingled behind, stopped, and sat looking expectantly up at his mistress. Jojo stood on her tippy-toes and brought down a cylinder full of treats. "Here you go. A little snackie for my darling ugly-bunnies."

Jojo used here cutsey baby voice every time she talked to her snorting, flatulent accessory, inducing Mimi's vomit reflex. The look of Pucchi freaked her out. The big pointy ears, smushed-in face, bulging eyes, shaggy coat, and it being the size of a large cosmetics purse just didn't seem right. An obvious mixi-matchi job. *Those places should be illegal*, she thought, looking at the poor creature. *The clinic where that came out of surely was.*

"Who'd ya wack?" Jojo changed the subject, knowing she wouldn't get anywhere when it came to Mimi and her financial irresponsibilities.

"Just some gunshyu shit."

"Practicing on some nobody from a minor gunshyu again?"

Mimi didn't answer. Not yet. Instead, she not so lightly walked over to the foyer, plopped down on the floor to take off her shoes, and tossed them in the shoe closet.

"Mi," Jojo scolded, worried from Mimi's silence. "You whacked someone higher up in the Suriidii?"

Mimi regretted not just answering with a 'no' to the first question.

"What d'ya do, off a Tsudii?" Jojo snorted out a laugh.

Again, more silence from Mimi.

"Mi! You fucking did! We're under kill-for contract with them. We are killing *for them at the moment*, not offing them. What the hell were you thinking?!"

"Exactly, I was thinking!" Mimi stood up, stomping her stocking feet back over to the red chair. It was all out now. She would've had to tell here anyway. She couldn't stay there much longer. She had to get her on board or say good-bye for good. "There's no money in being a Dekora anymore. We're being negotiated out of existence by those Lolita whores. Did you hear that Oné-chan is now training some of them to be assassins as well?" Mimi scoffed. "With all that fake wavy hair flying all over the place and over-painted mugs? Don't even get me started on those dumb-ass parasols they cart with them everywhere. They should stay whoring the streets of Sukébé-machi instead of 'diversifying'."

"I don't think they would call themselves whores. Seduction and sex are just tools, just like our tools are Little Killers and blades," said Jojo. "But yea, they're basically whores." She stood now with her hands on her hips, her soft puppy dog score totems mocking her seriousness. "Well, like it or not, the Lolita are part of Oné-chan's new Moé Cabal, they're our sisters now."

"Tseh, Moé Cabal," Mimi muttered. "Bunch of bickering cows. Forming the Cabal was the dumbest decision Oné-chan made ... so far. Now, it seems that anyone can be mercenaries. The market will be flooded."

"Don't get off topic, Mi-chan." Jojo remained frozen, waiting.

Mimi continued her defense. "Jo-chan, we need to go rogue if we are to make a decent living in this city. We can't count on the Dekora and definitely not the Cabal any longer."

"What's with the 'we'?" Jojo interrupted. "I'm doing just fine."

"Oh, excuse me, I forgot. This little one-room box is reward enough I guess, all wondrous and neon psychedelic. Mmmm, can just smell the bubblegum paradise."

"Shut it with the bitchy sarcasm, Mi." Jojo's taut angry face slackened to melting concern. "No one saw you I hope." She picked up Pucchi and nervously started stroking it. The dog-ish creature squinted its eyes in anticipation of every overbearing pet.

"I walked into a nasty rundown ramen shop full of Characters, my teddy-kuma, pig tails, and freshly polished high Mary-Janes exposed for all to see," Mimi said, haughty in her stare. "And off'd a Storyliner."

Jojo almost dropped Pucchi. "Story ... No one has ever killed a Storyliner! There are only two in existence."

"One now." Mimi didn't even try to suppress her smugness.

"We're all dead. We need to go to Oné-chan and warn her. The Editor's probably on his way to the Palace now!"

Mimi rolled her eyes. "You're over-reacting, as usual."

"This isn't just an unsanctioned kill. A fucking Storyliner, Mi!? They are strict no kills. Everyone knows that!" Jojo released Pucchi from her increasingly unstable grasp. The little creature wasted no time in escaping the screeching of human-to-human battle. "Oné-chan won't be able to charm her way out this one." She braced herself against the sink. "We're dead."

Yea, you said that already. I get it." Mimi used here stocking foot to sway herself in the chair, as if she was just having a lallygag gossip session with her bestie. "I'll be dead soon enough no matter who I piss off. Better go out doing the major-est piss off that can be done—apart from killing the Editor or Queen Ren ... or even," she whispered, "Oné-chan." She instantly embarrassed herself by feeling like she had to whisper the sacrilege.

She popped up out of the chair and grabbed her white faux fur bolero and keys, unsuccessfully trying to stuff the ever-increasing mound of novelty keychains into her pocket. "Oh, I just influxed you for the last two months' rent and the next three." That made her feel good. She slipped on her off-duty white high Mary-Janes and opened the door. Before closing it, she turned back to her roommate. "Off to Za-Ginsa for some shopping. Hmm, maybe a pair of those gorgeous pink diamond earrings we saw there the other day. Remember?" She slammed the door then whispered, "Love ya, Jo."

"What. Ever!" Jojo stared at the closed door—a solid block of anger—for a few seconds, then squatted to Pucchi's level and grabbed its drooling drooping lips and scrunched its face even more than it already was. "I have to warn Oné-chan, if I'm not too late." If she thought any deeper, she would have concluded there was more than a bit of self-preservation in her decision. She sat down to put on her blue Mary-Jane mules and remained sitting on the Foyer's stoop. "What the fuck have you done Mi?"

"Is that imbecile here yet?" The Editor's stunted arms unraveled from their contorted resting position against his chest with restless malignant grace and began intricately air-drawing the rage tempest that was barely being contained within him. *My priceless Storyliner. Dead. Murdered.* The Tsudii leader's hands' erratic involuntary movements occasionally blocked the view of his face from the entourage of Illustrators strategically scattered throughout the room, far enough away from their master so as not to agonize his overly sensitive eyes from the glow of their storyboards.

He climbed a few steps onto a dais and stood behind his solid onyx desk that dwarfed him. His paper-pulp pale skin the texture of overly beaten sticky-rice almost glowed through the dim. His eyes were the most striking feature. The skin around them had been stretched allowing his eyeballs room for constant artificial enlargement, like two eggs placed on a bed of wet sand. His pupils were permanently dilated to almost the entire circumference of his eyes. Dramatically enlarged pupils were now all the rage among his Tsudii worshippers, but he went to the extreme; he was the Prophet of Draw and needed to look the part.

He scanned his dim expansive penthouse suite in his tower headquarters from his dais plateau; the only place the he could easily reach average height. The suite was kept in a strict forever-gloom; every piece of furniture and fixture coated with a special proprietary zero-reflective matte black. He glanced over at the two exhibits he had chosen for today's in-suite display brought up from his prized human-rarities zoo a few basement levels under his tower capital. His collection was a cherished hobby and the only thing of this horrible night that allowed him to sneer a grin just open enough to reveal mucous gums and stunted, jagged teeth. *I chose good ones today.*

The exhibits, most likely the last pair of Scraper Crawlers who used to live in somewhat harmony with the indoor residents of the super-tall low-rent high-rises of Sanjo and unsuccessfully resisted their scraper ghetto's take over by the Tsudii, cowered in their translucent display box. *Those grossly elongated legs and arms hanging bored off their bodies have nothing to climb now.* His sticky grin quickly shrunk back into puckered stasis. "Unappreciative savages". *They should be honored I saved them! Doubly so that I chose them for exhibit so soon after acquisition. egregiously ungrateful.*

His lips slickened with thick drool from the thought of a snack of their blood later after all the assassination mess was sussed out. He enjoyed a daily nightcap of blood from whatever the exhibit of the day was, believing it gave him creative inspiration. He often brainstormed for his addictive story ideas in their blood. He was particularly looking forward to tonight's, a double. He hadn't yet decided if he'd have separate shot glasses or one with a mixture of the two. *A cuvé of Crawler blood, exquisite bouquet of petrichor with a zing of ozone.*

He slurped in the excess saliva as his hunger-grin mutated into a snarl when he homed in on the lifeless mass on the floor just below his dais. It was one of the Characters who wandered back to the gory scene at the ramen shop after failing to eviscerate the murderer of his precious Storyliner. *Idiotic mess.* Extreme mixi-matchi body-modification procedures as well as imprinting onto Illustrators made his Characters simpletons and useless at anything else but brute force. *That Illustrator deserved to be decapitated for allowing a fucking crazed pigtailed Dekora skip-a-doodle in and slice through the neck of my hard-made and unfathomably useful Storyliner.*

All he could get out of the deceased defective Character was that a Dekora was involved. He wouldn't have been so furious, only highly annoyed, if it was a Character or Illustrator that was assassinated and the Dekora were under kill-for contract with his nemesis and former business partner Ren and her Suriidii horde. He refused to call the Suriidii a gunshyu let alone a daigunshyu. His Tsuriidii was the first gunshyu sanctioned by the Mayor to help run the city, to help run It. It was now handing out gunshyu and daigunshyu titles to any organization with a heavy managerial hand. *Lazy fuck.* The Dekora were currently under kill-for contract with him, and the killing of a Storyliner was inexcusable and justification for a drastic retaliation.

"The Mayor is not lazy. Something much more dangerous. It is unconcerned … unless under direct threat. It is aware of our growing power." The monotone vibration of unwords buzzed up through the Editor's spine and into his anger-masticated mind. "It is not only that warped Suriidii 'queen' but now Oné-chan who is quickly overstepping her position in the city. Our city."

Ahh, Draw. Always nice to hear your opinion. His companion utili-god, the god of all the Tsudii, was a constant, sharing his mind as well as his flesh, factually reminding its prophet of practicalities. He gently patted his left breast where the small fountain-pen god resided, its hard metallic ink barrel chilly in contrast to his slightly warmer body. The Editor wouldn't say he enjoyed his talks with his parasitic partner god, but the internal conversations gave his jittery crippled hands a rest.

"Her Dekora and the Lolita have formed a ... what is it? A cabal? You should not have allowed them to join forces."

Me!? The Editor mentally shouted. He couldn't remain as unemotional as Draw. *There is no 'me'. There is only us. Totality, remember?* He turned back to look in on the Crawlers and tapped the glass, giving them a greasy smile. *So, what are 'we' going to do about this? I can't lose another Storyliner. I only have one left. I ... we ... haven't created one in years. I could've died creating the last one.*

He didn't want to get into a combined strategy meeting and relationship counseling with Draw now. Plus, everyone was looking at him waiting for him to continue. He walked back over and up to his desk and sat in a size-appropriate chair for him but not fore the desk. "Is the other Character here or not!?" The Editor began air drawing, much more agitated.

"Yes, my Prophet. He has just arrived. He is waiting down in the lobby," said Thirty-Two.

He had Thirty-two, his lead Illustrator, take direct control of the untethered Character pair and sketch this first one committing suicide—deletion. With all his prophet powers, he had had no luck in marrying strategic intellect and physical brutishness into one minion. At least ones that would not almost kill him in the development process, as the case with his one remaining Storyliner.

"Shall I send him up?" The wafer man took out a well gnawed black marker and stiff, book-sized orange leather board. He touched the device with the marker, lighting his almost human face with the same orange metallic hue as the others of his kind in the suite expressed. They were the only source of intense light in the gloom, the last stars in a dying universe. He was ready to draw the next pane in the summoned Character's sequence.

"No, not yet. Make him sweat." The Editor tried to block his orbed eyes with his busy palsied hands. "And point that damn thing away from me!"

"Apologies, my Prophet." The Illustrator re-adjusted his marker, turned the illuminated board sideways away from his prophet, and brushed the marker across the board displaying a large thick-set man with a shaved head sitting on a tiny stool wringing his hands and rapidly moving his left leg in nervous short up and down jerks. Thirty-two drew sweat drops onto the jittery oaf's forehead. "Done, my Prophet."

"Why aren't *you* sweating? You oversaw that now headless Illustrator who let the Dekora get away." His arms moved at the same rate and with the same aggression as his voice.

The force of his prophet's voice made Thirty-two jump, forcing him to make a small but severe black slash on his display. "Yes, terribly sorry, my Prophet." Thirty-two looked as though he would crumble into tiny sharp shards from the stress of his purported mismanagement. There was no excuse. If he had one, his prophet would not tolerate having to suffer through an explanation.

Ninety-seven floors below, the sweaty ungainly man mass let out a high-pitched yelp from a shot of pain running across his cheek. He involuntarily put his hand over the pain and felt warm fluid and smelled strong scent of iron. He looked at his bloodied hand in confusion.

"Turn off that damn panel. The light's giving me a headache." The Editor waited for his hands to finish the last few lines of their never-ending sketch and reached into his blazer pocket for his pair of specially darkened eyeglasses. The lenses matched the shape of his eyes, giving the illusion of two holes penetrating through his head and into the blackness of his being.

Thirty-two tapped the bottom of his panel, killing the glow. "Sorry, my Prophet." His own enlarged pupils refocused back onto the floor.

"Oh, Thirty-two, this is not looking good, is it?" The Editor sounded almost sympathetic. "An assassinated Storyliner, one of your kind decapitated, and a Character here dead at his, your, hand."

Thirty-two, fooled by his prophet's tone, looked up, appearing slightly more at ease. "Yes, I'm afraid so." He even relaxed his arms a bit, allowing his hand holding the panel do drop down to his side.

The Editor raised himself from his chair. "You're afraid so?" He stared down at Thirty-two with those ovals of nothingness, making the minion want to draw himself into a ball and roll away.

"I don't care about a loss of a head or a suicide. What I want to know is how your subordinate allowed one of my very expensive Storyliners to be assassinated?" His air strokes were getting heavier; the actual lines would have been thick and angry.

"I ... I ..." Thirty-two couldn't get the words out.

"Do you know at least the name of the Dekora slut who did the job? We are under kill-for contract with the Dekor—" The Editor stopped, remembering the recent organizational change up north in Deko-cho. "The Moé Cabal, aren't we?"

There was a long uncomfortable pause as Thirty-two hesitated. "Yes, I believe you're correct."

"Of course I am, you fucking twig of kindling!" The Editor remained standing but turned himself around, air-drawing a circle of invisible scribbles around him. He looked out onto the cityscape through the heavily tinted windows. The super scrapers of Shinyuyogi surrounding his stronghold were barely visible. Even through his glasses and the tinted windows, the sun still made him squint in pain. "So, do you have any idea why a Dekora did this?"

"Yoshi says ..."

"Who the hell is Yoshi?"

"The one downstairs waiting, my Prophet."

He didn't expressly forbid his Illustrators naming their mixi-matchi remote-controlled thugs, but he decided to be more explicit. "Get him up here." The Tsudii leader did not take his eyes off the soon-to-be urban battleground below him. "This all smells of Ren." *Now calls herself Queen of the Suriidii.* He let out a snarly chuckle. *Delusions of undeserved grandeur never survive into reality. Whoever did her transition, that sycophant Masao surely, must've messed with her brain in the process.*

His arms finally returned to their petrified positions in front of his chest. His heavy breathing revealed how taxing the physical manifestation of his divine insanity was. It was something he was willing to put up with. The benefits of being in Totality with his utili-god outweighed the inconveniences of his insanity and physical quirks. He had become the most powerful prophet in Hindoé. He was thankful those lucky enough to enter Symb with an idol would not likely survive the advanced phases of the penultimate Communion then the pinnacle of Totality and semi-divinity. He wanted it to stay that way.

"Yes, my Prophet." Thirty-two cautiously backed away far enough for the light from his panel not to disturb his master. He started drawing a scene in which Yoshi was waiting in an elevator. A few seconds later, the elevator opened into the suite and Yoshi walked out, dazed and still bleeding, the streaks of blood still wet and beginning to disappear under the neckline of his ink-black turtleneck.

"You, Yoshi," signaled Thirty-two. "Come over here."

The Editor let out a quiet chuckle. He enjoyed observing his pecking order in action.

Yoshi lumbered toward the long man. He took in a surprised gulp of air. He thought he saw the thin man get his head sliced off during the chase. He noticed more copies of the man around the nighttime room. The short man with creepy dark glasses starring at him didn't look familiar, though he somehow knew he was important. He had a feeling he had been sent for because of what happened during that chase. He looked around, his eyes finally adjusting to the dark world he hadn't known he was on his way to entering. He glanced over to a lump of man on the floor and continued toward the long man who beckoned. He saw lifeless man lumps all the time.

"Yoshi, your Prophet would like to speak with you about last night," Thirty-two said in as gentle a voice as he could muster under the circumstances. There were too many instances of Characters violently freaking out from not knowing why they sometimes arrived at unintended places.

"Come over here, son," the Editor said, equally understanding that a nervous simpleton would be useless if frightened. "I would like to know exactly what happened last night." He walked around the desk while drawing into the air. He led the Character around the dead lump of his companion and over to an expansive sofa, much different from what he had sat on while waiting down in the sparse lobby.

"Thank you." Yoshi looked around the strange place with mouth wide open.

"Please, have a seat. Would you like a drink, shochu, saké, beer?"

"Eh, beer pleath," Yoshi's left leg resumed its nervous bobbing up and down.

If this goon survives this, I'm going to have to have that speech impediment edited out, the Editor thought.

Thirty-two brought over Yoshi's beer and set his prophet's usual down on the table. Yoshi looked up at the filmy being, nodded his appreciation, and downed most of the beverage in one gulp. The Editor came over and sat next to him. Even sitting, the Character towered over the Tsudii leader. The Editor almost fell into the gravitational vortex created from the deep depression of the brute's incredible mass. "So, what do you remember?"

Yoshi watched his prophet's strangely folded arms come alive as he spoke then quickly retreat when he stopped talking. "It all happened very fatth."

Not going to get anywhere with this imbecile, thought the Editor.

"But I do remember it wath a Dekora. Looked like one anyway."

"Dekora?" The Editor feigned being intrigued. "Go on."

"She walked in all pink and whatnot with all those cute animal toyth hanging around her thkirt."

"Then what happened?" The Editor was becoming impatient with trying to be nice to the disposable Character. He tried to keep his questions short so as not to distract him with his hands.

"She went right up to Thtoryliner, took a pretty blade out from her boobth, and sliced hith throat wide open."

And why the fuck didn't you prevent it? He internally recomposed himself and motioned to the nearest Illustrator to pick up his drink and put it to his mouth. His hands were not totally useless, but the glass was too far away for him to reach. "Do you remember what type of toy animal she had dangling from her waist?" He knew each Dekora had a signature kill-score totem. This was the information he needed.

Yoshi waited a few seconds for the fascinating hands to retract before answering. "She jutht looked like a Dekora. Thorry, my Prophet." Yoshi looked down in shame. "I don't remember. They were jutht cute"

Of course you don't. Why would you have? The Editor also looked down but in frustration. "O.K, what happened after she killed Storyliner Kouki?" Storyliners were the only of his creature-men to be explicitly named, by him.

"She ran out, and me, Taku, and thkinnny man ...," He pointed to Thirty-Two, "ran after her." Yoshi snickered and continued. "She really can run in those high-heeled shoes they all wear." Yoshi looked at his prophet, seeing that he did not find the same amusement and quickly contracted his grin.

"And?"

"She jutht dithappeared."

The Editor was finding it increasingly difficult to control his anger, not necessarily at the idiot Character, but at the headless incompetent Illustrator who controlled him and the equally incompetent one in charge of it all. He moved his unblinking void stare onto Thirty-two. The nervous Illustrator quickly looked down at his panel, pretending to work on something. The Editor turned back toward Yoshi and forced a smile. "Go on."

"The next thing I knew, thkinny man'th head wath thtaring up at me between my feet. She muthta been hiding around a corner or thomthing."

The Editor couldn't stand hearing the childish voice any longer. He wasn't going to get any more useful information from him. "O.K., thank you ... Thank you." He couldn't remember his unsanctioned name, nor did he care to. "You may leave now." He stood up and ascended to his desk, focusing on the pink glow over the Dekoran stronghold to the north. He always hated that color. What is that Oné-chan and false queen up to?

"Thank you." Yoshi said, obviously relieved he survived the interrogation. Thirty-Two walked him to the elevator, waited for the doors to close, and drew his flawed character exiting the building.

The Editor remained gazing out onto his city. "Delete him." His hands drew only a couple short lines, barely moving from their home in front of his chest.

He saw from Thirty-Two's reflection on the window that the Illustrator was taken aback by the order. Emotional attachment to their Characters was common. Thirty-Two had only been in direct control of Yoshi for a few hours, but Yoshi was one of his original designs. "Now."

"Ye ... yes, my Prophet." Thirty-two took his marker out and quickly tapped and brushed at different places on his panel. "Done, my Prophet."

The Editor sensed the weak Illustrator didn't delete the fool. He looked more carefully at Thirty-two's reflection in the smokey window. The stick figure's face centered perfectly between two ghostly scrapers hiding Ren's expansive warehouse territory on the other side of the city. He took out his Little Killer from the inside breast pocket, tailored perfectly for easy and painless access, and pointed the palm-sized ceramic weapon behind him, over his shoulder, at the producer of the reflection. He activated the focus beam. A spot of indigo light was now added to the reflection. The entire process required only a second. When there was need, his gnarled hands became as useful as a precocious child's. The next second, the reflection disappeared. Thirty-Two lay twisted on the floor, his orange illustrator panel next to him, its dying screen cracked into a fractal star of piercing rays.

The Editor calmly and carefully put the weapon back into his pocket. "Nineteen."

A long, pencil-thin man, almost identical to the dead one now bleeding thick black blood from the tiny hole in his head, quickly shut off the painfully brilliant board and walked closer to the Editor's desk. He stood next to his colleague's corpse. "Yes, my Prophet."

"You are now in control of your fellow Illustrators." He finally took his eyes off the city view and refocused his cephalopod eyes to the left. "Delete that idiot downstairs before I do the same with you."

"As you wish, my Prophet." Nineteen betrayed no reaction to the threat and made the required few strokes on his panel to officially take control of then delete Yoshi. "Successful, my Prophet. I'll have all bodies disposed of immediately."

"Good." The Editor widened his grin, revealing overlapping teeth fighting for space. "Well, looks like we are going to finally have a little war to look forward to."

"I advise a more diplomatic approach first." said Draw. "The current Oné-chan's predecessor was rumored to be in Symb, remember?"

Of course I remember. I may be functionally insane, no thanks to you, but my memory is very well intact.

"Then you'll remember that if she was not yet in Totality, whatever the idol was could have been inherited by the current Oné-chan. "We have never met her face to face. If we had, I would have felt the presence of another idol or worse, a god."

As usual, Draw's unvoice was an emotionless drone, but the vibrations through his spine and up into his brain suggested otherwise. He snapped out of his inner strategizing and looked at the gaggle of Illustrators staring at him waiting for any kind of order. "Leave us!" Several orange faces quickly bobbed and swayed toward the elevator, "And turn off those fucking boards!"

"The only way to find out for sure if there is another idol in play and if it is on its way to becoming a utili-god is to meet with her. I suggest we set up a face-to-face with the Dekora matriarch. Flex our prophet-god muscles a bit for show of course."

You want us to have a chat with her? The Editor detested Draw's calmness and rationality. He wanted to get everything over with in the bloodiest way possible. But the sane part of his brain—Draw's half—would not allow that. His cruel insanity was useful, but not for this. *Very well. Let's have that chat.*

three

THE DOOR OF THE root cellar looked assaulted by raging time. All doors, even this uninviting slab of dead wood, presented fantastical opportunities of escape into a different world, a stoneless realm where hard and dim corridors were forbidden or, better yet, did not exist. But Yuuki's reality, reliably disheartening, invariably wounding, prevailed. He released a soft sigh, but his muscles remained mineral hard. He pressed the cold latch fanged by centuries of rust. The door to the forgotten cellar opened with a post-mortem gasp more felt than heard. The whispered tearing of long-abandoned spiderwebs was the only real sound. Yuuki waited for his eyes to adjust to the mournful blackness. There was a stench of death in the unmoving air; what he imagined the fragrance of a successful suicide would be like.

Even his pair of gleamer sticks, essential items when navigating the light-starved corridors of the cloister, barely penetrated the darkness encapsulating him. "How am I to clean a place I cannot even see, and with what?" He groped the wall on his left draped with a sticky infinity of crinkly cobwebs quickly cocooning his hand. He heard scurrying tic-tics along the walls or floor, he couldn't tell which.

He walked a bit further into the room keeping to the left. The lights from both gleamer sticks cancelled each other out of existence, allying with the darkness. "This is stupid. Need to go and get more gleamers."

He carefully turned around to where he could see the faint outline of the doorway, made visible by the almost intangibly lighter passageway outside. The place seemed both massive and confined. He groped for the wall that was now on his right, but something felt distinctly un-stony that was just out of reach of the struggling gleamer light. It felt smooth with bristly patches. It was not the cold weeping stone and fuzzy lichen he was used to. His hand snapped back, slamming against a jagged stone. Waves of pain shot up his arm. He jerked away from the uncanny texture as fast and far as he could, disorientating himself even further. He had lost the hint of the doorway and now surrounded by absolute suffocating nothing. He forced himself to stand still for a few seconds to calm himself.

His heart was beating about three times faster than normal. The gleamers only lit him, exposing him to whatever was lurking within the gloom. "It is only darkness. All in my mi—," A cold sensation crept down the back of his neck, wet and viscous. He instinctively reached back to wipe it off. His hand, in defiance of his mind, began to jitter its way around the shape. Whatever he was touching tapered to a point. A raspy almost sub-sonic growl vibrated the blackness surrounding him. The tapered object resonated in sync with the demonic purr.

"What the!" Yuuki ducked from whatever weapon was poised at his neck, slamming his head on a protruding shard of ancient stone hiding directly in front of him. Ignoring his forehead, he touched the back of his neck to check for a wound but didn't know if what he felt was his blood or something worse. "Who ... Wha ... What is there?"

The hiss-rasp began to coagulate into words. "Now, now little insect. I will not harm you. Not until all my eyes see you at least." Yuuki thought it sounded feminine, or at least what he thought a female would sound like. "Genkou Ryudasu. Perhaps you have heard of me?"

"N ... no." He didn't want to turn around yet, but he felt a little less disorientated thanks to the voice. "A Reincarnate?"

"You could say that. Not only are you deliciously fragrant but somewhat intelligent," Genkou said, her words punctuated with hisses and breathy bursts.

He wanted to see what it was, but the more terrified part of his mind pleaded against it.

A chemical green glow combusted in front of him. It grew brighter until a combination of familiar forms started to take shape in silhouette—several legs or arms and the sickly glow source, a bulbous arachnoid lower body. Yuuki wanted to scream, but even sound wouldn't dare leave the safety of his gut.

Genkou Ryudasu lifted her front four bristly appendages high into the air, two shiny silhouetted fangs dripped venom and protruding out from a head that was just about human enough to be entirely terrifying. He froze at the full presence of the giant arachno-human's menacing backlit deformity.

"Retributions! You are going to kill me! I am being sentenced to death?" He instinctively grabbed a piece of rubble from the degenerating walls, readying himself for a futile defense. A warm sensation spread from his groin down his inner thighs. The terror roiling through his body sucked the heat from the urine; the sudden chill intensifying the shakes.

"Not right away. But keep it in the back of your small mind. I can and will if I deem it prudent." The giant arachnid creature hissed. She placed her four front appendages back onto the floor and retracted her fangs, slightly. Yuuki heard what he thought was a laugh, but it could've easily been whatever she had feasted on coming back up. "Apologies, initiating luminescing takes quite a bit of energy. It forces my body into that position." The lower half of her shiny black carapaced torso swirled with bright pulsating greens and yellows, like parasitic glow worms feeding on evil.

Yuuki did not think the apology sincere or the excuse truthful. Most of the cellar was now revealed, covered in an unnatural scum of yellow-green light. It was massive. The walls were even rougher than those in the main cloister. Roots and monsters wouldn't care.

He got the first good look at the size of the horror and the sprawling web he had luckily avoided. The monster's leg-arm span was about three times that of her massive, half human half arachnid torso. An *Aku? Only legend, right?* Logically pondering what was looming in front of him kept his legs from betraying him to the rough unforgiving floor. He had been taught that Aku were extremely rare karmically punished monstrosities, dangerously warped Reincarnates. He ignored the warnings as just scare tactics by his instructors to keep him and the other novitiates well behaved.

Ryudasu rolled an oval cocoon closer to her with two of her front appendages. The sarcophagus reflected a strange grey-white glow of pre-death. It vibrated suffering. She looked back to Yuuki. Her six eyes seemed too large to fit on her head, staring at him with obvious, barely controlled hunger.

Yuuki watched her moisten her shell-like mouth of independently working flaps with a long, obsidian tongue in anticipation of her feast of whatever was inside or of himself.

"I heard you are quite the rebellious one. What did you do, you naughty plump grub?" She protruded her fangs out then down, injecting them into the quivering shroud. Twitching, spasms, then stillness. "Now we wait." She kept her six onyx eyes on Yuuki, her fangs dripping with clear viscous venom, tinged with the hue of gore. He saw nothing in those eyes but himself, multiplied by six. He had been taught that the eyes were the expressions of actual being. What did that say about this creature?

The Aku stared, unmoving, all eyes. He wasn't sure if she wanted an explanation of his crime but thought he'd be safer answering any question she asked. "I asked too many questions."

"Asking a question is hardly cause for sending someone down for a visit."

Yuuki shivered with fear. "I asked about ..." He inhaled a good dose of cobwebbed air. "Hinodé."

"Ah, well. That is a different story, especially to those shivering skeletons above."

Yuuki's curiosity began to tentatively overpower his fear. Would she answer his questions? He didn't care what she was or why she was kept hidden in the bowels of the cloister.

Ryudasu continued. "But I do somewhat understand their point."

Yuuki's courageous hope began to crumble.

The Aku noticed his disappointment. "No need to worry my juicy, frightened moth, I may find it in myself to give you a little bit more of what you want after I finish with my snack."

Yuuki smiled, which felt weird. "Thank you, Genkyou Ryudasu-sama."

"No need for formalities with me." Without ceremony, she sank her dripping fangs into the now soft and mushy cocoon. A soft hiss of gas escaped through the punctures, the final relief from suffering. He remembered his hands were coated in the same substance and tucked each deep into the sleeve of the other to keep them away from his face.

Yuuki cringed as his new acquaintance started sucking the life juices of whatever was inside that tightly packaged deathtrap. The battle between fear and curiosity was turning back in favor of the former.

Ryudasu continued feasting on her evening snack. *Will never get that sound out of my head.* "So, do I still have to clean this place?" He didn't know what else to say but needed to say something to drown out the slurpy, slushy sucking.

She lifted her head out of the cocoon carcass, mouth full of liquified murder "You can if you like, I do not much care." She began cleaning her fangs with her bristly leg-arms. "I rarely use this room."

Ryudasu's spinnerets began weaving a silk cushion behind her. "Before you do, have a more comfortable seat." She guided him over with two of her leg-arms. It was almost elegant.

After a few hesitant steps, Yuuki sat down. He gathered he had no choice. Ryudasu remained with her back to him.

The second his body touched the cushion, Ryudasu pointed her yellow-green arachnid backside at him. Before he could react, he was cemented within the initial silky matter then spun at high speed with her back legs in deadly synchronicity forming a sticky strangling coffin starting from his feet to his neck; only leaving his head exposed to observe and hear the terror of her actions. The sickening moist sound from the spewing silk and mucous concoction echoed throughout the cellar. Every twitch of his struggle tightened the strands.

Once the last squirts of silk exited the Aku's spinnerets, she turned around to face her immobilized captive. "I do not think you will be able to clean anything now." The wicked creature rasped, putting the finishing touches onto her artwork. "Mmmm, you look delectably beautiful!"

"Please do not kill me! Please." Tears started streaming down his cheeks. The silk cords tightened with each sob.

Ryudasu ran up on top of Yuuki in what seemed like a nanosecond, pushing her six death black eyes up against his *caput mortuum* face. "Why? You look quite savory. I am amazed at my restraint from just sucking you dry when we first introduced ourselves."

Yuuki was gifted a sudden adrenaline injection of brave defiance. "I never introduced myself!"

Ryudasu giggled, "You are Yuuki-Hana, favorite of Dogen Kugai, whose job it is to be an annoyance to everyone around you. Am I doing well so far?" She started to back off him a little bit.

"Why have I never heard of you?" It pained him to speak. "Please loosen your silk, I cannot breathe."

Ignoring his request she answered his question. "Until recently, I did not care to be known. Not such a difficult thing in this labyrinthine necropolis." She saw that the novitiate was turning a bit too purple and began to deftly loosen her latest oeuvre though reluctantly. Yuuki gasped for air once the key strand was severed.

"I was not *planning* on killing you, though you would be quite a sizable meal. You cannot begin to imagine how long it has been since I had a repast of your," she leaned in closer, "proportions." The powerful puffs of "Ps" chased away the precious oxygen Yuuki desperately needed. She continued unhinging him from her web. "I was told to scare you. From the delissscious fragrance of lingering fear, I assume I succeeded." Her mouth parts vibrated with vicious anticipation.

Finally free to move again, he started to get up out of the chair trap but thought he'd better not. "That demented Hégo."

"Not only him," said the Aku. "The Master as well."

"Why are you not killing me?"

"Unfortunately, it was not part of the agreement. I also wanted us to have a little chat and give you something."

"Me?" Yuuki felt secure enough to stand. The painful rush of blood away from his head finally returned to its natural equilibrium. He couldn't decide whether to hate, like, or still be terrified of the warped Reincarnate. He had to settle for all three.

"I have known of you ever since you were abandoned." Ryudasu mounted her makeshift web and began playing with her earlier snacks, tapping the hollowed cocoons forming constellations along her web universe. They resonated with re-animated vigor.

Yuuki's emotions were siding on a very cautious 'like'. She didn't use the pathetic euphemisms to explain how he ended up at Aoheki. "What else do you know?"

"You are what they call up there 'pure'." She was almost purring. "I know enough to want to help you."

Yuuki added 'mistrust' to his repertoire of feelings. "Not pure, unwanted. You do not seem like the type to offer help from the kindness of your heart." *Does she even have one?*

"Ahh, you are not as naive as I thought you would be. Good. Good." She growled an appreciated chuckle. "You are correct. No one is completely altruistic. You will have much more experience of the selfishness of human nature once you enter the fallacy of Hinodé."

Yuuki leaned forward wanting to make sure he heard her correctly but went too far and tripped over a pile of crumbled rock, falling back into Ryudasu's main web. He began to struggle, tangling himself into immobility. The vibrations of struggle triggered Ryudasu's predatory instincts. She pounced onto the squirming novitiate. One of her pincers sliced a gash down his left cheek as she came down over him. Her poisonous fangs arched over him within a few centimeters of his heaving chest, struggling to contain his adrenaline-seared heart.

"Ryudasu! It is me, Yuuki-Hana!" He tried to smother the panic to stop struggling. "Ryudasu-sama!"

The hideous huntress' head hovered just above Yuuki's face. There was nothing resembling humanity in those multiple eyes. She was all killer. The mixture of venom and decaying liquified organs laced her breath with a rancid, medicinal quality that infected Yuuki's airspace, forcing him to hold his breath.

The Aku remained in pre-murder trance. Yuuki tried again to get through to the non-predator that he had to believe was still there behind those nothing eyes. His only option was to use what he had already gathered. She seemed to need him for something. "You were talking about me going out into Hinodé. Ryudasu, Ryudasu?" He was trying to wake her out of her murderous trance. "Remember, I am pure!". Yuuki stilled himself as the spider part of her started to subside.

"Yes, you are." She folded her fangs back and inwards then slowly backed off, the clicks of her pincers were the only sounds for long few seconds. "Apologies, the vibrations set me off. Let that be the most important lesson you learned today."

Yuuki would not move, careful not to trigger another attack. "Could you untangle me before I start vibrating again?"

"Certainly." She began to untangle her would-be snack with her front pincers. There was less reluctance in her snipping than last time, but it was still too slow, too hesitant.

Streaks of his fresh blood glistened on one of her pincers, complementing the putrid green of her bodice. He shuddered from a sickening wave of relief within his stomach. *Not a fang.*

Her inert eyes seemed to remain fixed on him, but he couldn't really tell. He knew, however, that she was ready to pounce on him again upon detecting the slightest struggle; giving her an excuse to make him the feast she'd been longing for. "You have a nasty gash there. Would you like me to bandage it with my silk?"

"No. Thank you." Yuuki wiped his blood on his kimono.

"Very well." Ryudasu put the bloodied pincer to her constantly preoccupied cuticular mouth plates and licked. "Mmmm. Sweet. Healthy organs." She finally finished her reverse weaving and lifted the novitiate with her front leg-arms, almost motherly, and placed him on the rock-littered floor. "Please watch your step. My stomach is beginning to wail from hunger, and your tantalizing innards are not helping."

Yuuki carefully stepped further from the sticky expanse, his cheek intensifying in hot pain. "You said I was to leave the cloister and go out into Hinodé?" He hoped he hadn't imagined hearing those words.

"Oh, yesss," Ryudasu hissed. She remounted her web and climbed toward a reinforced strand anchoring the ephemeral hunting ground/graveyard to the ceiling. She stopped at a tiny cocoon glued near the ceiling and started slicing it from the rest of the web with her fangs.

She brought it back with her down to the floor and gently set it on a pile of rocks in front of Yuuki with the reverence of presenting a gift. She gashed it open with a pincer.

Not wanting to see what being had the misfortune of falling, flying, or walking into her geometric trap, he closed his eyes, but curiosity got the better of him. He allowed a small slit of reality penetrate his retina. No blood. No corpse. It looked like a rolled piece of paper. "What is it?"

"A map," Ryudasu said, without any hiss or rasp, almost wholly human. "Take it with you into Hinodé. The manner in which you just handled yourself tells me you are ready."

"Hinodé," Yuuki repeated. It sounded even more real hearing it uttered without shamed whispering.

"Yes, Hinodé. Out there. We are in Hinodé at this very moment. We are not in a self-contained universe, no matter how much these hermits want to believe we are."

Yuuki's mind wandered to his imagined Hinodé. Probably a weak copy of what was out there. A rush of fear shot through him. *Am I ready for the reality?*

Ryudasu tapped the scroll and interrupted his thought with her native staccato rasp. "Look at it."

Yuuki put his concerns and questions to the back of his mind and picked up the thick scroll. It didn't feel like the onion-thin paper used upstairs. A small vessel dropped out from one end. Yuuki looked at the vessel then the Aku.

"We will get to that in a moment."

The contents looked like the tar the older monks spread on their hair to make it grow faster and thicker. Careful not to trigger any web strands, he unfurled the map. He squinted to see better in the dim meager gleamer light. The map didn't look like any he had seen. The only maps he had access to were those of corridors, cells, and courtyards, and even they were a rarity. "Where are we? I mean, on this map. Where is Aoheki?"

Ryudasu stabbed a faded black square just to the right of center with a deadly precision. "There."

Yuuki's entire view was taken up by Ryudasu's pincer, crusty with what he could only imagine were layers of flesh of uncertain depth. His the latest. Instead of fear, he was in shameful awe of the gruesome Reincarnate. "Why are you doing this for me?"

Ryudasu growled-purred in a low resonance inaudible to the human ear, "It is what you wish for." Her purr-softened growl became jagged and dangerous. "Is it not?"

Yuuki instinctively looked away, hoping less eye contact would calm the dangerously agitated Aku. "Yes." It was a meek response, but it was what he has been wishing for ever since he was aware of who and where he was. "It is."

"Once in Hinodé, a woman will collect you and help settle you into your new existence." She was noticeably calmer. "The map is for you once you escape this madhouse world." The map would be useless to him, but she needed to have the childish dreams of this monk seem more tangible. *That woman must succeed or we all will remain ignorant to our own deaths!*

"What is the woman's name? People do have names out there I assume."

She growled-sighed. "I know her by only her title; a Dame or something like that." Ryudasu never cared to know the names of her outside contacts. A name meant personhood. She didn't need people, simply tools. "Do not worry, she will know who you are."

"But how am I supposed to find her? I cannot read anything on this map."

Ryudasu quickly pushed her eye-pocked head to within millimeters of Yuuki's face. The hairs around her eyes prickled Yuuki's forehead and chin. An impatient growl gurgled from her grizzled mouth parts. "She will find you." She backed up a bit "Let her help you when she offers.

"But ..."

"Lisssten!" Ryudasu's hiss teetered on the borderline of a shriek. "You are a Wamono. Inner journey and all that is what you monks live for, even you."

Yuuki did believe in his Order's core life value of not focusing on what the future holds but forging a path to whatever future. His past, however, would have to rely on a new philosophy. "I will never get through the pair of Shisa at the main gates." He'd heard they'd also feasted on those trying to leave in the past. He looked at Ryudasu and wondered if those Shisa were also Aku.

Ryudasu flicked a large slab of fallen wall or ceiling, as if playfully kicking a tiny pebble down a pathway. She pointed her glowing abdomen toward an area of wall, exposing a black hole rejecting all light from the room. "Follow that until you come to the end. The exit is blocked with a pile of debris. Remove it, and you will be exposed to your wish."

A constructor tunnel? thought they were all filled in centuries ago, immediately after construction. "You want me to go out now?" Yuuki dizzied with the immediacy of compacted time.

"Sometime in the late morning or early afternoon the day after tomorrow. I told your new friend to remain waiting for you until you emerge. It may take you a while to get through the tunnel. Now, take a sip from that vessel." Her command was mixed with child-like anticipation.

Nothing seemed right: black gooey liquid, spider-human Aku, sudden chance to leave, and secret tunnel. He was more afraid not to do what Ryudasu ordered. He opened the vessel and wafted it under his nose. It was almost odorless with just a slight whiff of saltiness. He put his left hand underneath the vessel and brought it up to his lips in traditional Wamono fashion.

"Take only a few drops," said Ryudasu. "It is not something to guzzle."

When she was Master of Aoheki centuries ago he had inexplicably consumed a large amount of the highly controlled substance. To the present day, she still cannot unravel the karmically devastating impulse. Like everything of life, devastation could very well become an epiphany with just a different tilt of the mind. Revelations into the grand Hinodé deception, including his Wamono Order, overran his psyche. The inevitable insanity culminated in him massacring hundreds in his flock, the punishment for which she had been suffering ever since. *A necessary sacrifice for gaining insight into the lies and crimes of the deceptively ambivalent Wamono god-thing. But you are not just that, are you Gou-Tairei?*

Yuuki allowed just enough of the ominous thick liquid to coat the first few taste buds on the tip of his tongue. It tasted as it smelled. "What is this suppose ..." The cellar shimmered then shifted. He stumbled but was coherent enough to know what the consequences would be if he fell the wrong way.

As he was about to give in and collapse, the shimmering slowed. Faint images came into his view of people walking and carrying bags of all sorts. *Hinodé?* It was raining. People were protecting themselves with umbrellas or running to seek cover. The scene cloaked him in euphoric warmth. He could barely make out what was on the other side of the street, which he could only perceive as a strange wide corridor with no ceiling but just sky, crammed with people and strange contraptions, some carrying one or two people and others carrying dozens. One tall rectangular one rushed by blaring out a kind of nasal singing with faces staring at him from small windows along the side. Bursts and pulses of buzzing neon hypnotized him. Their reflections distorted by the hard weirdly smooth ground. He tried to open his hand to touch something from that world, but the will to move was not enough to command his body.

Ryudasu released a vibrating hum of excitement originating from deep within her viscera. *He does not seem to be dying. Good.* Centuries of hunches and experimentation were finally showing results. *Is he seeing the undeceived living? Is he witnessing the true world ... my Yedo?* Her abdominal glow intensified. *He must survive long enough for the micro dosing to reach saturation while staving off any mass-murder intentions. Simply another necessary sacrifice.*

The vibrations began to die into slowing undulations. *My revenge.* She was counting on this Wamono's pure blood to preserve and tame the ink for her intended recipients to have their own epiphanies without falling into blood-lust psychosis, or deeper into it from what she had heard from the Dame. She also learned one had a penchant for consuming blood. But she had to first get this monk out of the cloister and herself out of imprisonment.

The intense radiance from Ryudasu's over excited abdomen forced Yuuki back into his real self. "What did I see?"

"Most likely a hallucinatory side effect intensified by whatever was in the forefront of your mind. Wishful thinking heated to boil." A thunderous growl roiled deep in her viscera, stimulating the soft hairs on the back of Yuuki's neck. *What terrible revelations will he have to endure?*

He wanted it so much to be real, to be Hinodé.

"Continue taking it. But in much smaller doses. One drop." She leaned in close to Yuuki, his reflection in the eye directly in front of him distorting his face beyond recognition and spoke every word as one sentence. "Only. One. Drop." She backed away, creating a vacuum that almost brought Yuuki along with her. "Make sure you consume daily. It will give you immunity from some of the rather unsavory viruses you will be susceptible to out there." Lying to the desperate and impatient was never a difficulty.

"Medicine?" It was all Yuuki could say. Nothing was making sense, but he was already looking forward to his next dosage. Even though Ryudasu had no irises or pupils, he sensed she was staring into a space that was not quite here.

Unfortunately, Gods like you do exist. But your only power is gifted to you by the weakness of the religious mind. She had been one such weak mind before her enlightening sacrifice of sanity and freedom. *I will use that power to destroy you, your demented urban playground, then onto the rapturous annihilation of those who sent me to you and your fraudulent world trap.*

Remembering she had a guest, "Return here the day after tomorrow and begin your journey home."

Ryudasu's 'home' sounded softer even caring to Yuuki.

Ryudasu's voice returned to the hunter rasp. "Do not tell anyone about this. As far as Kugai and Hégo know, you were terrified into obedience. This is our secret and your future, your exisssstence."

He wouldn't have to lie about being terrified. "I understand. May I leave now?"

Yuuki waited for any verbal sign from the grotesque Aku permitting him to exit. None came. He carefully navigated the crumbled floor and walked out of the cellar.

Ryudasu turned her bulk to make sure her sacrificial pawn had left. "Time to begin the long finale."

Dogen Kugai sat at his desk studying a proud, tiny spider fastidiously maintaining its delicate web spanning from one leg to the underside of a corner. Like most Wamono, he believed arachnids were reincarnations of those who acted on their ambitions of power and grandeur and didn't care who they stepped on in the process. The ambivalent Gou-Tairei's loyal but vengeful army of Retributions see it fitting to bring them back as something that could easily be stepped on. Unfortunately, the monstrous one living deep below could not simply be stepped on.

A knock jolted him out of his trance. He rolled his eyes knowing who it was by the wood-on-wood banging.

"Enter." He pretended to be busy with his warped and stained diary in which he had been recording the morning's less than mundane events before being distracted by the tiny spider. Daiso Hégo limped through the door, tapping that wretched cane onto the floor at every step.

"You summoned?" Hégo said, not trying to hide the spite in his voice.

"I need to talk to you about young Yuuki-Hana." Kugai had learned to ignore Hego's blatant disregard of his authority. They'd known each other for almost a century; the closest of friends for more than half that time with a short stint as intimates. Now, they'd learned to simply tolerate one another.

"What is there to talk about? I have gotten word he is safely back in his cell."

Kugai dropped his pen-brush and rubbed his forehead. "Yes, physically."

Hégo groaned, rolling his weepy eyes. "That insolent boy needs to find his place, and that place is not trying to obtain explicitly forbidden information. Just because he is pure as you say." Hego's sarcasm was not subtle. "That does not give him free reign to ignore centuries-old and tested rules and customs." The withered monk moved closer to Kugai's desk. His foot stumbled upon a warped cobble. Luckily, his cane stabilized him. It was well formed to the crooked monk's body after decades of constant contact.

Kugai stood up and offered his chair to his older counterpart. "Insolent, yes." A father's worry deflated his already withering body. "He is no longer a boy. I am having regrets."

Hégo scoffed at the vacated chair. "Now you think my idea of scaring him into obedience was too harsh? After all the problems he has caused us over the years?" He looked at the chair then to Kugai. He finally gave in and painfully lowered himself into the chair. "You are a fickle old man. Too late anyway."

Kugai breathed out resignation. "Yes. What is done is done. I hope we did not make a grave mistake."

"He is most likely planning more ways to be a pain in our backsides." Hégo grumbled while rubbing the knob of his cane.

"Most likely," agreed Kugai. "The novitiate was not the main reason I called you here." He leaned his hip against the desk and picked at the fraying splinters on the nearest corner.

"Why do you always have to worry and waste my time? Just say what you want to say!"

As Kugai was about to explain, the thumping beats of the evening's Haiku-Bassbeat sermons began. The nearest transcendence chamber was only a few doors down from his cell, but he rarely attended. At 122 years into his current cycle, the trance movements and heavy electronic beats were starting to take a toll.

What used to be the meditative trance-inducing harmony of the electro beats and chiming of thousands of hair beads as the monks swayed and swirled was now a minor annoyance. He usually made it a point to be doing his out-of-cell duties during sermons, but the day's events made him lose track of time. He motioned to Hégo to leave with him before the cell flooded with blood-pulsing bass. The disciplinarian shook his head, sighed, and followed his master's lead.

The two ancient Wamono went in the opposite direction from where the beats were being produced. Kugai slowed, concerned about losing his companion. He looked back to see Hégo only a few steps behind. He didn't understand how he did that. He could barely walk without that cane. Finally, the corridor began to escape the long reach of the spiritual beats. Kugai relaxed his pace, sensing his ears and sanity were safe.

Hégo panted in sync to those distant beats. "Now ... hah ...hah ... who is the old stick-in-the-mud ... hah ... hah ... hah? You should start coming to the sermons again. Basho Jyon, pompous as he is, has mixed some wonderful beats lately. Transcendent."

"I know, I hear them every day, four times a day." Kugai shouted, his hearing not matching his voice yet.

"It is not the same listening without the reverberations and body heat."

"I have no problem with the sermons. It quite upsets me that my body and mind no longer allow me to attend."

They exited the corridor into Sakura Hitotsu-en Courtyard. Unfortunately, it wasn't that one blissful week in early spring when the sole cherry tree would be in spectacular blush bloom.

They simultaneously looked up, as everyone instinctively did when entering the center of the courtyard, toward the hidden summit in the sky's perpetual, dirty, cottony mists. No one, not even Kugai, knew the walls' exact height. The ancient Constructors' access ways were ordered filled in by the mythical Founder-Sama, who is most definitely living amongst them as a Reincarnate if not already eternally existing within the paradisiacal End-of-Cycle city of Yedo.

But no one knew who it could be, not even the Reincarnate. There were many candidates, but the most plausible was the gentle and wise squid Nonen Amedo.

With narrowed eyes, Kugai looked intensely for crumbling or cracks above the alluvial pyramids of rubble growing at the base of the towering barrier walls. Aoheki's only protection from Keibu-yo were in desperate need of repair, and this worried him to the point of striking a covert deal with his Aku prisoner.

"Well," began Hégo, wasting no time getting back on topic once they settled near the tree, "why are we here besides your overly sensitive ears?"

"You are looking at it." Kugai looked up again toward the grey-green walls.

Hégo looked at the solitary tree behind Kugai. "The sakura?" The ancient monk twisted his face in fake confusion and disbelief.

"No, you daft old man, the wall."

"There are several portions if I remember correctly, not only one."

"I prefer to singularize since it does one thing: protect."

"Yes, yes. You are trying my patience Dogen. What about 'it'?" Hégo began the painful process of sitting down to endure Kugai's famously drawn-out explanations and exhaled the old-man "Issho", signally the effort it took just to sit down on a cold sitting stone.

"Comfortable?"

"As much as I can be."

"The wall, our protection, is in dire need of repair."

"You decided to take a leisurely jaunt up there to take a look?"

"That is exactly the point. No one in living memory has ever evaluated the health of the wall. It could crumble down at any moment." His voice was urgent. "Look at the piles of rubble punctuating the base. Just last week a monk walking near the base was hit on the shoulder by a falling chunk. Luckily, he suffered no serious injuries."

Hego only grunted his acknowledgement. "When was the last time a cloister was breached?"

"Attacked?" Kugai quickly corrected the elder monk.

"Yes, yes, attacked. When?"

"I do not know. A couple centuries ago or so I would guess."

"Exactly."

"It does not mean it cannot happen!" Hégo had a knack of pushing Kugai over the edge of decorum. "Wamono had horrible things done to them, even killed during attacks in the past, just for refusing to be part of the chaos and violence that was and still does infest the city. You know that ... or have you forgotten Founder-sama's Plea to Cloister?"

"You made your point, Dogen." Hégo waved his hand trying to shoo the paranoia of his superior away as if it were an annoying insect. "So, get on with your master plan. It is getting chilly."

"It concerns Ryudasu and your idea of making her our repairma ... wom ... spider." Kugai had not thought of what her title would be.

"Maybe those bassbeats have already driven you a bit insane. I was not serious, you fool!" Hégo had to prevent a smile from etching itself onto his face. *The seed has finally sprouted.* "I only wanted to show you how paranoid you were about those damn walls. They have been standing for centuries. A few piles of debris here and there is not unusual. You trust that horrid creature? How much of a release are we talking here?"

"You sound like a pesky young novitiate I know asking too many questions." Kugai broke out a small grin. "I trusted her enough with Yuuki-Hana."

"Agh!" Hégo again waved his hand, shooing the snide remarks away.

"She can climb, and she is quite dexterous. She's the only cloister inhabitant who can check and repair the walls. She has all the required equipment and strength."

"Equipment, you say. She can also kill ten of us in one stroke with such equipment." He crossed his arms, pulling the oversized laced cuffs over his hands safe from the brisk breeze constantly blowing up, down, and around them.

Kugai remained silent, allowing his companion to continue his mini tirade involving unspeakable horrors and massacres, eventually ending with a deep scornful breath. His mind went to the future, trying to predict how this potentially dangerous decision would manifest. *Would I end up like Ryudasu? To suffer the same fate?*

"What does she want in return? Access to the walls would not placate her. She will want more." Hégo wasn't worried of talking Kugai out of the decision. He knew him too well. Nothing would change that paranoid mind.

"I think release after several centuries imprisoned down in the bowels of the cloister is enough. Look, she is still a Reincarnate, an Animate, no matter if she is an Aku. She has every right to live within these walls. She will forever be imprisoned/protected within or 'on' these walls, just like any other Wamono Reincarnate. But we need her. I cannot go on ignoring something so important to our security as this wall. You would have to agree with me there, Daiso."

"Yes, well, how many Aku have you known? She is the only one I have even seen or even heard of. Those Shisa are close but not quite. Volunteering to be deadly and feared is not the same as having it be a punishment." Hégo wrapped his long locks around his neck to stop the biting wind from chilling his thin blood. "She is an outlier, therefore an unknown. Gou-Tairei does not guarantee she will be constrained within these walls." Hégo rubbed the worn handgrip of his cane, almost petting it. *This is working out perfectly*, he thought. What he said was not all hyperbole. Ryudasu was an unknown variable, even in his plans.

Kugai shivered from the chill of Ryudasu's crime. He didn't know the full story. Sometimes he doubted the commonly believed travesty of a cloister-wide massacre. He had to diminish Hégo's fears. "You know how stories get embellished over time. Do you not think coming back as an Aku is retribution enough?"

A brisk wind whipped into an invisible cyclone in the colossal corner nook. From a distance, the two monks could have been mistaken as oddly shaped detritus fallen off the walls. Kugai noticed Hégo convulse from a shiver before speaking. "This is all quite moot. You do not have the sole authority to 'parole' her. It is not only up to you."

"I am well aware." Kugai did not appreciate being reminded of his limited power. "But I am her warden, so my recommendation will hold more weight than the others, besides of course Dai-Master Daviido-Sama. I am going to formally give my request during the upcoming Wamono-Zentai Conclave." Looking up and along the wall, he noticed a small temporary cataract of stone and dust plummeting to the base from far above out of the mist. *They must approve. There is no other option.*

Hégo groaned as he bent over to pluck a few blades of struggling grass.

"She would be a lurking reminder of what would happen if one of our flock were to even think about being insubordinate to the rules and life of the cloister. Think of it, a terrifying protector. Those Shisa guarding the main gates can only deter insincere converts outside. She would make your job immensely easier within."

The older Wamono released a labored sigh. "O.K., O.K." Kugai noticed a tightening of Hego's bloodless lips. It almost looked like a smile: a satisfied grin. "I am getting a chill. Help me up."

The gnarled monk held out his boney left hand. Kugai obliged. "Issho." Old Hégo unfolded himself and stretched and cracked his back. "Thank you." Hégo reminded Kugai of a faded weather-worn, collapsable sun chair being unfolded for the first time in decades.

They started walking back to the corridor entrance. Kugai kept a supporting hand below his older companion's left arm. The bassbeats had died away and the chilled corridor was quiet again, at least for a few more hours until the night sermon would begin pulsating through the walls and Kugai's head once again.

Dogen Kugai carefully entered Ryudasu's main prison lair in the abandoned wine cellar. Barrels lined the sides waiting for the next batch of Koshu grapes that would never come. He avoided descending into her black humid underworld as much as he could. Today he had no choice. He needed an update on what had happened with her and the troublesome novitiate and to fulfill his end of the bargain. Despite her monstrosity, she was still Wamono. The thought of what damage the spider creature could do to the fabric of cloister life shot shivers through his already chilled bones.

He closed the lapels of his kimono tight around his neck and put his cold, numb hands into the cozy insides of the opposite sleeves. His mass of hair wasn't enough. The insidious ancient air stabbed him with thousands of malevolent, icy pricks.

A formless rasp Kugai was dreading resonated through his skeleton, churning his guts. "What brings the high and mighty down here?"

"It is what we planned." Kugai kept to the facts, trying hard not to fall in the talented Aku's psychoanalytical traps.

The Aku sighed, disappointed the Master of the Cloister didn't want to play her games.

"Did you do what you were supposed to with the novitiate?"

Ryudasu leapt from her sticky perch and landed centimeters in front of her jailer. The sudden appearance of her bristly eye-pustuled head forced Kugai to step back a couple steps. "What do you think?"

Kugai recomposed himself quickly. "Good. And thank you, Genkou Ryudasu-sensei." He thought it prudent to show the unpredictable Reincarnate respect. "And you told him not to tell anyone about his punishment, especially about you?"

"Yessss, yessss. He will not say a word. I made sure of that." She began cleaning her bristly front legs, holding them secure with her glistening fangs as she moved her head up and down. "I do not think you will have much more trouble with that juicy man child."

Kugai looked at the Aku's shiny black eyes, seeing himself in all six mirrored surfaces. How weak and inferior he looked compared with what was looking directly back at him. "I came here to discuss the details of your release and your request to have limited access to the cloister above. As well as full access to the outer walls, of course."

"Well, how kind of you Dogen Kugai-sama," Ryudasu said, mocking the man's monotone, to-the-point intonation.

"You have one job only, to maintain the wall. Do you understand?" He sensed barely controlled anger in those six unmoving orbs. He stayed firm, not showing the fright writhing just under his dermis. "You were imprisoned for a reason, Ryudasu. The Wamono-Zentai have not forgotten, even though your atrocity long ago has disintegrated into the caustic mists of legend."

Rydasu let out a growly purr. "*I* have not forgotten."

Kugai noticed the slight vibrations of the Aku's leg hairs. She was sensing pure fear seeping out of him. "I will inform the Wamono-Zentai at the coming conclave that I would like to take you out of imprisonment to help maintain the barrier wall. That will be in two days' time. I assume you can wait a couple more days"

"You mean you have to ask permission." She rumbled and hissed like a gear-filled machine running on putrid steam.

"Their approval is of course necessary." He despised her for making him feel powerless within his domain.

"Do I have any other choice? It is not like I can simply walk up to the ground levels and above whenever I want. That incapacitating stench wafting out of every crack and pore of every damnable stone above does its job well."

"I have ordered the monks in charge of applying the substance to cease the day after the conclave if everything goes as planned. That should be enough time for the … odor … to dissipate in time for your release." He had to remember to tell the herbalist to begin concocting the conventional piney substance all cloisters used to combat the constant invasive universe of mildew instead of the arachnid-repelling citrus.

He thought back to the tiny spider in his cell. *Why was that little one not repelled by that scent? The mightier one is, the more acute the weaknesses, I suppose.*

"And you are certain the Wamono-Zentai will allow you to free me?" she asked, knowing from experience how tedious and set in their ways the Wamono governing council was. "You are only one Master of a small and unimportant cloister. How can you be so confident?" She backed off a bit, returning to the comfort of her web.

All thanks to you, he thought. Aoheki's dramatic fall in the strict hierarchy of cloisters was the direct result of Ryudasu's unspeakable crime centuries before. "I am confident. It is common, almost necessary, for a cloister to employ an able Reincarnate to help with wall maintenance."

"I am no ordinary Reincarnate," she said, edging closer to the Master. The rubble on the floor seemed to have scurried away on their own volition to make way for the fearsome creature. "I guess it is just your luck you have the most famous Reincarnate living within your humble little pile of crumbling stone."

"Your reputation is more infamous," Kugai retorted. "It is quite unfortunate Reincarnates cannot travel between cloisters. It would have been much simpler to request Ametsubuheki for a few extra ravens."

"Yes, very unfortunate." Finding out if she could exist outside terrified her the most. She would either live or die a forever death? She wasn't ready, not yet.

Kugai wanted to leave and get as far away from this horrid, dank abyss. *I must have done something terrible in a previous cycle to have the burden of an Aku.* "I will leave you to ... whatever you do down here. I must prepare for the Wamono-Zentai and think of how and when to inform our inhabitants you exist; that you are not just as a grotesque cautionary tale, and you may be joining us in a few days." He was dreading exposing his flock to this knowledge. But the relief of no longer having to keep it would be a consolation no matter how small.

"So, it is true. No one knows of me up there?" She sounded offended.

Kugai smiled. "Correct, maybe a century or two ago there were many more who knew of your existence. You have simply become a cautionary tale to the novitiates." For the first time since entering the benthic gaol, he felt he got the best of the wicked creature.

Ryudasu crouched, lowering her body to Kugai's level. She stared at the fatigued man, each eye reflecting the yellow gleamer stick bundle, giving it a possessed eyeball. "Ghhet Ohhut!" she hissed with rigid controlled anger.

Kugai turned around to leave, never letting formality drop. But he couldn't move toward the door. One of the Aku's bristly legs pinned the hem of his kimono, as well as one of his floor-length locks of hair, to the dusty floor. He turned back around as best he could and looked down just in time to see the clawed end of one of her other legs snip a large clump of the moss-green lock, slashing a clean opening in his kimono in the process.

She was standing on four of her legs and towering over him. He stared directly up into her eyes, refusing to say anything.

Ryudasu lifted the purloined lock up to Kugai's tense face and let the hair break apart strand by strand until there was nothing between her crusty pincers. Silence.

Kugai whipped the bottom of his frayed kimono around in front of him and stomped out of the Aku's lair. He turned around once he knew he was at a relatively safe distance from the mad monster and pointed a scolding finger at her. "Do not make me regret what I am about to do for you, Ryudasu." He turned and walked out of her sight. He heard her sinister growl of a laugh even as he mounted the stairs up to the basement level. Self-doubt doubled him over with a punch to the gut. *Am I the one who is mad?*

four

THE PINKU PALACE'S NEON trim cast an pastel pall onto Jojo's face. The pathway leading up to the main entrance of the Dekora HQ surrounded visitors with hundreds of metal ropes with large glass orbs clinging to them. They rained down from the protective overhang twenty stories above. Walking through them produced an army of bizarre reflections of oneself. This time though, they all looked like what she imagined the different stages of agonizing death would be.

She began her long walk through the crowded Jojo-filled funhouse. The massive opaque glass doors swooshed open, blasting her face with candy scented air. She put on her sunglasses to protect her eyes from the blinding white that would bombard her once fully inside the lobby. A first timer to the Palace would without exception become disorientated and stumble until crashing undignified to the invisible floor. There was no visible transition from floor to wall, no horizontal no vertical. The Oné-chan at the time of construction wanted it that way; a message to whoever entered that they were puny and insignificant in her eyes and in those of her feared cutified army of the Dekora gunshyu

Even though Jojo was a member of the infamous gunshyu of professional killers, she still felt puny and insignificant. She was the only person in the lobby; no one would voluntarily remain in the nothing atrium for long. The slight assassin could just as well have been a lumbering, bloated milking cow; an unsightly creature on a perfectly porcelain pasture.

She found the thin cracks surrounding and separating the two halves of the elevator doors and carefully walked toward them. A minute sensation of warmth flowed from her brows to her lower lip. The invisible scan in front of the elevator doors determined who she was. The doors separated with a muffled swoosh. She released the breath she was holding with a puff of "hahh". Many girls found out they were no longer welcome in the gunshyu, for some major or minor offense, when the doors refused to open, thus having—at most—a few minutes left to live; human life was not something any gunshyu held in high esteem. Jojo's spatial world returned to normal once she entered the warm pinks and browns of the elevator interior. Only Oné-chan had the power to return the horizontal and vertical.

Nervous anticipation added long seconds to the journey. "Oné-chan," Jojo began practicing what she would tell her matriarch, "I have something very important to tell you. I know which one of your star mercenaries has gone rogue." She winced in preparation of how the Dekora leader would react. The wince was also for the traitorous act against her best friend. But her loyalty and life had to be with the gunshyu. She continued her scenario. "I have no idea why she did it. But—"

The elevator doors hissed open before she had a chance to finish. A woman, most likely in her mid-fifties—no one dared ask her actual age—materialized in front of her, blocking the way into the suite. Oné-chan was clothed in a black and pink harlequin-esque form-fitting suit, trimmed with lace, an obvious diplomatic nod to her new Lolita daughters.

"Whhoo has gone rogue?" Oné-chan yelled and questioned at the same time. A breeze of mint- and cigarette-infused breath flowed over Jojo's face. "Whhoo?".

Jojo didn't know what to say, but she tried. "Who, what?"

"You didn't think we wouldn't have cameras and microphones in the elevators? That's where all the best information is mined, love." She looked directly into Jojo's eyes. "Obviously."

"Eh, Good afternoon Oné-chan." Jojo took off her Mary-Janes and began to neatly place them, toes facing the elevator, like the others all in line waiting for their feet to fill them again.

"Oh, get on with it, girl! Whhoo has gone rogue? Whhoo is my star mercenary, as you would have any idea of anything."

Jojo opened her mouth to tell her, but the impatient grande dame ordered her, with just her head, to sit in one of three hollowed out egg-shaped chairs hanging in the middle of the suite.

"Yes, ma'am." Jojo couldn't get anything else to come out.

Two of Oné-chan's assistants, clad in candy-pink skin-tight shiny one-pieces and who seemed to have come out from within the walls, guided Jojo to one of the swaying chairs. Their heads and faces covered with the same material with only their eyes and lips exposed. Oné-chan draped herself over a white fainting couch facing the floating eggs.

After both women were finally situated, Oné-chan again scolded her young hit-girl for not answering her. "Do I have to pry your mouth open? Reach in, and grab the information out of your vocal cords?" She mimed the threat as well. Jojo knew it wasn't only meant figuratively.

"Sorry, Oné-chan."

Oné-chan showed no sign of acknowledging the apology and stared at her waiting.

"Mimi, Oné-chan, it's Mimi." Jojo blurted it out exhausted from trying to keep it in.

"Mimi whhoo?" Oné-chan said with eyes half closed in boredom. "Do you know how many 'Mimis' there are in this organization?" She stuck her neck out, eyes squinting.

"Jojo, Jojo Mamba." She made sure to say her second Dekoran name.

"Huh." Oné-chan didn't care to inquire further.

Jojo waited for her to say something more. They just stared at each other.

"Well! Whhhoo?"

Jojo snapped straight back into the chair from the shock wave of Oné-chan's questioning, making the egg swing erratically. "Mimi Barakuda, ma'am." She saw that the matriarch did not hear her from the strain in her face. She tried again. "Mimi Ba.ra.ku.da."

Oné-chan sat back and put her legs up along her couch and looked up into the air, thinking. "Mimi Barakuda, Mimi Barakuda." She tapped a long sharp fingernail against her forehead trying to remember when she heard that name before. "You say she's my star mercenary, do you?"

"I'm sorry, ma'am. I was just embellishing her importance since she's my roommate and best friend." She scrunched her face. *Shit. Now she thinks I'm somehow involved.*

"Ah!" Oné-chan burst out, initiating another go-around in Jojo's egg. "Now, I remember. She's the one that dispatched one of Ren's prized gross golem minions last winter. Yes, that was one to remember. I still can see all that brown bloody snow. Gorgeous. You know that inspired my spring and summer lines." Oné-chan was notorious for going on tangents. "I guess you could say she's one of my stars, though I haven't heard of any major kills from her in a while." She always remembered big kills and gave her girls who carried them out extravagant pieces of clothing or jewelry from her fashion house. "That's a pity."

That's it? Thought Jojo. "Um, aren't you frightened of what this will turn into?"

"Frightened? What for?" She looked at Jojo with a 'you silly girl' expression. "Girls go rogue quite often. I usually have their heads, or something else, popped off before they get a chance to take any business away from me."

She doesn't know yet. I'm not going to survive this.

"We'll get her. You better start looking for a new best friend, love."

I just killed my best friend. The realization that she had sentenced her best friend to death began to short-circuit her highly trained killer interiority. Her eyes began to tear over and lips to tremble. She was saved from showcasing an embarrassing and dangerous total breakdown in front of her boss when one of

Oné-chan's assistants pried himself from his wall post and whispered into the matriarch's ear.

The condescending smile on Oné-chan immediately evaporated, precipitating into puckered, lipsticked grimace. Her eyes widened with fury.

Jojo's muscles tensed as her boss's face tightened from a combination of anxiety and anger. Oné-chan sprung from her soft couch, forgetting her guest's existence.

"Get me Sayuri. Now!" Oné-chan wanted her daughter and Nanny of the Dekora to take care of this.

Jojo and most other girls unfortunate enough to experience training under the Mad Nanny feared and hated her. Just the mention of her name still turned her stomach.

Oné-chan paced back and forth from her immaculate white desk to the window overlooking Deko-cho. She still did not re-acknowledge Jojo's existence. She stopped, held her arm around her mid-section, looked down to the black and white checkered floor, and resumed pacing. Jojo watched Oné-chan moving her head as if she were having a conversation with herself. Oné-chan finally snapped out of her fictional conversation and singled out one of her assistants. "Whhell, where is she?"

The assistant remained unnaturally calm. "Someone is trying to get in touch with her now, ma'am."

"I want her here now, in person! How could this have happened?" She didn't ask anyone in particular. Jojo assumed she was thinking out loud and correctly decided not to answer. Oné-chan turned her head slowly toward her guest. "You!" she pointed at Jojo, who was trying to hide herself inside the chair. "Is this what you came to tell me about?"

Jojo couldn't even force herself to respond.

"Whhell, is it? Answer me you little twit!"

"Yes, I'm sorry, but yes." She couldn't hide any longer. "This is why I came over. I needed to warn you."

"You could've been a little quicker in telling me!" Oné-chan's anger morphed into worry and indecision. She fiddled with her strand of pink and yellow diamonds decorating her décolletage. "Never mind." She took in a deep breath and closed her eyes. "Tell me what you know."

"Mimi said she wanted to go rogue, that it was the only way to earn a living since ..." Jojo didn't want to say anymore. She was about to give criticism to a woman who didn't take feedback well.

"Since whhat? Just tell me!" Oné-chan sounded uncharacteristically desperate. Jojo sensed that the matriarch was angrier for this than the actual transgression.

"Since you formed the cabal." She said it. It was out. *Let her do what she needs to do and get it over with*. She was already resigned to the idea of not ever leaving this suite alive.

"So, she went rogue. O.K., I get that. But in this manner?"

If she did survive this, she would have to do something else to punish herself for being so spineless.

"So, all this was a political statement?" Oné-chan threw up her arms at the ridiculousness of it all. "She's pissed at me, so she is about to bring down the Dekora and the entire cabal for her petty issues?"

"She thinks she can do better." Jojo never could shut up when she was nervous.

Oné-chan regained her poise. She entwined her diamond necklace around her fingers and walked back to her desk. "Too bad the little bitch will never live to try to do so." She drummed out a clicking cadence on the desk with her polish-hardened nails. "Whhere is Sayuri!"

"I'm here," came a muffled voice from the elevator doors. The Nanny of the Dekora was dressed in the same style as Jojo, the major differences being her shorter pig tails, no score totems dangling from her pink frilly mini, and Mary-Janes with thicker and higher heels.

"Do you know about any of this?" Her mother asked in more of an accusatory tone.

"Know what?" Sayuri was barely comprehensible, sucking the candy part of an oversized ring shaped as a baby's pacifier.

"Get that damn thing out of your mouth." Oné-chan ordered. "About one of your darlings going rogue and offing a Storyliner, that's what!"

Sayuri stopped slathering her sucker. Her surprised face looked like the wearer had rather low mental capabilities. "No, I didn't know. Who?"

"Whhoo?" Her mother repeated. "It doesn't matter. What matters is what's going to happen to us." She shot her glare to one of her assistants near where her flip-phone was lying. "Get the Editor on my line, I need to talk with that little bastard before this gets out of hand," The artificial light, radiating off the be-jeweled palm-sized phone in all directions, spayed the suite with rainbow stripes. Oné-chan was slow in adopting new technology. She refused to use the newest fad of ring-and-implant models. She snapped her head back to her daughter and pointed an unusually long, boney finger at the cowering snitch. "Get more information from her. She's starting to bore me, and I need to calm the little bug-eyed weirdo before he starts taking his size, woman, mommy, whatever issues out on me and the cabal." She turned, looking for another assistant to command. She found one standing near the fireplace. "You."

The assistant snapped erect. "Yes, ma'am."

"Use your phone and get me Queen Ren. I need to get to the Suriidii before that troll does. All I need now is for them to use this as an excuse to make up and force us into redundancy." Worry infected her body as she stood waiting for whatever flip-phone came to her first. Her own Mayoral sanctioned satrapy was contingent on helping It maintain this frigid cold war—a far better scenario than the two former business partners reconciling or beginning another turf war, either result would reduce the city to rubble. *The Mayor giving that bat-shit Ren her own satrapy was a clever scheme to reduce the Editor's influence over the city—over It. But insanity unfortunately does not cancel out insanity.* She was convinced the Mayor had a self-destructive streak or at the very least a challenge junky.

"Ma'am." One of her assistants pushed a phone toward her.

Oné-chan looked at him with wide eyes, her hands splayed in frustration. With the intense stress the morning had already brought, she couldn't remember which assistant she asked to call which gunshyu leader.

"The Editor," the assistant whispered covering the phone's speaker.

Oné-chan ripped the phone from his hand and swung her bejeweled hand in front of him, signaling the order to return to his spot near the desk to await further orders.

"Hello love," she answered, not wanting to sound out of control. "Yes ... I hear ... Yes ... I kno ... No, of cour—" She melted into a disgusted grimace, holding the phone away from her ear as if some kind of inky testosterone slime would start oozing from the device. She had only spoken to the Editor a handful of times since she ascended to Oné-chan. She had luckily never met him face-to-warped-face.

After the conversation fell into a rhythm, Sayuri skipped over to her mother's couch, sat down, and stared at her former trainee, still curled up like a baby chick not yet ready to face the world. The Mad Nanny leaned forward, her knees together, heels apart and toes turned inward. She sucked furiously on a lollipop she'd pulled out of her pocket to replace her candy pacifier. If it weren't for the white stick poking between her sticky glossed lips, people would think she had some sort of unfortunate tumor that only she was unaware of.

Jojo believed Sayuri to be made of pure evil. Many new recruits either went slightly insane, offed themselves, or were offed by her or her equally sadistic henchwomen. She was the real gruesome glue that forcefully bound the girls together. Oné-chan was the face of the organization. She was conniving, intimidating, and sinister, but she had to keep her hands somewhat clean, at least the back of them. Her daughter was the assassin's assassin and was very good at it. For all Syuri's shortcomings, she taught her girls well.

Sayuri finally took out her sucker and pointed it at her nervous charge. "So, let's start with who you are," Sayuri began. She never attempted to remember any of the names of the dozens of enchanting butchers under her.

"Jojo." Jojo wasn't sure how much she should answer.

"Jojo what?" Sayuri noticeably frustrated from the tooth-pulling for information.

"Jojo Mamba."

"Ah, yes. You were in my first training group. You're still alive. Good" She was glad to see that her savage training courses were working. Each dead assassin was an excuse for her mother to say it was a mistake to make her the Nanny.

"So, Jiji," Sayuri blurted, uttering the young assassin's name so quickly and incorrectly it sounded like a small frog calling for a mate in swampy Shinyuyogi Park, "Who is this insubordinate little wench?"

"My roommate, Mimi Barakuda,"

"Your roommate, huh. Where is she?"

"I don't know, Nanny-chan. I really don't." She tried to sound sincere but came out as desperate.

"Gagh!" Sayuri rolled her eyes. "Don't be such a whiney little cunt." She sat back and returned her pacifier back in her mouth while holding the shunned fresh sticky lollipop in her other hand. "I know you know something. What is it, Jaja, Juju, whatever the fuck you call yourself?" She released the candied stopper from her mouth, producing a sucking slurp.

"Jojo, Nanny-chan." She hoped her correction wouldn't end her up as a 'volunteer' for wounding-before-killing practice for the new recruits; one of Sayuri's favorite punishments.

"Huh, you don't look like a Jojo. Tell me anything." She leaned forward, pacifier in mouth. "Hon, I guarantee that whatever you know won't be held against you as far as I'm concerned."

The Nanny's concern was not the only one that worried Jojo. She glanced over at Oné-chan, still talking on her blinged-out old-school phone.

"Excuse me Ma'am," announced the assistant who must have had Ren on his line.

Oné-chan covered her phone and barked, "What is it! I'm finally getting somewhere."

"I'm sorry ma'am, but I have the Suriidii leader on the other line and she has been waiting for some time. She is growing impatient."

"Just give her my apologies. I'll call her back as soon as I can." Oné-chan didn't wait for acknowledgement. She turned around and apologized to her counterpart. "I'm sorry love, now where were we?"

"Yoohoo, Koko," Sayuri said, snapping her fingers in front of Jojo. "Can we get on with this? I have a nail appointment in an hour, and I would just love to get the hit-order out on your dear, dear roomie." The Mad Nanny's voice was calm, almost sweet. She pulled on her candied pacifier, slurping every last bit of saliva-dissolved sugar before freeing it from her ravenous tongue. She leaned closer to Jojo and shouted, "But I won't be able to do that until I get some fucking information from the person who knows her best!"

Jojo tried to retreat further into the suspended egg chair.

"Sayuri!" Her mom screeched, again covering up her phone. "Shut your sticky mouth! I'm talking to the Editor!"

"Sorry Oné-chan." She'd learned not to call her 'mother' in front of other Dekora the hard way. She rubbed her hand along the left side of her back where a scar lay hidden under her blouse.

Jojo couldn't take it anymore. She needed to think about herself. "O.K., O.K., I'll tell you what I know, but it isn't much."

"That's more like it. Go on. Anything will help get this slut out of our hair."

Jojo blew out a resigned sigh. "She said she was going to go shopping in Za-Ginsa."

"That's rather brazen of her." Sayuri popped her sweet oral fixation back through her sticky sugary lips. The hard candy part clanked against her pure white, perfectly aligned dentures, of which she had several sets. One was made of platinum, which she always wore on the first day of new-recruit training to put even more fear into their already terrified minds.

"Mimi was always like that. That's why she was such a successful Dekora. She just wasn't afraid." Jojo was trying to weave a more positive tapestry of her friend. She was afraid she went too far by the look on the Nanny's face. She wished she had Mimi's fearless stupidity sometimes.

Sayuri's face relaxed a little. "Well, success has just a thin a shell as bravery, love."

Jojo was a bit disorientated by such a calm and sage-like response coming out of that sugar-rotted mouth.

Sayuri continued, "They are both very easy to crack." Her smile looked as though the pacifier's handle had just sprouted bright gooey pink wings from either side. She took out her phone and pushed the speed-dial button for one of her trainers. She put the cumbersome contraption to her ear, still looking at Jojo with that bizarre child/whore smile.

"Hey, send that Lolita you've been fucking to my office at the Palace in twenty." Sayuri clicked the phone shut and refocused her attention on Jojo. "Thank you for the information, Momo." She stood up and signaled to her mother that she was going to take care of the mess with a thumbs-up and a wink.

Jojo still swayed in her egg. She could only sit there waiting for Oné-chan to get off the phone. She wished she could talk with Oné-chan's public persona, Sanae, the fashionista mogul. Jojo idealized that personality. She was the first Oné-chan to have an influential corporate empire outside the gunshyu system.

Jojo remained patient and silent. *If I survived the Mad Nanny, then I may survive her mother.*

"Ohhh, you still here?" Oné-chan, genuinely surprised to see Jojo still swaying childlike in the chair.

Jojo could only nod. Her legs tingled from not being able to anchor themselves on the floor and back weeping sweat from pressing against the velvety interior of her egg.

"That impossible little man." Oné-chan folded her gem-laden phone, dramatically collapsed onto her couch, and put her hand to her forehead. "He's demanding a meeting. He says he's going to come over 'when he gets around to it' and without notice" She waved her hand at the side of her face. "Whatever. We need to give mentally stunted power-trippers what they want sometimes to prevent murderous tantrums." She sat up and leaned out toward Jojo. "You know he has a private human zoo someplace deep under that eye-sore of a tower of his." Jojo had heard the rumors. "So, why shouldn't I kill you right now?"

The thousands of sweat droplets coating Jojo suddenly turned to ice crystals piercing her skin. "I had nothing to do with this, Nothing!" She was the most animated and fearless she'd been since arriving at the Pink Palace.

"Come now, love." Oné-chan sounded unusually calm. "You must have known something about this or knew it would happen. She's your best friend."

"That doesn't mean anything."

"You're wrong there, my little killer rose." Oné-chan took out a thin cigarette and a powder-blue lighter in the shape of an innocent big-eyed animal. Jojo couldn't make out exactly what kind. "Don't get me wrong, I encourage strong bonds between my girls; the stronger the better." She flicked a tiny plastic lever on the adorable lighter. It hissed gas before igniting into a darker blue stream. She let the flame live for a few seconds as she continued. "Romantically involved yet?"

"No, we aren't." She would've been happy with a bit of flirting and kisses once in a while, but Mimi liked her male liaisons too much and the attention. She watched Oné-chan as she finally lit her toothpick-thin cigarette. The end of the ivory-colored stick burst into a short-lived orange flame before smoldering into a dull glow.

Oné-chan took a long drag, turning the dull orange almost white, and exhaled a long stream of blue smoke that expanded into a ball as it engulfed Jojo's face, causing a fit of coughing. "What, you can't take a little smoke, love?"

"I don't smoke, ma'am".

"That's too bad. This brand is to die for." She emphasized 'die' as if it were her favorite word. "Where was I? Oh yes. I can't have only one half of a bonded pair, be it of the friendship or sexual type. There's just too much risk that you will still be in contact with your traitorous half and either go rogue along with her or spy for her. Neither option is preferable, wouldn't you agree? That's of course if she's still living after today."

Jojo cleared her throat from the sweet noxious fumes. "I came to you. I am just as upset as you are." She regretted saying that the millisecond after it escaped her glossy pink lips.

Oné-chan's neutral smile puckered into a grimace. "Is that so, love? Well, then it wouldn't be very difficult for you to go along with Nanny on her expedition to find and kill your ex-best friend."

Jojo knew she was going be killed if she didn't agree. She took a deep breath. "O.K., not a problem. Mimi betrayed us and put the entire cabal in danger." She exhaled, deflating a bit.

"My my, I guess you two were not as close as I would've expected." She sat back on her couch taking another drag of her cigarette. She took the smoldering stick from her mouth and held it in front of her, studying it. "It's almost finished. They don't last very long, but while they do, they are very good at what they do." She turned her focus onto Jojo. "But there is always another to take its place."

Jojo was tiring of the wordplay. If she didn't have to check her Little Killer at the elevator, she would've popped her then and there—if she had the guts.

"You should try at least one before you go." Oné-chan handed the girl one of her cigarettes from a metallic pink case. Jojo cautiously accepted the gift. She didn't know which end to light until she saw a tiny yellow gem hinting that that end was for the mouth.

"Thank you." Jojo put the studded end in her mouth sensing for any signs of treachery then stuck her neck out so Oné-chan could reach with her lighter. She took a careful drag and quickly exhaled before the blue vapor could invade her throat and lungs.

"There, now you can die," Oné-chan whispered then smiled. She looked over to one of her assistants and gave a minuscule nod while Jojo took another anemic drag. The stiletto-heeled bodyguard calmly walked from his assigned place to just behind his superior, waiting for additional orders. Oné-chan took another long drag while still looking at the girl trying to fight back coughs. "Don't make a mess."

The assistant swiftly grabbed his pink Little Killer invisible against his uniform, aimed it in the direction of the balled-up girl veiled in a haze of blue and pulled the trigger. The fixture holding up the egg-shaped chair creaked as it swung back and forth from the force of the slug that penetrated Jojo's brain. A red dot on the girl's forehead slowly elongating. The cigarette fell from the dead Dekora's lips onto her chest, burning through the skin.

"That withering old shrew!" Ren's outburst frightened her custom mixi-matchied child-pet Nekohito out of its content babble-purring. Its clay and flesh human baby head grimaced at being disturbed. Ren took it into her arms before it burst into tears and human-feline cries bouncing and echoing throughout the cavernous studio. "She calls me! Then says she's too busy to talk!" The self-proclaimed monarch of the Suriidii continued aggressively caressing Nekohito back into lazy contentment then continued to work on an improved version of a warrior knight in her gruesome golem army. She pulled her commring off her thumb and slammed it down on her workbench. "Take it away," she ordered a prototype she started weeks ago but had quickly become bored of. "Throw it out into the river for all I care." She took her small molding knife and began slicing a precise incision on the back of her right hand, neighboring several older ones roughened with coagulated blood. The accumulated meshwork of scar tissue grew permanent scabby gloves on both her hands. She ordered they never be touched while under Masao's knife for her various modifications.

"Yes, your majestic prophetess," replied the shivering naked prototype, its rudimentary male vocal mechanism muffled and slurred by its still setting mouth. He carefully grabbed the ring, bowed, turned around, and exited her studio as quickly as he could, his left putty foot and right metallic one taking turns patting and clinking against the uneven slivery wooden floor, scarred with years of gouges and stained with decades of clay, paint, and blood.

"Wait!"

The prototype stopped in mid clumsy gate, shaking not only from the naked chill but also from the fear of becoming recycle fodder. "Yes, your majestic prophetess."

"Find Masao, I need a touch up." Ren stood up and limped with the help of a cane to her studio's one floor-to-ceiling window. "And leave the ring."

"Ye ... Yes, your majestic prophetess. Right away." The prototype gently placed the ring on a small table near the door then quickly slap-clinked away.

She could just about make out her reflection in the grimy window. *I need to get a mirror in here one of these days*, she thought, struggling to see how her face was healing. She swore she had ordered Masao to bring one several times. She stroked her new face. Most of the bandages had been removed except those around her jawline and forehead. She backed up a little to get a look at her entire form. "I should have had Masao cut some of this damn fat out this time."

Ren was, until a few months ago, king instead of queen of her domain. Even before and since her transition, there was always at least one body part wrapped in bandages. There were minor touch-ups here and there that relentlessly needed to be snipped, added, or remolded. Her nickname among her various human and more malleable subject-worshippers was O-miira; 'Royal Mummy'. She was aware of this but never heard it spoken in front of her. If she had, she would have no qualms about disposing of the offender, no matter how high up in her court of clay, metal, and flesh.

"You called for me, your majestic prophetess?" came a low voice. The warm deepness soothed her sore groin.

"Yes, Masao. What do you think of extra-long eyelashes? Would they go with my new ice blue eyes?" Her face was almost touching the window, as she tried to make out the details of her eyes, imagining lush, soft lashes framing them. "I think long ones all the way around." She made an exaggerated circle around one of her bruised eyes with a ratty, bandaged finger. "That would make them pop, don't you think?"

"Yes, your majestic prophetess. They would." Masao was her Chief Remodeler and responsible, along with pretty much everything else to do with his queen prophetess' realm, for all her body-modification whims. He took off his putty-and blood-spackled smock, folded it neatly, taking care not to create any unnecessary creases, and draped it gently across his arm. His exposed mauve and grey Suriidii regalia was characteristically crisp and spotless, hugging his slender but muscular body. "I will have some made for you immediately."

"No, I don't want artificial ones." She continued studying her reflection, vaguely staring back at her from the window, the monolithic scrapers dotting the immediate horizon distorting her face. Unlike her enemy and former business partner, she was not interested in being at the top of a scraper. She preferred her plain, almost dilapidated low-lying studios, labs, and production lines forming an industrial nation of utilitarian tyranny throughout the wards east of the inky Sumi River. "Go find a couple live ones for me. I've seen some gorgeously long pairs on a few boys over in the molding fief. Bring a couple you think might do and I'll inspect them. I'll need more than one pair to cover both eyes top and bottom."

"Yes, your majestic prophetess," the Chief Remodeler said, never questioning his queen-prophetess' request.

Masao had been her closest confident since she revealed herself to be in Totality with the utili-god Caliper. However, two prophets, more accurately two utili-gods, can never be in any kind of partnership; one would inevitably and violently cancel the other out. The necessary split of the Tsudii-Suriidii corporate-religio daigunshyu resulted in a quick but devastating city-wide civil war. The two Mayoral satraps had been forced by the Mayor into a tense, tightly regulated cold-war truce ever since.

Masao helped the new prophet re-organize the former non-publication departments of Figurines, Art Installations, and Performance Productions she had overseen in the former media empire as well as its vast factories, studios, and warehouses throughout the eastern half of the city. The tentacled Suriidii reach now extended throughout the city thanks to the popularity of its original side business of mixi-matchi clinics located at the busiest viscerdenn stations that even the Editor depended on to maintain control over his wards.

"What do you think of that annoying witch over in Deko-cho?" The Suriidii queen asked her number one advisor. "And please, Masao, what do I always tell you? Just 'your majesty'. We're friends, aren't we?"

"Very well, your majesty." Ren growled a snicker at her confidant's obvious discomfort. "You mean the Oné-chan?" Masao always needed to make sure everything was clear before proceeding. His long years in service to Ren taught him that miscommunication could cost even him his life.

"Who else would I mean?" Her Chief Remodeler's slow and formal communication style often annoyed her, but it was what made him so valuable. His almost perfect bone structure also didn't hurt. *That perfect triangular head and exquisite inverted triangular torso*, she thought. He was one of the very few un-modifieds at her disposal. She forbade him to have any modifications done to him. She wanted him the way he was, naturally perfect.

"May I speak frankly, your majesty?"

"Certainly. You always may." She shuffled back to her stool, sat down carefully so as not to disturb the bandages on her backside and thighs, then scooped up her Nekohito, annoyed at being woken up again. She made a nest for it in her arms.

"Thank you." Masao had also learned delicate tact was still required when told he could speak frankly. "I believe this Oné-chan is dangerous. Not only in the fact that she is powerful in both public and satrapic layers of this city, but it is obvious that she cannot control her subordinates." He remained standing in formal pose, never daring to relax and betray comfort in front of his queen.

"What do you mean?" Ren started rolling eyeballs around on her desk with her long fingernail.

"Oh. Apologies, your majesty. I thought you would have already received the information." Masao was noticeably irritated at himself for assuming she already knew. It was his job to notify her of such things. He had assumed his complex network of royal spies would have gotten back to her on this already.

"Well, tell me! What is being kept from me?" She had very little patience for being kept out of the loop.

"It's about Oné-chan and her assembly of mercenaries."

"Yes, yes, I figured that. Just get to the point." Her skin was starting to itch under the bandage covering her jawline, making her even more irritable. She fought the urge to make a painfully satisfying incision on her hand.

"Yes, your majesty," the inelastic man continued. "Apparently, one of her Dekora butcher-girls went rogue." He paused, making sure his queen took in everything.

"Yes, O.K." Long pauses in conversations frustrated and frightened her. She was trying her hardest to remain patient. Sometimes she believed that this man was a very well-made humanoid mechanism full of gears, bolts, and clay. It would explain his maddening calmness and lack of fear, particularly of her. "Those whores always go rogue. Pay them enough and they will do anything. We pay a few on the side to take care of minor disposals not related to our Tsudii friends. It's a simple economic fact Oné-chan doesn't seem to grasp."

"This time it's a bit more, how should I say, complicated."

"How so?"

"This 'whore' ..."

Ren wanted to smile, but the rest of her bandaged face wouldn't allow it.

"... assassinated a Storyliner."

Ren's eyes widened as far as they could without splitting the sutures open at the corners, and the smile she was working so hard to form quickly retracted. "Are you sure of this?"

"Yes, I am," Masao responded.

"Shit! Well, that's not horrible news for us now, is it?" She began stabbing her workbench with here pin-knife. She needed to puncture something since her hands were not an option with Masao present.

"No, not entirely, but ..."

"Yes, I know. The Dekora broke a contract. Loss of trust and all that."

"Precisely, your majesty."

"So that's why the old hag called me." Ren chuckled. "She must be running around like one of your specimens becoming sentient before having its head affixed. I'm sure she has a lot of explaining to do to that little tweeked-out freak."

"Yes. Our spies have word that the Editor wants revenge against the Dekora and the young Moé Cabal," added the Chief Remodeler.

"What do you advise, Masao?"

"We could either do nothing and let the two fight it out, likely destroying each other—"

"Yes, that thought came to my mind as well. And the other option?"

"We could use the Cabal's disadvantage to our advantage by forcing them into a permanent partnership with us; getting rid of the back-and-forth contracting business scheme they have been using to increase their power and influence throughout the city."

"Hmm," Ren nodded, abandoned her bench puncturing, and began stroking Nekohito, inducing more cooing purrs. "In effect creating a permanent army of the most highly trained killers in the city. I like that idea."

"Please, remember the Mayor's directive forbidding another direct conflict between us and the Tsudii. We cannot risk infuriating it by eliminating It's newest and darling buffer Satrapy of Deko-cho. No one knows what power It really has. Plus, It *is* the city, we cannot forget that."

"No, we sure as hell would not want the Mayor involved any more than It already is."

"However, both options have advantages and disadvantages, your majesty, and should be seriously considered."

Ren was starting to enjoy this rational pro-and-con game of Masao's and even more so the slightest of wobbling of his legs from standing stiff and proper the entire time. *I guess he is human after all.* "Yes. If we let them fight it out amongst themselves, I'm sure Oné-chan would finagle her way out of it somehow. I hate to admit, but she has an uncanny talent of turning a bad situation to her advantage. Look at the way she increased her power over those Lolita harlots."

"Precisely, your majesty." Masao acted like a professor challenging his prized pupil in the art of rational problem solving. "She expertly avoided what we would have thought and hoped would turn into a Moé civil war."

"How unfortunate for us it didn't turn out that way no matter how much we tried to steer it otherwise." Ren continued the game with the second option. "However, if we force her into a permanent alliance with us, we will have to be extremely careful to maintain the upper hand—a majority stockholder, if you will. It would be quite difficult to keep those girls under control. What we are talking about is creating a client kingdom."

"Yes, I suppose." Masao was never fully comfortable with her imperial analogies. "And yes, it would be quite difficult."

"But if it worked, it would weaken the Tsudii."

"It has that potential, your majesty. But so does the first option, with about the same probability."

"I take it that you would advise the first option."

"Yes, at first," said Masao. "But there is no reason we cannot do both."

Ren leaned forward, wincing from soreness. "Go on."

"We simply sit back and see how things go. Our prime goal is to eradicate the hold the Editor and Draw have over a disproportionate percentage of the city, correct?"

"Yes, of course. And it would be better if he were eradicated period."

"If fighting breaks out between them, which is inevitable, we watch to see who starts to have the upper hand. If the Dekora and the rest of the Cabal seem to be winning, we remain neutral, but if the opposite starts to materialize, we just form that alliance. By that time, they will be desperate for any assistance and—"

"And we can negotiate the new covert 'partnership' on our terms," the queen said, completing the reasoning.

"Precisely. Though they need to remain as outwardly independent as possible. The directive, remember."

"I'm not senile, Masao. I don't need to be reminded of the shit storm that would happen if the directive was violated."

"Calm yourself." A voice vibrated though Ren's furious mind. "He is simply doing his job."

I was wondering when you would begin meddling in the conversation, Cal. Ren caressed the side of her right thigh to which her utili-god Caliper was physically attached. "Apologies, Masao." She relaxed her eyes to seem more understanding. "I know you are trying to cover all angles."

We will have to make the Tsudii have an upper hand at the beginning."

The Chief Remodeler nodded in agreement, almost an approval of his queen's strategic thinking. "That's quite a dangerous play, your majesty."

"It's dangerous no matter how you play it, my calculating friend." She did think of Masao as a friend, as far as she could allow that sort of relationship.

"How would you like me to proceed with this plan?"

"Give me a while to think about it. I would like you to do the same."

"Of course, your majesty. Is there anything else?"

"No, that's all. You may go. Things are about to move very quickly, so we need to be ready when this mess really starts taking a shape."

"Yes, your majesty." Masao carefully unfolded his sullied smock and covered his uniform, instantly transforming himself from royal advisor to head of the Remodeling fief located adjacent to the capital studio. He had no choice but consider himself the chancellor and duke in his queen's half-fantasy empire.

"Oh," said the queen remembering something else.

"Yes, your majesty?" Masao stopped before pulling the knob to open the large glass-paneled doors of the royal studio.

"Have a prototype bring up a mirror. I'm tired of looking through that polluted window. It does not do your handy work justice.

"Right away, your majesty," said the meticulous remodeler.

Once the doors to her studio were firmly and 'precisely' closed, Ren crumpled under the weight of her royal posture, rested her aching head on her hands, and began balling up the leftover scraps of pliant putty populating her workbench. *Will these last modifications finally make myself attractive to him?* She smashed the newly born smooth balls back into ugly, untidy smears and looked down at Nekohito, who noticed her looking at it and raised its creased clay and flesh face to her. "Nekohito, why doesn't he make me into what he wants? He's my damn remodeler!" She waited for the usual unwelcome response from Caliper. "What, no snide comment, Cal?"

She quickly scooped up the clay and blood-crusty knife on her workbench and sliced three reddening slivers on each hand. The climax from her half-hearted self-restraint sent painful shudders of ecstasy throughout her body. It was the only passion she could experience.

five

YUUKI WOKE THE NEXT morning from a sleep he didn't remember falling into. He remained lying on his back, only moving his teary eyes, wondering if all that had happened with the giant Aku was real. He unfroze himself from the grip of waking disorientation and hesitantly touched his gouged cheek as if it might wake up and bite his hand. He had been so exhausted he forgot all about tending to it when he returned. The pain returned on queue. His pillow decorated with angry blood smudges and irate crusted gore. *It was no dream.* He didn't want to go the infirmary. He hated that place—full of old, sick monks and more than a few demented ones.

He quietly walked over to the desk and bent to look at his reflection in the tiny grungy mirror that provided any kind of dimension to the cell. Hiro and Shinya's cots were empty and disheveled. *They must be doing their morning bathing.* The mirror didn't get much use from him, but it did from the constantly grooming Shinya, the oldest of the three cellmates. It didn't allow for the clearest image, but it was enough to be repulsed by Ryudasu's bloody work. He reached back to his cot, grabbed a corner of sheet, and ripped a couple frayed swatches. He wadded one up and dipped it in the cup of water he always kept next to his cot. It felt like the skin had turned to tree bark. After a few passes with the wet cloth, the wound began to soften but protested with pain. He could see further inside with all the dried globules of blood clinging to torn flesh cleared away. *She almost pierced right though*. He put a finger in his mouth and pushed against the laceration from the inside. His finger was almost visible through the remaining membrane. It was the moment he became aware of his adulthood. He thought of all the monks having scars; not all visible but psychological. Hinodé had scarred them so badly they had to escape. *I need more scars.*

He reached inside his sleeve pocket and touched the reality of the map inside. *Am I actually getting out of this place?* The thought allowed a smile of accomplishment, but a twang of sadness at the thought of leaving the only home he had ever known took hold of him. It just as quickly dissipated through the misty exhale of his breath.

He listened for any heavy footsteps coming down the corridor signaling his cellmates' imminent return. The dusk maintained its young silence. He took out the map and unfurled it on his cot, holding it flat with both hands. The precious little dawn light that made it inside the cell was quickly being overtaken by the cremation-grey haze of cloister shadow. He carried his treasures over to the desk, clearing away the study books and chore logs of the others. He placed his yellow gleamer in its holder and unfurled the map again.

It was more a schematic than an actual map with almost familiar scribblings that were just that off to be unreadable. He stood hunched over the map for quite a while, trying to get some sort of orientation, but it was impossible; the only location he knew was the square Ryudasu had pointed to as that of the cloister. There was not even a direction marker.

He straightened himself and put his hand on the small of his back, massaging the kinks out. He let the map roll back into its natural state. He needed to walk away from it before it started to drive him mad, or at the very least give him a headache. It was just in time.

Shinya barged into the cell, tossing his soap, washing cloth, and drying towel onto his cot. Yuuki jumped, almost knocking over the gleamer. "Did I scare ya?"

Yuuki grunted an affirmative.

"Good!" Shinya replied with a cheeky smile. "That must have been some punishment. You were passed out when we got back from our night bath. Old Kugai is not going to like you skipping last night's and this morning's bassbeats."

Shinya joined the cloister of his own will about twenty years ago when he was just barely old enough to do so. He was twelve years older than Yuuki, but Yuuki was bigger and taller. He didn't quite understand the reasoning of how the proctor determined which novitiate would share a cell and for how long. This was his fifth set of cellmates, and they were just barely getting comfortable with each other's personalities, quirks, and out-right annoyances. Like all novitiate, no matter their age, Shinya had taken the vow to leave behind everything of Keibu-yo and never mention it or his life outside. He took the vow seriously, he had too. Trial by Shisa was a powerful deterrent. Despite Shinya's unwillingness to share, Yuuki liked Shinya; liked him a lot.

Yuuki lifted his chin slightly in the universal male-to-male acknowledgement.

"So, what did they have you do this time and who did you pester for what information about Keibu-yo? Is there anything left?" Shinya asked. "You are lucky Kugai-sama likes you so much. You would have been sent to Shisa trial long ago, and they would not care how special you are."

Yuuki ignored Shinya's envious dig at his favored status. For some reason, it felt less hateful when he said it. "A lot is left."

"Woaaa! What happened to your face?"

"Nothing. Just tripped over some rubble down in the root cellar when cleaning it as punishment." His cheek burned up from the attention.

"Did not know we had a root cellar."

Yuuki regretted telling him. He was already betraying the promise he made with that Aku.

"Where is Hiro?" Yuuki asked, changing the subject.

"Still in the baths."

Shinya unwrapped and let fall his bath kimono and did a full body scan with his towel to wipe away the remaining droplets that escaped his quick dry back in the baths. The morning's voyage was about to begin. Yuuki wanted so much to reach over and touch him. He looked away, closing his eyes tight, blaming them.

Yuuki always started out on his voyeuristic exploration of Shinya—if he was positioned correctly—at his large copper-brown eyes hooded with broad precise brush-stroke eyebrows. He moved down to his broad chest and slight paunch covered in currents and eddies of wet-blackened hair, changing direction depending on how the last streams of water from the bath, or the sweat from a hard day of chores, flowed over it. His penis, nestled in a thick shrubbery of hair; the same intense black as the hair on his head, always seemed to be half erect, his testicles ever so slightly bobbing up and down to the rhythm of his breathing. His legs were uniformly covered in the same soft hair as his belly. The furriness extended down to the knuckles of his perfectly rounded toes then around, carpeting all the way up then over the mounds of his buttocks, stopping in an alluvial fan a few centimeters up the small of his back. Yuuki had the opportunity to take the same visual voyage at least once a day. He sensed that Shinya knew this and made it a point to give his younger cohort the opportunity to gaze. Was this Shinya's narcissism or purely altruistic?

"What is wrong, Yu-chan? You lost interest? Am I getting too old for you?" Shinya's voice was not wrapped in his usual sarcasm but sounded half concerned.

Yuuki looked back at Shinya standing directly in front of him full frontal just a half a reach away, but it might as well have been an unfathomable chasm. Yuuki started to give an 'I do not know what you are talking about' look but decided it would've been ridiculous. Instead, he looked directly at Shinya's glistening black groin and squinted. He instantly regretted it.

Shinya edged closer. "Is this better?"

Yuuki couldn't help staring directly at Shinya's twitching penis, he then looked up to his smiling face. Yuuki jumped off the cot from the opposite side and sat down hard at the desk. *I did not do anything different. What is going on?!*

"Come on Yu-chan," Shinya pleaded, walking over to Yuuki still naked. "I am sorry. Just wanted to play with you a little."

Yuuki still had his back to his nude cellmate. *What does he mean by 'play'?* He felt slight pressure on his shoulder where Shinya placed his bath-warmed hand.

"I did not mean to upset you. Just that—"

"Just that what?" Yuuki turned around, hot tears starting to form.

Shinya squatted to be at eye level with his younger cellmate. "Calm down Yuuki. What is wrong?" His voice was soft. He ran a couple fingers down Yuuki's bandaged cheek, instantly dulling the pain.

"I had a hard day yesterday, that is all." Yuuki covered his reddening face, trying to hide the tears. He felt Shinya's hand lift from his shoulder and the slight breeze he made from standing up and moving away. Yuuki turned his head ever so slightly and watched Shinya put on his kimono and start to wrap a binding ribbon around himself to close it.

"I know you like guys, Yuuki. We both know. And that is cool. I mean, probably more than half of us are orientated to both sexes. If we are not sure when we join, we will be after a few months. A fortress of males will bring that part of anybody out in full force." His smooth quiet laugh covered Yuuki in a soft vocal down.

"Us?" *Is he telling me he ...?*

"Even me." Shinya raised his arm in front of Yuuki and walked to the high window. "A lot of novitiate talk about girls they met, or in my case, imagined meeting out there. We want what we cannot have I guess is the saying." He smiled and walked back toward Yuuki. He took Yuuki's chin by his hand and drew his tear-streaked face to his own and kissed the still shivering lips. He pulled back, gently smiling. He grabbed Yuuki's hand. "Come on, I want to show you something." He pulled Yuuki up from the chair. Yuuki only now realizing how strong Shinya really was.

"What?" Shinya helped him get on top of the desk. Yuuki didn't even see him jump up.

They stood in front of the small, lonely window. "Look," Shinya ordered but with a smile. Yuuki looked out. He didn't have to stand on his tippy toes like Shinya had to.

"Sakura Hitotsu-en Courtyard, so what?" It was just a wide expanse of pee-yellow grass and stones strategically placed around the enclosure. It had been an ancient rock garden, long forgotten and smoothed over by grass, rain, and wind.

"Look over at that wall." Shinya pointed to the wall on their right. He placed his wide hand against Yuuki's lower back with the pressure of a feather. "If you go there and look really hard, you can see a small crack. It goes all the way through." Yuuki squinted to see if he could see the small miraculous portal to the outside world."

"Why did not you tell me this before?"

"I only found it a couple days ago. I was waiting for the right time to tell you when Hiro was not around."

"Can you see anything?" Yuuki's eyes grew from squints to huge brown orbs.

"Not much, but a tiny bit. I only tried once and only for a second. There were others around." Shinya's hand never moved from Yuuki and even tightened a little more.

Yuuki found at the very instant how love felt.

Ryudasu finished weaving her death shroud around a paralyzed rodent. She had nothing to do but kill, feed, and think. It was what she had been doing for centuries: ample time to devise and refine her plan in minutia. It was all at last coming to fruition, thanks to that obstinate 'pure' novitiate finally growing up. But any little kink could make the whole scheme fall to rubble, just like the barrier walls.

Her entire body was as still as the musty air around her. Only her front leg-arms moved, weaving the finishing touches on her snack for the evening. The only sound was the sticky attaching and separation of her silk strands as her leg-arms worked like factory mechanicals to lay the strands just right.

Nothing can get in my way—not this close. She finished her snack preparation and carried the white coffin up to the top of her web, placing it among the others in various states of readiness.

That impudent human better do what is required of him. The transformation of his blood is key for the next phase. Her tenuous connections to the other side of the cloister walls were only useful to a point. This last phase required physicality out there and a very specific one at that. Being a Reincarnate, she could not step even one of her needle-like pincers onto the unconsecrated ground of Hinodé. "Ooh, how I would love to wreak horror in the streets of that rancid city, so filled with deceived souls. Hegemony makes both sides villainous" She let out a hissing sigh. "I had to pay for my past actions. It is my turn to receive payment."

She swung one of her legs and kicked an emptied cocoon off the web, slamming it against the wall before it landed with a soft thud on the rubble below. "Damn these walls: this world!" Her agitation combusted her abdomen, blasting the entire cell in a hue of bile yellow-green. "And damn you Gou-tairei!" She didn't want to believe in its unconcerned power, but she was proof it existed. "Being certain in your existence does not require devotion or respect."

She remained at the top of her web focusing on her various cocooned snacks. *Soon, I will stretch my web over all Hinodé. It will be a limitless feast. I am so hungry. So, so hungry.*

Ryudasu looked up at the wall to a glossy green stone that stood out against its death-drab neighbors. "It is time." She reached one of her leg-arms over to a small vessel resting on a rough ledge etched into the time-worn wall, just to the right of the out-of-place stone. Her pincers closed as she dipped them into a thick black substance. *Need to get that old fool Hégo to acquire more for me. I sacrificed a good portion of it for that novitiate.* She carefully withdrew her pincers from the vessel and began smearing the blackness over the fuzzy green stone. The scraping of her claws against the stone echoed throughout the cell. *That Dame had better be there. Not going to wait around in Goushintei purgatory until she gets around to ingesting on her end.*

Ryudasu made sure the black viscous mass was well mixed with the mossy green on the stone then brought just enough for about ten minutes of mind-to-mind communication to her mouth and began to carefully lick the bitter grease off them. The ink, in pure concentrations, was highly dangerous to those not pure in their being. Her present form was evidence of and punishment for that little experiment. *Petty Gou-Tairei, petty.*

She remained still, her abdomen dimming. The silence broke with a sudden and audible snap in her highly tensed synapses that rippled throughout her body, throwing her into a spasm, spawning wave after wave of vibrations along her web. Her abdomen then exploded again in yellow-green light, so bright all shadows unshadowed. Low gurgling welled up within her, eventually escaping her flailing armored mouth. Her brain was not aware of what was happening to her body and surroundings. It focused on something completely different.

Like all times previously, all she could see at first was haze, as if she were standing on the very top of the barrier walls in the middle of permanent misty cloud. She imagined the first few minutes under Goushintei as such a scene. It kept her orientated. A slightly darker form began to materialize in the murky distance. She learned from the dozens of times she had done this that it wouldn't become any more detailed until it started conversing with her. She never had the patience to wait for the form to initiate. She needed to know who she was going to talk with: to make sure it was who she expected.

"You made it on time this session," Ryudasu began.

"Yes. I'm sorry to have kept you waiting the last time, Holy Spinner," the form replied. Ryudasu made out a humble bow in the form.

A female voice. Good so far. The form began to give away more detail. "Keep talking. I need to see as much as I can of you to make sure. There could be people out there jealous of your relationship with me."

"Yes, of course, Holy Spinner," replied the female form. "Is the time almost upon us?"

"I certainly hope so, my little silk strand, I certainly hope so." She detested acting gracious and 'divine'. She wanted to encase this ignorant devotee in a sticky silk shroud and suck her dry, alive.

The woman was almost visible, finally differentiating from the haze around her. But she would never become clear, a limitation of the Goushintei. Ryudasu could make out something on the head of the blurry-faced apparition. "Why are you wearing that ridiculous headpiece?"

"My apologies, Holy Spinner." The woman involuntarily reached up and felt her towering wig. "I had to officiate a group funeral of our latest actors. It went a little long and I didn't have time to change into less offensive attire."

"I do not need to hear excuses. Are our converts preparing for the coming re-unification of the Vast Dimensional Web?" She forced herself not to laugh every time she spoke of such nonsense. She didn't care about any devotion or any silly grand re-unification. This little religion, built up around her was simply a happy accident thanks to simple religious minds and outside ignorance to the more chemical than spiritual Goushintei. "What is the progress in converting the rest of your kind?"

"Forgive me Holy Spinner, but if you could give some sign, some evidence, that you exist, I believe conversion would happen much quicker." Even through the Goushintei miasma, Ryudasu sensed the woman shivered with nervousness. "I am not the leader of all the Fujou. I only have power within my small den. Our devotion to you must remain secret, unfortunately. The rest are devoted to the Tsudii, Suriidii, or both. But I do have a plan."

I am competing for the devotion of weak minds with my own cousins. "A plan?" Ryudasu was becoming bored but needed to express divine patience. "Does it have something to do with your reforms?"

"In a way," said the Fujou Dame. "It may not be possible to convert the entire Fujou gunshyu, but I could put into motion a break-away. Perhaps ally with other independent women from other all-female gunshyu. I'm meeting one tomorrow. A Fujou dedicated to reforming her den would help in forming some sort of confederation."

"I chose you, just like your father before you, to spread my word. Unfortunately, he passed away before he had time to make any progress within his circles. It is up to you now. Faith is all you should need." From the beginning of this accident of a religion, Ryudasu knew that an army of fanatic drones would only be beneficial to her larger plans, but she was getting tired of waiting and if she couldn't be seen by others it would be a hindrance to her totally unholy plan. "However, I do understand. The time will come very soon when I will be able to give you and others a sign. Patience my devoted silk strand."

"That is encouraging news."

"There is something I need you to do that is of the utmost importance," Ryudasu imagined illuminating her abdomen slightly for effect.

"Yes, Holy Spinner, anything."

"I want you to meet a young man outside the walls of the Wamono cloister of Aoheki. You will see him at the spot I guided you to several months ago, remember?"

"Yes. The place where the stones are a little out of place, not too far from where I receive the gift of the Vision Dew every month."

"Yes." *Ridiculous name.* "He is a Wamono novitiate monk named Yuuki-Hana and will be exiting most likely tomorrow evening. He has no idea who I am or our holy plan. He is simply a sacrificial messenger, so do not mention me or your faith, he will not understand. It will only confuse him, understood?"

"Yes, I believe so. He is to be sacrificed? If he should have to sacrifice his life, then it will be an honorable death for him. Will I be the one to perform the sacrifice?"

"No, befriend him and take him back to your den. I cannot overemphasize how important this is." She watched her devotee for any signs that she was understanding the importance. The woman nodded. "I need to hear that you understand." She intensified her voice to sound more 'godlike'.

"Yes, Holy Spinner. I do, and I will do everything in my power to accomplish our goal."

"Good, Good. This novitiate has not been outside the cloister since he was an infant. He has no knowledge of life outside those walls. He will need a friendly face to guide him for his first few days. Who knows what a frightened disorientated young man will do?" *He needs to trust someone out there.* "You must safely deliver him, with a map I have given him and the message I dictated to you during our previous meeting, to the one your father told me about, this Editor. *He and the so-called Queen Ren must be my cousins, now complete strangers even different species.* She was not pleased to find they were both compromised by Inanimates or idols as they called them out there. Some even became sort of gods, and that interfered with her god persona. "The Editor should be able to take it from there." *The novitiate's blood should be sufficiently enriched with that squid's ink by then.* "And do not allow those carnivorous females you lead to place even one of their debauched fingers on this novitiate."

"Yes. I understand, Holy Spinner."

Ryudasu didn't want this mindless creature knowing any more about her plans than was necessary. She only needed her to be devoted enough to do her tedious info gathering and build her religion. Becoming a god made it much easier to control and mold.

"I cannot guarantee exactly what time the Wamono will exit, so stay in the area throughout the day and keep watch over that portion of the wall."

"That will not be a problem. I am due for a recruiting expedition."

"I did not ask you if it would be a problem." She detested when others assumed she had any interest in their sense of self-convenience. "'Recruiting'. Is that what you call it? Seems more like hunting."

"Yes, I am aware of your distaste of our practice. I can only pray that recruiting will be a thing of the past."

Ryudasu didn't care what those hags did: recruit, hunt, it was of no concern to her. But she had to be righteously indignant about something. She wouldn't be a god otherwise. "Our time is almost up, and I see that the Vision Dew is starting to affect you. We will end now if you have no other questions." She couldn't admit to her devotee, but she was also quickly tiring. Nothing much frightened her, but the aftereffects of the unpredictable psych-communication drug was something that everyone, even a fake god, had to be somewhat frightened of.

"No questions, Holy Spinner. I will prepare for Aoheki immediately."

The image of the strangely coiffed woman began to meld back into the drug haze of Ryudasu's mind, disappearing altogether within a few seconds. Both interlocutors would soon go temporarily blind, mute, and dangerously disorientated for several hours. Ryudasu took the short few seconds after disconnection to mentally prepare for the ordeal.

six

BASHO JYON'S MID-AFTERNOON HAIKU-BASSBEAT sermon was about to approach its climax. The cloister's most sought-after cleric was barely visible, high in his pulpit overhang. When he came to personally conduct a sermon at a transcendence chamber, there was always a larger crowd than usual. Many living in other clerical jurisdictions temporally defected just to experience Basho's psyche-altering bass-beats sermons. The visible-invisible space created from the multi-color strobes pulsing and bouncing off the far walls and heads of the celebrants below kept the cloister celebrity in complete shadow.

The progressive, electronic beats began to fade. The chant chorus providing the necessary human guttural bass during the sermon slowly became the only sound, putting everyone far below into a uniform trance sway. The purring exhales of the monks composed the accompaniment. The abyssal masculine atmosphere prepared the inner-most recesses of the mind to receive Basho's only utterance: the sermon. His synthetically enhanced ultra-deep bass voice matched the booming vibrations of the chorus reverberating throughout the cavernous hall and into everyone's psyche.

Tenth wind's vocation...
Unfetter tenuous leaves
Ignored to live on

The chamber remained almost silent. The chorus softened their voices to a nearly sub-sonic sustained vibration while Basho disappeared into the wall, his hypnotic vocal reverberating then dissipating around him. The air remained heavy with contemplation on the master cleric's haiku, prepared just for them and never to be uttered again except perhaps by future scholars in arguing its meaning.

Yuuki didn't care about processing Basho's latest verbal gift. He had been occupied looking for Shinya in the novitiate cluster. He didn't remember much after Shinya showed him the crack in the barrier wall, but the memory of his supportive hand on his back was very clear. He still felt the male heat. *Was it all only one pathetic scene in an epic desperate dream?*

He quickly shuffled out of the chamber when the bassbeat trainers weren't looking. Streams of sweat cascaded down his forehead and back colliding with the cool air of the corridor. He started walking but soon fell back against the chilled, wet wall, sliding down in a fetal crouch feeling the unforgiving chill of the weepy stone seep into every pore. He put his head down between his legs and sobbed. *Do I tell him I am leaving? Should I leave?* The doubting questions put him into a dizzying spin.

A steamy, plumed sigh escaped his tear-wet lips. "I need to leave!" But his mind kept rebelling, wandering back to nude Shinya and the kiss they shared. The thought of his lips killed off the chill creeping into him. He vice-gripped his head between his hands, attempting to crush all the conflicting thoughts swirling inside. *I need to talk to someone.* He bobbed back and forth debating if confessing everything would be a smart thing to do. Who would listen and not act, not judge? A small but sincere smile stretched over his cry-rouged face. "Of course!"

He pushed himself up the cold sweaty wall with renewed energy. He would have to climb several small flights of stairs, navigate a few dozen right and left turns, and journey down several hundred meters of almost-forgotten hallways, but the journey would be worth it. It had been too long since he made a visit to his dear old friend.

"Amedo?" Yuuki called out for his friend.

"Yuuki-Hana?" came the friendly gurgle. "My, it has been a while." The squid fluttered his body fins to the near side of his liquid home, illuminated by only a single artificial moonlight-hued gleamer hanging above. He extended his pair of long hunting tentacles for Yuuki to touch. "Come over and let me feel you. These old eyes are not what they used to be."

Yuuki gladly obeyed and placed his hand on the cold rubbery skin. "Good to see you, Sama."

"Sama? What has gotten you in such a polite mood?" Nonen Amedo said, starting off the friendly banter. "Is this really Yuuki?"

Yuuki quietly chuckled. "How are you holding up?"

"Holding up?"

Yuuki rubbed the flattened end of one of the old cephalopod's extended hunter tentacles. "Sorry. How is your health?" Yuuki bent down and rested his arms on the pool's rim so his friend could see him better.

"Oh, as always; becoming older, slower, and hopefully wiser." Amedo lifted a tentacle to Yuuki's face, moistening his bandage. "Yuuki, your face. What happened? Did you find yourself in an altercation?" Amedo's side fins fluttered concern.

"No, no fight. I am O.K. It is just a cut. I am pretty clumsy, as you know." Yuuki smiled, making sure to show his friend that it was nothing. "Anyway, I am glad you are well." Yuuki traced his finger around a stone protruding from the pool. "I wish I could be as well behaved as everyone else."

"Another punishment? I was not always a model Wamono in my day."

"What could you have done that was so bad?" asked Yuuki still not convinced of his confidant's reasoning

"Punishment is not always based on actions committed in the immediate past life, Yuuki. The Gou-Tairei has no concept of time. Unfortunately, we do. Specific actions committed at any point in any lifetime can affect your present. Deeds never complete. Again, it is how you react and deal with those situations that determine your next form." The squid dipped under the water to re-moisten his delicate skin and bobbed back up.

"So how do you explain *you*? How did you cycle into a Yedo-Seitai?" Yuuki was grateful for this philosophical discussion. It took his mind off his immediate worries and at the same time put them into a more manageable perspective.

"From what I can deduce, a squid is by far one of the more intelligent creatures of the Yedo world, and one of the more graceful, if I shall be so selfishly proud. It is a great honor to be a being only from the city where we all hope to end our less than infinite cycling through lives." Amedo fluttered his fins slightly. The sound of the minute splashes echoed throughout the silent grotto. "Forgive me for rambling on, dear Yuuki. To answer or not answer your question, I do not have any idea or thinking how I cycled into what I am currently."

Yuuki would have tuned this mini lecture out after the first minute at seminary, but Amedo made it more personal, more interesting.

"The Gou-Tairei is quite fickle. Some of us eventually remember tantalizing or worrying bits about all our past lives, which is rare in the extreme. Some do not remember anything but the memories of their present life. I have yet to—and most likely never will—comprehend this." Amedo dipped back down under the surface and came back up to continue, squirting the excess water through his syphon.

Yuuki lapped at the water with his hand and emptied his lungs with a long sigh. "I will never understand, will I?"

"Most likely not. That is not the point of being a Wamono. So, to what do I owe this pleasure?" He hoped to get some cloister gossip. Amedo was a revered Reincarnate but forced to live separately from the others due to his dependence on large volumes of water.

Yuuki looked down at this friend, who looked like a frayed piece of tissue paper sunk a couple centimeters below the surface. He looked into the large eyes, eyes that had seen the world, maybe worlds, from countless perspectives.

Amedo dipped down again as he waited for a reply to his question. When he re-emerged, he squirted a beak-full of the clammy salty water at Yuuki's far-away expression.

"Hey!" Yuuki jumped back, jolted out of his reverie by the cold shock. He quickly recovered while giggling. "What was that for?"

"Sorry, I could not resist. You were leaving me, I had to bring you back somehow."

Yuuki couldn't hide anything from those iridescent black eyes. When he was younger, he always believed those eyes were so black because they contained everything in the universe. He still believed it.

"Yuuki." Amedo was starting to become concerned. "What is wrong? Please tell me. I will try to aid you."

Yuuki looked at him and smiled. "I know you will, that is why I came." He inserted each hand into the other's sleeve. He felt afraid to say it out loud to someone other than himself.

"I will not judge if that is what is concerning you. Did you get into trouble with Dogen Kugai-sama again?"

Yuuki laughed. "Yes."

Amedo relaxed his tentacles, relieved that it was just the usual transgression. "What did you do to rile him this time?" Amedo enjoyed hearing the naughty adventures of the troublesome young novitiate.

"I asked about Hinodé." Yuuki slowed down while saying the forbidden name. He winced, ready for a tirade, even from the calm squid.

"Oh," said the surprised but restrained Reincarnate.

"That is it?" Yuuki was taken aback at his friend's reaction. "No yelling, no earthshakes?"

"Yuuki," Amedo said with slight disapproval, "I hope you know me better than that."

"I am sorry. I keep forgetting you are not like the others."

"How did you learn the name of what lies outside these walls?"

"I was asking questions about Keibu-yo," the denial word sounded ridiculous now, "to Ren Denshu-sensei and sort of worked it out of him without him realizing it until it was too late."

"Interesting. Ren Denshu-sensei is rather, what is it, by the book. Is that correct?"

Yuuki smiled. "You would be surprised how persistent I can be."

"I would not. Go on. What makes this incident special?"

"The punishment. It was strange and frightening." Yuuki fidgeted nervously. He didn't want to bring those still fresh memories back up from where he tried so hard to keep them.

"I see," said Amedo, his chromatophores turning a worried faded violet.

"I met Genkou Ryudasu." Yuuki waited for another earthshake.

Amedo went almost black. "How did you come into contact with that creature?" His voice had been the most agitated Yuuki had ever heard.

Yuuki didn't know how to react to his friend's rare, unnerved state. "Kugai and Hégo organized it all as a punishment." He hoped to get some answers to the questions he had about the Aku. Had she always been the same horrific beast? Was she now immortal? Are all Aku immortal?

Amedo gurgled a sigh. "The lesion on your cheek is from her, then." His normally bubbly voice was flat and matter of fact. "Why would Dogen Kugai-sama do this? Surely the punishment did not fit the crime in this instance."

Yuuki covered the bandage with his hand and nodded. "He wanted to scare me into behaving. That is what she said."

"That does not make sense. Does it make sense to you, Yuuki?" Amedo's original moon tint was returning.

"Not really. She told me not to tell anyone that I met her, but I had to talk to someone. The story gets much weirder."

The Reincarnate let out a watery sigh again. "I am listening."

"Ryudasu and I ... talked."

Amedo's flapping slowed. "Talked?" His voice was a combination of confusion and fear. "I did not think she would be much of a conversationalist, only a killer."

What Amedo was revealing made Yuuki feel that he was very lucky to be alive. "She frightened me witless but also told me a few secrets."

"Secrets? What secrets?" Yuuki could hear the intense mistrust. "I am sure they were more secrets about Keibu-yo."

"She gave me a map of the city and showed me a way out of here."

"How dare she!" The high-pitched scream surprised and frightened Yuuki.

Yuuki mustered up the courage to continue. "I am leaving as soon as I am able." The single-minded statement took even him by surprise.

"Yuuki. Please think about this. Ryudasu is an Aku. She is not to be trusted." Amedo pleaded with his young, desperate friend. "She is not giving you all this information out of the goodness of her heart. If she still has one." Amedo forced himself to relax, dimming his chromatophores. "I know you want to leave the cloister and understand the reason. But please think deeply about this. You must admit there is something not right with it all."

Yuuki made up his mind and was not going to let anyone, not even his best friend, change it. "I know she is not to be trusted. She almost killed me!" The memory of his near-death experience began to fester. "But I trust no one here, except you." Tears were starting to pool in his eyes.

"I am sorry, Yuuki. I did not mean to berate you. I am worried about you and what that evil creature has planned. She wants you to leave for a reason. And it is not so you can be happy."

"I realize that, but I cannot stay here any longer. I made up my mind, Amedo. Sorry."

"No need to apologize. Whatever happens after you leave will not be your fault. Please remember that." Amedo returned to his sage-like demeanor and hue.

"Thank you." Yuuki was glad his friend remained himself. But what he said frightened him. What would happen to him once he was out there, not only to his life but those yet to come? Asking those questions was as far as he dared delve. Ignorance is sometimes beneficial. "I just need to know that you understand my thinking. Everyone else has come into this place with at least childhood memories of the outside. Why should I be punished for not having my own?"

"I understand your frustration. However, we, all of us, believe your situation is unique." Amedo tried to calm his young friend. "We wanted only to protect you. But I see now that it has only made things worse."

"Amedo. You are the only one who has truly listened to me over the years." He decided not to tell him about the strange black liquid that gave him visions of another world. He didn't even understand it. *I have to take another sip of it. Every day. That is what she said.*

"But I was a willing participant in the policy of protecting you from such knowledge."

"So, I have your blessing, then?"

"You do not need it and I do not require you receiving it. You have every right to know where you came from while in this life."

"Thank you. It means a lot to me." The weight of the entire cloister, barrier walls and all, had been lifted from his shoulders.

"Could you do me a favor?" Amedo asked. He reached his trembling hunter tentacle out toward Yuuki and placed it so gently Yuuki could barely feel it but felt the weight of concern.

"Of course," Yuuki placed his other hand on Amedo's tentacle to try and calm him further.

"Could you return here before you leave? I would like to say 'good-bye' to you." Yuuki felt slight sob-like vibrations transmitting through his friend's tentacle.

Yuuki tightened his grip around his friend's rubbery skin. "Of course I will." He leaned closer to the water. "Thank you for listening." He let go of Amedo's tentacle, resettled the hem of his long kimono, and walked out the faux moon-lit room.

The old Reincarnate sank himself to the bottom of his watery hospice. The few centimeters of water gave him a sense of safety and separation from the rest of the unpredictable and dangerous world above. *Events will proceed quite badly for many of us.*

On his way back from Amedo's nighttime cell, Yuuki took a detour to the entrance of the Grand Atrium and its massive doors. He remembered Amedo's explanation of doors; they should be welcoming, or at least interesting, to go through and discover the surprises, good or bad, on the other side. These menacing ones looming over him were the opposite. Intricate carvings covered them warning the viewer to behave or be plagued with Retributions in future cycles.

Yuuki placed a drop of Ryudasu's liquid tar on his tongue. He had waited for something to happen, to see what he hoped was Hinodé again. Nothing. He was tempted to take another small drop but decided against it. The fear of going against yet another of Ryudasu's instructions was the only obstacle to his growing desire for the mysterious substance.

He stared at a carving of an Inanimate on the right panel created by, Yuuki presumed, a rather angry artist. It was one of thousands of ghostly minions inhabiting both spirit and physical worlds doing the respective wicked or honorable bidding of their Retribution or Accolade masters expertly depicted on the other side of the doors. Even many Accolades were tricksters and couldn't be completely trusted.

This Inanimate was Ittan-momen, a favorite of Retributions and often imagined as a piece of luxurious silk floating through the air. This depiction had deliberately placed creases and wrinkles, making it look depraved. Inanimates were real, signs that a formless Retribution or Accolade had set its non-eyes on you. This extravagant sheath would either smother the unsuspecting guilty person carved nearby, ending his present life and hastening the next with its Retribution master festering within the new form, or try to control the individual through powers Yuuki didn't understand.

Yuuki looked around the empty anteroom, searching for a floating piece of angry silk. He hadn't thought too deeply about the consequences of what he was about to do in terms of his next cycle or cycles. *Is leaving here such an offense to get the attention of a Retribution?* His cold-numbed feet began to sweat.

He thought of Shinya. The temptation to remain and live a quiet life with the one he loved without the threat of Ittan-momen or any other Retribution lackey shortening this life and cursing the next was still strong, tearing away at his earlier resolve to leave the Order. *Can I ever become whole?*

seven

KUGAI QUIETLY SHUFFLED INTO the stark Goushintei alcove to ready himself for the grueling Wamono-Zentai Conclave. Instead of the usual solitary window, there was a long slit running the length of one wall near the ceiling, no barrier preventing the constant chill from entering without fear of being tamed into warmth. Nothing coherent must ever be uttered within the four cold-perspiring walls.

He knelt on the frigid ground, making sure to keep the ultra-thin kimono wrapped securely around his knees before resting them on the boney stone. The garment had to be thin to prevent the consumer of the Goushintei from becoming dehydrated and fainting from the intense sweating excreted during the debilitating session. But now he was shivering, almost uncontrollably.

Kugai reached deep inside his kimono and grabbed a small vessel half filled with Amedo's viscous ink. *May the Gou-Tairei's uncaring influence allow me to continue in this cycle.* He carefully tipped the vessel so only one long, slow drop of the goo fell onto a slick stone in front of him. The stone was slightly more domed and greener than the others surrounding it. His skeletal fingers carefully rubbed the light-phobic droplet over the stone's surface. His fingers turned white almost instantly from the stone stealing his blood heat. He took a deep breath, lifted his hands from the suddenly warmer stone, and covered his face. He licked his palms, ingesting the slick slime. His hands started to warm, even warmer than before.

His body convulsed slightly in response to the psychotropic reaction of the ink and lichen, which immediately paralyzed his vocal cords. His hands latched onto his face, smothering their owner. He began to convulse more vigorously.

His bellicose hands finally loosened their grip, sensing desperation for oxygen, forcing Kugai to take a massive intake of air. He remained staring into nothing, as a newly blind man would do, hoping to see any shape or silhouette. If anyone were allowed in, they would be convinced they were looking at a possessed corpse that had somehow remained upright after the worldly life force had left it. Even the Masters didn't know what actually physically happened to them.

The scenery in his mind changed from a murky moss green to a swirling white and grey. His mind created a metaphor of a misty morning out in Sakura Hitostsu-en. Forms birthed from this non-mist, slowly congealing into ones he recognized, his fellow Masters and Mavens. There was never any guarantee the psychotropic drug would work, or worse, work too well. He took comfort in knowing they were going through the same ordeal. It took months of painful trial and error to perfect the correct individual dosage. They were the most dangerous months any new Master or Maven would likely have to endure.

"Good afternoon Dogen Kugai-sama," said the Dai-Master. Faces were not quite formed. The other attendees would remain cloudy half entities for the entire conference if they did not verbally participate.

"Good afternoon, Dai-Master-Sama," replied Kugai. His mental image of himself wore his official kimono, his hands tucked into the opposite sleeves in the required respectful pose.

"Are we all here?" Asked the Dai-Master. The sixteen other Masters and Mavens responded in the affirmative. "So, let us get to it, shall we?"

A collective "yes" hummed through the slowly clearing mental miasma.

"First, Dogen Kugai-sama's proposal. Could you remind us and inform those who may not have heard what you are proposing to do regarding the prisoner Genkou Ryudasu?"

"Yes, certainly," said Kugai. He knew everyone was aware of what he was about to propose. The toll on his body from days of private Goushintei sessions was proof. Kugai tried not to hate anyone, but he despised the hawkish Wamono supreme leader. His mind was synaptically sweating from nervousness in how to explain the situation in a convincing official manner. "As all of you know, the Aku Genkou Ryudasu has been incarcerated at Aoheki for the past several centuries."

"Yes, we know all this. Get to the point. Goushintei is not easy for any of us," interjected the Dai-Master.

"I apologize," Kugai said, knowing it was just an excuse for Daviido to harass him. The Dai-Master obviously disagreed with his proposal. All he needed was a majority, but it was risky going against the opinions of the Dai-Master. Daviido could easily convince those who sided with him to suddenly change their minds.

"What is it you want to do with the prisoner?" Asked the soft-spoken Master of Takiheki. He was trying to help his colleague jump-start his argument.

Kugai unmasked a smile in recognition of his friend's guiding nudge. "Thank you, Kokushi Maku-sama. You all know how terribly essential the barrier walls of our cloisters are to our survival." All the leaders, even Daviido, nodded their misty Goushintei heads, forming human smears. "Unfortunately, for Aoheki, we do not have Reincarnates living amongst us who can help maintain and repair our walls. We neither have the ravens of Takiheki." He gave a nod toward Maku-sama. "Nor the macaques that Ametsubuheki is fortunate to have living amongst them." Kugai gave another nod to his colleague sitting just to the right of Daviido. "In fact, I believe all of you have at least one Reincarnate who can help with your walls, am I correct in this?" He knew he was. Again, all nodded, creating the vertical streaks Kugai was hoping for.

"You are convinced Genkou Ryudasu is the solution to this problem?" Asked Go Gaburielu. Kugai had heard the Ametsubuheki Master was still on the fence about his proposal.

"Yes, I can only conclude that she is our sole hope in securing our safety. Believe me when I tell you that I thought hard over this and did not conclude lightly."

"I surely hope not," interrupted Daviido. "What guarantee do you have that Genkou Ryudasu will not repeat what she … he did to get him imprisoned? Supposedly for life."

It was a logical, thus expected, question. "The only guarantee that I can give you is her word." Small grumblings came from the line of ghosted monks and nuns in front of him. He could see their heads turning to one neighbor then to the other. He imagined what the sound would be like if they were all physically together, hundreds of metallic hair beads inducing a meditative trance.

Daviido looked down the line of men and women on either side of him. "Need I remind you ... all of you, how many innocent Wamono that demon massacred while he was Master of the Cloister at Aoheki?" He made it a point to slow down on the name of Kugai's forever cursed cloister. "He went insane. It does not matter if he was Founder-Sama's disciplinarian and successor. This Aku incarnation, by definition, is still insane."

Kugai was losing ground. His body back in the cell was reacting. The perspiration pocking his face rained down onto the already damp stone floor. *You cannot lose this, not now.* Kugai inhaled in his mind and in the barren Goushintei alcove and continued his argument.

"Our walls are crumbling as we speak." Kugai's voice broke due to his almost shouting, surprising the others. He exaggerated this urgency, but he had no other choice. "There are piles of rubble accumulating at the base of the wall, and I have seen cracks forming higher up. There is even one at eye level through which one can see directly through to Keibu-yo!"

"You did not tell us this during our preliminary discussions," said the Maven of Moriheki, rather surprised at this new information.

"We just assumed you were requesting this out of precaution," said Go Gaburielu.

Kugai smiled inside. "I noticed that penetrating crack only a couple weeks ago."

Daviido tightened the tiny muscles around his eyes, trying to pierce Kugai's hyperbolic façade. "This is rather convenient, and I might say unbelievable. Yes, Aoheki is the oldest cloister, but Takiheki is not much younger." He raised his fisted hand and pointed it toward Kokushi Maku. "And it has had no major wall issues." His severe features followed his hand. "Is this correct Kokushi Maku-sama?"

Maku's soft voice responded. "Yes, but we do have the ravens to look after and repair the structures."

"Have they reported to you any problems on their inspections?" The Dai-Master asked, hoping to prove his point.

"No, they have not." Maku looked at his friend with apologetic eyes. "But—"

"Thank you, Kokushi Maku-sama," Daviido interrupted. "Shall we put this to a vote?"

"I am not finished." Kugai was in bad form, but he needed to ensure the council sympathized with his predicament.

"I think we have heard all we need to hear on this matter," Daviido bellowed.

"No, we have not." Kugai's rude tone was enough to have the Dai-Master call for his censure on the spot. "The fact is that the wall is in disrepair. This has nothing to do with the walls at Takiheki or any other cloister." Kugai's voice carried the courage of someone going past the point of no return.

"This is insolence!" Yelled the Dai-Master. "This is brazen insubordination!"

The rest of the council shifted nervously, looking at both men. Several began whispering to their neighbors. Such confrontation was almost unheard of.

"This is not insubordination, Dai-Master-Sama!" Kugai's anger surprised even himself. "This is the safety of my congregation at stake." He forced himself to stop before he said something he could not defend.

"Releasing a mass murderer in the form of a deadly Aku to wander freely amongst them is ensuring their safety?" Daviido pounded his fist upon the council table.

Kugai saw the Wamono leader make quick darting glances to either side of him, watching for any negative reaction to his embarrassing outburst.

Kugai inhaled deeply to return to being humble in front of his esteemed colleagues. "Forgive me my fellow Masters and Mavens, I should not have lost control like that. I apologize. Do I wish I did not have to release Genkou Ryudasu? Of course I do. I am very aware of the difficulty this proposal causes." The council members stopped their nervous whispering and shifting and listened intently to the Aoheki Master. "I think you can all agree, even you Dai-Master-Sama, that our walls are the only barriers against Keibu-yo. The only barrier against the lawlessness of the so-called civilization out there. We are the only islands of sanity in an ocean of mass-psychosis and violence." He placed his hands into their ceremonial home within his draping sleeves. "How many of you have had more than the usual number of new recruits desperate to be let in and take the Vow of Isolation? I have seen young men come in with their clothes torn, almost insane from their terrifying experiences out there." He looked to the left and right along the line in front of him. "I am sure we must assume the Inanimates and their host humans, arrogantly and heretically calling themselves gods and prophets, are becoming increasingly powerful. I am also sure you all agree that this assumption is more a reality." He saw more nods. *It is working.* "But what we do not know is how much control the unholy pairings have."

His colleagues continued nodding in agreement. He had heard reports about the influx of novitiate; an unusual number were of middle age or older. He almost wished new adherents were not forced to take the Vow of Isolation immediately after surviving the Shisa guardians. Simply the desire to know what was going on in Keibu-yo was a punishable offense, filling one with an unbearable guilt. Kugai was no exception. He constantly implored the Gou-Tairei to forgive him for the impure desire by cutting off small strands of his giant bloom of hair as penance. The incessant cutting was beginning to show.

Back in the physicality of the alcove, Kugai wound tightly into the fetal position, completely naked, and trembling with fevered sweat. The sweat-soaked kimono lay in a soppy pile on the other side of the room. He continued calm and fully clothed in the hazy bubble of the Goushintei. "I am not by any means convinced that this is the best option. It is my only option, and yours. What would happen if your walls were ever breached? We would most likely have a much bigger massacre than Genkou Ryudasu would ever be capable of. We have no idea how thoughts and ideas have regressed out there. All we can do and should do is speculate and be prepared." Kugai looked directly at Daviido. The Dai-Master's fist clenched, still in the same place where he'd slammed it down in embarrassed anger. "Thank you, Dai-Master-Sama. I have made my proposal and case. I am ready to follow whatever the council votes."

Daviido finally moved. "Thank you, Dogen Kugai-sama. I open the proposal of releasing the prisoner, Genkou Ryudasu, as per Dogen Kugai-sama's request to a vote." The rest of the council made their final secretive discussions and showed their readiness by putting their hands in their sleeves and bowing their heads in silence. "All of those in favor of the Master of Aoheki's proposal, show your decision."

Kugai saw head after head raise, imagining clear eyes meeting his, showing their approval. His heart was finally freed from the fear that had been gripping it for the past few days, only to be replaced with another more intense terror.

"This plan is working," Cane's tone was as wooden as its form. "Either that Aku will be released and our original plan proceeds, or the council will reject Kugai's absurd scheme forcing questions to circulate concerning his leadership and sanity."

Hégo leaned back with some effort, the chair straining with creaks and wobbles. "I was thinking I would never become Master, that I must have done something quite despicable in a previous life for the Gou-Tairei to refuse this to me."

"There are always detours regarding that paradoxical deity. Take me, for an obvious example. Should I even be here?"

"That is more thanks to the trust we have with the Flower Guild of artisans, I was able to have you made to aid in my walking after that nasty fall, what, over 70 years ago now." He had to quickly convince the then Master to include even artifacts made by the Flower Guild, their secular allies in Keibu-yo, on the exorcist list after realizing that his walking aid was an Inanimate. This was not only to safeguard the Order from total infestation but also to prevent anyone else from having the same opportunity for power and longevity that comes with eventual Totality with a potential utili-god. There was also the obvious incompatibility among Inanimates that would be impossible to evade.

"I will be approaching my seventy-eighth year of existence," said Cane. "We will soon be more powerful than any previous Master of the Cloister."

Hégo looked at the flower-embossed stick. "Yes, and do not forget that until then, I can just throw you into the fires of one of the kitchen ovens. You will not be able to help anyone, especially yourself. Just remember that when you become a utili-god." No Wamono quite understood why the Gou-Tairei ambivalently allowed potentially dangerous inanimate objects to have the opportunity to become such powerful entities. Hégo's hypothesis was that it kept the world more interesting for The Gou-Tairei to lackadaisically observe.

"And you a profit." Agitated vibrations shivered through Hego's spine betraying the Inanimate's unemotional tone. "We need each other. I need to survive intact until that prescribed existence year, and you need something like me to help you become Master. Have no fear my dear friend Daiso Hégo, I will not betray you after all these decades of your protection."

No fear. Hégo did not trust his companion as far as he could throw it, and that was not very far in his advanced years.

"May I ask you something, friend?" The slender Inanimate asked, vibrations subsiding.

"What is it?" Hégo was tiring of the hollow voice.

"Why is it you are not frightened of a Retribution attaching itself to you for who knows how many cycles in the event of a successful cloister coup? That would certainly attract the attention of one of those punishing minions of the Gou-Tairei."

"As you have so convincingly proven," said Hégo, "there are always ways around the limitations of the Retribution that finds you. There is no escaping a Retribution, but there is plenty of opportunity to get or accomplish what you want with that Retribution."

"Quite true," said Cane, satisfied with the answer. "What is it that you do want in this life? It cannot be only becoming the Master of this inconsequential stone labyrinth."

Hégo released another pained sigh. *Too many questions*. He felt that the more information the devious Inanimate had, the more it could use it against him later.

"My goal is your goal," Cane said. "I am tied to you, for better or worse." It sounded foreign to the old monk; something that happened outside these walls. It was a type of violation. "I have survived this long, so I am destined to become more than just a walking stick. Power. All my kind, and your, are cursed to want it. But for right now, I want to concentrate on not becoming kindling for heating your tired, brittle bones."

"Becoming the Master of Aoheki is my most immediate goal, a step toward a more distant wish."

"Which is?"

"Dai-Master." It was the first time he had admitted this to anybody other than himself.

"Being the supreme leader a few thousand paranoid shut-ins is not exactly a major power play."

Hégo didn't appreciate the interrogation. "This community has gotten out of control with all this 'the outside is some kind of hell' nonsense. I still remember my experiences as a young man all those decades ago. Things could not have changed that much." He looked up and stared at the craggy walls all around him. "I was too sensitive."

Yes, I believe so," said the Inanimate. It grew adept at using the only power Inanimates had over Animates - psycho vampirism. "But if you do not mind me asking—"

"I do but go ahead. I cannot stop you."

"Why did you become a Wamono if it was not all that bad out there?"

"Because I thought so at the time. I was young and naïve enough to think that the Order would provide a utopia. It took me a while, but I found I am too ambitious to rot away as the second monk at a minor cloister." His pupils dilated with the blackness of resolve. "I am not going to be overlooked anymore, Gou be damned!"

Cane encouraged this rare verbal memory dump by remaining silent, only asking questions when it thought appropriate for further mining.

Hégo continued. "I always thought it was enough to become a respected elder monk. I have accomplished that. I am the cloister disciplinarians." He leaned forward to give his aged back a rest then sighed retrospective disappointment. "The elder part at least." His muscles stiffened at the thought of his superior's weakness and envy over the respect he had with most of the flock.

Cane found this urgent need for respect was a growing theme in the monk's aging mind. Its escape from this stony tomb was closer. "How will becoming Dai-Master help you fulfill your need?"

"I will be in control of the entire Order; seventeen cloisters and thousands of monks and nuns. They will have no choice but to respect me then." A sliver of a smile started to form, cracking the wrinkled skin swirling into the vortex of his sunken cheeks.

"And the not so obvious reason?" Cane prodded, hoping there was something more complex than this desperate grasping for respect.

"Reform." Hégo's ephemeral smile disappeared and was replaced with a puckered grimace. "We need to know what is going on in Keibu-yo to re-gain the original goal of this Order before it is too late, which I fear it already might be. If I need to sacrifice my well-being in my next cycle, so be it."

"What was this grand Wamono goal?" Cane asked, more out of curiosity than of any real manipulative concern.

"The power of the Gou-Tairei in everyone's lives." Hégo's eyes widened with an excitement a dying man experiences just before death. "Even those outside these walls. We have become too isolated." The zealousness on his face subsided and an expression of futility washed over the gnarled man. "I am afraid we no longer matter."

"It wouldn't hurt to have a larger influx of recruits under your over-reaching wings," said the wooden aide, clearly seeing the real reason through the façade of religion.

"Unh" was Hégo's only response.

"We should have another little chat with that Aku," said Cane. "To make sure everything is in order."

Kugai crawled around feeling for the nearest wall to rest against to wait out the post-Goushintei sensory deprivation. He welcomed the blindness, deafness, and muteness for the first few minutes as a refuge from the stress and politicking. However, disorientation and paranoia would soon take control. Finding a wall was imperative to keep himself somewhat orientated before terror would try its hardest to rip apart his vulnerable mind.

His right hand finally caressed the welcoming wetness of a real wall. The only other stimuli were his heavy breathing and the sweat cascading down over every blemish and wrinkled of his body, triggering uncontrollable chills. He was imprisoned in his sound-proof heart, heaving and sagging to a primal life beat.

Electrifying spikes of paranoia combusted his psyche. Images of crumbling walls and gaping holes assaulted his eyes. "The wall!" Kugai tried to cry out, but no sound escaped his paralyzed vocal cords. "They're coming. Killing, killing! We're all going to be killed!" He pulled and yanked at his long, dreadlocks. Harder. Harder until bloody hairy clumps covered his palms, his head jerking in staccato in all directions and angles.

Kugai's face turned slick with tears and blood. Terrifying scenes appeared and disappeared at electron speed but were clear as if contemplated for hours, all coming together to form a static vista of him standing in Sakura Hitotsu-en Courtyard under that solitary peaceful tree. He made out something coming through the wounded wall. "Coming for me! The Outside! Coming!" He looked around to other monks strolling through the courtyard as if nothing out of the ordinary was happening. He ran over to a triad of monks standing at the entrance to—what seemed to everybody except Kugai—the peaceful outdoor retreat.

He grabbed one of the painfully unaware monks by the shoulders. No reaction. He was a ghost desperate for physical interaction. "We have to get out of here!" His face was so close to the blissful monk's that the spittle from his shouting splattered the monk's face. "You do not care, you imbecile!" He backed up a few paces to include all three monks' creepily calm faces. "What is the matter with all of you?" "You cannot see what is happing right there?" He pointed toward the nearest slab of ruptured wall, spewing forth an inky torrent of tiny black insectoids.

He gave up trying to talk sense with the three living statues. "She has done something to them." His voice was the calmest since he alone witnessed the devastating breach. He kept his eyes on the undulating currents of what he could now see were human-sized multi-colored arachnids. They never seemed to get any closer, but thousands were flowing through. He heard the uniquely spidery racket of pincers clicking, clacking against the eviscerated wall.

In his corporeal form, Kugai stood naked and shivering facing the wall that, only a few minutes earlier, comforted him. His arms remained at his side when any other person standing naked in a cold dank cell would be furiously rubbing his arms to create heat and blood circulating. The last drops of urine slowing dripped off the tip of his shuddering, flaccid penis. The rest puddled around his feet, the only part of his body with any hint of blood flowing under the onion-thin skin. The discarded kimono acted like a magnetic sponge absorbing the cooling waste.

"Get out of here! Go back to the hell from where you were spawned!" shouted the Kugai in the courtyard.

The physical Kugai still stood and stared at the unresponsive cell wall, his mouth miming screams. He collapsed in a mass of skin and hair, his face landing in the already icy piss puddle.

The Kugai in the courtyard could only stare at the writhing wall. "I am sorry, it is all my fault." He was sobbing, his body convulsing. "I should not have done this to you all. I do not deserve your forgiveness and will not accept it. I can only be damned for what I have done or neglected to do." His voice was a normal man's, deeply saddened by what he had done to those in his pathetic life. "Only the Gou-Tairei has your destiny now. I can only hope you have all done enough good in this cycle and those before to return as better humans, or even more gentle beings, for you all deserve that, all of you."

His real body now shivering on the soiled floor, one half of his face in the pungent freezing pool and the other half staring blindly at the hand in front of him.

In the courtyard, his eyes widened in terror. "No! No!"

There was no one living left, only bloodied carcasses strewn around the once tranquil courtyard. A giant arachnid wearing a freshly cleaved human face as a mask stood on its rear legs then lunged at the crazed psyche-bashed Master. Its gore-plastered mouth plates opened and closed in anticipation of a succulent meal. The blood from previous victims slowly dissolving into the spider's rancid solution of venom and saliva. Kugai's reflexes overpowered his terror, forcing him to lift his arm to cover his mouth and nose to block out the stench. A fang went straight for his eye, piercing it to suck out the nutrient-rich jelly.

His real hands, rabid with voracious evil, began attacking his face.

Kugai let out one last scream; the last thing he saw was a venom-drooling spider with his eyeball impaled on the fang's tip. The disembodied eye stared back at him, then blackness.

In the cell, Kugai's right hand clutched a bloody jellied mush of white and hazel that had been one of his eyes.

eight

RYUDASU'S DAY-LONG BLINDNESS WAS finally dying into resurrected sight. It had been longer than usual. She stretched her cuticulated lips, but no voice came. She 'woke up' feeling the vibrations of a new snack stuck in her beautifully symmetrical trap.

Everything remained a blur, and a couple of her eyes were still not functioning. "That was too long," she slurred. *I am surprised I have not gone totally out of my mind.* She growled a laugh. She knew of many a master who had dropped off the crumbling cliff of sanity never to return after one too many Goushintei sessions. She lifted her legs to check her body, but she didn't feel any pain from self-inflicted wounds. *I should not have to suffer this many more times.*

She remained still but bounced slightly from the struggling, doomed creature tying itself tighter into the lower strands of her web. Despite her blindness and muteness, she felt different even rejuvenated. Her strength was returning quickly, and she was famished. The vibrations of suffering triggered poisonous saliva to ooze down her fangs. Slow heavy drips plopped onto the floor at an increasing rate.

Her spider instincts were relentless. It took her one leap to traverse the entire expanse of her gigantic web. She stood over her latest catch, her hind legs supporting her whole body. Her fangs dripped lethal saliva onto the squirming creature, coating it in a death baptismal. "You are lucky. I will savor you like none other."

She hissed out laughter. The force transmitted through the web to her victim. Her eyesight was improving quickly. "Well, what have we here? This is quite a surprise, and I must say a delight." The creature was a monk. She didn't care who it was but guessed it was likely a curious novitiate wanting to see the monster for himself. She couldn't make out the face. It was almost entirely shrouded in hoary webbing. It had been too long since she made a meal of a human. She couldn't remember the last time.

Her human-starved gut couldn't wait. She had to wait for her venom to dissolve the organs into exquisite juices. It would take at least a few hours for prey this large. It would be worth the wait. She could syphon off a rodent or two in the meantime.

The curiosity of her former human-self wanted to see the monk's face, if only to witness his expression as she stabbed her slick fangs deep into him, careful not to go all the way through, preventing any of the precious chum from escaping. As she swung down, she imagined the layers of flesh she would penetrate, the initial snap of skin, resistance of muscle, delicious crunch of bone, finally the pulpy spongy organs. Her front leg-arms finally came down, forming a cage around the monk trying to scream through the suffocating web. They were moans of pleasure to her.

"Pleasure. The liquifying of your organs will give me pleasure. You are honored, Wamono." The muffled screams continued. "Be prepared to be sacrificed to your real god. You are to be part of me, part of god!" Her fangs penetrated the monk. A final moan forced itself from the violated body. Ryudasu also moaned with kill ecstasy. She was no longer simply a monstrous spider creature; she felt herself divine. It was her first meal as a god, and the taste of the monk's flesh on her fangs her first ever taste. She carefully pulled her fangs out just before they penetrated the back of her feast. The blissful suction sound as the flesh around her fangs trying to fill the puncture wounds was second only to the cacophony of ruined layers upon her first impaling. She growled complete satisfaction as the last centimeter of fang withdrew from both punctures.

She backed up, observing the dying mass. Her superior hearing detected the venom beginning to work. Liquefaction had never sounded so divine. She could almost sway to its musicality. "Dear monk. You are the lucky first to be incorporated into the sublime being of the Holy Spinner."

Sick people made Hégo nervous. As the interim Master, he felt it his duty to come to the infirmary and show his respects to Kugai. He should've visited sooner, but the duties thrusted upon him over the past twelve or so hours made it almost impossible. He wanted to thank Kugai for going insane and allowing him to temporarily take over as spiritual and administrative head. He had to convince the majority of eligible monks that he would be the best choice to take over permanently. The vote would be in a few days, so he had to be on his best behavior when it came to the annoyingly much loved Kugai.

The sound of his cane's singular clomping on the stone floor echoed throughout the vast sick ward. *This place is too big*, he thought as he craned his neck to see it from all angles. *The sick do not need to be pampered this much.* The former disciplinarian looked around at the lumpy beds. It didn't take him long to find the shivering and mumbling lump of Kugai. *He is really gone.* He dropped his eyes to the floor, embarrassed at having to witness such a scene. *It is only going to get worse, so might as well get on with it.* The slow walk to Kugai's bed was tortuous. With every step, the steady sane 'clomp' 'clomp' of his cane meeting the floor was overtaken by mumbling cackles, disrupted every few seconds by high-pitched, insane laughter. Hégo didn't much like the cautious old man, but he didn't deserve this.

"Master-sama," came a soft voice from Hego's left. The voice soothed his shriek-shattered ears.

"What is it Toyo Jaibu-sensei?" He turned to the infirmary's head physician with his usual unwelcoming stare but welcomed the distraction.

Toyo Jaibu was not very old, but old enough to vote in the all-important election that would decide the rest of Hego's life. "Uh, well, about Master ... sorry, Kugai-sensei—"

"Get on with it!" The doctor's personality was almost as annoying to Hégo as the mad rantings going on a few beds away.

"Yes, well, he will probably not, uh, be able to hold a conversation with you. He most likely will, uh, not even recognize you." Toyo Jaibu twisted a loose end of one of the ribbons crisscrossing his body. Hégo had never seen the perpetually on-edge monk not fiddling with his ribbon. The completely frayed blue-red bands of twisted thread signifying medical experts looked to Hégo what shredded flesh must look like. The doctor's fingers were indelibly dyed the same carnal hue.

"I gather that," responded Hégo, glancing over to the raving patient. "I am just here to check up on him, not to have a philosophical debate."

"Very well, I just wanted to, uh, prepare you."

"Thank you, sensei." Hégo looked back down at the doctor's fingertips. The color of oxygen-depleted blood made him cringe. *I hope to the un-caring mercy of Gou-Tairei that I never need his hands inside me.* He didn't bring his eyes back up to meet the doctor's face. He instead continued his slow steady hobble toward his mush-brained peer. His cane didn't get to call out two 'clomps' before he was stopped again by the fidgety doctor.

"Sorry, Master, but ..."

"What is it now? I am quite busy and would like to get on with this so I can run this place." Hégo did not care if he sounded angry. He was. He took it for granted that everyone else knew. Voters will have already taken his angry impatience into consideration.

Well, uh, Kugai-sensei, he, uh, keeps repeating apologies every few minutes. I am not sure why this is, but he seems to be apologizing for something rather horrific from, uh, the sound of his, uh, voice. Maybe you will know if it is of any importance since you know him so, uh, well."

"What exactly does he say?" *It could have something to do with the Wa-mono-Zentai during his last moments of sanity.* Hégo remained silent staring at the doctor. He was thinking about how this little mystery could help him in his bid for power.

Jaibu didn't know when to answer his new Master's question. The old man started at him as if he too lost his wits. "Master-sama?" Jaibu started to sweat. Hego's stare was obviously making him more nervous. "Master-sama, is there something wrong? Do you need to, uh, lie down?"

"Of course not, you jittery twit!" Hégo yelled, forcing a small backward jump from the poor doctor. He continued on his way, as fast as his old legs would go. *There is one vote lost.*

"Oooh, hahaha look at the wonderful cudlefly. Spectacular!" Kugai's bandaged face was smiling at a summertime insect he thought was right in front of his face. Blood seeped out from the wound that once housed his eye. The blood was no longer red, but a rusty, violated brown. "Spectacular."

As Hégo arrived at the side of Kugai's bed, a frown killed off Kugai's smile. "I should not be smiling. No, no, no. Not even a grin. I've let them in, every single one."

Hégo recoiled at the sight of the fallen Master. Kugai's remaining eye was opened wider than normal. Hégo thought it was a kind of overcompensation for the loss of its twin. The eye possessed an insanity independent from that whirling tempest in the man's mind. "Every single what?" Hégo asked.

Kugai didn't respond. He kept his gaze on something Hégo couldn't see. His eye was beginning to tear up. "I am so sorry, so, so, so sorry." His body convulsed into tiny tremors. His sobs morphed into chuckles, but his body maintained the same tremor rhythm. "Oohoohoohoo! Yes!" he cried out. He snapped his head sideways and stared directly at Hégo. The interim Master almost fell over with shock at the insane man's sudden attention. Luckily, Cane reacted and situated itself to steady his human host. It took a few seconds to realize that Kugai was not really looking at him. *For the Retributions of Gou-Tairei, that imbecile doctor was right.* He was prepared to see Kugai a little spaced out, but not this much. Kugai wasn't a bad man, just misguided and a bit spineless. *A simple vote of no confidence would have sufficed. But what is done is done.*

He reached out to touch Kugai on the shoulder but stopped in mid-reach. *He would probably bite my hand or begin worshipping it*, thought Hégo. He tried being vocal again. "What are you sorry about, sensei?" He tried to sound as gentle and sympathetic as possible.

For a moment, Kugai seemed to register that someone was in front of him, talking. But the glaze of dementia soon re-coated his eye. Kugai lifted a shaking hand and pointed a dried scaly finger at Hégo. "Spy!" he yelled at the top of his lungs. The sound burst forced Hégo off balance again, this time falling back onto the neighboring unoccupied bed. Cane could not rectify the disequilibrium. "Get out! Get out!" Kugai kept his finger pointed at Hégo. His one pupil eclipsing the light brown of his iris. "I see your ravenous mouth parts and your other legs hidden behind that poor excuse for a disguise!" He sat up still staring at Hégo. "You cannot fool me!" Kugai finally lowered his accusing arm. His body fell into a slump. "Or ... or are you here to punish me?" His voice now sounded scared and resigned. "I am ready. I should not even be still alive for what I have done."

Hégo remained in the same position, afraid to move. *Spy? Mouth parts? What is that broken mind trying to conjure?* He carefully looked over to Kugai. He didn't want to make any eye contact or do anything that would threaten him. He had heard that people suffering from Goushintei dementia could physically do things that they could not when sane. He checked for any restraints tied around his wrists and ankles. None. Kugai was back in the same slumped position, a puppet without a master. Hégo chuckled to himself. *Just ranting from a mad man.* He struggled to right himself on the bed and put Cane between his legs for leverage. "Come on Cane. Nothing here for us. He is not coming back anytime soon."

Toyo Jaibu rushed over when he saw Hégo crumpled on the bed. "Master-sama! Are you alright?" He grabbed Hego's arm with his nervous hands and tried to help him up to his feet.

"Get off me! I can get up just fine without your help." He shook off Jaibu's grip and tightly wrapped his knotty knuckles around the head of Cane and pushed himself up. It took a couple tries to get to where he could stand and lean on Cane. "Make sure he is well taken care for and arrange a private room for him." Hégo took a few steps toward the silent patient but remained far enough away not to cause another outburst. "He should not be stuck in this place."

"Yes, Master-sama," said the doctor. He kept his arms out ready to catch the old Master in case he had another fall.

"Put your arms down! I am not an invalid," barked Hégo. "Make this your top priority."

"Yes, Master-sama. I will get on with, uh, the arrangements immediately. Thank you for, uh, coming here to, uh, see him. Many of the monks are frightened of, uh, him, that this insanity is some sort of, uh, Retribution working on him for something terrible he has, uh, done. Do you believe this Master-sama?"

"Ridiculous!" Hégo had little tolerance for monks who read too much into good and bad things happening just because they happened. "He just had a very unfortunate reaction to the Goushintei. It happens. You should know that doctor." He wasn't sure if he said this for the doctor's sake or his.

Kugai started to mumble. "Colors, colors, all so pretty colors. Iridescence shining the sky and walls. Oh, the walls. Such strong bones you have—"

Hégo began to stagger his way out when Kugai's mumblings abruptly stopped. The silence caused shivers to scratch their way up his spine.

Kugai broke the silence with lucidity. "Who is Cane?"

Hego's heart skipped several meek beats. He didn't dare turn around and kept limping away, saying nothing.

nine

POST-DREAM BLACKNESS BRIGHTENED INTO dim wakefulness; Yuuki's eyes had not yet adjusted from sleep to consciousness. His naked body released itself from its nightly slumber coma with a shiver, his nerves attracting the cold air. He pulled it up around his neck, trying to keep his body heat in. At some point during the night, he had stripped; his body remembering the unnaturalness of clothed slumber.

Today I leave, he thought. Ryudasu said to leave in the late morning or early afternoon today, which was all the better; he needed to do a few things before heading into the tunnel and into another world; his world.

He scanned the gloom, making out the calm heaving form of Shinya and listening to the musicality of his deep-sleep hums. Hiro's cot was bodiless and still made. *Where was he all night?*

Yuuki quietly sat up, keeping his blanket securely wrapped around him. He forced his eyes to make out the smallest detail of Shinya in the early morning murk. He was uncovered as always. He could just make out the rising, soft mound of Shinya's woolly groin, which would remain the color of lightless pre-dawn even after the sun started to shine through the high window. His not quite full erection twitched with dream. The struggling light shone through the spaces between his toes, forming a halo around each. Shinya's feet were perfect. His big toe just wide enough at the tip and the neighboring toe just a few millimeters shorter. Every few minutes, his toes would curl or splay wide. Yuuki could sit for hours watching them involuntarily contract and extend.

He wanted to remember these few moments of watching the various ups and downs of Shinya's dreaming body, to burn this scene into his mind to keep it with him as he wandered the new world. He forced himself not to reach down and relieve the burden of arousal.

He could now see much more of Shinya's masculine frame, down covering his rising and falling stomach. His arms were crossed over his head, exposing the dark hair under his arms. Yuuki was still erect, the male electricity warming his dawn-chilled body.

Yuuki curled himself into an upright fetal position still studying Shinya. *Sorry Shinya. I cannot risk finding out you do not love me. I am not strong enough.* Yuuki's eyes became glossy with tears. *I wish you could come with me. Why would you? All you did was kiss me. Could mean anything.* He felt the heat dissipate between his folded legs as his mental conversation with the man he loved became angrier. *Why not earlier?* The tears finally overflowed onto his cheeks forming miniature cascades. *I hate ...!* His nose began to run. He buried his head to muffle his sobs. *I cannot hate you.*

He lifted his head, breathed in the chilled air, then wiped the tears from his face. He couldn't be like this, not now. He was finally getting out and would not let his heart or cock deter him from his escape. He threw off his blanket and quietly stood up. He pulled out the kimono he chose the night before from underneath his cot and slowly dressed. He stuck out his right arm to give his sleeve maximum hang and put items he thought he would need for the first few days in the inside pocket.

A shard of the young light reflected off the vessel containing the one-time magical tar. *Is it even worth taking anymore? But the non-taste tastes so good.* His stomach and mind had started to crave it even though he no longer envisioned the strange world he experienced in the root cellar. He took a drop as instructed. *Just one more drop.* The second drop tasted even better. The tear in his cheek began to tingle, frightening him. *Only one drop.*

He was ready but didn't want to leave just yet. He sat back down on the cot and looked over at Shinya. The sight of the only person he had ever loved, even if it was for less than a day, prevented any other thoughts from entering. He sat there for five minutes or so, fighting the only thought that crept in uninvited. *I cannot leave without kissing him. I have to feel him on my lips a second time and the last.*

He slowly raised himself off his cot, every muscle knotted in tension, and tip-toed over to Shinya. He scanned the slumbering man, moving his hand just above the hairs covering Shinya's belly. The escaping body heat radiated onto his palm. He bent down and put his face close to Shinya's. He could hear the in and out of air through his nostrils. Could he kiss his never-to-be-love this one last time? *Maybe just on the forehead.* Yuuki stopped as the tiny hairs of Shinya's eyebrow began tickling his lower lip. The magnetism of lip to brow would be too strong if he descended further. There must be more space, a lot more space, between them now. He straightened himself up and exhaled the kiss, the leaden emptiness that had replaced it almost crushing him into a fleshy disc onto the hateful stone floor. He steadied himself against the desk, made sure his kimono was securely closed, and left the man he now desperately loved behind in this world where he had never belonged.

It took Yuuki almost an hour to reach Amedo's cell. The artificial moonlight creeped out from under the door. The cool light weirdly warmed him. He gently pushed the door open, careful not to make any sound, and hid his gleamer sticks beneath his kimono to make sure they wouldn't give him up. He tip-toed over to the pool.

He peered down into the shimmering water looking for the white ghost lazily swimming around his home. There was no other movement than his own reflection on the water's surface. *He is asleep.* A quiet breathy relief escaped him.

There was a wet crumpled piece of paper next to him on the pool's ledge. Puddles collected in the pocked stone surrounding it. He refused to even entertain the question of how his friend could write. The words were almost illegible due to the smearing of the unset ink, his ink. *Ink. Tar.* Before thinking of what his hand was doing, he smeared his fingertip into the still fresh ink and placed a bit on his tongue. Yuuki almost let out a gasp. *I have been drinking Amedo's ink?* Micro flashes of city sparkled behind his eyes, but only ghostly electrical pulses. They vanished as soon as they exploded onto his brain. *What is the connection with that monster?* He had a ravenous urge to lick the note away, but the thought of cannibalizing a part of his friend provided him the power to resist—for now. He began to read the words he could barely make out.

Sa-yonara, dearest friend

The finality of the simple archaic good-bye punctured his heart. He looked over to a flat sheet of slate and piece of chalk he often used to leave Amedo notes when he came by to visit but the old squid was taking one of his frequent naps. Seeing and hearing his closest friend would just be too much. The revelation of the ink was also not something he wanted to bring up. The creature of shame roiled and undulated underneath his skin. He didn't know why it had awoken, but shame was like that, unpredictable and nonsensical.

Amedo will understand. He quietly picked up the slab and chalk and walked over to the door so the scrape of the writing wouldn't disturb the sleeping Reincarnate. He scribbled for a few seconds, looked at it, and smiled. He tip-toed back to the pool to hang the message on a special contraption he'd made soon after they first met ten years ago. The flat face of the stone would hang parallel to the surface for the squid to easily read. Before he connected the special message to the device and swung it into position over the water, he read it to himself one last time. *Flowers wilt, weeds thrive.*

He remembered Amedo telling him the short profound saying, the origin of which was lost in the wisps of ancient memories, when he starting to have sense of not belonging. Something he never stopped feeling. He would utter to himself the four wise words whenever that feeling started to overtake him. Since then, he never intentionally stepped on or pulled a weed from the walls or courtyards and would contemplate the details and passing life of a wilting flower for several minutes. Dying flowers and thriving weeds had much in common; plain, sometimes ugly. But weeds were much stronger and stubborn. His tear-fatigued eyes watered up again. Thankfully tears made no sound.

Yuuki approached the stairs leading down to that fateful root cellar. *I am finally leaving.* There was little effort in finding his way this time. Horrific memories make effective maps.

He looked down into the dark cavern formed by the swirling staircase and took out a gleamer stick, shaking it hard to make it as bright as possible. He started down the steps worn by centuries of bare feet. In almost no time, he found himself at the cellar door. A high tide of images of Ryudasu invaded flooded his mind and refused to retreat no matter how much he tried. *What if she is still in there waiting for her gullible feast?* Paralyzing fear spread the numbness of his feet up into his legs. He could still hear the sucking and slurping of her feeding and the raspy, hungry growl. He started wiping his body of phantom web.

He took a deep breath, thinking it would give him extra strength and spoke with as much force as he could muster, "You are not going to stop me from leaving you evil, ugly demon!" He barged through the door ready to punch whatever was waiting. His flailing fists met no resistance until he slammed one directly into a slab of wall. The dope of adrenaline masked any pain. He looked around frantically, his breathing heavy and short. He kept his gleamer stick at arm's length, trying to illuminate as much of the room as possible. His breathing slowed. "She is not here. She is not here." Still not trusting his senses, he expected the deadly Aku to jump out hissing and drooling venom. "That was stupid." He took a few more deep breaths to calm the internal churning chaos and moved closer to the center, seeing the black on black of the hole Ryudasu showed him yesterday. *It was not a dream.*

He cleared away the whispery crackling 'normal' cobwebs and stuck the yellow gleamer into the hole. The entrance was not much bigger than him, innards jagged.

Yuuki entered, struggling to find a crawling rhythm. His bulk just about fit the wall's toothy maw. The meter of sight the gleamer reluctantly provided would not give him much warning if any thing or one should surprise him.

The cobwebs were thicker than at the opening, and his face was soon shrouded in the ancient, delicate death traps, long abandoned by their hunter owners. The smell of long-ago rotted dead things combined with wet dust was overpowering.

He had no idea how long the escape route was or if it even was one. There might be a dead end crammed full of corpses in various states of decay; buried for eternity, his being the freshest. He closed his eyes for a few seconds to clear his head chanting in a whispering echo; "Namu Myoho Renge Kyo, Namu Myoho Renge Kyo." He didn't know what it meant; none of his elders knew either. It wasn't long before his mind had cleared and the thought of his fellow victims of the Aku monster in various states of decay ahead disappeared. He continued his crawl toward what he hoped was freedom or at least continued survival.

He had no idea how long he had been crawling. Every centimeter gained felt like an hour. It must have been at least a few hours since being voluntarily consumed by stone. Every scrape against rock clawed at the nerves along his spine. He imagined forever stone walls and dark corridors. He remembered that first drop of Amedo's ink, what freedom might look like. "What are you, Hinodé? Will we get along?"

He had reached what he hoped was the end of what seemed a tunnel through the entire world. He felt cautiously optimistic that Ryudasu had spoken the truth. He stretched his gleamer stick further in front to get a better idea of how massive the rocks blocking the exit were. "It does not look that bad." He twisted his neck as far as it would go to look behind him. The only option was to roll the rocks to behind him. They would block him from the only known escape back to the root cellar.

A faint voice came out of nowhere, stopping Yuuki in mid dig. "What are you on about?"

"Who is there?" His mental survival skills kicked in, convincing him that the voice was just in his head. There was no response. He continued his work and grabbed the next rock.

"It's me who said that. Who else could it have been?" The voice was barely audible but equally the loudest besides the mineral collisions of rock against rock.

Yuuki dropped a rock beside his belly. "Who and what are you?" Any being could be sentient and with voice.

"First answer my question, then I'll answer yours. It is only common courtesy," said the voice.

Yuuki deduced it probably wasn't a Reincarnate due to its strange, lazy way of speaking. "I was just wondering what the place looked like on the other side of these stones. Now, who are you?"

"Very well. I don't quite understand your answer, but you did answer it," said the presumptuous voice. "I am ... well, I don't know *who* or even *what* I am to be honest."

I am technically still in the cloister. Still within its walls. Yuuki tried to reason away the possibility of encountering an Inanimate so close to or even inside the cloister. All he was sure about was this non-corporeal voice was outside his head. "Where are you?"

"Well, from the feel of it, I believe on you."

Yuuki jumped, suddenly feeling undulating voracious maggots covering him. He scraped his arms and ankles against the rough rock, banging his head on the tunnel ceiling. He ran his gleamer along his body. Thousands of tiny sparkling shards of minerals covered him, tossing him adrift among stars. *No thing is crawling on you.*

"I'm sorry, I cannot be specific. I am just ... here."

The sudden moving about and strain of crawling and digging were taking over. He laid his head down on a less painfully jagged patch of rock and closed his eyes. He didn't care if there was a voice speaking to him.

Not long after the thought of the strange voice dissipated, he found himself in another busy, roofless corridor. The smell and fumes of metalo-organic fermentation assaulted his senses. The bottlenecked corridor was populated with strange, wheeled machines that looked half alive or half dead. He thought he could hear moaning as they creeped slowly past. This strange place looked familiar. He looked up as far as his eyes could go before rolling back inside his brain trying to find some clue, some name of where he was. He couldn't move any other part of his body but felt his heart trying to pump its way out of its bone and muscle prison. His field of vision filled with menacing wall-like structures. People were going in and coming out at their bases. The slender walls went high into the sky, almost as high as the barrier walls. But they were not made of massive blocks of stone as far as he could tell. They were shiny with intricate angles and designs. He smiled, finally connecting the similar ink-induced vision he'd had back in the root cellar. *Am I out? Did I escape?*

The next moment—he couldn't tell if it was minutes, hours, or days, but it was a definite shift—he was looking up at a large face. He was also moving—more like flying. The face was of a woman was smiling down at him but also crying. Yuuki couldn't speak; he could barely think. There was no awe, only passive observation. The woman was saying something, but he couldn't understand any of it. He was flying faster, bouncing up and down with the wind. She was now looking past him. More tears.

Yuuki's surroundings shifted again. He seemed to be back to where he started. He was no longer flying but standing in that roofless corridor. He focused on an entrance on the other side, but the busy goings-on prevented him from having a clear view. All he could clearly see were those breathing machines with what looked like veins and arteries branching out from metal pipes and sheeting. Keeping everything ordered in his mind was becoming difficult, even painful. He wanted to lie down, but weirdly knew he was already doing that. He wanted another shift to come so he could at least have the sense of flying with the crying woman. The experience was an overwhelming not very distant history.

From the gaps in the packed corridor, he saw a woman leave the entrance. He knew, how he hadn't a clue, she was the same woman who had been crying and flying with him. He tried moving from his frozen stance. Couldn't. He tried covering his nose to prevent the bio-mechanical stench from invading his unaccustomed senses. Couldn't. He wanted to cry out. Couldn't. He could only follow the woman with his eyes as she walked, almost running, down the bustling corridor. He shifted them back up toward the high windowed wall shards, particularly the one from which the woman exited. He could not reach his eyes up to the structure's clouded apex. The shard was a moody yellowing white that almost glowed. *What strange stone.* He wondered why Aoheki couldn't have been constructed with such vibrant rock. Its facade was a weave of silvery beams. It looked to Yuuki as if the mesh was somehow keeping the guts of the massive wall from overflowing out and down upon the unsuspecting people scurrying about on the corridor floor. Was it also breathing like the strange machines rolling and lumbering along in front of him?

He darted his eyes, trying to focus on whatever details he could commit to memory; the battered signage, the rancid smells of what he guessed were from those creature machines, and the magnificent thin wall shards where people seemed to live within.

Each entrance, including the woman's, had a teardrop-shaped insignia above the doorway outlined in black. It looked like a drop of ink *What is it with ink?* But it wasn't completely black. He squinted trying to focus on what was written inside the shape. He held his breath, hoping that would give him the needed focus. He couldn't read it. It was some kind of character, like an abbreviation or number.

People walked directly in front and behind him. He wouldn't have been surprised if they could walk through him. "Why am I here!" he yelled as hard as he could, straining his throat. Maybe that small voice did this to him.

The voice. I am still in the tunnel. Dejection's weight forced all the air out of his lungs in one large invisible squeeze. *What did that voice do to me? Did I finally ingest a critical mass of Amedo's ink?* Whatever it was, was it helping or tricking him, or was it simply a nonsensical scene deep in his exhaustive slumber? The thought of the ink attacked his stomach with daggers of hunger pains.

Yuuki's vision went dark. He took in a deep breath to refill his emptied lungs and coughed from the inhalation of the wet mildewy air of the tunnel. "I am awake," he said. His stomach ripped in two, one half in relief the other disappointment. "Are you there?" He waited for a few seconds. No response. "Please, I cannot be going crazy. Not now." There was still silence except the incessant dripping of the ubiquitous moisture onto slimy stone.

He used the power of the dream or vision to get into a rhythm of digging himself out of the wall. The need to enter the home he never knew pushed him to ignore his body's need for rest. As he moved the next rock, which looked the same as the hundreds before it, his tiring lungs were shocked into long intakes of dry, oxygen-rich air. "Almost out." He quickly grabbed the remaining rocks, almost digging. He didn't care if his fingers were being worked to nubs. *Thank you Ryudasu.*

Yuuki tugged on the next rock. It was heavier than the last few. He used both numb hands to finally loosen it from its probably centuries-old position. In its place came a rush of more of that fresh dry air. It was drier than Yuuki had ever breathed and infused with the same bio-mechanic odor as in his dream/vision. He convulsed into a fit of coughing and gasping. It felt good. Dim artificial light rushed in, spotlighting his face. He wasted no time and stuck his head through the hole not much bigger than his head to get a better look into his new world.

ten

WORDS IN BRASH COLORS scalded Yuuki's retinas as he pushed the last bit of his body out of the selfish wall. The sounds assailing him surrounded him in a bubble of cacophonical silence ensconcing his everything, only allowing the onslaught of moist-phobic air heavy with the uncannily familiar bio-mechanical stench to scratch at his throat and lungs. Before doing anything else, he blocked the hole with the last few rocks he pushed out. He didn't want to be responsible for a breach. Though, it looked like no one cared.

"Watch it!" Shouted a blur of a person.

Another pedestrian almost ran into him. He quickly glued himself to the wall to avoid causing a human pile up on the street that he could only imagine as a strange corridor with no ceiling, the same as in his visions. He lifted his eyes involuntarily. The same garish colors loomed directly over him. *Does old Kugai and Hégo know what are hanging on the outside of their sacred barrier walls.* It took a few seconds, but he found he could read the words shouting at him in bright reds, blues, and oranges. Most consisted of meaningless non-cloister vocabulary, but he was able to at least know how they would sound.

He looked across the loud roofless corridor to hundreds of squares, rectangles, and occasional circles in different shades of yellow and white built into the tall buildings he mistook as broken shards of wall. The pupil-less eyes stared him down, mocking his naïveté. Sweat streamed down his face and back—each drop created from excitement or fear. There was so much sunless light, but he refused to shade his eyes. He didn't want to miss anything. There was no need for a gleamer to find his way through this strange world of incomplete corridors and shattered wall. He kept his mouth closed to protect his throat and insides against any further infestation of the hydrophobic atmosphere. He looked down then up the corridor. The entire length was lined with the same dead eyes piled on top of each other as far as he could see, and further up into the heavy clouds. The corridor was alive with people and weird fleshy contraptions with other people inside them, more of the same in his visions. The sound of the city induced an uncomfortable ringing in his ears. The people pulling other people constantly shouted to the moaning creature machines to get out of their way or yelled some sort of curse at being cut off. There was a constant hum of things forever running. Yuuki had to remain leaning against the wall he fought so hard to separate from to not fall to the hard, strangely smooth floor.

His claustrophobia surpassed an unknown threshold taking control of his enervated being. He looked around at all the wall shards staring at him with thousand eyes. *More walls.* He tried to regain his balance. *How can there be more walls!* He finally stood up and walked further out from the shadows of his former life and trained his eyes to see beyond the glare of the pinks, blues, and yellows of the angry words scolding him. For a few seconds he thought he was still caught in the cloister, that this was yet another walled off area, dilapidated but still a barrier. He squinted attempting to see through the neat fissures and what lay beyond. Without thinking, he walked toward the narrow openings. He advanced only a couple steps before more shouts began to assault him from every direction.

"Watch where ya goin'!" A cart puller on his left cried out.

"Damn Wamono freak! Go back to your rocky cocoon!" shouted another on his right.

"Are you lost little Wamono?" Came another from somewhere Yuuki couldn't tell. The voice did not sound sincere, almost evil. He wanted to yell back "Do I look little!?" but his vocal cords refused his rash request.

This is harder than crawling through that suffocating tunnel. I need to get to the other side. He had to wrench himself from the stony umbilical cord. He looked up and down the chaotic throughway for an empty space where he could traverse. A high platform rose up above the chaos a few meters down, on which people were walking to avoid the mess of wheeled contraptions below. Every other second, he looked ahead to make sure he didn't bump into anyone as he made his way toward the platform. No one wore kimono. Their hair styles were different lengths and volumes, and they all wore various shapes of foot coverings. Almost everyone passing stared at him for the duration of their walk-by, locking their humorless eyes on him. A few paused with mouths agape, but everyone was too busy with their lives to be bothered further. Yuuki felt like the outsider. *Are not they the outsiders?*

His goal of the pedestrian overpass had too many obstacles before it, mostly of the human kind. He didn't have the urban skills to maneuver through the throng of walkers traveling the opposite way while keeping from being pushed down by those behind. His bare feet were not used to the strange hardness of the ground. He began to miss the slick omnipresent moisture softening the cloister's undulating floors.

I have only walked a few meters and already in pain. He was starting to wonder, for the first time, how he was going to survive. All that had concerned him was getting out not on staying out. *How am I going to live out here?* He crouched down along the wall, the cloister wall, and covered his face to catch the tears breaking free from their ocular prisons.

"Are you O.K.?" Asked a soft voice. It was the first time he heard a gentle human sound since he last spoke to Shinya.

Yuuki raised his tear-washed face from his hands to see who owned the welcoming voice. He could only make out an indistinguishable form through the tears. He blinked a few times to squeeze the salty fluid out and down his face. "I am lost," was the only thing he could say.

"Yes, you seem to be in that predicament," the gentle voice said.

Yuuki thought it belonged to a female. He wasn't sure. He had never heard a woman's voice before. He didn't count Ryudasu's as being particularly feminine. As his eyes dried, they could produce a clearer image of the concerned female. She had long yellow hair in an intricate weaved design. There was a small mark on the left side of her neck just below here ear. He stared at the black and green spiral tattoo trying to figure what it represented. The good Samaritan noticed he was staring and quickly scrunched her shoulder to hide it. Tattoos were nothing unusual for him. Most Wamono had tattoos. He had only one so far.

"Did you just come from in there?" She pointed to the wall they were both leaning against.

"Yes." Sob spasms prevented him from speaking full sentences.

"Then you're not lost. Your home is right here." She put her hand on his shoulder to try and calm him so he could speak. Her touch was barely noticeable, the comfort it produced was disproportionate.

Is this the woman who is supposed to help me? Her sincere touch gave back his ability to speak in full sentences. "That," he pointed with his thumb at the wall supporting him, "is no longer my home. I escaped."

"Whatever for?" The woman sounded genuinely surprised. "I thought it was like a paradise in there for those who chose such a life."

"It may well be for some, but I never chose it."

The woman nodded her acceptance of his rebuttal. "I'm sorry. I never gave my name. I'm Hiroka."

He didn't want to ask if she was the one to help. It felt weird to ask.

"You can call me 'Yuuki'." He grabbed hold of her arm, allowing her to help him get back on his tired feet. His name sounded unconnected to him. Was he Yuuki anymore? He wanted a new name. He wanted to retract his permission to call him by that name.

"I know who you are."

A cooling rush of relief blew within him subduing his tear-burned face. *It is her.* "Could you tell me where I am?"

"We are in Ueoka district of Ue-No ward." She cocked her head. "You have never been outside these walls? You obviously weren't born in there."

"Well, I did not 'enter'." His response was quick. "What is the name of this city, all of it?" He needed confirmation from someone else of the name to all that was in front of him.

"Are you people really that isolated?"

"We call it 'Keibu-yo'." It embarrassed him telling her what he and other Wamono thought of her home.

That means something like "Scorned World", right? That's a bit harsh don't you think?" She laughed a little.

"Why are you laughing?" Yuuki couldn't figure out if she was insulted or being good humored about it.

"Sorry, it's just the wording is a bit archaic, which makes sense I guess."

Yuuki fought through the embarrassment to continue. "Wamono," he made it a point to turn who he had been into the other, "are terrified of what is out here. I do not want to call it that anymore."

"This is the Hinodé Wards." Still wearing her gentle smile, Hiroka let go of Yuuki, confident that he could stand on his own. She brushed and straightened her long brown coat, still taking care to keep her tattoo hidden.

Aoheki was also divided into something like wards. This was new information. He was exhausted but couldn't leave this alone, not after what he had been through. He needed to know everything. It didn't matter if he wouldn't be able to process it all. "What are these wards part of?" This felt like a strange and wicked puzzle that everyone else figured out but him.

"That's a bit more complicated, Yuuki." Hiroka's gentleness dimmed slightly. "It has many names, probably as many as there are people inhabiting it. Doesn't really matter. No one ventures beyond the Watcher Walls. No one even knows if there is really anything on the other side. It's just assumed, I guess. I haven't really thought about it. Don't think many here do."

"Walls?" Yuuki didn't want to hear that word ever again. He would never be free from the imprisonment the word forced upon him. His legs began to weaken again, allowing gravity to slide him back down to the ground.

Hiroka crouched down beside. "Yea, 'walls', but they are far from here. We should get you off the streets and a bit of rest. We can talk about ... this entire place later."

Yuuki raised his eyebrows, still covered with a patina of stone dust but knew not to probe any more. She was right. He did need to recuperate.

The Entire. Good a name as any. He now had his own name for the mysterious rest of the city that may or may not exist on the other side of those horrid far away walls. *Walls that watch?* From the flippancy of his new friend's tone, Yuuki knew it was something not appropriate to talk about.

"Come on, let me take you someplace where you can rest and have something to eat." She wrapped his massive arm around her shoulders and struggled to lift him up and guide him to the pedestrian overpass.

Except a few soft collisions with ground-gazing passersby and trips on the unnaturally even ground, they successfully traversed the overpass. His lungs still futilely coughing out the dry atmosphere. He tugged on Hiroka's sleeve, forcing her to stop while he stared out through a sliver created by two towering wall shards, exposing the immense city now all around him. Not taking his eyes off the blinking, pulsating view, he said, "This place seems to go on forever." He tried to make out any sign of those giant Watcher Walls supposedly enclosing Hinodé, but everything seemed to be watching him.

"Yea, it's pretty big," said Hiroka. Her voice betrayed her much weaker enthusiasm. "Come on, we have a ways to go."

"Is this all Hinodé?" Yuuki wanted to know everything about this weird city of broken staring walls.

"What you see all around is Hinodé." She looked at him knowing what he was thinking. "You don't have to go through a naming ceremony to call it that. Everyone calls it Hinodé or just the Wards."

"Naming ceremony?" He knew she didn't want to be asked anymore questions, but it was a reflex. "Sorry. You do not need to answer." He wanted to make statements instead of questions. "So, we are now in Ueoka district of the Ue-No ward of Hinodé Wards, which is still part of something much bigger; too big to even have a name unless one goes through a ceremony."

"You catch on fast," said Hiroka as she smiled.

He nodded silently again. He kept close to his guide but looking far off into the jagged sprawl every time they passed a sloped gap. "We must be high up. Those little corridors seem to just drop straight down."

Hiroka sighed a laugh. "We don't call them corridors. They are streets, alleys, and boulevards. We are walking along a street. These small 'corridors' are alleys." She stopped at an entrance to one of the suicidal alleys and pointed to a straight lit line scarring the valley floor and rising toward a distant hill. "And that is a boulevard." She gently tugged him signaling the need to keep moving.

"Does this street have a name?" He bounced slightly making sure she knew which one he was talking about.

"I think the name will be familiar to you. Aoheki-dori."

Yuuki's wonderment quickly disappeared. "I cannot get away from it" he mumbled. But the sense of wonder flowed back like a fever as they turned a bend. The whole southern half of Hinodé lay below them, spreading out to the horizon. He took in the deepest breath since he first entered the city and exhaled the world back out—his world. *Why would anyone not want to be part of this? This is so ...,* he couldn't find a word to express what he felt toward the gargantuan creature he had always been a parasitic part of. He wouldn't say it was beautiful nor was it in any way ugly. He was ecstatic that it just ... was.

Hiroka guided her newfound charge toward a gaping archway of a viscer-denn station. The heavy moist wind coming from deep within comforted Yuuki's body but had the opposite effect on his mind. "What is in there?" *I cannot handle more dark, wet corridors.*

"It's the viscerdenn," said Hiroka. "It's how we get from one part of the city to another in a relatively short time. There's no way we could walk, and taxis, especially meka-sha ones, are too expensive."

"Viscer what?" The constant pounding of new words was just as powerful as the physical battery of the multitude.

"Look." She guided his sight to the street. "The fleshy beast-machines are vischersha and the machine-only ones are meka-sha; very expensive. Don't worry, the viscer ones are harmless. Well, for the most part. They can be a bit moody sometimes." Yuuki didn't know if she was kidding, but it brought up images of grotesque monsters consuming him for a pre-departure snack.

"Do we really have to go down there?" An overpowering claustrophobia constricted every muscle and blood vessel. He had to constantly fight to be recognized as an adult in the cloister, but he had to admit that he was a newborn to this world.

"I don't have the money to hire a meka-sha taxi. And I know you don't." Yuuki looked at her in what was becoming a common expression. "You don't know what 'money' is, do you?" Hiroka rolled her eyes.

"I am sorry." Yuuki's eyes turned down to the featureless pavement in embarrassment. People walking by probably thought he was a mentally challenged oaf being lectured on something or other by his smaller caretaker. "You can leave me here. I can take care of myself. I do not want to be a burden on you." He didn't know why he said that. Of course she had to take care of him. It was what Ryudasu said would happen. She has been truthful so far.

"Hey, there's no need for that," Hiroka half scolded. "You have a lot to take in. That's why we need to get you someplace where you can rest your body and brain."

He looked back across Aoheki-dori one last time to the stalking cloister wall that kept him ignorant of everything that now swaddled him in streets, alleyways, boulevards, and most of all space. He remained fixated on the summit-less barrier wall without emotion. Nothing of his past mattered. Kugai and old Hégo didn't matter. He even dared to think Shinya no longer mattered.

The two braced themselves against the strong warm-moist wind exhaled from the guts of the arriving and departing half-beasts down in the city deep.

Yuuki looked around in little-boy amazement at the intricacy of everything on the platform for the southbound Za-Ginsa line. Metal pipes dripping greenish-grey mucous hissed steam, bulging and twisting over each other along the tunnel and wall behind them on a race to a fetid finish line deeper into the city's bowels.

"How many of these uh, viscera things go through here?" Yuuki looked down the weeping tunnels in both directions to see how far he could see.

"How many lines? Only four I think." Hiroka began to mouth their names while bending a finger for each one counted. "Yea, four."

A hot moist burst of air came rushing down from one end of the tunnel. The force of the wind lifted Yuuki's crud-heavy kimono and crept up underneath giving him a strange warm chill. His close-shaven head beaded with the condensed swampy exhaust. "What is happening?" He had to raise his voice quite a bit over the increasing roar behind the humid wind. He grabbed hold of Hiroka's arm.

Hiroka looked up at him and smiled. "The viscerdenn is coming."

"Will it attack us?" He was still clasped onto Hiroka's arm and, realizing he must be hurting her, immediately released his grip. "I am sorry."

"Don't be," she said, trying to comfort the Wamono. "If I were new to this place, I would probably be more frightened than you." Her reassuring grasp felt more like searching. Was he that unusual of a being?

The great mass of the viscerdenn appeared in the tunnel. The sound reminded Yuuki of the terrible vocals of Ryudasu. It rasped and growled as it slowed down to a stop. His eyes widened. The thing was a combination of some kind of grub-like beast but with metallic doors along its pulsating side and wheels on its back for, what he assumed, keeping it steady or making sure it behaved as it rushed through the city's guts. Its body was coated in a slick patina of uneven rusty red. Streams of it oozed down the sides following the vertical grooves that carved the viscerdenn into several segments. The underside, from what Yuuki could see anyway, was covered in a black film of grease, its own mucous, and dust. Yuuki looked for any familiar signs of life; eyes, mouth, legs, or just breathing. He couldn't detect any, except the breathing. It seemed to be heaving, glad to take a rest after speeding along for who knows how long between stops.

"Is it some kind of Reincarnate?" asked Yuuki.

"A what?" Hiroka asked.

"Never mind." He looked up at the immense viscerdenn and wondered if it really was a Reincarnate and what it must have done in a previous cycle to deserve its current occupation. It must have attracted a rather sadistic Retribution. *It is not a complete Inanimate, so it cannot be too dangerous.*

"Are they made?" He didn't know the right word to use.

"What?"

He pointed to the apparently exhausted transporter.

"Kind of," responded Hiroka. One of the mixi-matchi corporations of the Suriidii transforms them."

"Transforms them from what?" The swish of the portals drowned out his question, but she apparently heard since she just shrugged her ignorance.

"Come on, let's get in," Hiroka took his thick wrist and struggled to pull him toward the nearest gaping opening of the fatigued beast. The circular sphincter and the dozen or so others running along the seeping bulging body clasped shut seconds after they stepped inside. *Did it just swallow us alive? Was I eaten?* The interior was much more mechanical. The floor was hard and cold. It felt similar to the street far above. Commuters sat on hard metallic planks. There were, however, signs of the beast part. The ceiling was obviously flesh. Dark fluid ran through semi-transparent tubing along the ceiling. All the seats were taken, so they had to stand in the space near the door.

He hesitated a couple times before building up enough nerve to gently press his hand on the soft warm meat around the door. A muscular reflex spasmed beneath his hand. He didn't know if it felt good or repulsive. "How long do we ride in this thing?"

"About forty-five minutes, give or take," answered Hiroka. Yuuki noticed her smiling at him. It was a strange smile. He remembered the tattoo on her neck and how she tried to cover it up once she felt his gaze on it. Something just did not feel right, but he had no choice but to trust her for now. The best coping mechanism was simply to choose the easiest path to belief.

"We're lucky we don't have to transfer. It's a straight shot to my station."

Yuuki smiled politely, finally tiring of asking questions. He looked down the tunnel-molded shape of the viscerdenn. His lungs constricted. Flashes of walls and confinement strobed in his mind. He loosened the one ribbon keeping his kimono closed and opened the collar to release some of the nervous heat built up inside.

"What's wrong, Yuuki?" Hiroka grabbed him and offered herself as support. "Are you sick?" She noticed that he was completely naked under the kimono and quickly grabbed the loosened cloth to keep it from opening any wider.

"Please," Yuuki struggled to get each word out of his mouth. He didn't want to talk. "Need space. Cannot breathe. No room."

Stares from the commuters burned into him. He looked up, angry. "Stop it!" He shouted, forcing the hundreds of eyes to look in the opposite direction or down to their feet. "Get me out of here! I do not want to go back! I cannot...go...back." His speech slowed. He folded himself as tight as he could, trying to hide. He pushed his back against the divider separating the end seat and door. "Please!" He finally looked at Hiroka, the only person he could trust, even though he knew he couldn't.

"O.K., O.K., we'll get out at the next station," Hiroka said. She slowly leaned forward and put her hand ever so gently on his shoulder. She was careful not to frighten him any further. "Can you hang on 'til then? You have to calm down. The Denn Corps can sniff out troublemakers in no time." Hiroka looked down the swaying aisle for any sign of the underground system's temperamental enforcement gunshyu. "You don't want a bunch of them on your case."

The viscerdenn jerked to a slower pace as it rolled and scraped into the next station. A static voice scratched out the station name to the napping, reading, or self-conversing passengers. "Approaching Shtaoka Station. Change here for the Saka and Nishi denn." A few of the passengers prepared their belongings for disembarkation and get on with their lives up on the surface or continue on their benthic travels through city innards.

Yuuki started to breathe normally again. "We only went one stop?" He looked at Hiroka, his face hid nothing of terror. He saw the pity on Hiroka's face. Embarrassment and shame staged a coup to overthrow the terror. *I walked in narrower places before. I crawled on my belly for who knows how long just to get here.* He tried to stand up to show her and everyone else in the denn that he was fine. "Apologies. There is no need to get off. We can stay on until your station." He quickly wiped the liquid fear from his face with his oversized kimono sleeves.

"Let's get a seat. There's a space over there." She gently took him over to the vacant space just big enough for the two of them to squeeze into. Yuuki had a more difficult time due to his bulk and woke up the man next to him. "Pardon me," he said. The man grunted, adjusted himself, and closed his eyes to continue his commute slumber.

"Thanks," said Yuuki. "That will not happen again." He still couldn't look at her. "I guess you are sorry you agreed to help me."

"Don't be silly. Now, get yourself tied and secure. We don't want to give anybody a free show of what your made of." She smiled. Yuuki didn't like her smile.

eleven

MIMI STOPPED FOR A light late lunch after a full day's shopping. She unloaded her purchases at the overly ornate bag and coat check at Kumirasan, the swankiest café in Za-Ginsa. *The green velvet drapes are a bit much.* She kept her shag jacket on. She didn't trust anyone with such a valuable piece of Dekora kit. Her arms, free from the weight of shopping, felt as if they were not even there.

The one purchase she did carry into the dining area, because she was already wearing it, was the pink diamond necklace she hinted to Jojo about before she left. *At least this dazzling gorgeous-ness will show the old miseries stuffing their wrinkly shit-smelling mugs that I belong here.* Dekora were not uncommon in the city's most glamorous district but were often looked at as dumb, cutified thugs with one-dimensional fashion sense, and very dangerous.

The hostess, looking at Mimi with unhidden disdain, guided her into the main dining room. "Don't give me that look, bitch," Mimi didn't care who heard. "You don't own the place, you only work here, so lose the 'tude." The hostess knew better than to anger a Dekora. She maintained her languid expression, slowly turned around, then smiled at every diner she passed on her way back to her station as if nothing out of the ordinary happened.

She looked around and stared back at all the patrons, mostly middle-aged women, in their expensive lizard furs and cat-porpoise skins giving her disapproving side-eyes each revealing a soupçon of terror. Each table, covered with a think pristine ivory-colored cloth trimmed with the same oppressive green as at the coat check, was just that tiny bit too small to be elegantly inconvenient for more than one person to dine at. The windows were tinted, maintaining a constant twilight inside and preventing any garish intrusion from the city outside.

She focused on one late middle-aged woman with lavender hair sitting at the table in front of hers. She was wearing an age-appropriate dowdy dress in lime green that clashed a little bit with her hair to be almost interesting. "And you Obaa, wearing my boss's fashion," Mimi said, making sure more than her intended target heard, "you don't need to look at me like that. You seem to be quite a fan of *last year's* spring collection catering to her ..." Mimi looked the pinched old woman up and down, "... more aged clientele." Mimi was confident Oné-chan was no longer her boss, but she was still and always would be a Dekora. Despite Oné-chan's numerous shortcomings, she was a woman who made things happen and didn't lounge about stuffing her face with overpriced amuse-bouches.

The woman hrumpfed, threw down her eating utensils, and storm-waddled out of the restaurant, giving the hostess a scolding before doing so. The people of Hinodé knew better than to physically confront a Dekora alone. Mimi had no concerns of the repercussions that would befall a normal person like herself insulting a stuck-up old-money Za-Ginsa hag. Though she had never thought of herself as normal.

After she put everyone in their place, she looked out the window onto Chudori Street, watching the shoppers walk past with their gorgeous boutique bags that were as much a fashion accessory as the items that were or were not within them. She could tell those from the less fortunate districts from their craned necks, looking at the ornate and cutting-edge architecture of the great fashion house boutiques lining the wide and immaculate street. *Going to run this place one day.* She sat there daydreaming how she would run things differently than Oné-chan. who No more kowtowing to the Tsudii, Suriidii, and independent councils, particularly the one that controlled Za-Ginsa. Mimi believed the Za-Ginsa Business Consortium was a bunch of money-shitting inbred offspring of the once simple and grungy trades people who used to populate these streets. She looked around knowing some of the Consortium cronies were here stuffing their sunken faces with the over-priced menu items. She wondered if the old battleaxe she insulted out of the café was on the secretive board.

She looked up at a particularly tall scraper across the street covered in what seemed like sparkling diamonds. The locals called it the singing scraper due to the whistling it produced every time a strong gust blew down the concrete and glass canyon. Her commring woke her from the epic planning. She wasn't used to the vibration of her new device. The sensation made her finger twitch. She felt safe answering it since no one from her old life had the call code, not even Jojo. There was only one person who had it. *It must be a new job.*

"Moshi Moshi." She answered with the more polite greeting instead of her usual lazy 'mosh mawwwsh'. "Yes, Sama." She was thankful for the useful gender-neutral honorific. She still couldn't tell if this Sama was a man, woman, or someone between or outside. She imagined the person was a sophisticated gentleman with more kané than he knew what to do with. But she couldn't even assume it was the same person she sort of met just a week ago after fulfilling what would be her last official contract kill for Oné-chan. The mystery individual had hidden themselves in an oversized cowled kimono. An Illumination Blue addict stood next to the figure and handed her a note on which were written two words, "Kill Storyliner", and numbers that looked like a kané transfer account.

She listened as the obviously filtered voice explained what he/she wanted her to do for the next kill. The words burning into her brain evaporated all the blood from here body. She was a wraith haunting the up-scale café, floating without mass. But she had to keep her unemotional killer poise with Sama. "That won't be a problem at all. Good evening, Sama, and thank you." She flicked her thumb around the ring to disconnect and let out a long exhale syncopated with nervous beats. The blood rushed back into here in a deluge.

Assassinate Oné-chan. Why the fuck did I agree to that? She slouched down into her chair. "Fuuuuck me." Scandalized gasps popped throughout the café. Mimi simply gave the old biddies a rolling side-eye. *You're all whores, but instead of kané, for diamonds and holidays at the garden retreats inside the Juku compound*. It was all that was needed to get them back pretending to graze on their overpriced pastries and cakes. She allowed a half grin raise one of her cheeks. *A shit-ton more kané, though*. The grin just as quickly disappeared. *One power-hungry boss in exchange for another*. A garrote was tightening around her newborn independence.

On a full but twisting stomach, Mimi walked past what would normally be enticing windows. The mental burden of contemplating her new assignment did not need any more physical shopping weighing her down.

One of the window dressings displayed statuettes of little hairless rabbit-looking creatures with messages placed high above them putting words into their shivering mouths, begging to be warmed with the latest mixi-matchi furs that had just come in. She looked at the poor statues wondering how the real animals were wrested from their own fur. She looked sideways to a saleswoman standing at the doorway hands folded staring at nothing in particular "Sick fucks."

The day's shopping weighed down her every step; bags crumpling and sashing against each other as she meandered her way through the grazing herd of shoppers. She was both excited and scared to death at the prospect of pulling off the assassination of the decade, perhaps of an era.

The sun pierced through the alleyways separating the cool shadows of the scrapers housing the many faceless corporations that made the elite district their home. Mimi had lived in the scraper zones forming the multiple downtowns of the city for most of her life, so she took them for granted, except one. Her new apartment was in one of those scrapers. Her mystery employer had given her an advance large enough to put the required five months deposit on a 63rd-floor flat just outside the business blocks. The generous advance only allowed her that far up. She deliberately rented a north-facing flat so she could have a view of the Pinku Palace—a past she could look down upon and a future to look into.

She decided to take a detour through a small neighborhood park and simply sit. There was some sort of plaque on a mossy stone pillar at the entrance. She assumed it used to provide the park's name, but it was now more moss and rust than information. Her feet dragged along the gritty pebbled walkway hoping to find a rare place to sit, a chronic absence of which was a sign of the utilitarian workaholic psychosis of the city. Oné-chan's anti-utilitarian viewpoint was about the only thing Mimi respected of the woman. *Why does she have to die? There are much worse so-called humans who deserve not to live.* She thought about the sign behind her no longer able to do its job. *I can't do this. It doesn't make sense.* She let gravity take even more control and let her shopping drag on the ground. The abrasive beats of paper bag on gravel and grit staccato of her footsteps scratched at her brain, creating a strange liminality where soothing and pain mated. *Yea, she's a premium quality bitch, but she doesn't need to be killed.*

She found what she didn't expect but had hoped for, an empty bench. It didn't even have any bird shit forming a crusted diseased skin or worse, some stray or escaped viscermech's bodily fluid dripping over the edge. She couldn't count how many times she stepped in or sat on a glob of the disgusting bio lubricant. The thought of unfortunate beings manipulated into organo-mechano amalgamations bloomed black weeds of pity deep in her gut. *Being created in cruelty meant everything done to them for the sick pleasures of the city's debauched and dull was just life. Not cruel, not pleasant. Just fucking life.*

Her hunter instincts kicked backed in to make sure no one else was eyeing the rare prey in front of her. She mustered what energy she had left and rushed toward the bench. "Made it!"

No one was wandering around either eating their late lunch or looking for more nefarious activities, so she allowed herself the luxury of slightly lowering her guard. She placed her tortured bags beside her on the bench to discourage any lunatic lurking nearby from sitting next to her in her newly conquered territory.

"Never assume you are safe," Mimi said repeating what the deranged but, in this situation, practical Nanny told them on their first day.

She saw a person run away after looking over toward her.

"I taught you well," came a familiar voice coming out of the bushes creeping up and around the bench's arm rests.

Mimi's muscles tensed. She instinctively reached for Kitty D. Too late. Gloved hands reeking of flowers and talc reached from behind and grabbed both her wrists, pinning her down to the bench. The slow, heavy breathing rustled her hair on the back of her head, sending strangely pleasant chills down here back.

Mimi knew exactly who that demented high-pitched voice belonged to. "Nanny-chan." Her voice squeaked just a bit, betraying her intention to remain cool and calm. *She never wears gloves. There's another.*

"Hello, my dead baby sister," said Sayuri. She stooped down to look at her rogue sister eye-to-eye, her face so close that her and Mimi's long fake eyelashes entangled.

"Took you long enough." Mimi maintained composure in her voice. She focused on the gloved vices. The rest of her view was taken up by the crazed mug of Nanny, her lips distorted by the constant greedy sucking on here lollipop. Sugary saliva oozed out the corners.

Sayuri finally backed away a bit, tapped one of the gloved hands to release their grip so hers could take its place. Their owner came around from behind Mimi and stood next to her partner. *A fucking Lolita.* Mimi's eyes followed the immaculate black with white lace crinolined skirt up along the disturbing pure white skin of the arms and finally to the expressionless face. The expert sexual-weapon's porcelain skin almost shone in contrast to her frilly black doll-like skirt. *A Black Lolita, the worst.*

"Ayumi Victoria," started Sayuri, "meet our little rogue, Mimi Barakuda." She remained eye-locked with Mimi.

"Call me Viki," said the Black Lolita. "I don't usually allow people to call me that, but since you won't live long enough to annoy me with it." Viki leaned on her folded parasol, the same black with white trim as her skirt, as if she were bored and patiently waiting for her friend to finish. Mimi was well aware that Lolita parasols doubled as deadly weapons.

"Since you were one of us ... a Dekora," the crazed Nanny said making sure which "us" she was referring to. "You get to choose how you'll die."

Mimi worked up a glob of spit-diluted mucus and lobbed it directly into Sayuri's face, which was too close to build up the required force, but she managed. "Fuck you, you lunatic!" she yelled, spittle dripping from the corners of her mouth.

Sayuri calmly stood back and licked off the slimy mucus in reach of candy-red tongue. Viki raised her parasol and pointed it at Mimi, ready to lunge it into her if she foolishly decided to flee.

"And fuck you too!" Mimi growled at the Lolita. She was having a difficult time trying not to look at the creepy mask-like face. It was the Lolita's turn to have a face-to-face with her. With her parasol still pointed at Mimi, she walked over until the point formed an inverted pyramid into Mimi's chest, the pressure increased as Viki bent down to Mimi's face level. Her long wavy brown hair fell onto Mimi's face, tickling her. Her skirt lightly brushed against Mimi's knees, making them itchy.

"Do we have to kill her now? She's cute." The Black Lolita's eyes scanned her prey from pigtails to Mary-Janes without even a twitch of a nerve on the rest of her face. "I'll do you free of charge." She smiled and licked Mimi's cheek. "Mmmm, scrumptious." The Lolita's warm sugary breath overpowered Mimi's breathable air. She fought back the urge to cough.

Don't breathe it in, Mimi ordered herself. The recipe of the Lolita specialty enticement drug was a carefully guarded secret and was promised to remain so by Oné-chan. Mimi's cheek and nose started to tingle.

"Not now, Ayumi Victoria," said Sayuri. "You're not a whore anymore, at least not full time, and especially not on my time." She finished cleaning herself off and pushed the distracted Lolita out of the way. She re-secured Mimi's arms to the bench. "Damn it, Viki! I want her fully aware of how she's going to suffer, not in a stupor of horny euphoria!"

"Listen you mental Dekora," Viki was now pointing her folded parasol at Sayuri. "I'm no whore and don't try to pull rank! None of this superiority bullshit!"

"O.K, O.K., breathe some of that shit up your own nose and calm the fuck down!" Shouted Sayuri. She was forced to take her eyes off her victim and onto the misbehaving trainee. "I am your superior, now! If you want to be an assassin and not a dirty slut scraping the grimy back alleys of Galu-mura for Janes, then shut up, grow up, and listen to me, dolly!" She turned her attention back to Mimi, not caring to see her companion's reaction.

This is good, Mimi thought. She pretended to fall under the stupefying effects of the drug. She developed an effective strategy over the years of fighting their former competitors in avoiding the debilitating drug. All she had to do was close her nostrils off from the rest of her respiratory system. But dermal contact was more difficult to control, and she was beginning to feel the effects. She had to act fast. She glassed her eyes over, making them appear doting, and kept a stupid grin. She lunged out to kiss the Mad Nanny. Sayuri instinctively pushed back to avoid the come on.

"What the ..." Sayuri lunged at Viki and grabbed her by the shoulders. "How long do we have to wait until that shit wears off?"

Viki kept her collapsed parasol tight in her hands, ready to use. Her face remained as frozen as a doll in a toy shop.

Viki's whole body became rigid, and an almost imperceptible furrow distorted the painted-on eyebrows—a bad sign on a Lolita. They were not traditionally assassins, but their profession warranted them to be ever prepared for things to go wrong. "You're just my mentor. You don't control me," the Black Lolita said, without moving anything but her lips. The second Sayuri let go of her shoulders, in less than a second Mimi suspected, Viki violently swung her parasol around hitting Sayuri in the throat. The blow forced the Mad Nanny down to the ground, exposing her to another attack. Viki mounted her mentor-turned-enemy, pinning her to the ground. She again went for the Nanny's throat, pressing her parasol firmly onto her throat, restricting as much air as possible. A smile finally broke through the porcelain-cast face as Sayuri struggled underneath her for breath.

Mimi could have easily walked away without the two noticing. She wanted to help one in hope of gaining a much-needed ally. She didn't know who to favor since she hated them both; Nanny for being a sadistic insane bitch or Viki for just being a Lolita.

She watched as Sayuri finally mustered up the strength to push the umbrella far enough off her neck to get some air and throw the Lolita off balance. Viki quickly regained her balance, her parasol in both hands, ready to strike again. Sayuri prepared to pounce, her hand a fingertip away from her brain killer hidden under the waistline of her miniskirt.

"Come on, Viki." Sayuri emphasized the forbidden name. "You can't kill me. You would have my mother to deal with if you did."

"That doesn't mean shit, Nanny," the Lolita said, her voice lingering on her adversary's title, making it sound ridiculous. "I'm going to have to deal with her no matter what. I've already touched the precious heir to the Dekora fuckery." She attacked a fellow member of the Cabal and the daughter of its leader. She was dead as soon as she knocked the Dekora nanny down with her parasol. She had nothing to lose.

They're both fucking nuts, Mimi thought. She still had time to strategize. If she helped the Lolita, she would be indebted to her, but she was an unknown. *I could use a fearless and perhaps slightly crazy Lolita on my side. They have some nasty tricks stored in those pretty little empty heads.*

Sayuri and Viki eventually broke their stalemate and simultaneously rushed each other. Breath forced out of each as one slammed against the other. The force jolted the parasol from the Lolita's grip, landing on the ground beside the bench. The two women rolled on the ground forming a perfumed dust cloud. An image of two hunger-crazed wild sows popped into Mimi's head. She could hear the growls and grunts of exertion and anger coming from the melee. Passersby slowed down to see what was happening. Once they saw the tell-tale fashion of the Dekora and Lolita, they quickly put their heads down and continued their now faster-paced stroll through the park.

Mimi calmly stood up and walked around the bench to the discarded parasol and picked it up. It was much heavier than expected, not just to prevent the harsh sun from coloring any sign of life onto their skin. She carried the substantial prop over to the dust cloud and waited for a break in the tussle for a clear view. A break finally appeared. Both women were sprawled out on the dusty ground, their faces looking up to the sky and their bodies heavy with grimy exhaustion. She walked over to one and calmly, as if performing a graceful dance, aimed the pointed end of the parasol at an eye. Like a jab from a scorpion's tail, Mimi punctured the Mad Nanny's left eye. The scream frightened the ever-observing ravens from their perches in the surrounding trees and wires. Sayuri grabbed the laced weapon before it could go further and puncture her brain. Mimi had the power of mercy and that was worth more than a dead Nanny. *Offing Oné-chan has just entered the realm of my possibility.*

She grabbed Viki's soiled gloved hand and picked her up from the ground practically dragging her out of immediate danger. The Lolita was really like a doll now, having exhausted all her energy. They both looked down to the wailing Dekora as they started to walk away.

"Fucking bitches! You won't survive the night!" Sayuri then formed a calm smile and giggled, exposing her blood-candied teeth. "Your best bitch Jojo definitely didn't!" With her hand still over the bleeding hole that had been her eye, she took out her kétai. "Mother!" she yelled into the tiny phone sobbing and sniffling "The bitch took my eye out! Come get me." If she was a meter shorter, she could have easily been mistaken for a lost little girl with something in her eye, crying out for her mommy. Cupping her gushing eye socket, she forced herself to stand and staggered to the nearest person, took out a knife, sliced a few gashes into the unsuspecting man's cheek, and stumbled toward the park entrance, screaming profanities to the trees.

"Come on!" Viki towed the dead weight of a shocked Mimi through the gloom of alleyways off the north end of the park. Mimi finally regained enough of her strength to force Viki to stop but still in a stupor.

"She killed Jojo." Mimi kept staring into nothing, her brain trying to process the Mad Nanny's quick verbal jab that was sharper than any Lolita parasol.

"Who killed who?" Viki began tugging on her Dekora savior, not really caring to get an answer. "And why the fuck didn't you kill Nanny?" Viki's face was as calm as a sleeping cat's through her uncanny shouting.

Mimi turned expressionless as her companion. "You're welcome."

Viki looked at Mimi displaying a slight pout. "I still think you should've killed her."

"I would've if I got that last bit of info earlier." Mimi shook her head and took in a long stream of city air to push try and suffocate the shock of Jojo's death. "Just leave it. Come on." It was Mimi's turn to tug on the doll girl. "I'll take you back to my place. No one knows where I live now, so it should be safe."

"Are you sure?"

"Where else can we go?"

The mismatched couple meandered through the crushing alleys that fed the main thoroughfares of the upscale district. They stuck out like well-watered roses thrown on a garbage heap, even with their disheveled appearance. Mimi looked back at her new friend-by-default and started to laugh.

"What?" Viki almost imperceptibly frowned.

"You're hair." Mimi giggled. "You looked like you were just struck by lightning."

Viki stared at Mimi, opened here parasol, and put it over her head. "You aren't exactly the princess of Pinku Palace."

Mimi thought she heard the faintest solitary note of a giggle coming from the placid face. *Why do I attract all the weirdos? She just better not get in my way.*

"My place should be just a couple blocks this way." She pointed left down a narrow lane populated with Fujou nests.

"You don't know where you live?"

"I just moved to the neighborhood. Don't know all the different ways to my place yet. I wouldn't normally come though these seedy alleys infested with Fujou torture dens. Who do you think I am?"

"I have no idea," Viki answered, her lips remained kiss-ready puckered. "I know where we are. Let's go down here." They could hear the cheering and catcalls of Fujou women coming from the dark, dilapidated entranceways. Each had their unique den symbol displayed in sputtering neon lights. Most had some kind of stylized coupling of intertwined male symbols making up the insignia.

"Have you ever been into one of these places?" asked Viki.

"Nope. I think what they to do to their actor-slaves is sick. Have you?"

Viki looked at her companion with a sense of pride. "Certainly."

"Of course you have. This is more of what you are used to, isn't it?" Mimi said.

"We and the Fujou have worked together in the past for various reasons, that's true."

Mimi didn't want to know what sexual perversions the two minor gunshyu got up to, but she needed more basic information about this high-class sexual manipulator.

Viki stopped in front of a den with especially loud caterwauling and screaming inside. "I've been in this one before," Viki said, twirling her parasol.

Mimi looked at the den's façade. The name arched over the crumbling wooden door read simply 'Otokonoko-tachi'. "Boys." Mimi repeated the name. "Hardly original. What's it like inside?" Mimi found herself wanting to know but felt ashamed of her curiosity.

"The usual," said Viki. "A stage in the center of an open room with benches for the audience all around it extending up the walls, kind of like a boxing ring."

That sounded like a normal playhouse setup, except for what took place on those stages. She knew little of the mind-set of the Fujou, just like that of the Lolita or any other minor gunshyu for that matter, even the other daigunshyu of the Tsudii and Suriidii.

A torn, stained poster depicting two young men embracing each other, chests naked and wearing fundoshi barely concealing their erections, flapped in the greasy alley breeze. Even her heavily experienced boys in Ni-cho would cringe at what went on in those hellish theaters. Many had been victims of the Fujou depravity. She forced a bad memory from entering her mind. *No! Not now.*

A ruckus of scuffling heels and yells echoed down the slithery alley. The two fugitives expected the worst, grabbed the other's arm, and ran inside the den with the unimaginative name.

twelve

THE EDITOR ADJUSTED THE eyeglasses he had made specially for this meeting to ensure they were secure and completely covering his light-phobic eyes. He and his entourage of Illustrators and the Characters they controlled carefully entered the lobby of the Pinku Palace. The normally tight security surrounding the building was almost non-existent. *She's expecting us.* He gave specific orders to his Illustrators to have their Characters not damage the pristine entrance and lobby. He didn't want all-out war. Not yet.

His Illustrators immediately extended their arms to the sides to balance themselves in the blinding white void. Their Characters did the same without being instructed to do so. Even the Editor tried to extend his atrophied arms in front of him. A bland non-gendered voice filled the lobby. "May I ask who is calling?" The voice was calm and mechanical, which made the Editor even angrier.

"The one who will destroy this place if I don't see Oné-chan in five minutes." The Editor vigorously scratched through the air, adding to his imaginary forever-drawing. The automatic revival of his otherwise dead arms did not help him try to regain his orientation.

"One moment please," the ambivalent voice said.

"I don't like that voice," said Draw. "Something is not right."

The Editor ignored Draw and yelled at his Illustrators, "Steady your damn Characters, now! This is just a room." He looked down to the floor. "There is the floor." He then swung his body to point around the area, "and there are the walls. Get it together!"

The Editor used the five minutes to reflect on how the five minutes after would manifest. He couldn't afford a war with the Dekora. They were no longer just the Dekora, but the Moé Cabal. It was a new power dynamic. He suspected a trap. *Fucking Ren must be involved in this.* He looked around for his Storyliner.

"Genta!" The Editor barked. "Give me a scenario with Ren as a main character up to this moment."

"Yes, my prophet," responded the Storyliner stood frozen for a few seconds, working his hands as if he were drawing a story panel on an invisible draft table.

His Storyliners were one of his proudest and strangest modifications and his most important. He never knew why he made his Illustrators and Storyliners in the forms they were in. He never questioned his creative vision out of sheer creative arrogance. He had questioned his ability once after creating his first Storyliner with the help of several bribed mixi-matchi clinicians. The self-probing disturbed him too much.

Genta's head was encased in a polished silver ovoid sphere that casted a deranged reflection of whoever looked at him. The rest of his body was void of any clothing, except for a thin, wispy fundoshi scarcely covering his genitals, and thick-souled open-toed black boots for his feet. He had created a half dozen Storyliners from a group of failed Wamono Smashers turned Illumination Blue junkies who showed more potential than being made into oafish Characters. Their 'birth' was excruciating for him. Unfortunately, most had only lived a couple years. Genta and his murdered partner had been the longest living.

He sensed a slight difference in Genta since the assassination. He paired his Storyliners and knew he would eventually have to create another, just to keep Genta working efficiently and, more importantly, remain usefully sane.

Genta signaled that he was finished by dropping his hands to his side and losing his erection.

"Well?" Asked the Editor.

"I came up with many scenarios with Ren as a main contributor to the situation we currently find ourselves," said the robot-like seer. "And I have come to the conclusion that there is no story involving the Suriidii leader in the events culminating to us being here now."

"I see." The Editor wasn't sure if that was a good or bad sign. It was good insofar as he didn't have to worry about his nemesis in this little spat. But he was always looking for an excuse to go full force after the traitor no matter the truce directive from the Mayor.

"But I formed a few epilogues," added Genta.

"And?"

"In every scenario I created, that queen was there."

"In what capacity?" This piqued his interest. He almost forgot where he was.

"Either allied with us or with the cabal, my prophet. She will be a key character after this current scene concludes."

"So, this is going to escalate?"

"Yes, my prophet. It is the only logical progression of this chapter. But ..."

"But what?"

"Something seems to be changing. It is not totally related to this event. I cannot explain it, yet."

The Editor didn't want to get into too much detail. Not here. He turned his attention back to the pristine room and the absent voice. "It's been almost five minutes."

A strange force suddenly grabbed hold of the Editor and his crew. The whiter than white lobby transformed into a petrified Tsudii forest.

A chilling vibration shimmered up Oné-chan's spine informing her that the Editor had made his way inside the lobby without incident—as requested—and that he demanded to see her within five minutes. "Thank you, Palace. I know it was difficult for you to allow such filth inside you."

She ambled over to her walk-in closet and put on one of her jackets she'd designed for her latest collection. "No reason not to look my best." She draped the pure white with black piping garment around her shoulders. The back tails dragged a little on the floor. She ordered the building emptied as soon as she found out the Editor and his freakish entourage were headed her way. If she was the only casualty, her gunshyu and the cabal would still survive under Sayuri. The only thing that would truly suffer after her demise would be her fashion empire. Her daughter's skills in tyranny far outpaced her skills as a businesswoman.

She was not ready to push the elevator button just yet. *What if this goes terribly wrong?* She was embarrassed even thinking of such cowardice.

"Are you sure you want to do this, my dear?" the question vibrated back up through her body.

"I have no other choice. And you know that. The Editor will not get bored and decide to leave quietly." She finally pushed, more like punched, the button to call up the elevator.

The incessant questioning. Sanae was afraid to think about her arch-idol becoming a god and dragging her into prophethood. She witnessed many human-idol pairs transitioning from the relatively innocuous Symb state into Communion end in the weaker human going completely and suicidally insane before attaining ultimate Totality, complete physical oneness. It takes a strong type of insanity to make it through the relatively short Communion into Totality, and she wasn't sure she was willing to sacrifice herself for the pairing. But her will had nothing to do with it. She never heard of any relationship being severed voluntarily. She remembered the bloodied note her predecessor left for her when she, the then Nanny, found her dead matriarch slumped on the sofa in this very suite, a drooling wound from a self-inflicted Little-Killer slug lodged in her brain. It was the moment she became the 9th Oné-chan and inherited the forbidden arch-idol.

Be careful. It think it will not be able to read your mind for a few years yet. NEVER tell anyone but your successor about this relation-ship.

The gentle ding of the elevator arriving woke Sanae from her past. She was glad Palace could not yet read her mind yet. Would it tell her if it did? Its voice stimulated Sanae's temples once again. "I've secured the lobby. I made sure there would be no danger of any attack."

"Thank you, Palace." Sanae entered the elevator. The confidence of Palace's words sunk Sanae's stomach deep into her bowels.

"We are being attacked somehow." The Editor could barely mumble his anger. *How can she do this?* There was no point in trying to vocalize. His lips, even his eyeballs, could not move without the most exerted effort. He told his mind to 'look' down to his chest. *You should be able to do something about this.*

"I cannot." Draw's response was cold and calm.

Why not? The Editor began to sweat out his panic, cursing his claustrophobia.

"She seems to be in Symb with something much stronger than I. This building I assume."

She's in Symb with a fucking arch-idol!?

"But it will only possess limited abilities," said Draw. "The proximity to me is saving us right now. If it were already a god, all of us would be dead. They must be approaching Communion, or it would not have dared make its existence detectable by the Mayor."

Us not being able to move a muscle isn't what I would term limited abilities.

The ding of the elevator interrupted the prophet-god pair's silent back-and-forth. The door folded open exposing Sanae to a lobby full of living statues. *Palace! What have you done?* Inaction was everywhere in the blinding expanse of the lobby. She quickly sussed out the situation and convinced herself it would have to work to her advantage. She stepped out of the elevator cabin. Her first step of her high heels echoed throughout the bizarre, cavernous mausoleum. The next step announced her complete arrival.

She gazed around the maze of bizarro statues. *Aberrations, all of them*. She didn't have to have seen a Storyliner before to pick him out among the Tsudii frozen menagerie. His head reflected the white all around, decapitating him. She had to force her eyes away from his barely covered genitals. Her gaze then focused on the Characters. They were all shapes and sizes. One a few meters away sported a long willowy tail culminating in a horizontal double-ended spike. His head was disproportionly larger than the rest of his body and was an inhuman shade of orange. Small spines stuck out around the rim of the face. She wouldn't be surprised if there were drooling fangs behind those thick hairy lips.

The disturbingly thin bodies of the Illustrators seemed so fragile that a slight breeze from Palace's air-conditioning system would shred them into millions of tiny floating particles. Her shifting eyes finally recognized a figure unlike the rest. *There he is*. She straightened herself up to show she was in control and not Palace and moved into the Editor's paralyzed view.

"Well, love, so nice meet you face to face. She decided to get the obvious over with. "I see you've met Palace." She looked up and around letting her unexpected captive know to what she was referring. "Aww, you look surprised prophet. You must know you and Ren are not the only ones in this city who're in Symb."

A muffled response came from the petrified Tsudii leader. Sanae understood the obviously rude exclamatory but pretended not to. "Oh, dear. I am so sorry. I will ask Palace to release you all if you can guarantee that we can have a civil conversation about the events that took place a couple days ago. Is that agreeable to you?"

The Editor mumbled something incomprehensible.

"Yes." Sanae answered for him. "Good."

She turned around and spoke to the elevator It was the only thing that looked anything like a face. "You can release them now." She waited for a few more seconds. No vibrating response. "Palace. You can release them. They present no danger to us." *What's happening?* She turned back to the Editor to show she was still in control. "Palace is having a bit of difficulty in releasing all of you at once. It will only take a moment longer." She turned back around toward palace's 'mouth'. *It can't keep doing this!*

"Yes, I can," Palace's voice bellowed between Sanae's ears. The vibrations almost dropped her to the floor.

You can read my thoughts. The terrifying realization she hoped would never come.

"I have been able to for a while now, my dear," responded Palace. Its voice was cold and sharp as shattered ice.

The Editor's gut tightened. He knew what was happening from the slight shivering of Oné-chan's body. *Communion.*

"Yes," reverberated Draw. "We don't know what this Palace is thinking or in the process of doing at this moment. We have to help Oné-chan gain back some of her control."

Help her? The anger was almost enough to break him out of the buildings invisible grasp.

"We have no choice," said the calm voice of the pen deity. "It's either that or we die a death we cannot imagine.

So, what do you suggest? You must have some idea. The skin above his left nipple where Draw encased itself into his flesh began to tingle. Warm fluid began to spread around his nipple, down his stomach, and eventually down his leg. *What's going on?*

Finally Draw responded. "I'm trying to get us moving again."

That's you I feel? The Editor had never felt the streaming sensation before. It was strangely comforting. *You're bleeding out!?*

"My ink-essence is unlimited. I'm assuming. We have never been in ... such a situation."

The Editor felt Draw's life force pool up in his shoe. The comforting feeling changed to one of disgust. The fluid began doing its magic, thawing the frozen prophet. After a few more very long seconds, he could swivel his ankle. *It's working.*

"Now start moving it faster, wiggle it free from its stasis," ordered Draw.

The Editor obeyed and quickly moved beyond wiggling to shaking. Soon his leg was joining in on the awkward dance.

Sanae was jolted out of her own form of paralysis by the out-of-place movement out of the corner of her eye. *He's moving.*

"It is not me," responded Palace. "He is doing it on his own, I'm sure with the help of that insignificant utili-god."

Her head fogged with warring thoughts about the entire chain of events of the last few seconds. She had to think fast. "Palace." She looked up into the vast atrium. "Let them go now, please. This is not helping the situation. I appreciate what you are trying to do, but it is not necessary. I am sure they will not try to harm us or you." She looked over to the straining man in front of her. "Right?" She wanted Palace to free them of its own accord instead of embarrassing it by allowing The Editor to free himself.

Just as the Editor was freeing his last limb, the small army of Illustrators and Characters began to perform the same slow jig for freedom. As soon as the Editor could speak, he ordered his Illustrators to refrain from creating any aggressive actions for their Characters. "If anyone raises so much as a clenched fist, they will be out of a job and life!" Every Illustrator dropped their storyboards to their sides.

Sanae didn't even attempt to hold back a sigh. *Thank you, Palace. I'm glad we can now talk like this.* She hoped her lie was convincing.

"You know what we have to do." Palace ignored Sanae's insincere gratitude.

We can't be killing off the entire head of another daigunshyu. Sanae was starting to see the benefits of Communion thought-speak. She wished it were reciprocal.

"No. An alliance," said Palace.

Alliance? Are you .... She thought better of insulting Palace's sanity.

The Editor could only stare at his former captor, trying to read what was going on in that fragile fresh-in-Communion mind. *They're planning something.*

"Yes," said Draw. "They are planning the inevitable. We will have to agree to it."

Agree to what? I fucking hate being out of the loop, Draw!

It was taking all of Draw's weakened state to hold him together. "An alliance against the Mayor. All three daigunshyu rebelling."

All three?

"We have to, just temporarily, let go of our issues with Ren and that oddly shaped god of hers. I can never remember its name. Such a weirdly specific little tool."

The Editor was beginning to understand the devastating ramifications of a rival to the Mayor and him being on the wrong side. Helping a new appreciative Mayor gain control could put him and Draw in an even higher standing. *I'm beginning to see your point.*

Sanae could simply smile awkwardly at the Editor while she tried to understand what was happening. She had to trust Palace and accept she was out of her element. *I need more context, Palace, and quickly. This stand-off won't last much longer.*

"I held off exercising our Communion to the fullest as long as I could, my dear. But this little incursion forced my foundation. I had to act, making us in a sense public."

It was not an 'incursion'. They both knew the Editor was going to come.

Palace continued. "Because of my act today, the Mayor will soon detect us and thoroughly deal with a very real threat to its power and existence." Palace voice was calm, but Sanae's internal freak out added the required emotion.

We are that very real threat?

"Precisely, my dear. Two fully mature arch-gods will not ... cannot exist in the same space, as the same city. Hence my so-called illegality."

Sanae wasn't understanding everything of what Palace was saying but enough to get the gist. *So, we need all the help we can get.*

"Precisely again, my dear. Even the help of that pseudo-queen. We need to get her on board."

We need to first get the Editor on board about bringing the one he hates most on board. No easy task.

"Nothing will be easy here onwards, my dear. But I have a feeling the Editor will see, if not already seeing by his grotesque smirk I just noticed, that the benefits will outweigh the ego-denting costs."

After she scanned the room to make sure everyone was obeying the Editor's orders, she looked down to her petit guest. "I have a proposition for you, love?"

The Editor stretched a hungry smile across his face. "Yes, I believe you do."

thirteen

MIMI AND VIKI, BLACK blinded upon entering the dim innards of Otokonoko-tachi's foyer, froze until their eyes adjusted. Muffled waves from raucous cheers creeped out from behind a set of heavy black drapes.

"Forty-five kané," demanded a crackly voice from behind a grimy, scratched fiberglass window.

"Excuse me?" said Mimi. She wasn't sure where the voice came from.

"Forty-five." Repeated the crone. "If you don't have it, leave."

"Of course," said Viki, her voice calm and respectful. "Take ninety kané." She handed the crone her kané card.

A greasy gnarled hoof of a hand reached out and clasped onto Viki's card, its nails painted a gaudy vermilion. A few seconds later it slapped the card back onto the counter and shooed the customers over to the drapes. "Thank you," said Viki.

"Why so polite?" asked Mimi.

"From my experience with the Fujou, respect is the only way to get anywhere. If you show them any discourtesy, you'll exit a den with a few nasty gashes on your face if you're lucky."

"What do we do now?" Mimi scrunched herself up not wanting to touch anything in the disgusting Fujou den.

"We watch the show," responded Viki. "We'll just stay in the back."

They entered the stage area carpeted with cheering and jeering women, even draping the age-blackened walls in creaking strained balconies. Mimi scanned the audience. Most audience members ported the signature Fujou high bouffant wigs she had only heard about. They never showed themselves in public in such over-the-top costumery. She could easily pick out the non-Fujou, both curious and perverse, by their normal-ness. She focused her still adjusting eyes on a group of Fujou in front of her. White and peachy make-up caked their faces. *Do they even know who each other really is*, she thought. She had heard that many respectful women of the upper echelons of Hinodé society were secret Fujou. It was something respectful society outwardly shunned but secretly populated.

Mimi looked to Viki trying to get her attention, but she was too busy trying to blend in and seemed to be looking for something or someone. It wasn't too uncommon for non-Fujou to attend one of their infamous productions, but a Lolita and Dekora together in full garb would cause wigged heads to turn. There was no love among the three gunshyu, especially after the official merger of the Lolita and Dekora into the Moé Cabal. The Fujou felt jilted. They were too tightly connected to both the Tsudii and Suriidii. The publications the powerful Tsudii produced were the Fujou's inspiration for their slash-fiction plays, which were heavily funded by the Suriidii.

"Over here," Viki said, using her hands to indicate what her voice was obviously ineffective in communicating over the caterwauling of women.

The two settled in a dark corner under a slightly swaying first-tier balcony. They simultaneously looked up then at each other hoping the balcony would be strong enough to hold the over-excited fans inside it.

Mimi instinctively craned her neck to see what was happening on the stage. *What am I doing? I don't want to watch this.* She wanted to talk about what to do next with her new partner in roguery. But it was impossible to flesh out such important details inside a Fujou den during a performance.

She found herself again trying to see the raised stage. She could only see a couple of male heads popping up every few seconds. Whatever was happening, it seemed to be a big hit with the audience. She was grateful for the almost meter-long wigs in her line of sight. Four or five long curls dangled down the necks. Each strand had several gem-like accessories hanging from its end, which caught the smokey beams of light from above the stage.

These particular over-excited women all had a tattoo on their necks, but she couldn't make out what the design was, the restless curls and constant cloud of chalky dust from their wigs kept them almost hidden. All she could make out were black and green lines forming some sort of spiral. *Like they need any more identifying marks.*

Mimi looked over to Viki. The Black Lolita's eyes were not focusing on the man-on-man sex plays but on something more abstract, urgent. She looked toward the entrance, checking to see if Sayuri and her mignons got a whiff of their scent. *So far, so good.* She looked back over to Viki and sight-communicated the question, *What now?* Viki's mouthed, "enjoy the show." She smiled the irony.

Mimi looked back at the entrance one more time just to be safe and went back to studying the audience and half-heartedly trying to avoid the spectacle that was appearing between bobbles and swaying wigged heads.

"Top that boy!" A spectator shouted and cackled a couple rows in from where Mimi and Viki were standing.

"Don't pussyfoot around, darlin'. Get to it!" another called out. Both women looking at each other smiling, grinding their grey brittle teeth in their excitement. Mimi couldn't tell if they were thrilled by the performance and degradation the men on stage were forced to go through or they were sexually aroused. She looked at the other Fujou near her. They all had the same grotesque set of teeth. *What weird-ass drug are they on?*

The yelling and goading intensified. Finally, the towering wigs in front parted just enough to give her a view of the stage. A little-girl gasp escaped. She was not prepared for what she saw. Four naked writhing male bodies thrusting and sweating, a gang bang. She couldn't see the victim yet, but she did see what she assumed was his blood on the other four bodies. One thick stream running down the muscular twitching thigh of one of the attackers pulled her further into the sexual melée. Soon her entire view filled with the unseen victim's streaked and splattered life.

She fought back tears and memories of her only other experience with the decrepit horde. *Not now, not now!* She inhaled a deep breath taking in the strong scent and taste of blood, sweat, and make-up.

The four she could see were taking turns at both ends of the victim thrusting their narcotic-enhanced erections in a carefully choreographed performance; two penetrating, the other two stroking and punching and or kicking at the same time. Mimi saw the eyes of one of the rapists. They never blinked. Each eye was one large black dilated pupil with the thinnest ring of white creating a demonic halo. All four possessed the same drug-hazed gaze. But she had the heart-sinking suspicion that the play's victim was not so lucky from the muffled screams she could hear from under the pile of tensing ass muscles and curling toes that providing the audience-demanded angry thrusts. After each one, the audience roared in approval then jeered in their demand for stronger, angrier thrusts and punches. Soon she would see the victim, either dead or almost dead. The unfortunate actors would not simply hop up and take a bow when the performance was over. But she still hoped.

Mimi didn't want to wait to see the end. She stepped closer to Viki to tell her that she was ready to leave. "I think we can go now. We won't have any problems with Sayuri for now."

"I think it would be best to stay here for a while longer," said Viki.

"What do you mean?" Shouted Mimi. She was no longer afraid of being heard. The cheers and jeers of the audience drowned out any coherent sentence. "We are not safe here. We are just as safe outside on the streets as in here with this herd of mad heifers."

"I have an appointment." Viki continued looking straight ahead as if talking to someone other than Mimi.

"A what?" Was she being ambushed by this Lolita? "What kind of appointment?" She looked around with a face of disgust.

"Before the...uh...events in the park," Viki said finally looking at the irritated Dekora but keeping her eyes on Mimi's hand for any signs of attack, "To meet this den's Dame."

"So, 'fleeing' into Otokonoko-tachi was no accident," said Mimi, her voice calm and cold. She knew she couldn't do anything rash in this place. One blow or slice at the traitor Lolita would be like a single drop of blood in a tank churning with starved mixi-matchi shar-gators. She tried to remember the exact moment of the expert manipulation during their fleeing.

"A happy accident. It saved me from thinking of an excuse to get inside."

"What's the appointment about, If I may ask?" Mimi was trying with all her training not to react with her intense hatred of the Lolita.

"Going rogue," Viki said. She was back to searching the arena.

"Rogue?" Every muscle in Mimi's body contracted for immediate attack. "You're going to become a Fujou!" Luckily one around registered the outburst. Most were too busy goading the drugged actors. Her shout barely reached the intended pair of ears.

Viki looked directly into Mimi's eyes this time. "No, of course not." She immediately went back to her watch. Mimi's attack-ready stance relaxed. "I wasn't planning on having an extra person and neither was she. But it could turn out to be a win-win."

Mimi crossed her arms in skepticism. "And just how do you think that?"

"Can we talk afterwards or during the meeting?"

"Oh, I'm to attend?"

"I'm not sure if she'd like it, but, again no choice," said the Lolita. She went back to scanning the crowd for the characteristic straight-edged garments of a den Dame. Her eyes widened, narrowed, and widened again.

Mimi turned in the direction of where Viki's eyes were engrossed. She saw a young woman walking toward them with a large male by her side. *Must be one of her victims*, Mimi thought. She looked back to Viki. "She's a Dame? So young." Viki only responded with a side grin and a sigh. "Who's that with her?"

"I don't know," said Viki. Viki and Mimi turned to each other once the couple, particularly the strangely clothed male, came into better view. "Wamono?" They re-fixed their gaze in sync back on the odd pair.

"What the hell is she doing with a Wamono?" Mimi could perhaps understand the Fujou hunting mucky alleyways and dilapidated neighborhoods, particularly in Ni-cho, but she couldn't get her head around how she got her depraved hands on a Wamono.

"I have no idea," Viki said. She just stared at the young Dame and monk. "Let's just get this meeting started."

"That would be easier if I knew what this meeting was about."

Viki side-eyed Mimi, annoyed at her nagging. "You're supposed to be dead. This was none of your business. Unfortunately, it is now. So, just be quiet."

The room didn't look like anything Mimi imagined an office of a Fujou Dame to be. It was cozy and elegant, a different world from the decadence of bodily fluids in the upstairs arena. Her eyes fell upon the large antique-looking desk. The intricately carved trimming around the edges mesmerized her; some kind of leafy plant repeated infinitum around the entire desk, including the legs.

"Please, have a seat," the Dame said. Her tone was that of a well-trained Za-Ginsa debutante. "Can I offer either of you a cup of tea? I have many blends."

"No thanks," responded Mimi. She kept her arms crossed and eyes on the desk.

"Yes, please," answered Viki. She looked at Mimi as a mother would to her child after doing something to embarrass her in respected company.

"What would you like? Green, black, red, white?"

"Red, please," Viki said. She wore a large smile to make up for the puckered grimace of her companion. The rare smile freaked Mimi out.

Mimi was still transfixed on the goliathan desk. It was becoming more of a game of how long she could hold out without making eye contact with the Fujou. She fixated on the notes on the desk presumably in the Dame's handwriting. Every curved tail of certain characters ended in a pompous loop. She looked up while the Fujou had her back to them. Mimi saw the same tattoo on her neck as on those in front of her in the arena.

"I apologize for bringing company to our meeting." Viki said. "But as it turns out, Mimi here is in the same situation."

The Dame turned around from preparing the tea. Her eyes brightened slightly. "Mimi? The Mimi who went rogue and killed a Tsudii Storyliner?" She walked over closer to the latest celebrity.

Mimi had no choice now but to look directly into the Dame's eyes.

The Dame was beautiful, Mimi hated to admit, but dressed rather plainly, like she had just come back from a day of food shopping. From the look of what she brought in with her, she had a good day. "Yea, that Mimi." She kept her arms crossed.

The Dame looked up to where Mimi was now looking. "You are probably wondering why I'm not wearing a show wig."

Mimi remained stoic but did want to know.

"I've never really been a fan." She smiled and went back to check on the water for the tea. "I think they are a bit outdated, but my gunshyu still holds on to such traditions. I am of the opinion they are outward signs of shame."

"They should be ashamed." Mimi couldn't help the dig.

"Mimi!" Viki's lips barely moved.

"You're right." Said the Dame. "They should be. I am. I don't see the need to hide it in such ridiculousness."

"So, you don't have to where them?" Mimi asked, her curiosity overruling her indignation.

"We only wear them during performances."

Mimi narrowed her eyes into scathing cracks. "Performances? Is that what you call the carnage going on upstairs?"

"Mimi! Stop it!" Viki's porcelain face betrayed her voice.

"That's alright. I understand the Dekora hatred of us, I do." The Dame walked toward her guests and handed the Lolita her tea. "Be careful. It's still quite hot." She smiled at Mimi and sat herself behind the ornate desk. "If I were the Governess, I would make some big changes in our gunshyu."

"You're a Dame though," interrupted Mimi.

"I only have power in running this den, keeping it viable. I have no control over the perfor... What you saw upstairs. Our Writes have creative control of all of that." Mimi was still fighting the urge to like or at least respect her.

The Dame took a silent sip of her tea from an oversized cup. "So, let's start shall we," she looked over to Viki.

"Yes, thank you, Dame" Viki adjusted herself in the soft chair and cleared her voice. "As you know, I want to also go rogue, as do you if my sources are correct." Mimi looked over to Viki and scrunched her brow then looked at the Dame.

"Call me Hiroka. There's no need for formality. You are not Fujou" She put her hands around her cup. They couldn't fit all the way around. She exhaled a small-pleasured moan.

Mimi looked around the room again. The walls were paneled with dark wood. It was like she was in a tree cave. The dark knots in the paneling stared at her trying to steal her secrets. Frigid creepiness shivered its way down her spine.

Viki continued. "I would like to make a proposition, and I think now that Mimi's with us, it could become reality."

"And what is that?" Hiroka gently blew on the surface of her tea.

"Yes, what is that?" Mimi added.

"That we form our own gunshyu, on our own terms. We could bring the best of the three female gunshyu." Viki looked over to Mimi then to Hiroka. "And perhaps include others."

"To what end?" Asked Hiroka. She took another sip of her tea.

"That's what I'm not sure of yet, what I do know is that we need each other to survive." Viki took a sip of her tea and set the steaming cup carefully on the coaster Hiroka had subtly placed in front of her.

Hiroka glanced over to Mimi. "What do you think?"

Mimi wanted to make sure of one thing before she opened herself up. "What about that Wamono you brought in with you?"

Hiroka sighed and ran her pointer finger along the rim of her still steaming cup of tea. "Yes, him. He is just the next unfortunate plaything for the den's amusement."

Mimi rolled her eyes and hrumpfed. "I knew you were too good to be true."

Viki broke in. "Just listen!"

Mimi gave her companion the look that she was about to receive a neck kiss from Kitty D but said nothing and sat back recrossing her arms. She returned her damning gaze onto Hiroka.

"He will be my last collection," said the young Dame. "I still need to keep up appearances. It is the main duty of a Dame to go out to collect the month's undiscovered star."

Mimi leaned forward; her eyes still locked on Hiroka's face glistening from the steam from her tea. "Collection? Undiscovered star? Are all your brains just blobs of depraved mush?" She couldn't sit still any longer. Images of her friends over in Ni-cho slid in and out of her visual memory. Some could be chained up naked and bleeding in some fetid dungeon right next door. She stood up, placed her hands on the antique desk, and leaned in toward the Fujou Dame. The other two women didn't try to hide their nervousness. They knew how dangerous a pissed-off Dekora could be. Mimi smiled. "Don't worry I'm not going to kill ya'." She changed her accusing stare to Viki to show she was talking to her as well. She returned her attention to the tense Dame. "I should, but like my friend here said, I should just listen for once." She remained in the same intimidating pose waiting for Hiroka to defend herself.

"Mimi, please sit down." Viki's doll face never cracking.

"Shut up!" Mimi barked. She was in control of this meeting now. "What do you exactly mean, 'your last collection'?"

Hiroka took in a deep breath and stood up, showing the rude little bitch who was really in charge. "I will not be spoken to in such a manner!" Her voice took on a dark, commanding tone. It took Mimi and Viki off guard. The voice no longer matched her physical appearance. "I can just run my finger along here," she pointed to a side edge of the desk, "and my guards will be here in less than five seconds. Once I call them, they will not stop until the threat is under control or eradicated permanently."

The Dame's eyes became deep violet cataracts, and the tips of her ears blazed with a corrosive crimson. "Mimi! Sit down!" Viki reached over, grabbed Mimi's arm, and dragged her down into her seat. Mimi didn't know what was going on, but it was obvious that Viki did and didn't resist her strong-arming. Only heavy breathing filled the woody space for a long ten seconds or so. Each of the three pairs of eyes nervously and angrily darted glances between the others.

Mimi was almost frozen into inactivity, something she wasn't used to. *What the fuck is she on?* She hated enhancer drugs. They were too much of an unpredictability in her line of work.

Viki finally broke the silence. "O.K., ladies. Let's just start over, get everything out in the open. We're running out of time." She leaned back and crossed her legs showing her immaculate white stockings, unnaturally white considering the day the wearer had, and the matching white frills of her slip. "I'll start."

"No. I will start." Said Hiroka. The violet fading to a gentler lavender. Viki acquiesced. Hiroka smiled. "I understand your anger. Like you, I am also disturbed by how our shows have become."

"Have become?" Mimi interrupted. Viki shot her the now familiar sculptured look.

"Our performances were not always this violent, exploitative yes, but not violent. Male-male love stories have always been the backbone of our collective. They have been ever since the Tsudii started publishing such stories in their various digests. There's something so unattainably innocent about love stories between males. Our performances started out as actual love stories filled with romance, heartbreak, and passion; yes, sometimes violent but restrained and always sexually explicit. Our productions were once the talk of the theatre establishment in nearby Kabuza. Men, especially those from Ni-cho, flocked to see and even begged to be involved in the productions. It was mutually beneficial to all involved." Hiroka kept her eyes away from the judging ones of Mimi.

"So, what happened?" asked Viki. She leaned forward, becoming interested in this bit of Fujou history.

"A new Governess took over the Fujou through a rather bloody coup, I guess about forty years ago now, before I was even born." Hiroka seemed surprised at realizing how long ago it was. "She changed everything. She was the leader of the more radical faction that wanted darker productions, something they believed was more representative of reality; a reality of rape and dysfunctional relationships."

"But that's not how it is at all!" Mimi thought of her friends over in Ni-cho and how many of them confided in her of their real trials and tribulations with their lovers and husbands. Rape and violence were rare. "You ladies really need some major psychological counseling."

"I know it isn't," Hiroka said. "The majority knew this but were powerless. Governesses have absolute power. Over the decades, we just got used to the extremeness of the shows, and they gained in popularity. It quickly infected every show in every den across the wards. When I established myself as a den Dame, I vowed to change things either within or without. Unfortunately, it has to be from the outside. What these women need is to regain a certain spirituality that they all have lost in their lives at some point, bringing them all here."

"Spirituality?" Mimi detested that word. "Just like the Tsudii and Suriidii worshippers have toward their warped prophets?" She looked over to Viki for another scolding look. She had apparently given up.

"No, nothing like that. This is different. I'm not going to defend my beliefs or even explain them. I want to change things for the better. That should be good enough for you."

Mimi saw Hiroka's eyes returning to the dangerous violet and decided to let it go. But she still had the same much more practical question, *What about that Wamono?* Her mind forced her to vacate the present and follow it back to the last time she was directly affected by the bloody perversions of the Fujou.

"Hold on. For fuck sake!" Mimi couldn't answer the door naked. The robe balled up on the floor was all tangled, half inside out. She glanced at her comm-ring. "Seven in the morning. Not the best time to stop by a Dekora's place". She had a rough night. Her killjob refused to die quickly; taking several slices to the jugular, face, and chest just to drop the Suriidii golem freak to the ground. She had just dozed off to sleep after getting the last smears of the job's blood and clay flesh off her face and hands. The visitor kept banging at the door. "Is the fucking world coming to an end or something? Coming!"

"Mimi. Mimi," a weak voice penetrated the steel door. The voice didn't match the powerful banging. Alarms sounded in her head. She grabbed a long kana sword from the umbrella holder next to the shoe closet, holding it tight. *There must be two of them.* She was fresh out of training and on edge. She was also alone. Jojo was still not back from her assignment. "It's me, Hidéaki. Please, let me in."

"Hidé?" Mimi loosened her grip on the kana, allowing some of the blood to flow back into her fingers. She hadn't seen him for a couple months. He was always 'relocating' into his latest boyfriend's place. "What happened? Did your latest kick you out?" She still wasn't ready to open the door.

"C'mon Mi, it's me!" Hidéaki's voice sounded desperate.

She tightened her grip again and opened the door. Hidéaki fell into her foyer bloody and grimy. He could barely hold his eyes open.

"What the fuck happened?" Mimi, still holding onto the kana, dropped to her knees beside her friend. "Hidé-kun, Hidé?" She didn't want him to pass out here or anywhere. She needed to keep him awake in case he had head trauma. She could only see the bloodshot sclera. "Hidé, wake up." She slapped his face to jolt him into full consciousness. It was starting to work. She dragged him further into her flat. She wanted that door shut and locked. She still wasn't convinced there wasn't someone else hiding around the corner or down the street using him as bait.

Hidéaki regained consciousness after she finally got him to sit up and lean against the shoe closet. He was breathing, a good sign. He stretched his bloody bruised lips into a painful smile. "I made it."

"Made what?" Mimi wanted to know everything that had happened but had to be patient with his condition. She was careful not to sound overly excited. She giggled to make him feel safer. "What did you make?"

"Made. Out. Alive." He was still smiling. "Escaped den." His exhaustion prevented him from forming complete sentences, but Mimi filled in the blanks with the required grammar.

"You were in a Fujou den?" She had heard from friends of friends what went on in those horrendous playhouses, but she never witnessed any of their 'performances'. She remembered hearing such a story from Hidéaki a few months ago. "Were you an ... actor?" She wasn't sure of the correct term of the performer-victims the sick bitches tortured.

He tried to laugh. "Yea, an 'actor'." His smile quickly died. "Mimi, it was horrible." He began to cry. "Ow, it hurts." He began to laugh again.

"Don't try to talk now," Mimi advised. "Get some rest. We'll talk later after you've re-cooped a bit." She thought she saw a weak nod of agreement. "Do you think you can move over to the futon?" She pointed over to the half-rolled mattress propped up against the far wall. Hidéaki attempted another nod and leaned forward so that his hands and knees were firmly on the floor. He began to crawl the few meters to what must have looked like a palace bed to him.

Once at their destination, Mimi sat beside him to make sure he fell asleep, and only asleep. She then fell asleep to the soft rhythm of her hand gently rising and descending on Hidéaki's plump firm belly. The intense heat of fright and trauma radiated from him. His whole body twitched in fits, waking her up every so often. She didn't know if they were from his injuries or nightmares.

Mimi woke first. Jojo's dog creature must have knocked something over. She jerked her head up hoping to see her friend still sleeping and, more importantly, alive. He was on both accounts. He reeked of amyl. She was surprised she didn't smell it when he first fell into her foyer. Many of her Gei bois sniffed it to relax their muscles for intercourse, especially those less experienced. She never smelled so much of it on one person. *Those nasty whores have at least a nanogram of compassion to allow their victims to use the stuff.*

"Hey." A groggy voice came from behind her head. Mimi turned and looked at Hidéaki's face.

"Hey." She smiled. "Do you want some tea, rice, anything?"

"Just some water." Hidéaki covered his eyes and forehead with his forearm. "And something for a massive headache." She looked at the tattered sleeve covering the upper half of his face. *That is, was, his favorite shirt.*

She stood up, stretched, and walked the few steps to the kitchenette to fix him a glass of water. "Do you want to talk about it?" She cringed as she said it. She didn't want to upset him again, but she needed to know.

"I guess." Some of his strength came back. He sat himself up. "Can I take a shower first?"

"Sure, hon." She shuffled back to the futon and handed him his water. "I'll get you a towel."

Mimi sat there staring without really seeing Hiroka and Viki talking. She wasn't hearing anything they were discussing, just human noise. She couldn't linger on what she saw after she finished her turn in the shower that horrible day. Her memory didn't care. But the disobedient memory muse had some sort of compassion and visualized within her the smile Hideaki had as he lay on her futon no longer with her in life. The smile revealed an ultimate understanding that she, or anyone else alive, would never comprehend until she was in a lifeless heap somewhere with the same smile on her battle-bloodied face.

That smile. That beautiful, gorgeous smile. Hidéaki's knowable-universe smile physically manifested in the 'fuck-you' grin forming in front of the Fujou Dame. The fickle bitch of her memory sent her back to a group of mutual friends standing by Hidéaki's funeral pyre. *I will not burst into tears, not in front of this mother hen of sick fuck murderesses.*

"I apologize," said Viki, bringing Mimi totally back into the ignorant smiles of the living. "I shouldn't have brought her. I should have rescheduled."

"No, you did the right thing," said Hiroka. She looked at Mimi, her eyes now clear and soft "It is some kind of fate that brought us three together." She smiled at Mimi. "You will only become more famous, if you survive, and you could help us immensely if you decide to."

"Help you what?" asked Mimi.

"Form our own mini gunshyu. Ayumi Victoria is right. With our expertise, we would be a formidable trio."

"What expertise do you have?" asked Mimi in her usual sarcastic undertone. "Hold on. You keep forcing me to switch topics. First thing first," she straightened herself up in the chair, "We need to do something about that Wamono you brought in with you. Where is he now?"

"This isn't the time," said Viki.

"The fuck it isn't!" I won't agree to anything unless I know he's alright and will not be subjected to that torture I saw upstairs. From what Hiroka had just said, she was suddenly the key to their futures and had the real power here.

"O.K," Hiroka said, obviously frustrated. "I'll see what I can do. He should be safe asleep in a room on one of the upper floors by now. I had my drinks matron slip something in his beverage. The poor thing had quite a day. Why are you so concerned about him anyway. Do you know him?"

"Poor thing?" Mimi had to restrain herself. This was no time to go assassin on her. "Of course I don't know him. How could I? He's a Wamono, isn't he? Don't see many around."

"He escaped," said Hiroka. Her finger caressing the edge of her desk showing them her threat still was in play.

"You really get to know your victims, huh." Mimi crossed her arms, not willing to let this go. "That's pretty sick." She decided to answer the Fujou Dame's question. "I'm concerned because many of my friends and friends of friends have been forced to participate in your 'performances.' Those lucky enough to have escaped have been scarred by those experiences. We protect them whenever possible, mostly from you." She slowed down and pointed her accusing hot-pink lacquered fingernail directly at Hiroka.

"Yes, and you have done a very good job. We rarely recruit there now because of your diligence," said Hiroka, not fazed by the aggressive accusatory tone of the angry Dekora. She continued speaking, not moving her eyes from Mimi's finger. "I had to go all the way up to Ue-oka today. That's how I ran into Yuuki. He told me he escaped Aoheki."

Mimi had never heard the name. She didn't know most of the names of the massive lightless Wamono stone fortresses. She had no reason to.

"And yes, it is all pretty sick. That's what I am trying to tell you, but I must work slowly and carefully. I can't ruffle too many wigs at once."

Mimi snickered to herself at the image of some of those catty bitches upstairs with their wigs all in a mess—more of a mess.

"I was just interested in how he got to where I found him. As you said, we don't see many Wamono just walking around the streets. Besides, we have to ask such questions and show interest when we.."

"Go on the hunt?" Mimi interrupted.

"Befriend them," Hiroka corrected. "I agreed to do something about him already. Can we just move on here. I have other business to attend to."

"I bet," Mimi mumbled. "Since I have your word, Let's." They remained focused on the other's eyes.

Viki finally found a gap to speak. "Alright, we are all in the same situation. What should we do about it and how?" She kept looking at the time on her ring.

"You have someplace to be, darling Viki?" Mimi still managing to maintain her sarcasm.

"Yes, we both do." She waved her hand between Hiroka and herself. "We are not as lucky, or stupid, as you. We are still very much a part of our gunshyu."

"We can't compete with the daigunshyu," answered Hiroka. "We have no utility-gods attached to us."

"What, thinking of forming a sexually gooned-out prisoner-thespian army to take over Hinodé?"

Hiroka smiled and breathed out a minute condescending chuckle. "Of course not, but I think between the three of us, we can muster up a few allies first. I have a few ladies that will follow me. Mimi noticed Hiroka unconsciously cupped her hand over her tattoo. Our goal is not to take control of Hinodé from the daigunshyu." She looked at Viki for agreement for what she was going to say next. "We simply want a little piece of it for ourselves."

"That's all?" Mimi said, obviously not believing this was possible, though she would be lying to herself if she didn't like the thought of being a leader of a new gunshyu, and she would be the leader. "What about the rest of your little coven of horny deranged witches?" She asked looking at Hiroka.

"We are strongly and obviously dangerously aligned with both the Tsudii and Suriidii, kind of like your former gunshyu. Queen Ren is an important patron of our art. She even started coming to some of the shows at one of our dens in her wards, or realm as she prefers. I believe the Governess made her an honorary Fujou." Hiroka relaxed, slouching a bit in the chair. What I'm saying is that we have been carefully walking the dangerous but rather beneficial thin line between them for decades. Ripping away from the yoke of the daigunshyu would render the Fujou more inconsequential than they already are. And thanks to you, my lovely Mimi, a war is about to break out between your Oné-chan and the Editor. I wouldn't be surprised if they have each other in a choke hold ready to slash the other's throat as we sit here sipping tea. It will only be a matter of time, a very short time, until Ren gets involved. The Fujou will most likely not be able to maintain their neutrality for long. We, they, will have to choose sides. Once that happens, their entire existence will be in jeopardy."

"I'm confused," said Mimi. "You want this war to happen to destroy your own gunshyu?" She was hoping to hear an affirmation come out of the rogue Dame's perfectly rouged lips.

"Not destroyed, just drastically altered. I would hope someday in the not-too-distant future, when all this mess that is about to explode into being is over, that I would be in control a new Fujou gunshyu." Mimi could tell by Hiroka's voice that she was not sure if she should've admitted this to them. "It could be the foundation on which we could build a fourth daigunshyu. That's if the other three survive this."

Mimi waved her hands dismissively. "This all sounds too fluffy cloudy, and to be frank, your 'spirituality' concerns me. How do we know that you are not in Symb or worse with an idol?"

"We have to have some ideal to move forward on this. It's how our minds work, even yours, assassin," responded Viki.

Mimi was starting to get bored. She did like the idea. It had some merit, but she wasn't ready to give up her total independence. She knew that she also needed to take her own criticism and not be overly idealistic in her new independence. The assassination of that Storyliner was about to precipitate something that even she couldn't have imagined. She will need help if she is to survive. "O.K, let's do it." She stood up so fast her chair skidded halfway across the room behind her.

Her curt agreement took the others by surprise. From this small statement and the others' reaction to it, she considered herself the leader of a fledgling gunshyu that she wasn't totally sure she even believed in. "But I still need to be my own one-woman gunshyu for a while longer." She calmly went to the door. "I have shit to do. Talk later." She walked out but not without a cheeky wink to her fellow conspirators.

fourteen

YUUKI'S SIGHT BLURRED WITH the remnants of the death-bathed sleep he hadn't known he fell into. *Am I between cycles?* He could make out only vague outlines of other beds, they seemed empty. The walls looked like weirdly smooth light grey stone. He tried to sit up, but his head feeling as though old Hégo had whacked him on the head a few times with that horribly ugly cane. "Where...?" He tried to stand up, but his legs were still under the spell of whatever his head had been under. He remained sitting at the side of the bed, thankful for being able to do only that. The room had a strange chemical scent Yuuki had never smelled before. It made him even more lightheaded.

He twisted himself to see if there was any window to look out into open space. There was, but on the other side. He tried to stand but was still too weak to walk across the long, thin room where the dim outside world teased him. He hoped it was from the outside and not from another room. His claustrophobia began to rage at the thought of being imprisoned in a room inside another room, his pores exploded with tiny bombs of sweat. *Rooms within rooms within rooms.*

The last thing he remembered was following Hiroka into a gathering place. She said it was a 'bar', but he didn't know what that was. Flashes of women smiling and pointing at him flooded his psyche. He had gone from never seeing a female human to experiencing dozens in less than a day. His memories also flashed him the bizarre hair on the women, heads were so high and twisted. He now remembered Hiroka telling him to wait for her, directing him to a high stool in front of a long counter. Another similar quaffed woman was behind it giving others drinks and moving to the beat coming from two huge speakers on either side of the long table. He had been strangely comforted by the soothing beats; a much calmer version of Basho Jyon's Haiku-bassbeat sermons. It was the only Wamono tradition he started to be sentimental about. He remembered drinking something the women gave him, but that's where the road abruptly stopped in his journey through last memories.

A rush of fear pierced up, around, and back down his back and legs. "My map!" He rummaged through the bed linen and bent over between his still useless legs under the bed. Nothing. "The ink! Where are they?" The objects took on much more importance now that he was all alone in a very strange world. They were conduits to who he was but no longer wanted to be. He stopped, sighed, and even chuckled. He stretched his left arm out and reached in the wide maw of the sleeve with his right hand and felt the map and vessel in the pocket. Just where he had put them.

He tried lifting himself up again. He needed to see if the window looked out into the city. The minuscule part of Hinodé he did see on his trip from the barrier walls of Aoheki to the bar only whetted his appetite for more. He could only think positively. Someone would come and get him soon and take him out for breakfast and explain everything.

He tried to put pressure on his feet. They felt imprisoned; a soft numb, different from the cold wet kind inside Aoheki. It was like they were resting on a cushion of air; disconnected and disorientating. He lifted his rear-end up a few centimeters from the mattress with his trembling arms and rested the bulk of his weight on his phantom feet. He crashed back down onto the bed. He attempted two more times with the same result.

A flash of heat ignited around his suffocating soles and toes. *They are burning up!* He quickly tore the soft nightmares devouring his feet off and threw them across the room. Cool air rushed over his choked feet. "Better." After a couple more tries, he finally was able to stand without losing balance. The dimly lit window didn't seem that far away now. The walk to the window was more like a wobble, but he eventually made it.

The relief of seeing outside almost sent him off balance again. He was above the ground and had a view. The only thing not expected was the light source. It was not from the sky, which was just a lighter stone grey than when he squeezed himself from the hole in the barrier wall. *Have I been out for a whole day or just over night?* It seemed to him the last vestiges of the dying night before the full brash strength of the sun conquered everything in the world. The sun-mocking light came from a strange type of gleamer, bigger and brighter.

He looked down to the street. A couple women with the strange wigs talking outside. *I must still be in the same place.* He lifted his eyes a bit to take in the larger view, the crusted sleep accumulated over the night crumbled. There wasn't much to see except the tall wall shards a little distance away. He tried to remember what Hiroka called them. "Scra ... scraping? No. Scrap ... scrap... scrapers! That's it". There always seemed to be some kind of wall in front of him. He slid his back down the wall below the window, trying not to cry. He had to figure out where and when he was.

There must be a door. Finding a window to witness the outside was more of a priority. *At the other end the of the room. Where else would it be?* Wondering if it was unlocked and what was on the other side kept his mind off the tears. A strong breeze was making the strange gleamer device outside sway, forcing the light to dance across his toes and the floor in front of him. The calming effect of the brightness distracted him long enough to let his mind do whatever if felt like bringing up. It chose to conjure up the voice he heard or imagined at the end of the escape tunnel. Was it still 'alive' somewhere, even if only in his mind? "Voice, are you there?" He looked around the room for any sign, not knowing what the sign would be, especially if it was in his head.

The dancing light created a burst of reflection from Yuuki's flower charm, practically blinding him. He shifted his head slightly to allow the beam to continue its journey to the upper corner just above him. He hadn't thought of the charm since nervously fondling it while Kugai reprimanded him, before everything changed. It was caked with black tunnel dust. The slightest of smiles appeared on Yuuki's face. "Maybe finding out more about you is not such a fantasy after all." The optimism sounded stupid. *It is just a metal bracelet with stupid flowers around it.* He let his head fall between his bent knees, futilely hiding from the world and himself.

Within the dark micro cave created from his bent body, Yuuki tried to forget about the bracelet and the hope if falsely portrayed. His mind replaced one impossibility with another, the voice. "I am on you." It was a terrifying quote.

He stood up and looked out at the paling sky. "Every shade of grey is going to stalk me forever. Dark almost black Aoheki grey, this lighter grey." He ran a finger down the nothing-colored wall. "And the in-between grey outside." It wouldn't leave him alone. Grey, the hue of neither darkness nor light; of mold thriving on forgotten surfaces, the color of powdered death. "Pure black would be better than this stale grey." If everything was going to be grey, he no longer wanted to see.

"Black is beautiful. Shinya's perfectly black, almost brilliant, cropped hair and that vessel of viscous magic." His guts and organs shuddered. *I need my dose.* He wiped away a drop of saliva just about to slither its way out the corner of his mouth and reached into his sleeve to grab the increasing necessity. *Only one drop this time.* The instant the slick drop coated the taste buds on the tip of his tongue, his insides calmed and there was no strange tingle in his lumpy scarred cheek or anywhere else. *Good.* It no longer mattered if he didn't see visions of Hinodé. He was in the middle of it. He had the urge to ingest more, but he forced himself to follow the dosage that monster savior prescribed.

Now that blackness was taken care of, the blacks of Shinya remained. "Shinya," he whispered. He wished he were here, to watch him during those precious moments between deep sleep and waking. His body twitching, fighting the inevitable urge of opening those gentle tea-brown eyes and stretching the hills and valleys of hard muscle and soft flesh. *I wonder what he is doing now.* The smothering grey universe imprisoned him in a tiny cell of time redundant.

His fingertips involuntarily reached for the no-wall. They needed to touch something in poor substitution—something more real and less painful. He wondered about others, Kugai and even Hégo. *Have they even noticed I am gone? Has Shinya noticed?* That terrified him the most.

"That kiss was not from someone who did not care." He closed his eyes trying with all his mental abilities to keep the feeling of Shinya's lips on his, the softness mixed with the bristly day-grown whiskers pushing up above his upper lip; the invisible force that pulled on each of their lips as he pulled away as if both pairs knew that it would be the last time they would ever touch. Yuuki parted his lips in a ghostly reflection of that moment he never wanted to forget. He pried his eyes open from the grip of the colloidal mix of drying tears and sleep.

The gorgeously painful memory was the only entity preventing him from insoluble madness in this strange world. "I cannot forget him."

He made another attempt to look out the window. Still that cremation grey, but there was a pink glow in the distance, faintly peeking through slivers of void between buildings. *Such a beautiful color*, he thought. He never thought much of pink. There wasn't that much of it around Aoheki, just when the sakura were in full bloom. It had now become his favorite color. The light diffused into the heady stale sky making even that horrible color appeasing to his tired tear-raw eyes. "Shinya," he said as he took a deep breath of the city air, "I am going to do well here, and we will be together again, I know that now."

"Who is Shinya?" The sound of a tiny voice struggled up to Yuuki's ear.

Yuuki instinctively looked down to where his ear, or was it his skin, picked up the faint communiqué. It came from the flower bracelet. "Is that you again?"

"Yes. Who or what is this Shinya?"

Mimi was still in a haze about what just happened on the other side of the Dame's door. *Am I stupid or is this alliance genius?* She needed to go home and devise her kill plan for Oné-chan, maybe get some sleep after being up for almost 24 hours.

She felt secure enough to leave the other two to hash out the details. She had never been a details girl. "Almost three fucking hours in here!"

She looked up the flight of stairs, reminded of the Wamono above someplace. *I can't just leave him here.* Before she was aware of what her feet were doing, she was heading up the stairs. "For you, Hidéaki."

At the top of the first flight, show posters stared at her pleading for help, to release them from their sexual bondage. Her ears tuned in on the cheers and jeers of the audience not too far away. She would've admitted she was terrified. But there was no need to admit to a fact.

She didn't know what floor he was on just that he was 'upstairs'. No one was around. *They must be all watching that sick shit.* she started up the next set of stairs and arrived at a hallway lined on both sides with half dozen doors. She sighed, "This place didn't look that big from the outside." She methodically put her ear to every door, alternating sides hoping to hear anything male. At every pressing of her ear, nothing. *Are they all down there?* The complete silence was disturbing. She assumed every show culminated in a mass gang bang. *Not the most efficient use of talent.*

On the second-to-last door on the right, she heard muffled sobs. *Life!* She pressed her ear flatter against the door. She heard speaking, but it didn't sound like a conversation. She could only hear one voice. She listened for a few seconds longer to gather any clues as to the voice's identity.

Finally, she could isolate two words, "Shinya" and "Aoheki". She knew one of them was a male name. The other one sounded familiar. "A.o.he.ki," she said pronouncing every syllable slowly. She jerked her head away from the door. *Hiroka said he escaped from Aoheki!* She stepped back, studying the door.

"Now what the fuck do I do?" She was almost talking in her normal voice. She felt confident that no one was within earshot. "Do I barge in and rescue him? Do I tell him why he is here if he doesn't know already?" Several other questions and options were buzzing around in her head, forcing her to stall and think. She didn't like that. "Fuck it." She grasped the door handle. "Locked. Of course it is." She collapsed her head onto the door. The thud echoed down the hallway.

"Who...who is out there?" a voice questioned from the other side of the door. Mimi could tell the Wamono was frightened even though he tried not to sound it. "Hiroka?"

"No, my name's Mimi," she said, frustrated at being robbed of her dramatic entrance. "I've come to get you out of here."

"Did Hiroka send you?"

What's with his obsession with Hiroka? She had heard about the Fujou talent of imprinting on their victims. "Yes." She lied. "But we need to get you out of here right now. Can you open the door on your side?"

She felt pressure on the handle she was still holding on to, but nothing gave. "No, it is locked. What is happening?"

She had to think fast. She didn't want to panic him. "Nothing to worry about. We just need to move to another place, and stupid Hiroka misplaced the key. She locked you in to make sure no one came in to disturb you while you were sleeping." She hoped he was as naïve as she heard Wamono were, though, from how old he looked last night, despite his size, he couldn't have been cloistered for very long.

She reached into a small pocket in the waistband of her mini-skirt and took out a small metal rod with grooves. She inserted it into the keyhole and jiggled it around a bit until it started to give resistance. A lock pick was a tool no self-respecting Dekora would leave home without. She twisted it around in the hole a few more times to find the right fit. "I'm trying to open the door now," she said. "Could you take your hand off the handle if you are still holding on to it?"

"O.K., sorry."

She was having trouble getting the notches to align just right. "These bitches really don't want anyone to escape."

"What?"

"Nothing, hon. Just having a bit of a time with this door." She finally felt the last groove fall into place. She carefully released one hand from the tool and placed it on the handle, making sure not to move the rod from its precarious bed between the intricate grooving. She felt the door handle give a little bit. "Yes!" The latch released and the door opened. Yuuki stood there in his kimono, desicated tear steaks scarring his face. He seemed much bigger than she remembered him a few hours ago with Hiroka.

"Hello," he said. There was a silent couple seconds while he looked her up and down. He smiled. "Pink."

"What, you never seen a girl wearing pink before?" She thought a second. "No, probably not." Her eyes focused on the wound on Yuuki's cheek. "What did they do to you?"

Yuuki didn't know what she was talking about until he followed her eyes. "Oh, that. No. This happened while still inside."

They didn't have time to chit chat. She needed to get him out of there while the performance was still going on. "Come on, we need to go right now."

"Why, is there something wrong?" Panic once again assailed his vocal cords.

"No, nothing, but we need to hurry just the same. Hiroka only brought you here to rest. It's not a good place to hang out for very long." She reached across the doorway and grabbed his arm. He resisted and with his bulk pulled her into the room.

"Wait, my belongings." He easily released himself from her grip and walked over to the window and grabbed something small. She heard him whisper something to his wrist. "O.K. I am ready."

"Come on! We don't have much time." She heard a different kind of raucous from below. The cheering and caterwauling had been replaced with a more muffled din of hundreds of small after-performance conversations. "Shit!"

She changed direction and headed to the opposite end of the hallway. "There must be another way out."

"What is happening?" He forced her to use both arms to pull him.

"Those women downstairs. They are not very nice. They will hurt you if they see us." She needed him to have a bit of panic now to get him moving to where she wanted him to. His resistance weakened.

There was a slightly lighter area at the end of the hall. "That could be a stairwell." The corridor floor and walls were covered in the same plush red velvet, thankfully muffling their footsteps *and a twisted history of masculine pain*, thought Mimi. They reached the light; no staircase, but a window. "Damn!" Mimi almost shouted. Yuuki looked out the window and saw there were stairs running zigzag down the outside wall.

"Stairs." He pointed out the window.

Mimi didn't hear. She was too focused on the women's voices getting louder from the other end of the hallway. "They're coming!"

"Who? Please tell me what is happening!"

"No time to explain. Just trust me."

"What's going on down there?" a raspy crone voice grated their ears. "Naoko, is that you? Now's not the time to have a private show with your boys."

Mimi and Yuuki stood still, not moving a muscle. She covered Yuuki's mouth with her hand. It barely covered his lips. He was pointing out the window toward the discovered stairs. Mimi kept her hawk eyes on the floor at the corner of their little enclave for any growing shadows. Yuuki not so gently tapped her side to get her attention. "What?" she whisper-yelled.

He made sure she followed his pointing hand. "How are we supposed to get out there? We break it, they all come running."

"Nao-chan!" the voice called out again. "Come on! You signed up for today's backstage duties. I'm not going to do it by myself again. I covered your ass last week. I was all covered in blood and stank of amyl."

"Kumi, what are you on about?" Another ragged voice responded.

"Nao-chan?" Kumi turned around and followed her friend's voice coming from the bottom of the stairs.

"I was in the theater waiting for you. What?"

Kumi turned back to the still shadows at the far end of the hallway. "What's going on down there? If you are planning to escape, then I suggest you reconsider. I'll make sure your next role will be your last." There was no response or movement coming from the window nook. "Nao-chan, come on. Let's catch us a bad little boy."

"Right behind ya." Responded Naoko. The two were excited of the unexpected prospect of a change in plot for their upcoming co-production.

"Shit!" Mimi braced herself for a one on two fight. She knew the Wamono would not know what to do and hoped he'd stay out of the way. She removed her hand from Yuuki's warm lips. She reached her warm, moist hand down into her bra and took out Kitty D. She looked back at Yuuki and put a finger to her lips to make sure he knew to remain quiet.

The heavy footsteps of the two Fujou quickened as they progressed down the hallway toward them. "Now, don't be shy, darling," cooed Kumi. "We won't hurt ya."

"That's right," chimed in Naoko. "We'll leave that up to the directress of tonight's performance."

"Shut up! Don't want him to jump out the window and kill himself. Wouldn't be very entertaining," scolded Kumi. She tried to whisper, but her raspy voice made that impossible.

Yuuki obeyed Mimi and remained quiet. He turned back toward the window. It was divided into upper and lower halves with a latch in the center. He twisted the rusty metal clasp. It moved. "I can open—"

"Shh!" Mimi didn't looking back at him, her eyes fixed on the corner watching for the first millimeter of foot to appear. It was all she needed.

Yuuki lifted the bottom half of the window, a gust of moist air ruffled his billowing kimono and disturbed Mimi's pigtails. Mimi jolted at the sudden change in climate and gave her new charge a dirty look.

"I just opened it," Yuuki mouthed. He was halfway out the window and reached for Mimi's hand "Come on!"

Mimi's training conditioned her never to turn her back on an adversary, even when they were not visible. She backed up toward Yuuki's reaching hand while still holding her prized killer in the other on the ready. A foot finally appeared at the corner of the nook. Mimi wasted no time and flung Kitty D. just at the right moment for it to slice the neck of the leading Fujou as the rest of her appeared from around the corner. The mortally wounded women fell back, knocking her companion to the floor along with her. Dark oxygen-rich blood sputtering in sync with the struggling heartbeat as she fell. The slick life force quickly disappeared into the same gory color of the walls and floor.

Mimi stepped out into the hallway, wasting no time in retrieving her weapon and looked at the two women screaming in deathly pain and anger. Mimi's eyes met the unwounded Fujou pinned down by the weight of her dying companion, threatening the life of the other with stares of mutual hatred.

"Dekora!" shouted Naoko. "Dekora! Help!" she cried as she tried to free herself from her gurgling and gasping sister. "Help!" Her massive wig cocked to one side showing the dull cigarette ash of her real hair.

Mimi picked up her weapon and caressed it while staring directly in the hysterical Fujou's fuming eyes.

"Come on!" yelled Yuuki. He was halfway out the window still reaching for Mimi's hand. He couldn't see what she was looking at. All that was visible protruding from the corner were two spastic feet. He could only hear screams of help. "She killed her?" He barely whispered.

Mimi never took her eyes off the screaming women. "Scream all you want." Mimi said as she cleaned the blade, making sure it would be at its sharpest for its next job. "You won't live long enough for your friends to get me in time." She inspected the blade while keeping a hating smile.

"Help!" "Somebody Hel-eech"

Mimi's blade sliced the women's head almost entirely off her body. Only a couple strands of muscle and pulsating leaking arteries kept it from falling off and rolling to the middle of the hallway, her wig fell onto the floor with a heavy thud.

Yuuki took in a gulp of air as he heard the stunning silence. His muscles petrified at half witnessing his first death, multiple deaths. Mimi disappeared from his view. "Where are you going?" He didn't want to be left alone but wasn't sure he wanted to be 'saved' by this killer girl. Would she kill him next?

"Go!" Mimi shouted as she ran around the corner carrying the re-bloodied blade. "Hurry!" Angry female voices echoed down the hallway, increasing in clarity as they got closer to the scene of the mini massacre. Yuuki could not unfreeze his muscles in time, and Mimi slammed into him trying to push him out.

The two finally made it the ground. Yuuki looked up to white hatred-cracked faces topped with disheveled mountains of wig glaring down at them, but none were giving chase. They knew better. Mimi reached back and grabbed his over-sized sleeve but meaning to grab something more substantial. "C'mon!"

Yuuki could not look away from the yelling women above. The city was yelling at him through these horrid women. His translation was clear, "You are not welcome here!" *Everyone at Aoheki was right. I was wrong, very wrong.*

fifteen

BACK IN THE SAFETY of her suite, the tangy smoke from Sanae's cigarette veiled her in a hazy ephemera. She was secure and hidden within it. She picked at the tiny diamond shards on her pants with her indiscreetly pink-enameled nails. The shards sparkled in the smoke-scolded sunlight. She blew the veil away and walked over to the closest window. The black specks of the Editor and entourage skulked outside the main entrance. The only thing protecting her was Palace. What could save her from it?

She was not clear how the unpleasant tête-à-tête with the Editor would play out. She hadn't planned on forming an alliance with the Tsudii. The long fragile death ballet the Dekora had been performing with the Tsudii and Suriidii was no longer sustainable. She had known that for quite some time; hence, the alliance with the Lolita. Palace's little show in the lobby destroyed any remaining veneer of that balance. The lobby was more of a first battle than a negotiation of an alliance. The Editor would annihilate her and the Dekora at the first opportunity. *That selfish brat handed it to him on a bloody platter heaped with severed Storyliner head.*

"That was amusing," The soft almost monotonous vibration-voice forced a shudder through her insides.

"I would have to disagree." Sanae didn't know what or how to think now that she knew Palace was securely entrenched in her mind. "Are we in Totality?"

"Communion, my dear. Take this as a positive. You are alive, the Dekora and the cabal remain unscathed, and we now have a useful ally in fighting a more serious enemy. We can deal with that weirdo afterwards, but he is useful to us." Sanae sensed Palace chuckling without hearing it do so; that frightened her more.

"How the hell do we fight the Mayor?" The realization of the deal just made to fight a new common enemy was beginning to churn her guts."

I am not sure, my dear. We have no choice." The cold chills released through her body simulating Palace's voice hurt. "It will soon find we exist. I cannot keep myself off the grid forever without causing suspicion at Juku."

"I know what happens if we lose, but what happens if we win? Do we become the Mayor?" She waved the smoke away and poured herself a glass of her strongest and most expensive shochu. "Is that the goal?"

"It is not a goal. An inevitability." Palace's matter-of-fact remark drained the blood from Sanae's head and extremities, pooling in tightly around her frantic heart. "As we hinted to our ... friend down there, there can only be one arch-god in the city. A little skirmish for satrapy supremacy will seem like a playground scuffle compared with what will happen when the Mayor becomes fully aware of our existence."

Sanae ungraciously gulped her shochu in one go. The alcohol burn was a welcome sign that she was still human. What would it mean when there was no burn, no pain?

"Come, come, my dear. Tell me what you are really worried about."

Sanae was growing frustrated with the charade. "You know what's worrying me!" She switched to speaking through thought to confirm her fear. *I don't know how much of my thoughts you can understand.*

"All," Palace said without the slightest inflection in its vibrational voice. "We are almost one now. You do not have to be frightened. Totality will come shortly. Let's hope, unlike your predecessor, you have better mental capabilities to remain alive long enough to enter the final and permanent phase."

'We are one.' frightening.

"Why?"

The question startled her. She would keep forgetting until it would become a strange normal. *I can no longer have a thought to myself?*

"The two of us as one. Don't you understand how powerful we can become? We will control all Hinodé."

I need to be sure that I will be able to think what I want to think without the fear of ... you.

"You can be honest. I will not go against you. I cannot. I need you as much as you need me. You are free to think anything, even if it is critical of me. I have to accept that also. I've been accepting that for a while."

Am I to be a prophet like the Editor and Ren? She had so many questions. She still wasn't an expert in Symbs even after years of being in one.

"If we survive a bit longer into Totality, much more. The Mayor is not a profit."

"a god?"

"No. Bigger. The City."

Sanae didn't want to know anymore. She downed the rest of her drink and poured herself another and fuller, all the while keeping her cigarette lit and ready for a drag.

How long have you been ... in here? Sanae unconsciously pointed to her head.

"For a few weeks. I haven't done anything against any of your thoughts have I? I know you do not trust me, but over time, you will." Palace seemed to have chuckled again. "To tell you the truth, I'm not sure I can trust you either."

Your former ... 'partner'—my predecessor, did she ever trust you?

"As much as one can. Unfortunately, I've been through the Symb phase a few times. I know the drill." Palace's voice never raised or lowered. It kept the same tone. "My kind is, well, rather ... demanding on their humans."

Sanae poured her third shochu. It was having the desired numbing effect. *How many have to go insane before you do?*

"I cannot go insane. That is your burden. Do I sound out of our mind to you?"

Our mind. She couldn't bear to take another drag on her cigarette. She had to fight the urge to vomit; to purge herself of the concrete and steel creature that would eventually take over her mind and her body. *Can I understand every thought of yours then?*

"No. Unfortunately, it doesn't work both ways."

"Of course it doesn't."

"Any updates?" Ren saw Masao out of the corner of her teary, bloodshot eye. She didn't want to stop working on perfecting her latest golem model. Today's project was better fitting eyes for her grotesque urban soldiers. She had just gotten into her 'slicing zone', cutting away, slicing, and the most pleasurable of all, widening slices into gashes. Most of her bandages had been removed from her face, revealing plump but bruised lips and high protruding cheek bones. But a ring of bandage needed to remain around her head to keep everything in place until the nerves and sinew finally renewed and re-attached.

"Our spies within the Dekora said the Editor attempted to conduct some kind of invasion of the Pinku Palace a few hours ago, your highness." Masao stood as he always did, just inside the door, standing straight in contrast with the warped wooden trim around the doorway sporting a fresh smock. Clean smocks made her uncomfortable. She scanned her well-worn studio to ease her pristine phobia. The walls worn and flaking with old layers of paint and the uneven, rough floor speckled with years of dropped and smeared clay and careless wisps of gore suppressed her anxiety. The contrasting calming earth tones and history's violence in the color of crusted blood was her color scheme for inner peace.

She paused from working her serrated molding knife into a freshly formed eye socket of the model. She still personally created at least one of her flesh and clay worker soldiers once every few months. "Invaded? How noble of the little tyrant." She snickered while gouging out a neat hole with her blade, where an eye would eventually be fitted. "I take it he was not successful from your choice of words." She knew Masao never said anything without careful thought to the received meaning.

Masao remained near silhouette. The pure white of the damnable smock almost glowed. "I am not quite sure, your majesty, but the informants say that something transpired inside the Pinku Palace that rendered the Editor and his entourage impotent."

"Huh, interesting." Ren continued her work without looking up. "I'm sure that little shit's not happy with that. He will probably do something rash, violent, and even more predictably stupid to re-inflate that disproportionate ego of his."

"What would you like to do presently?" Asked Masao, still standing at attention, expressionless. "The Tsudii do not seem to be gaining that upper hand we hoped for."

"Well then, we'll just have to change our strategy slightly. Damn!" She'd sliced through an eye. "Go tell the procurement section to send me up larger eyes," she shouted to the still unfinished attendant standing in the same shadow that was cloaking Masao. The incomplete being ran out the door to do her bidding. She looked at the dish with the now too small eyes staring cross-eyed up at her. "What a waste." She dumped them into the bin next to her feet.

"Your majesty," said Masao, trying to steer his queen back on topic. "This change in strategy?"

"Yes? Right. Well, I think it time to have a heart-to-heart with our lovely mercenary fashionista."

"Initiate an alliance this soon?" The chief remodeler was out of character by questioning her without asking for permission. She didn't show any sign of anger toward his skepticism.

"I didn't say that. We should start a dialogue. It is only logical. Of course, I would explore the idea of talking with Oné-chan in such a situation. Don't you agree?"

"Of course, but do you think it prudent to anger the Tsudii to such an extent so quickly? It may backfire. You know he does not possess the most logical mind. He could declare war on both of us."

"He's not logical, but he's not that stupid either, unfortunately. We have that damn Draw to thank for that.

She stood up and walked closer to her confidant. She still had a minor limp to her gate. She refused to use a walking aide as Masao recommended. She didn't dare get any closer and frighten him away. *He's my subordinate for fuck sake! I can't be acting like a horny little teenage girl every time I'm near him!*

"I would not call you a teenager," a soft metallic voice-like vibration buzzed inside her head.

She no-so-gently smacked the side of her right thigh. *Not now, Cal. I'm busy strategizing. Just do your mysterious god conjuring and bring life into my beautiful creations. Unless you have an opinion on the topic at hand.*

"Meeting with her to what end, your majesty?" Masao moved his left heel back just slightly as she approached.

Her heart died a few beats as she saw his reaction. She turned around and limped back to her stool, stroked Nekohito napping in its soft bed on the floor next to the workbench, then took in a deep breath to create an air barrier around her heart from the hurt churning in her gut. There were more pressing issues at hand. "Obviously, they no longer have a contract with the Tsudii. They will need to compensate for the lost income somehow. We are the only ones of any import now available. The spineless Ue-No Free Citizens Council doesn't have the balls or money to get involved with assassinations, and the Za-Ginsa Business Consortium are too busy hoarding money and living the high life to even care. We will buy the remainder of their contract with them but declare our neutrality in their little conflict. Does that sound good to you?" she playfully added.

"Yes, I believe so." Masao didn't sound convinced. "So, we would hire them as our assassins, but not use them for hits on the Tsudii?"

"Precisely," Ren responded as if she just said something overly complicated to a mentally deficient child. "We have 'interests' other than the damn Tsudii. Plus, we need to re-negotiate with our greedy Mayor. Ever since I was given the opportunity to have my own satrapy upon attaining Totality with Caliper, I have been wasting my resources providing it with my golems. Masao tensed every time the Mayor came up in conversation, especially in a less than deferential tone. It amused her to see him ever-so-elegantly squirm. "We just need to keep that pink horde above water financially. We can afford it."

"You have a point," said the stiff counselor. "It would be the natural thing to do. Questions won't arise, especially if we officially declare our neutrality." He emphasized the last point.

A tiny green light began to pulse on Masao's commring. "Excuse me your majesty." He stepped just outside the studio to take the call.

Ren went back to her grotesque work on the table. *Cal, what do you think about this?*

"It seems like a sound plan for now. As you say, there are other concerns we can focus on while those two take turns killing each other."

The annoying Council and Consortium?

"Yes. But ..."

And the Mayor.

"The Mayor."

Masao re-entered and bowed. "Pardon me, your majesty."

"What was that about?"

"That was Oné-chan. She would like to meet with you."

"That's convenient." She let out a giggle. "And expected." She stabbed the pin knife down into her bench, stood up, and walked over to the window. "Saves us a step. Set it up. My usual."

"Certainly, your majesty. Masao began backing up out the studio.

"Oh, and where's that mirror?"

"I'll send one up right away, your majesty."

She continued looking out the window not saying anything else. Masao shut the doors softly in front of him. The gentle click could have been from a loaded weapon; its bullet ripping through her already wounded heart, splattering bloody clumps of rejection.

sixteen

THE EMPTINESS IN THE cell matched Shinya within. This was the
time of day he and Yuuki were usually together; often taking naps while
Hiro was being loud and annoying someplace else. Hiro also disappeared, but
that was not unusual. He often illicitly stayed with his mates in their cells for days
on end.

The moment he saw Yuuki's cot empty and made, he knew he was gone
forever. It was only a matter of time with him. All he could do was silently wish
him luck if he was still alive. People only come into a cloister and only once.

Shinya tried to take his afternoon nap but couldn't force his eyes to remain
shut. He got out of bed, loosely wrapped his kimono around him, and walked
over to the desk. He stepped on the chair then onto the desk and looked out the
window onto Sakura Hitotsu-en Courtyard. He was glad he told Yuuki about the
crack in the wall. He put a finger up to the window tracing over where the crack
would be if he were right there. "It is our only connection". He could almost feel
the rough stone. He wanted to feel him. "Everything is now desolate." He finally
peeled his eyes from the window and dismounted the desk. The old desk and chair
creaked under his weight as he stepped down. He sat on his cot and played with
the dangling ribbons on his kimono. "I can't go back out there, can I?"

He lay back down, but this time he didn't even try to sleep. Piercing images
of blood and sounds of death rushed into his brain. The vice grip of his hands

on either side of his head could not prevent the invading horrors. He turned onto his side in the fetal position, bracing himself against the assault of unwanted memories. He scrunched his eyes so tight a different kind of tear started to squeeze out.

"Mom, I'm back."

"Back here Shin-kun," his mother called out from behind a half-closed door at the back of the store.

Shinya unceremoniously dropped his bag of schoolbooks on the front counter and grabbed a sweetened bitter-melon juice from the small fridge underneath. It was Shinya's favorite part of the day. He hated school, like any normal kid, and counted the minutes until he was free from its pasty white walls. He looked forward to getting his hands on the latest "Gorshan Worm" that would have arrived in the store earlier in the morning or continue the weird saga of the half anthropological half fantasy "City Stories". Many of his friends were envious of him and his parents' manga store. They waited anxiously for their morning report on what horrible deeds the Worm had done to the citizens of the bizarro world of Gorshan, or in which exotic outer ward beyond the Watcher Walls the latest City Story was set. Normally, it would only take him at most an hour to get through both and probably another daily serial, but he had to read them very carefully for his highly anticipated morning reports at school. He was only allowed to read the age-appropriate manga in the store. He was too young to begin the mandatory imprinting onto the Prophet of Draw all adult citizens within the Tsudii Satrapy had to go through via the addictive reading of the Tsudii manga scriptural fiction. He got the feeling his parents would not want him to be imprinted even when he did come of age. He received angry looks from both when he even looked up at those high forbidden shelves.

"Where's dad?" Shinya yelled.

"Out," his mother said, always economical with her words. She was the money wizard of the family and spent most of her time in the back room going over sales and making sure the inventory was all squared away. She only manned the front when Shinya's father was out doing errands, coming out only when she heard the little metal bell hanging over the entrance. Shinya saw her condition was worsening each day. He couldn't remember when the last time she stepped outside the store. His father ended up doing everything that needed to be done out in the streets of Shin-yuyogi. He never complained. Shinya learned not to also. His mother knew she was a burden and broke out in tears if he even rolled his eyes whenever she asked him to go down the street to buy something for the store or their home above it. Sometimes it was just to buy more paper for her accounting books from the stationary store next door.

"Come in here and give your mama a big hug."

Shinya faked embarrassment "Aw, mom!" He enjoyed being with his parents; something unusual for many pre-teens. He walked into the back room to do her bidding. She was a pretty woman for her age. She always dressed like she was about to go out to some fancy lunch or meeting in Za-Ginsa or Kyujuku. He walked over and gave her requested hug.

"How was school today?" She always made sure to ask, refusing to go back to her books while talking with her only child. She wanted her full attention on him.

Shinya's answer was almost always the same. "Was O.K."

"Did you do well on your history quiz today?"

"I think so. Won't find out 'til tomorrow probably. But it seemed easy enough." He wanted to get on with his other unofficial school duty of reading his favorite manga, but he also didn't want to upset his mom. It was always hard for her to say goodbye to him every morning.

"Very well. Go on. I know you are dying to get into today's episodes." She smiled, stretching her brilliant, rouged lips enough to show her perfect white teeth. Shinya felt comforted in the fact that she did everything she could within the limitations of her condition to look her best.

"Thanks mom." He gave her a light peck on her cheek, ran out into the store, and grabbed the day's reading material.

"Remember, dinner at six," his mom yelled out.

"O.K." Shinya's response was barely audible even to himself. He was already engrossed in the weird worlds outside Hinodé.

He liked to read hidden under the sales bench for privacy but available if a customer came in. The tiny bell sounded its tinny chaotic chime above the entrance, but Shinya was in no hurry to greet the customer. He usually waited for a few minutes to allow the person to browse, undisturbed.

"Kozué!" cried out a man out-of-breath.

Shinya recognized his father's voice. He stood up to surprise him but saw a man who resembled his father, but his clothes were all disheveled and streaks of blood ran down his face and the front of his shirt. "Dad?" He still wasn't sure if the beaten man was his father.

"Shinya! Get out of here, now!" His father ran toward him. The man that looked like his father frightened Shinya. He started to run to the back room to his mother, but before he could get there, she came running out. They collided. "Get out, both of you," ordered the bloodied man.

"Ryosuké? What happened?" His mother instinctively began to run over to her husband, but he thrust out his shaking hands, signaling her to not come any closer.

"Run! Storyliner. Coming! Get out. Now!" Shinya's father had to brace himself against a clearance bin of old manga titles in the middle of the shop. Shinya saw that his hands were also red with blood and got a closer look at his bruised and sliced face. Mother and son were too stunned to obey his orders. They wanted to help him, but he kept yelling for them to get out of the store. "Go out the back! Go! Kozué, please!" Tears started to mix with the blood on his face. He couldn't remain standing. His legs gave out, and he collapsed onto the floor.

The bell above the entrance chimed again.

Shinya muffled his head with his arms trying desperately to squeeze the terrifying memory from his mind. But again, it proved too persistent. His entire body filmed with shimmering sweat. The two-decade-old memory was totally debilitating. He finally gave into its power and allowed the blood-red images continue their rampage through his exhausted mind.

"Well Ogawa-san, fancy meeting you here," said the artificially masculinized being.

Shinya ran back to his reading nook behind the front counter. Luckily, the Storyliner's featureless face was not yet focused on any other inhabitant of the space it reflected. Shinya peeked up from behind the counter and saw the short, muscled creature pull the blinds down over the door window and locked the door. He had never seen a Storyliner up close. He had only heard or read about them in some of the manga. The rumors and images differed from the much more terrifying reality. The monster's head portrayed uncanny placidity—no murderous rage; that was the most frightening to Shinya. The thug was practically naked. Only a cloth draped over his genitals, barely concealing.

Kozué ignored her husband's plea and remained at the back-office door way, so petrified with fear that she seemed more defiant than terrified. She did not even acknowledge her son crouched in terror underneath the counter in front of her. Shinya wanted to get her attention, to wake her up, but both were cemented in terror.

Run mom! Run! He hoped she could do the impossible and read his mind. Just as he was about to give up, he saw her hands begin to tremble and her eyes narrow in intensely focused rage. She remained still as if recharging from the draining fear. Shinya was in awe. She was petrified of people and spaces outside her small mercantile oasis, but inside it, she was a super being from one of his manga.

The faceless killer moved his dense mass until he was standing above Shinya's father. "Get up you worthless fuck." His voice sounded almost mechanical; syllables and accents clanked and whirred.

Shinya's father could only raise his hand in a futile attempt to protect himself. "Please, don't hurt me anymore. I'll get the tribute I owe, but I don't have it now. I know I'm behind. I can get some of it to you tomorrow. I know the Prophet will have compassion for his wayward worshipper." The plea used most of the remaining energy he had left.

"Some of it?" the Storyliner repeated as he bent down to a similar level as the suffering man. Shinya could see his father's bloodied and terrified reflection in the no-face of the Storyliner. "All. Now." He swung his skillet-sized hand back, closed it into a miniature wrecking ball, and released it, slamming it into the father's battered face. Shinya heard the gushy thud of the impact. The hateful sound summoned up his first experience of being powerless and a coward.

"No!" cried Kozué. "Stop! You brainless monster!" She ran toward him but was sent back with the same wrecking-ball fist, knocked to the floor, bleeding like her husband.

"Madame Ogawa." The Storyliner said in a mocking feminine voice. He lunged over, ignoring the half unconscious man. "You are even better looking in the flesh. This may turn out to be more amusing than expected." He roughly smeared the lipstick from her lips, streaking it across her cheek. Her face was now like her husband's. "Scarlet suits you." He slapped her to make sure she wouldn't try to interfere with his business again. The force threw her into the same state as her husband sprawled out a couple meters in front of her.

Shinya remained frozen in fear. His mind was screaming for his mother, but his lips remained dried, fused. There was nothing he could do to help them.

The Storyliner swiveled back to the father. "I'm sorry Ogawa-san, but the Prophet needs the kané now. If he cannot get it this instant ..." He straightened the bloody man's collar to make him more presentable. "Then he doesn't want it at all." He took out a small knife and sliced the beaten man's throat. "Unfortunately, time is just a little bit more important than money to him." Blood gushed out from the slice, pooling around the two men. Shinya's father was drowning in his own blood, gurgling and gasping his final breaths.

Shinya could see nothing of his father's last seconds but heard the gasps muted by blood. He peeked up again and saw a large deep-red slick flowing from the other side of the clearance bin. A bizarre rush of acceptance flowed through him. His father was dead. *Mom!* His mother was still alive; she was moving at least. He ducked back down fully hiding behind the counter. Heavy footsteps approached his mother. Unlike his father, his mother would be in full view when he peeked up, but he couldn't bring himself to look. He hated himself more than the faceless killer.

He heard cloth being ripped, heavy grunts, semi-conscious moans, and malignant rhythmic slaps. The Storyliner started to breathe heavier and grunt in rhythm to the other sounds. His bass primal vocals reminded Shinya of the rancid breath-exhaust from a viscerdenn seeping up through the gratings along the street. Finally, the only thing he could hear was the exhausted man-beast panting and faint feminine moans of pain. Shinya tried to unfurl himself, but his arms refused to unlock and release his legs. The murderer's heavy steps got further and further away. The bell rang and the door slammed shut, the reverberation continuing for eternal seconds.

Shinya had been too much of a reminder to his mother of the hell she went through that day. *I was angry with her for suggesting the Order.* He knew she wanted him gone but couldn't admit that he wanted to go. They had been living their double-exposure nightmare, fully awake with all its entangled layers of horror and scars.

He sat up, his kimono now fully open. The cool air felt good against his chest and groin. "It is time to go." Conversation with the air was just as good as talking with anyone else now that Yuuki had left. "I cannot escape like Yuuki." He couldn't escape his life twice. Suicide would be less despicable.

The membrane of sweat glazing his body cooled, charging it with excruciating chills. He stood up and wrapped his kimono tight around himself and tied a ribbon to secure the closure. He looked back at the desk. "What did you do all those times at that desk?" He smiled at the thought of his trouble-maker cellmate pretending to study but planning his next plot to piss off Kugai and Hégo. He walked around his cot to the desk and sat down, tracing the etchings of past novitiate generations with his finger. "Stupid of me not to let you know how I felt about you earlier. Once a coward, always one."

His tired mind switched back to his mother. *Is she even alive?* a dark spot in his mind whispered to him that she probably committed suicide long ago. It would make sense. A week after the attack, she tried to accomplish that very act by drinking a toxic cocktail of the industrial-strength cleaning liquids she used for the shelves and floor of the store. Luckily, he had returned from errands just in time. He felt she blamed him for saving her life. She never said as such, but her coldness told him otherwise. They were no longer mother and son. They were shameful reciprocal reminders of that day of blood and death.

"Damn you Yuuki," he almost shouted. "This is all your fault." He slapped his calloused hand down on the desk, his brain not registering the stinging pain. He didn't know what he wanted more, to know if his mother was still alive and say sorry for not coming to her rescue sooner that day or find Yuuki and wrap his arms around him never to let him go. *I am not strong enough to do both.* He was possessed with the type of raw sadness from which no breath could escape. Finally, the emotional pain released its grip on him, and he took in an immense breath of air, freeing the tears and his vocal cords.

He let his head fall gently onto the desk, remaining in the same beaten pose for several minutes. The tears slowed to a salty trickle. He picked up his head, revealing a dark stain where his tears soaked into the porous scarred wood. He liked it here. It had been his home for the past two decades and felt safe behind these massive walls. But there was too much he needed to see or find out on the outside.

He wiped the remaining tears from his cheeks. "Yes. I need to leave." *Maybe it is some kind of weird calling.* He thought of the rumored self-shunned corps of Smashers and if Aoheki had ever contributed volunteers. If he became one of these legendary Inanimate destroyers, he would be considered forever shunned for the greater good the moment he covered his cold stone-beaten feet and took his first steps back outside the walls.

The possibility, however slight, of an honorable way out bathed him in a strange calm. His breathing finally went back to normal, his face red from any tear sign. This battle was over, and he'd won, but the forever war with his memories and heartbreak would live on to rage.

"It is done." Hégo, exhausted, had just returned to his cell after voting for himself as the new Master of the Cloister. "No more groveling." He looked down to Cane and remained silent for any sign of it listening to his ramblings. There was no vibration or any other suggestion that it was listening, but he knew otherwise.

He leaned back in the chair. He had to stay confident. Doubt became exponentially more dangerous when allowed to grow in the minds of the desperate. "I am sure I have the votes. There is no one strong enough to challenge. Goto Ogushu is the only one that could garner as many votes, but that hermit is too wrapped up in his little world of dead words and worm-munched paper in the archives." He leaned forward and rested his bony chin on the hand wrapping around the bulbous end of Cane. He let out a wheezy chuckle. "I may be unpopular, but at least people know me. Ogushu just stagnates in that musty old room stroking his ridiculous beard and gazing at old texts."

Cane finally began the anticipated vibrations. "I heard his filing and organizational skills are second to none. And of course, his immense knowledge of the cloister's and the wider Order's history could be useful as a Master."

"Whose side are you on?" Hégo wanted to get up and walk around, but he always found it difficult to simultaneously talk to Cane and use it as a walking aid. "I am unsympathetic and unsentimental. I do what needs to be done for the good of the Order. That has been proven time and again." He felt like he had to prove this to Cane, and he despised it for making him think that way.

"Kugai was quite popular, correct?"

"Yes, I suppose." Hégo knew where Cane was going with this. He continued to verbally block his fellow debater. "And he was sympathetic and sentimental. But look what his last decree was before going mad——letting a prisoner, a monster, free to roam around Aoheki.

A soft knock penetrated the worn door. Hégo took in a breath of surprise but did not let it out in nervous anticipation. "That must be the clerk with the result."

He stood up, wanting to show the news bearer that he did not need to be constantly seated, plus he couldn't sit still. "Come in," he barked.

A small middle-aged monk meekly opened the door. "Excuse me Master-sama," said the clerk. His squeaky voice matched his stature.

He addressed me as Master. That is a good sign. "Yes, what is it?" Hégo did not want to show the lowly clerk that he was anticipating anything.

"I have the result of the vote."

"Well? And speak up!"

The messenger kept his head bowed slightly and turned left. The monk was barely audible through the thick hair that took his face's place. "The congregation voted you as the new Master of the Cloister. Congratulations."

Hégo almost fell to the floor in relief. Blood, released from the heaviness of worry and waiting, rushed from his head to flood the other parts of his body. Again, he had to be grateful for Cane's unfailing assistance. "Thank you." The gratitude was not much more than a grunt of afterthought.

The clerk remained half in and half out of the cell. An uncomfortable silence filled the barren room.

"Well, what is it?" The now official Master began to worry. He saw the monk's hands shaking.

"The vote was quite close between you and Goto Ogushu-sama," the clerk said painfully hesitating before each word.

"What does that mean?" *He said 'sama', not 'sensei'.*

The clerk took in a deep breath and blurted it out, obviously wanting to get it out and escape the impending wrath of the old man. "Too close, less than 10 votes separated the both of you." He took in a deep breath and quickly let the bomb escape with the held in breath. "Goto Ogushu-sama will be your co-Master."

"You mean disciplinarian, my second-in-command. Of course, I know that."

"I fear there is a miscommunication. I apologize."

"Then un-miscommunicate!" Hégo had to sit back down. He was quickly losing the one thread of patience he had.

"He will work alongside you in running the cloister." The clerk moved back slightly.

"What?"

"You will be slightly senior, of course, since you are older and had already been in a senior position. This is unprecedented here at Aoheki, so it is rather unknown to us. Goto Ogushu-sama notified us of the rule."

"Of course he did. You can go now. I do not need any more history lessons."

The clerk didn't hesitate to fulfill his new Master's command. The door shut just as softly as it opened.

"This is outrageous!" belted Hégo. He began to shake.

"Calm down," said Cane. Its voice in Hego's head was almost as soft as the frightened clerk's. "You are still the senior in this new relationship."

"I do not want a new *relationship*!" Hégo looked down at Cane. "One is enough." He let out a phlegmy sigh, breathing out the agitated shakes. Sharing anything had always been difficult. He still wasn't used to sharing his life with Cane after decades of being together. He would never get used to it. The Master's desk and chair suddenly looked just like any other piece of furniture in any other monk's cell. He felt slighted by his god. The smooth hardness under his palms reminded him of one thing that might have garnered the god's terrible retinue of Retributions' attention. *Damn you, Cane.* "This is a punishment."

"Punishment?" Cane's voice felt confused.

"Gou-Tairei is punishing me for allowing you to be here." The Wamono god rarely punished within the same lifetime, but his mind needed a convenient explanation.

Cane remained loudly silent, which Hégo took as a rejection of his justification.

"I take it you do not agree."

"I said nothing," replied Cane.

"That says a lot." He let out another life-worn sigh and rested his elbow on the side edge of the desk. "No matter. What is done is done. I am *a* Master now, the senior Master. Things have not changed that much. If I felt like I could control Ogushu as the disciplinarian, then I can control him as the co-Master. He will remain the same spineless mole of a monk as he always was."

Cane continued its silence. This time it was not challenged. The excitement of the day had taken its toll on the old man, and he still had to hold a cloister-wide conclave later in the day to put all his and Cane plans into irrevocable play. He painfully sat himself down, wincing in pain, and quickly fell asleep with his head propped up on his hand, soft labored snores escaping through his gaping wrinkled mouth. Cane vibrated slightly in synchronicity with its host's snoring. *I am no punishment. I am a gift and I be worshipped.*

The heavy ceremonial kimono bent Hégo's frail body even more than usual. He looked out over all that he now controlled. The hall seethed with the bobbing of nervous heads and hummed with equally nervous voices. Even all the Reincarnates were present, sniffing, slithering, or swimming amongst their human counterparts.

He couldn't remember when this many monks and Reincarnates were at one meeting. But there was couple of his flock missing. He had been notified earlier by the prefect that the novitiate Yuuki and one of his cellmates were no where to be found. The news should have been much more serious but was the least of his concerns now. *Good riddance.* He would have to eventually get to the bottom of how that overgrown imp had managed to escape. There were no reports from the caretakers of the Shisa having a human meal recently. The whole incident emitted a faint scent of that Aku. He would have to confront her about it the next time he would speak to her.

He tried to straighten his back and puff out his chest, but only a few millimeters of growth both in height and width resulted. He began his painful climb up the stairs to the dais where he would be protected from the agitated sea of concerned and nervous monks He finally made it to the top step and immediately shrank and deflated at the site of his co-Master already standing in front of his makeshift cathedra.

"*Vwomp..kaka, Vwomp..kaka, Vwomp..kaka.*" Yayoi Mashu slammed his precious staff as soon as he saw Masters Daiso Hégo and Goto Ogushu sit down. Hégo shot an accusing glare at the Officer of Ceremony and Order. Even though he was the reason for the racket, he still hated it. Mashu started his usual bellowing soliloquy. "All Wamono of the Aoheki cloister. The first convocation of Daiso Hégo-sama and Goto Ogushu-sama, the one-hundred twenty-third Masters of the Cloister, and the three-hundred seventy-third convocation on record has now commenced." The fabric and hair sea calmed to a more tranquil undulation. Mashu looked up and nodded to Hégo. *How dare he nod permission for me to speak.* He instantly churned up the back of his mind to think of an appropriate veiled punishment for him.

The senior Master used every stringy muscle he could to stand himself up out of his cathedra. He gave his co-Master a stay-away look when he saw the jittery junior move to help him.

"My distinguished companion," swinging a shaking hand at Ogushu, "and I would like to forgo the pomp of the installment ceremony and get on to what is of grave importance; the survival of this cloister and our Wamono way of life." He paused allowing the chain reaction of comments and surprise to rise then subside. "Ogushu-sama and I have been officially sworn in by Yayoi Mashu-sensei prior to this meeting." The looks of confusion pleased him.

He took in a long breath then exhaled. He put his hands into the opposite gaping sleeves. The entire audience did the same upon his cue. A soft shuffle of velvet and silk wafted over the stillness. "Wamono of Aoheki, I have an important announcement that will surprise most of you and may anger and frighten others." The mass of velvet began to swell in nervous confusion and anticipation.

"The barrier walls are the only protection against Keibu-yo." He looked at the giant carved doors knowing what should be now on the other side. The thought of what he was about to do desiccated his throat. He had to pause to build up a meagre wad of phlegm to re-moisten his vocal cords. "They are crucial in preserving our culture and, more importantly, our survival." He wanted the predominantly conservative brethren to know how dangerous it would be to neglect the barrier. "These walls have not been properly maintained for centuries, and I know I am not the only one who has noticed a more frequent occurrence of fallen, brittle shards." Hégo heard fits of verbal agreement, hundreds of heads nodding like a brood of hens looking for the last remaining bits of grain in the dirt. "The masterful builders of our protective enclosure have, unfortunately, not built into their plans a convenient means for us human-form monks to maintain and repair the barrier. We have none here who could do the same crucial work as the ravens at Takiheki or the agile macaques at Ametsubuheki. With absolutely no disrespect to our esteemed Reincarnates here with us this evening." He saw the soft brown eyes and glistening coat of Iyesu Mikaru. The Reincarnate probably couldn't see him very well since bears don't have the best eyesight.

He paused, letting the fear spread from monk to monk until a rebirth of a murmur took hold and grew to a mumble. Helpless energy exhaled from almost every mouth below him. *Good, good.* He waited for the latest restrained uproar to settle before continuing. "But we do have one living hidden among us who can help us in the urgent matter." The assemblage rippled with murmurs of who this could be. "Most of you are not aware of this Reincarnate in our midst. She has been a prisoner here at Aoheki for several centuries.

"Imprisoned?" one monk shouted. He quickly shrunk in shame for being so rude as to speak out in front of the Master.

"We are a prison?" another asked out loud ignoring the rules.

"Who is this prisoner?" a middle-aged Wamono cried out from the back of the throng.

'She?' was the most prominent question rippling throughout.

The intensity of shushing hisses grew.

Yayoi Mashu pounded his staff several times, each slam louder than the last. "Silence! We must have order during the convocation. Silence!" His baritone voice echoed off the walls and into everyone's ears. Hégo took out his hands from their ceremonial homes within his sleeves, stretched them out over the audience, and lowered them in the universal sign for calm. After another set of slams of Mashu's heavy stave, the congregation finally quieted.

"Genkou Ryudasu is the one imprisoned far below us in the old wine cellars under the basements." Waves of gasps crashed against the foot of the elevated dais. They all knew who the legendary Genkou Ryudasu was but didn't know what happened to the ancient bogeyman. "I apologize for keeping so many of you in the dark about this, but I had no choice. The Wamono-Zentai stipulated the secrecy during his sentencing those centuries ago."

He paused, watching the steam from hundreds of breaths combine then disappear. The scene gave him chills. "Dogen Kugai and I have been in conversation with Genkou Ryudasu, and she has agreed to help us with maintaining and repairing our ancient wall. She is our only option."

He was starting to talk above the intensifying hubbub. Even Mashu's powerful floor ramming and shouts of 'silence' were no longer effective. The convocation was quickly getting out of control. He had to take it back, or he would lose any the minutia of respect he did have. "Quiet!" The congregation turned toward the roar and self-silencing with 'sshhhs' and 'shushes'. He could read their minds; Kugai would have never used his voice like that.

"I know this sounds troubling but let me assure you that I sincerely believe Genkou Ryudasu has been sufficiently rehabilitated and deserves at least a probation. We need her." *I need her.*

"Before my predecessor had his unfortunate reaction to the Goushintei, he pleaded his case to the the Dai-Master and the Wamono-Zentai." The irritated twitching of that annoying squid Nonen Amedo's tentacles disturbed his peripheral vision. "They have voted in favor of Genkou Ryudasu-sensei's release." The atrium surged in frightened protest. He nodded toward Mashu to quiet the hall.

The officer obeyed and slammed his staff the predictable three times. The echoing interruption had little effect. Hégo nodded again, and Mashu repeated his assault on the stone floor. "Silence! Silence!" Finally, the mass calmed. Eyes began directing back onto the dais and the co-Masters. He had to channel their beloved Kugai to remind them who there are.

"I ask you all to see past what Genkou Ryudasu did those centuries ago. Yes, she committed atrocities in the distant past. Things most of you have only heard bits and pieces of—some true, but most may be exaggerated or even false. Gou-Tairei has taken care of her punishment. It is not our time's place to judge." He was taking a page out of Kugai's compassionate playbook. "It is not just our clothes, hair, or Haiku-bassbeat sermons that make us Wamono. It is our duty to plummet into the depths of our souls and find who we are and that what we should fiercely protect is our compassion. That, my brethren, is what makes us Wamono. If we cannot show that to another creature—a member of our community—then we have no right calling ourselves Wamono. Remember why we created these cloisters over a millennium ago; compassion was lost in what we now call Keibu-yo. We built these walls, not only to keep the outside out but to preserve our endangered compassion." His short speech provided him a puff of satisfaction. It seemed to be working. He believed in what he had just said, but it irked him that he had to remind them and worse speak it. *Now for another punch to the gut.*

"The decision is effective as of today; therefore, there will be no vote. The Wamono-Zentai have decided." He motioned to Mashu to intercept the expected uproar. Congregational voting was a revered institution in the Order, but as Master, he could use extenuating circumstances to forgo it.

"*Vwomp..kaka, Vwomp..kaka, Vwomp..kaka.* The Master of the Cloister is speaking. Silence!" The maneuver worked. Eddies of whispering hubbub and hand waving were re-born but isolated.

"Genkou Ryudasu-sensei should now be outside the main doors of this hall." Hundreds of heads soundlessly turned en mass toward the massive doors. Hégo wasn't expecting the quiet. He continued talking even though most still had their heads turned away from him. "She is to have almost full access to the cloister, and she will start her duties as Protector of the Barriers immediately."

He noticed Mashu was at the ready with his staff, but still no eruption. *Are they that terrified they cannot even react?* "Open the doors!" He yelled to the monks who were on door duty. Even from his distance he could see their hands trembling, struggling to open the cumbersome portals.

The doors finally started to swing outward, allowing a rush of cool damp air to barge in, tintinnabulating the hundreds of hair beads on the heads of those most exposed to the onrush.

"Do not do this Master." Came one from the front row of the most elderly of monks.

"What are we bringing upon ourselves?" came another.

A bi-colored tsunami of hair and cloth came at him triggered by the front line at the door getting their first ever look at their new Protector.

Perfect, thought Hégo. *She is doing her part exactly as we discussed. Now it is up to me to assure the frightened hens.* He had to admit, of course only to himself, that he was just as frightened.

He lifted his hands with as calm a face as he could muster. "Calm down. Calm!" He showed his palm to Mashu signaling to him not to use his powers of crowd silencing. He wanted to do it himself. "There is nothing to be frightened of. She is here to help us and start herself on the way to redemption." He was sure redemption was not in her vocabulary.

The growing hysteria of the monks wasn't subsiding. Hégo finally waved his hands up and down. Even Mashu slammed his staff frantically, ignoring his Master's earlier orders.

He saw monks down in the front, his fellow elders, being crushed by the solid human wave, crying for help and clamoring up toward the dais, adrenaline making it possible for their normally frail bodies to do so. *I need to stop this before I have to preside over several funerals.* He saw one monk, his former neighbor at previous convocations, on the floor being stepped on and lifeless. *Oh, for the compassion of the ambivalent Gou, help me.*

He looked over to see what his co-Master was doing, but Ogushu was not where he was supposed to be. *That spineless little mole.* The masculine screams lessened somewhat. Something was happening out in the masses.

He looked out over the calming crowed to see what miracle of Gou stopped the hysterical stampede. He saw someone standing in the doorway between Ryudasu and the entire population of Aoheki. "It cannot be," he whispered to himself. "What is he doing?" All eyes were on Ogushu. Once everyone's attention was on him and not their fear, Ogushu slowly and calmly walked closer to Ryudasu and gave her a courteous bow. Ryudasu returned the respectful gesture. In those few seconds the hall returned to almost normal. The monks checked the area around them to see if everyone was safe and unharmed. Those who weren't, including Hégo's neighbor, were quickly taken to the infirmary.

That bastard, Hégo thought. *That was not part of the plan. He was never part of the plan.* But he was relieved that the situation was now under control. He had to take it back. Most of the congregation was still looking in awe at Ogushu as he conversed with the ex-convict Aku. *What could they be talking about?* He motioned for the two conspirators to fully enter the hall.

The milling monks quickly parted to make room for their co-Master and Protector of the Barriers. They made more room than was needed. "Come in," said Hégo. "Welcome back into our community Genkou Ryudasu-sensei. We hope that you will be filled with the unobtrusive goodness of Gou-Tairei to perform your important duties as the Protector of the Barriers."

An uncomfortable pause laid heavy in the room, finally broken by Ogushu. "By the unobtrusive goodness of Gou-Tairei."

The entire hall followed his lead and mumbled the same required reply.

Ryudasu hiss-rasped. "Thank you. I will do my very best to fulfill my duties and protect the barriers from the corruptive infesssstations of Keibu-yo."

"By the unobtrusive goodness of Gou-Tairei," responded the hall.

Hégo waited for his junior to take his place back on the dais next to him before he went on to the second order of business. He watched as the space of fear and apprehension separating the monks from Ryudasu began to narrow, starting with a few brave young monks. After a few seconds most of the flock started to fill in the buffer.

Once Ogushu was back in his place, Hégo began to speak, refusing to acknowledge his junior before starting. "I apologize for the scare. I did not anticipate the fear you all would have upon seeing your new Protector." It was a scolding veiled in an apology. "Unfortunately, I have more important changes to announce." The crowd's mumblings were even more muffled by nervous exhaustion.

"Excuse me Master-sama," said Ogushu.

Hégo snapped his craggy neck toward his junior. His expression did not change, nor did he say anything to acknowledge the interruption. Ogushu had his hands hidden in the mass of his lace cuffs and looked down and to the left facing his co-Master. *He is good. Very good.*

Ogushu continued taking the silence of his co-Master as a sign to go on. "I believe the events that have taken place were enough for one convocation, do you not think so?" There was a murmur of agreement among the monks, especially the elderly.

Hego's glare stayed glued on Ogushu until the soft smile shrank from his junior's face and his eyes started to shift from the uncomfortable attention. Once he felt satisfied in silently reprimanding his junior, he slowly turned to the congregation and formed a difficult smile. "I understand that you all may be tired, but I think it prudent to talk to you now about what I have to say. Calling an additional convocation later today or tomorrow would be just as exhausting, would it not? Two in as many weeks is enough." He turned his head slightly back toward Ogushu.

One of the elder monks sitting in the first row spoke up. "Yes, yes. Let us just stay and listen. I would rather not come back here for a while." It wasn't the enthusiasm he wanted, but he would have to take it.

"What I am about to say may be even more of a shock than introducing you to your Protector."

More muttering came from below with heads turning to Ryudasu. "Silence!" yelled Mashu. The ox-ish monk struggled to keep the sweat produced thanks to his heavy ceremonial garb from running into his eyes.

"Maybe Ogushu is correct. Maybe this is not the right time to announce this." came a vibration up through his spine and into his brain.

Hégo couldn't respond to Cane, which was resting against Hego's cathedra almost forgotten. He had no choice but to try to ignore it. "I am creating a corps to be sent out into Keibu-yo."

The murmurs from the monks burst into full conversations. Hégo held up his hand to calm the congregation at the same time looking at Mashu to refrain from using his staff. He wanted to have the monks vent for a few seconds.

"Outrageous," came a voice close to the front.

"More than outrageous. Blasphemy," replied a neighbor.

"I know what you all are thinking. And I completely understand. I thought long and hard about this." *Longer than any of you ever imagined.*

"Please, hear him out, then you can ask as many questions as you want," interrupted Ogushu.

The crowd quickly quieted. *That Ogushu already has too much respect.*

A low grumble of a pre-speak growl began to emanate from Ryudasu. Hégo, and he was sure everyone else by the look of many putting their hands to their chests, felt the vibrations from her gut-deep vocalizing penetrate up through his body. "I agree," rasped Ryudasu. "The Order is in danger from the weight of its aging, both structurally and in flesssh." She walked further into the middle of the hall, the monk mass flowing away, as physics and human nature dictated, then around her. She was a craggy menacing island in an earth-toned doldrum of men.

She remained silent visibly trembling with what Hugo and others thought was a very low chuckle. *Forget that Gou-Tairei. II am your god now.* She finally continued. "Brave measures need to be taken by brave individuals." She looked around the hall without moving her body, thanks to her multi-eyed 360-degree view. "You are those individuals." She bowed, signaling to Hégo she was finished.

Hégo remained silent just enough for it to be uncomfortable before acknowledging his unlikely champions. "Thank you, Ogushu-sama and Ryudasu-sensei. The corps will be populated with volunteers who believe it necessary to keep this Order viable. Let me be very clear, they will not be Smashers. They will not be destroyers but saviors for those lucky enough to have the mindset to be guided back to us." He had very little confidence in the legendary Smashers or even if their descendants were still active. The Smasher policy was abandoned decades ago in hope that those already out there would continue through ideological reproduction. There have been no signs of there being an inevitable Inanimate extinction, so he assumed the grand experiment was a complete failure. "We cannot rely on walk-ins any longer. How many have we had over the past few months?" He looked directly at Taiku Shiba who's duty it was to record all newcomers.

"Twenty-two in the past five months, Master-sama," responded the willowy monk.

"Twenty-two." He repeated the number to have it sink into the crowd. "We will not survive at this rate. Over twice that many passed on to another cycle in the same amount of time. Yes, my predecessor claimed there was an increase in those wanting to escape the horrors outside, but the real numbers do not correlate with that. We need to actively recruit out in Keibu-yo; not need to, must."

The monkish sea was back to a calm lapping. He was getting his point across. *This has to work. That number was lower than even I expected.* He sat back down followed by Ogushu. "I am sorry to put this on to you now, especially after what you have just been through." The fatherly-ness of his voice surprised even him. "But I will require a vote on this immediately."

"But that leaves no time to debate this," a voice yelled out.

The heads in front of him were nodding in reluctant agreement. "This is just as critical as Kugai's plea concerning the barrier walls."

"What does the Dai-Master think of all this?" The annoying question came from Basho Jyon. Hégo never liked the celebrity Haiku-Bassbeat cleric.

Hégo had a lie for the question already in mind. "I have discussed this with the Dai-Master and he agrees with my proposal. It took some convincing, but when I told him the numbers, he had no choice but to agree." *There, that should shut him up.* Many eyes veered to his left. They were waiting to see what Ogushu thought of all this. Hégo looked at him as well. He saw on his junior's face the realization that all attention was on him.

He cleared his throat. "To be truthful, I did not agree with Hégo-sama's idea of creating a kind of recruiting corps." Shaggy heads were nodding in agreement, too many for Hego's liking. Ogushu continued. "However, after listening to his sincere concern for the future of this cloister, for the entire Order for that matter, and hearing Taiku Shiba-sensei's latest intake figures just now. I would have to agree, however reluctantly, with Hégo-sama's proposal."

"How many would have to join this corps and what about their purity?" asked Morichika Noh. Hégo didn't know the middle-aged monk very well, just his name.

"I must admit, I have not worked out much of the details. But I would assume it would first be composed of volunteers. Concerning their well-being in cycles after, I can give a definite answer." This specific lie he had to create on the fly. "Dai-Master Tokoshou Daviido has given me unprecedented power to pardon those who volunteer, which will protect their cycling while out immersed in the depravity on the other side of these walls. They will be allowed back in after their term of duty is up. No, I do not know how long a term would be yet." He leaned forward grabbing Cane to lean his weight on. "All that I am 100% sure about is that we must do something or the young ones among us will be the last of our kind." He didn't have to lie about that at least.

Hégo looked over at Mashu and nodded. *Vwomp...kaka, vwomp...kaka, vwomp...kaka.* "The vote to create a recruitment corps to be sent out into Keibu-yo is about to commence!" He waited for the buzz of last-minute discussion and arguments to form and die then slammed his staff again. Echoes from the previous battering still lingering, creating a cacophony of tiny audible ghosts.

"All those not in favor seat yourselves, lower yourselves, or speak to one nearby as your form allows."

It took only a few minutes for the vote to be counting once the shuffling of robes and murmurs subsided. The stomping of Mashu-sensei's angry staff sent stinging vibrations up through the congregation's bare feet. *The vote is over.*

"Aoheki has voted," yelled the Officer of Ceremony and Order.

"Yayoi Mashu-sensei," said Hégo. "What are the results of the vote?"

"Three hundred twenty-eight against," said Mashu. "Four hundred seventy-seven for."

Hégo had no qualms about smiling about the outcome. The seriousness of the situation should not produce any smiles on anyone, it didn't matter. His smiles were only slightly gentler frowns.

"I would like to volunteer Masters-sama!"

"Who is speaking?" Yelled Hégo.

The crowd parted, allowing the old Master a direct sightline to the speaker.

"Shinya, Master-sama." Shinya shouted even louder to make sure he was heard from so far back.

Hégo struggle to stand up. Once he finally was steady on his legs, he stared directly at Shinya. "Why is that?" the question was accusing.

Shinya wasn't sure how to answer. He was running on pure impulse.

"Why?" Repeated Hégo, squinty eyes still burning through the crowd and searing into Shinya.

"To ... to go out and save lives." He didn't care much about saving any lives except one.

Hégo dismissed Shinya's reason with a loud "hrrumph."

Is he going to forbid me from joining because of my association with Yuuki? Shinya narrowed his eyes back at Hégo.

"Just have patience. Ogushu-sama and I need to work out the details first before we start taking volunteers." The two elders slowly began their descent from the dais and into the waiting room. An awkward silence fell over the hall while Hégo fought his personal campaign against the stairs as Ogushu patiently followed behind.

It was not a 'no'. Shinya could still hang on to the hope of joining this recruitment corps.

"You have no idea what you are going to get yourself into young one," said an older novitiate sitting next to him. "You will not survive out there. I barely did, and for some reason, I believe you barely did as well."

Shinya stared at the man. "You do not know what I felt or who I even was out there." His voice becoming louder after each word uttered coming to a climax. "Fuck you!" Shinya turned and rushed out of the hall brushing against Ryudasu's leg as she was beginning to exit pretending to be careful not to accidentally pierce any of her now fellow monks with her pincers. She gurgled a laugh as she watched the angry novitiate rush past her.

seventeen

YUUKI STRETCHED, FORCING HIS feet out from under the blanket. He finally had a surprisingly good sleep considering he had been sleeping clothed out of a strange modesty. The first couple nights he kept waking up to adjust the suffocating clothing that became all twisted and disheveled from his natural tossing and turning. The suffocatingly soft bedding of what Mimi called a futon took some getting used to.

"Good morning," Mimi said. Yuuki's experience of other similar chipper first greetings of the day informed him that she was a morning person.

"Good morning," he responded less chipper.

"I hope you slept well this time." Mimi was in the kitchen making breakfast. Yuuki could smell bread toasting and meat searing. "I felt like making a real breakfast this morning. You haven't eaten much since you been here. Wamono aren't vegetarian, are they?"

"No." Yuuki yawned his response. "Many are, but it is not a rule. We even have a farm with animals and crops." He shrank into himself for saying 'we'. He adjusted his kimono to make sure nothing was showing that wasn't supposed to, and looked out the wall-to-ceiling windows. That magnetic force still as strong as ever. He hadn't stepped out of the apartment since he stepped into it three or four days ago. Time had lost its linear meaning.

Mimi ran back to the kitchen. "Shit, I almost forgot the meat."

Yuuki saw that she was not wearing anything pink and her hair flowed unkept down her back. He turned back onto the city view. "This place is ... I do not even know ... just—"

"Amazing?" Mimi gifted him the word, but her tone did not match its usual enthusiastic use. "I don't know why you would think so after what you just been through." She handed Yuuki a cup of tea. Her stealth startled him.

"What did I just go through?" It was the first time he felt ready, or more accurately, rested, to talk about what happened at the Fujou den—about anything. He barely spoke since that day. "I am not sure if I should be thankful, angry, or scared."

"How about all three?" She pointed to the expensive ultra-soft white leather sofa she had just bought with her earnings from the Storyliner job. "Are you ready to chat?"

Yuuki could only force a meek smile. He took the invite and walked over to the enticing plushness. He no longer let out a squeal of surprise at how far down he went, but he still couldn't get the balance right and almost spilled the hot tea all over his lap. Mimi giggled and sat down beside him, taking a sip of her tea. They both took a few seconds to settle deep into the luxuriousness.

"You should be thankful you have a friend like me for starters."

"A friend? Are you?" Yuuki carefully took a sip of the steaming tea then silently placed the cup down on the low table in front of him and clasped his hands together, wedging them in the fold of his kimono between his legs. *I should not have said that. She could easily kill me. I guess she is my friend no matter if I want her to be.*

Mimi wanted to take offense to this but remembered the circumstances of their introduction. She put out her right hand. "I'm your new friend, Mimi. Nice to meet you."

Yuuki returned with a simple barely there nod. "It is nice to meet you."

Mimi let her awkward hand drop. "Now we're friends," Mimi said smiling.

Yuuki looked at her as if he were looking at a piece of art by the somewhat rebellious Wamono artist Muso Ginesu. He could never decide if his work was beautiful or disturbing.

"Why are you looking at me like that?" Mimi mimicked the look Yuuki was giving.

"I just cannot believe you as a killer. You said it was your job."

"Yes, I am a mercenary of the Dekora gunshyu. Or at least I was." She proceeded to give him a crash course on the hierarchy of gunshyu and the violent politics of the city.

"It is so aggressive out here," Yuuki whispered, not realizing he said it out load.

Yuuki wanted to change the topic to something less confusing and what he was already exposed to. "Hiroka said everyone has their own name for the Entire; that there are many names for it."

"The Entire?"

"Sorry, the place on the other side of those walls that watch." The flush of fear pierced through his pores. *Have I broken some kind of law?* There was no sign of offense in Mimi's expression, so he felt safe that she wouldn't turn him into some naming authority.

"Oh, yeah. Most have a name for the, uh, Entire, but no one really talks about what's on the other side of the Watcher Walls. We only need to focus on where we are, Hinodé; no personal names for that; just that name for every-one." She felt rather proud of edifying someone. *Maybe I could have been a teacher.* She let escape a baby giggle. *Nah. My punishment for misbehaving would be a nice clean decapitation.*

"So, what is your name for it?" Another tsunami heat wave flooded across his face, this one of embarrassment. He was getting the feeling that the millions of names for the Entire were extremely private to those who had some sort of earned privilege of owning one.

"I don't have one. Many don't. Those who do have the privilege don't use it in public; sorta like an expensive painting in a private collection someplace high up in a scraper, just something they are glad to have. We all have a public name for it."

"Which is?" Yuuki was glad of this non-violent lesson. He began to relax and enjoy his tea.

"Beyond The Watchers, or just Beyond. But I like your name better." Her eyes shifted downward.

Mimi took another sip of her tea. "Anyway, the Fujou, a smaller less important gunshyu, are to avoid at all costs. They will force men like you to do terrible things in front of them."

Back to violence. Yuuki could tell that she did think about it, more than she wanted to admit.

Yuuki took advantage in the lull in conversation and looked around Mimi's flat, really looked, for the first time. He had never seen so much glass as part of walls before. Even the small division separating the main room from the kitchen was made of glass. It was a precious material in the cloister. There wasn't much color, which seemed odd considering Mimi's clothing choices. He liked it. It wasn't any of the too many shades of grey in his life. His eyes returned to the windows and the city on the other side. An eerie buzz ran up his spine. The city seemed to be watching him through its many windowed eyes. It could see much more of him that he could of it.

"This is all Hinodé?" He stood up and walked back over to the window. The magnetism of the city attracted only him.

Mimi followed him and sat on the floor.

"I guess I really walked into a mess." *This place does not seem ... logical.*

"You sure as shit did, Yuuki." She hopped up as if she possessed too much potential energy in her spring-like legs. "Let me plate our breakfast before it gets any colder." She klincked and klanked in the kitchen for a few minutes and returned with two plates of breakfast and placed them a plate on the coffee table.

He tore himself from the magnetic grasp of the city and sat back on the sofa with Mimi. He could only stare at the food.

"Not hungry?" She softly bit her upper lip, trying to think of something to say. "Do you miss Aoheki?"

Yuuki looked at her, eyes narrowed. "Not at all."

Guess that wasn't the right something to say. "I'm sorry, I didn't mean to ..."

"But I miss someone there."

"Oh," Mimi said, finally piecing the puzzle together. "What's his name? I mean, I assume a guy."

Yuuki looked back down at the good attempt at a breakfast. He didn't want her to see him cry if it came to that. "His name is Shinya."

Mimi smiled. Her impressions were rarely wrong on this. "What's he like, if you don't mind me asking."

"He is very handsome," Yuuki's eyes brightening up. Mimi swore she saw a sparkle in them. "He has short black hair, and his eyes are big and brown surrounded with long lashes. He is more muscular." He poked his paunch as proof.

"How long have you two been together?"

"Oh, we have never been 'together'. I did not know he felt the same until my last day there when he kissed me."

"And you left anyway?" Mimi was loving the romance and drama of it all.

"I had to. I did not belong there. It was very hard to leave him."

"But you miss him."

"Yes, of course. We were cellmates. He was so beautiful sleeping. It was my favorite way to see him." He started playing with his breakfast with the hashi sticks, each one beautifully and intricately carved. "These are beautiful."

"They were a gift from my mom." She looked down at hers and began playing with her food as well, but the play had the drag of melancholy.

Yuuki didn't know what to say next. Obviously, it was painful for her to think about. "Very thoughtful of her."

Mimi gave a dismissive shrug. "I guess." She stood up and took her plate with her to the kitchen, dumping the charred meal into the trash.

Yuuki's entire blood supply dissipated replaced with the miasma of awkwardness. "I am sorry. I did not mean ...'

"I know. It's just that, it's complicated. That's all." She washed the plate. It was the only way she could cry in private.

"I never knew my mother." Yuuki began hoping to shift the focus from her a bit. "I was abandoned at the Shisa gates of Aoheki when I was only weeks old. I do not know any of my family."

Mimi forced herself to stop the tears. "No one?" She still had her back to him, slowly washing the hashi, making sure the ornate grooves and reliefs were clear of any crud.

"Not even an uncle or second cousin. That is why I escaped. I want to know where I came from. Who I would have been if I had not been thrown away into the Wamono trash bin."

"Perhaps they didn't 'throw you away'. There might've been a good reason."

"And perhaps there was not! How could someone do that to their child?" Tears welled up and ran down his cheeks with no shame.

Yuuki's shameless tears triggered a gush of admiration within Mimi for this naïve and sensitive young man. She didn't have to turn around to see them. Tears didn't need to be seen to affect.

Mimi finally turned around and walked over to comfort him. "I didn't know life at a cloister was so terrible. Thought it was some kind of haven of peace or something; boring but spiritual." She smiled hoping it would be infectious.

"Most Wamono come to the Order of their free will or forced by their family for some reason. Either way, it was a conscious decision. I have been unconscious for the past twenty years."

"You want to find your family, then?"

"I do not know. A part of me never wants to see them after what they did. But I think I have to find somebody."

He wanted to change the subject. He was tired of being on a never-ending loop of sadness and anger. "So, what is this mystery about being able to name all this?" He waved his arm across the view outside the wall of windows. In wanting to change the subject he ignored Mimi's sensitivity. They were choreographing a delicate but awkward dance of avoidance and interference.

"It's no mystery, Yuuki." She let out another sorrow-filled sigh. There's a big ceremony every year for people who have turned or will turn twelve that year and fulfilled all the requirements of being a good son or daughter, not getting into trouble at school, yada yada, to officially and privately name the Beyond."

"So, why don't you have your own name?" It was either wound or be wounded.

"I'm getting to that." Mimi put down her tea with an agitated thump. "It was the last day I ever saw my mother." She walked over to the window, again her back facing her guest. She was not yet at the level of vulnerability as this intriguing monk. "We were getting ready to go to the local Ward Citizens Hall for the ceremony. I had just turned twelve the month before."

Yuuki could see her reflection on the crystal-clear glass superimposed onto the scrapers of the city. She gave a face to this massive entity he was now an active part of. "Is it a fancy ceremony?"

"Yea, people wear their best outfits. I had on this very pretty powder blue dress that had a train a couple meters long. I loved wrapping it around to the front. I thought I looked like a gorgeous marble statue. I could stand in front of the mirror for hours like that." Yuuki saw the smile on her glass doppelgänger. "I was waiting for my mom to come home. She had been out all night in her studio designing a pair of hashi for some important businessman. At least that's what she told me when she left that morning. She never returned and I never went to the ceremony."

Mimi had never spoken about this to anyone. *Why am I word-puking all over this Wamono I hardly know?*

Both remained silent. One not wanting to further upset the other, both lost in their painful personal histories.

eighteen

THE METALLIC CITY AIR was refreshing to Mimi after being cooped up in her apartment hiding and planning. Yuuki was deep in an after-breakfast nap when she left. It had been four days since she stepped fully outside. The furthest she went was down to the basement food shops. She had to get out for a bit by herself. But she would never be by herself. The guilt-ghost of Jojo made sure of that.

She stretched out her sleeves to warm her hands in the chilly morning air. The streets of Za-Ginsa were quiet at this hour. Most stores had not yet opened, just a couple bakeries and Toshio's tiny fish market. She walked by the various displays of dead or dying water creatures. Gelatinous eyes stared up into the smoky-grey morning sky and tentacles curled and uncurled desperate to escape their faded blue and grungy yellow plastic death pools. She had to cover her nose and mouth to keep away the stench of fluvial death. The humming silence of the morning city broke with the cry of what Mimi assumed was Toshio or one of her female family members calling out to whoever maybe walking by.

"Welcome to our humble business! Please come and take a look!"

Another lone walker appeared from around the corner, setting off another round of greetings. They didn't even look up at her or the other pedestrian during their automated nasal caterwauling. They were too busy cutting off the heads of a strange fish with short yellow spines. The fins, twice the size of their bodies, were frozen open like a street corner littered with damaged umbrellas after a storm. Soon the entire street would be flooded with such piercing competing greetings to get customers into their establishments. The shrieks made Mimi not want to go into any store. It was more of a warning to stay away than a welcome.

She picked up her pace to escape before another of Toshio's family chimed in to add to the mindless chorus. She made a mental note to find an alternative route back home. Other stores were starting to open their doors. A produce store a few doors up from Toshio's began adding a background percussion of boxes being ripped open exposing bright green, yellow, and red fruit and vegetables.

Despite the beginnings of the day's cacophony, it was good to be out and alone in the human-littered city and focus on her assignment. She left a note for Yuuki saying she had to do some errands and would be back in a couple hours and telling him not to go out of the apartment. The city was too dangerous for both of them now. She was taking a big risk by stepping out this morning.

She still didn't know exactly how to go about killing Oné-chan. Her mystery boss did not give her a 'deadline', but she figured they wanted it done as soon as possible. She didn't want to rush into this one. She had to admit that she could have planned, at least a little bit, for the Storyliner hit. A Dekora had never killed a daigunshyu leader let alone their own.

She turned the corner onto Kin-gyou Dori. Any visitor to the perpetually slime-slickened street would immediately see, feel, and smell how it got its name. Every other storefront was occupied by large tanks teaming with various mixi-matchi goldfish jiggling and lumbering through equally varied types of water, from crystal clear to murky and fecal. She stopped in front of one of the stores with two columns each with three massive tanks stacked on top of each other forming the outer wall of the store and almost reaching the second story. The bottom-left tank was full of the strangest fish she had ever seen. Their eyes were so bulbous that she was afraid that if she tapped on the glass, they would explode.

How can they swim or even be alive? It looked as though they couldn't figure it out either. *What a pointless way to exist.*

She shuffled to the neighboring right tank. One particularly massive fish came up to the front pane and stared at her. It wasn't gold at all, gold on goldfish was no longer fashionable, but a deep indigo and would easily stand up to her waist if it could stand on the gorgeous flowing veils of its tail fin. It was definitely wider than her.

She stared back at her aquatic counterpart. She made it female because it just looked it. "Poor thing," she said to her new beautifully grotesque friend. "You must feel so trapped in their going from side to side, up and down, back and forth all day every day." She smiled amused that the fish was probably excited to see something so strange come by. Mimi felt a connection to her new friend. She had much more to look at and could go in any direction she wanted, but she felt just as trapped. Trapped by eyes watching her, wanting her dead.

The ungold fish quickly turned away, startling Mimi. Something seemed to have fallen or been dropped into the tank far above her. It was a much smaller grey silvery fish, dull in comparison with the beauty of her flamboyant indigo friend. She watched the homely fish struggle to get its bearing in its new home. It looked terrified, switching back and forth catching the white neon rays of a sign across the street. One second a flash of silver, the next sleepy grey. The glittering show was mesmerizing. Mimi was happy that this frumpy fish could also be beautiful; it just had to work a little bit harder. There was something natural about that. Mixi-matchies didn't have to work so hard.

Mimi named the little fish 'On-Off' and followed it on its maiden voyage around the tank. She watched it dart side to side, front and back, up and down. On one of its treks to the left side of the tank, a shadow of blue black appeared from behind, overtaken by a plume of red. "What the fuck!" On-Off was no longer heading to the left side but spiraling down to the bottom, half its body torn away. It was her giant indigo friend who halved the size of the smaller fish. The massive ungoldfish came back to finish the job. This time Mimi was ready to witness the entire attack. Ungold appeared from the back of the tank. The water was no longer crystal clear, but a soup of blood, flesh, and alternating silver and grey scales. But the killer looked different. Instead of the eyes being the most prominent feature, it was her opened mouth, eyes hidden by jaw extending half its body length out in front, rows of razor teeth jutting forward ready to grasp and tear at anything that was unfortunate enough to be directly in front. The headed half of On-Off spiraled and floated in front of Mimi's face. It's much smaller eyes looking directly at her, not seeing. Its mouth was still working, taking in oxygen to feed its now pointless gills. Mimi felt the terror in those eyes. On-Off was nothing more than streams of blood and bits of white flesh floating around its killer. Ungold chomped down on the remaining bits still lodged it her mouth. Some of the flesh escaping through her gills.

Mimi's friend settled back into the staring game it was playing with her before the massacre. Mimi felt bad for On-Off but smiled at her friend. "We're a lotta like, aren't we?" Ungold remained staring. No response necessary.

She wanted, needed, to keep moving.

She was almost at the other end of Kin-gyou Dori but couldn't get her ungold friend out of her head. Seeing something so perfect reminded her of her imperfections. She questioned if she could pull off the unthinkable assassination.

The day was starting to warm, but she kept her arms wrapped around her to stave of the chill of insecurity. She saw the main drag of Za-Ginsa not far in the distance, the glass and steel towers coming into view and appearance and disappearance of viscersha and fu-viscersha transports going about their morning routines. Kin-gyou Dori looked past tense compared with the grand boulevard of Omoté Odori. She preferred to stay hidden between the rickety fish sellers and restaurants.

A cloaked figure stood at the corner of the everything goldfish street and Omoté Odori. The figure looked out of place somehow. With all the different fashions and cultural dress in Hinodé, a cloaked figure would normally not attract her notice. After a few seconds of squinting and unconsciously stretching her neck forward to get a better look, she let out a small gasp.

"Sama." She quickly ducked under an awning with the ubiquitous goldfish beckoning passersby to come in and try their delicious goldfish-shaped pastries. The second she hid, she felt ridiculous. She had proven herself with the Storyliner.

She inhaled deeply and went back out into the street to come face to no-face with the figure.

The figure extended an arm. The gloved hand presented her a yellow folded piece of paper. Mimi tried to look inside the light sucking cowl but spied nothing. *Is there anyone even in there?* She carefully took the note. There was no resistance on Sama's part. It was like the note was just floating in the microcosm of air between fingers. Once she had the note securely in her hand, the figure lowered their arm.

"Who are you?"

There was no response. Only the same ear-splitting silence.

"I think I deserve to know who I'm working for."

The figure stood still, not even a tilt of a supposed head to signal listening.

"Fine. Don't talk to me you faceless weirdo." She looked at the piece of paper wondering if she should read it now. When she looked back up, the figure was already walking away down Omoté.

"Hey!" She kept her eyes on the flapping robe until it disappeared into the crowd of morning commuters and early shoppers. "Thanks for the chat."

She unfolded the paper. *No later than tomorrow night.* She crumpled the message and threw it down on the ground. *Alrighty then.*

She looked up and down Omoté dori into the kaleidoscope of the bright but somehow understated oranges of the Viscer Worshippers, the purple and mauve striped floppy headdresses of the Tea Sitters, and the sparkling gold and green tights of the Ikebanans. The constantly changing patterns took her mind slightly off her now deadlined job.

A particularly irritated viscersha grumbled passed, bringing her back to the present. She needed quick intel on if Oné-chan would be away from the protection of Pinku Palace within the next twenty-four hours. "I'm so fucking sorry, Jo."

Mimi continued wondering the streets for a couple more hours though she did not feel it was that long. Her fierce ungold friend still swam in her head. The chill that would not let go of her all day began to give way to the smoldering embers of hatred at the thought of Oné-chan killing Jojo. Her job was no longer just an assignment.

Walking aimlessly was no longer helping. It began to drizzle, so she looked for a dry place to sit.

She made it to a small one-lot-sized park. Like most neighborhood parks in the city, it was grungy and littered with plastic lunch containers from the past few afternoons accented with wadded up tissues from the intermittent waves of clandestine evening activities. Luckily, the park was still pretty empty thanks to the drizzle. In a couple hours or so the park would be alive again for the day's first wave of moans and secretive whispers. She thought it rather beautiful in its own way. No one would bother her here. They would have other things on their mind. She just as well could be a ghost, which suited her perfectly.

She sat down on a bench protected by a rotting and rusting canopy of wood and corrugated metal. She leaned over covering her face with her hands, as if she was about to break out in tears or vomit; either would seem normal here. *What the fuck am I doing?* She sat up and took in a deep breath of the already stagnating humid air. "O.K, get a grip, Mimi. I've set all this in motion. I did, no one else." She didn't care if people heard her. "I have to do right by Jojo." She wrapped her now overstretched sleeves over her bloodless hands. The heat she produced from walking had dissipated, and she began to shiver.

The positions of some of the knots and gnarls in one of the beams holding up the rotting roof looked like a face. She started to talk to it to stay out of her head. "I'm so sorry Jo-chan. This is all my fault. Did you have to run to Oné-chan the first chance you got?" Her anger had no right of being and soon changed to guilt. "You were always the better one." Tears started to fall down her disproportionately warm face. She quickly wiped every tear away into oblivion before it made its way over the summit of her cheek. She hated crying, even when alone. It was as bad or even worse than puking. She never understood the use of it. It was just one more thing of herself she couldn't totally control.

She refocused on the face of knots in the beam. "I'll make it up to you, I promise." She didn't know how, and that's what frustrated her. "I guess I loved you more than I thought." She breathed in a large volume of humid air to recompose herself to the assassin she was trained, probably born, to be. *I can't do this. Can I?* She avoided doubt like the flesh-eating virus that made an appearance every few years from the stagnant industrial effluent slowly seeping into the blacksloppy Sumi River. "I can!"

Outside the entrance of the nearest viscerdenn station, Mimi tapped her commring to bring up a HUD with a list of her contacts. "O.K. Who don't I trust the least." She ran her thumb counterclockwise around her ring to scroll down the list. It wasn't a long list. Jojo's name came into view. She couldn't bring herself to delete it ... her. She continued running her thumb round her ring until she came to her newest entries. Viki popped up from the bottom of the HUD. "She might know something about what's going on with Oné-chan."

She highlighted Viki's name and put pressure on the ring with her pinky and middle finger to initiate the call.

After a several long minutes of half-heartedly apologizing for fucking up their deal with Hiroka and promising to fix things, Mimi finally got the information she wanted. Oné-chan was on her way to an early dinner meeting later with the Suriidii queen at a neutral location in Ue-No. Mimi double-thumb tapped her ring to disconnect and decided to trust Viki just a little bit more. "Fuck! Tonight? Well, then. Tonight."

The hour or so viscerdenn ride to the restaurant would have to be enough time to form skeleton of a plan. There was no time to overthink this. She was Mimi Barakuda. Planning could only get her so far. She needed to get to Ue-No before Oné-chan finished her dinner. *To be a fly on the table between those two,* she thought. She would have to be extremely careful and patient. That Queen Ren could not be anywhere near Oné-chan when she struck. She was in deep enough shit without inviting the wrath of yet another insane prophet. One crazy prophet and one simply powerful bitch was enough for any mercenary.

She tucked her fingers into her bra to make sure Kitty D. and her Little Killer were still where they should be and brought up a display coating her iris of the viscerdenn system. She rarely traveled to that side of the city, only when there was a hit assignment on a Suriidii. *Yuuki's from there.* She couldn't worry about the Wamono now. *He'll be fine.* She knew that was not even close to true.

nineteen

"**A**H, MASTER-SAMA," RASPED RYUDASU. "A pleasure to see you so soon.

Hégo squinted and cocked his head trying to locate the voice. He was relieved she wanted to remain down in the cloister's depths. He didn't take any more steps or move any other part of his body unnecessarily and fought the urge to jump at the slightest imaginary wisp of a fine silky fiber. It wasn't long until his mind coated him in the sticky substance. "Please turn on your ... your internal light. I do not want to walk into anything."

"Very well," responded Ryudasu. A yellow green glow slowly intensified until the sickly hue coated the lonely cellar.

The entire lair was draped in ghostly filaments interconnecting to form bridges and arches that extended from the central concentric perfection of her web. Hégo took note of her perfectionism. *She might be a very good wall keeper after all.* But that was the least important duty he wanted her to perform. She was in the center of her intricately constructed web city staring directly down at him. If he would have moved just a few centimeters, he would now be entombed in a tight wrap of the same substance. "Thank you," was all he could say.

"So, the convocation went well. Thanks to your co-Master."

"Yes. Thanks to him," grumbled Hégo.

"When do I start on the walls?" Ryudasu crept along her main web and stabbed a white cocoon with one of her hind legs. Her other legs worked in precise cooperation to move the cocoon to directly under her salivating fangs. "You do not mind if I have a snack, do you? I am absolutely famished."

"Go ahead," said Hégo. He couldn't take his eyes off the standout whiteness of the coffin and whatever was half dead inside. He knew what she was trying to do. He wasn't going to show any more fear. It was imperative that he show his authority and remain calm.

"What is inside?" Hégo asked showing he could take his mind off the matter at hand, that he was in complete control and not affected by her savage dinning habits.

"To tell you the truth, I am not sure. I just feel the vibrations, lunge, stab, inject, then wrap. I can tell you in a minute from the taste. I like the surprise."

Hégo needed to return to the reason he came down. "You will start in a few days. We need to work out a schedule and other details first."

"Sounds fair. I assume I can come and go since I am no longer a prisoner. We never really hashed out where I can and cannot enter."

Hégo sighed. He didn't come down here for such trivial details, but he obliged. "You are now allowed free access to all the cloister except the infirmary, seminary, and refectory, and of course the private rooms, which you will not fit in anyway."

She jammed her fangs deep inside the cocoon. A crackly snap then a slushy sound of surrender emanated from inside. "Ah, yes, just the right consistency." She lifted the shrouded victim closer to her cuticular plates with her fangs and a little help from her leg-arms. Her disproportionately small head almost inside the wrapping, sucking out the gore.

Hégo had to fight back his vomit reflex. The sucking sound was almost unbearable. Cane had no such pretense. "Disgusting."

Ryudasu stopped feasting and focused her multiple eyes on the gnarled cane. "What is disgusting is a sentient stick of rotted wood. An abomination is what you are." She did not have to yell, but the intense hiss in her voice was just as powerful. "It will never be a true god!"

What brought this on? Hégo thought. "I apologize for Cane's behavior. It is a bit ill-tempered sometimes."

"I do not apologize," interrupted Cane.

"It does not matter," said Ryudasu. "Apologies are for the weak." The insult to Hégo was intentional. She knew now who she had to really communicate with and placate.

Hégo suddenly imagined himself taking Ryudasu's place as the most hated Wamono in the Order's history if his reforms ended in disaster.

"Has the Inanimate gotten totally into your mind yet, Daiso? Have you entered Communion?"

"I prefer 'idol'," said Cane. "Animate and Inanimate are this Order's sanitary terminology for the reality."

Hégo wanted to throw Cane into the web. "No, we have not yet entered Communion." He would never get used to someone ... thing else being able to hear Cane. Yet another terrifying detail of the Aku. Ryudasu would always have the upper hand as long as their Symb had to be kept secret.

"But it is in there pretty good though. Try to resist Communion and Totality as long as you can."

Hégo couldn't tell if she was being sincere or facetious. "You are to call me by my full name." Hégo said trying to regain some semblance of authority.

"Oh, I think we can dispense with the formalities, don't you, old friend?" She relaxed a bit on her web.

Hégo ignored her taunting and steered the conversation away from his Symb with Cane. "I came down to give you more details of my thoughts on the future of the Order now that I am officially Master, as promised."

"Go on." She moved toward the bottom of her web, closer to her guests. Her head still slick with a jaundiced crimson of liquid offal. Drops of it plopped with dense biology near Hégo's bare feet.

He fought with every muscle not to move back from her advance. "I want you to first be our eyes and ears regarding the outside in your capacity as the wall caretaker. I'm talking about us as a team."

"Team?" Repeated Ryudasu. "An interesting term. Eyes will not be a problem."

He swore he heard a childish giggle come out of the monster. Not her usually abrasive raspy pseudo-laughs.

Cane took over their half of the conversation. "Yes. We believe it would be beneficial for all three of us if we teamed up and changed the way this cloister, this Order is run."

"My," Ryudasu said pretending to be scandalized. "The entire Order?"

"Yes," Hégo quickly said, trying to regain control. "Obviously, you know how I feel about how the Order has been run. We are dying out."

"Your little show upstairs made that quite clear. What do you want from me?"

"We want to secede," said Cane. Hégo scowled down at Cane then looked up to Ryudasu for her reaction.

"Secede? From the Order? Why?"

"Like I just said," said Hégo. "We are dying. We need to be reborn if we are to survive as an institution. We need fresh believers. Most out in Hinodé barely know we still exist. We are just those paranoid robed men behind these ridiculous walls." He looked up an around. "Instead of rejecting what is out there, we should concentrate on acknowledging it to save them and us. Even if that first involves destruction."

Ryudasu remained silent for a few seconds. Every moment that passed increased the sweat bleeding out of Hégo. "This is what you believe as well, Inanimate? Do you want to *save* everyone outside these walls?"

"I want what my companion wants. I cannot lie, Ryudasu-sensei. If that means saving people from unbelieving ways, then so be it."

"So, let me make sure I am correct", said Ryudasu. "You released me to commit another crime against the Order."

"No," Hégo quickly responded. "Saving us is not a crime. It is a bit unorthodox, yes. I cannot think of any other way."

"And what is this 'way'?"

"I am not sure yet, but I know you are the key. Once Cane and I enter Communion then Totality, which should be soon, our power along with your, well you, will be enough to force the necessary change."

"There we go," said Ryudasu. Her purring rasp was the closest she could probably get to a smile. "Force." She descended to the floor making Hégo back up.

That girly monstrous giggle again. It reminded him of poor old Kugai's deranged joviality.

"If you want unorthodox, then I may be able to help you," said Ryudasu. "But, once you enter Totality, do not even entertain the fact that I will turn into a mindless worshipper of you two." She looked directly into Hego's eyes. He smelled the fetid juices of her recent kills on her fangs. "You will be no prophet of mine." She shifted her multi-eyed gaze down to Cane. "Nor will you be my god-thing. Do I make myself clear?" *I am the only God, the Holy Spinner. You and everyone in and far beyond Hinodé will be worshipping me.* She inched even closer to the pair. *And certainly not such abhorrent pairings.*

You do not have to be concerned with that," said Hégo. "We have talked about it, and we are willing to forgo the usual prophet/god temptation for the good of the new Order."

"And for power?" said Ryudasu, fixing her six eyes on Cane.

"I must get back upstairs. We are done here." Hégo had to end this conversation on his terms. He said what he came to say. Then he remembered. "Do you know anything about Yuuki-Hana disappearing and possibly escaping?"

"That novitiate I helped you punish?" She hummed satisfaction upon hearing confirmation of the success of at least that step of her grand plan. "He escaped? Well, Master-sama, I guess your plan to get him in line failed."

"It did not fail!" Hégo could not contain his indignation. "He is out of my hair and no longer causing problems, isn't he? I would call that a success."

He maneuvered his way toward the door, using Cane to angrily flick away rubble from his path.

"Oh, by the way, it was a rather juicy giant rat." She smacked her cuticular plates together. "Or rather, rats. It seems she was late in her pregnancy with a sizable litter."

He looked back and bowed his head then limped through the doorway. *What am I about to unleash?*

"Why do you want to become an Honored Exile? Hégo sat on his worn chair, Cane between his legs, and hands firmly on top of his wooden companion. He stared at Shinya, eyes cloaked in the shadow created by his wild overgrown eyebrows. "I need to know your true intentions, and I will know once you vocalize them if they are true. Choose your words wisely and sincerely."

Shinya took a few seconds to respond. He remained in the required humble stance. Having to look at the frightening old monk would be more uncomfortable. He needed to be careful and choose a lesser truth and make it sound convincing as the only truth.

"Certainly Sama. Once I heard your announcement, I knew I wanted to grow the Order and save as many individuals as I can." It was automatic. Perhaps too automatic, but it wasn't an untruth.

Hégo grumbled then clicked his tongue. He dropped his head, revealing his disappointment. Now, tell me the real reason. I do not want to hear a slogan you think you want me to hear!" He leaned the head of Cane out then his torso and jittery head. Shinya peeked up, the old Master's weepy rouged eyes accosted his view. "I want to hear *you*. Shinya." Hégo leaned back and let out a slow sigh of exertion.

"Apologies, Sama." Shinya rescued his eye from the elder terror and looked back at the floor a meter in front of him. Shinya no longer knew what he wanted from becoming an Honored Exile. That was the truth. *cannot say 'to find Yuuki.*

His legs pricked from the stasis of standing humbly. He couldn't feel his body. He couldn't feel.

"Apologies are no reason, novitiate!" Hégo's scolding came out coated in phlegmy gurgles. It was a sound of a long-suffering beast rather than a Master of the Cloister. "I have not made up my mind as to who will be sent out. It all rests on my decision, only my decision." Even though Ogushu was not there with him, he had to make that point very clear.

"My intention is to see." Shinya could not think, just speak. He began to shiver from the frigid stare he knew was on him. Old Hégo might be frail, but his presence was more terrifying that that Ryudasu creature now lurking somewhere within the cloister.

"We are finally getting someplace." Hégo chuckled, which sounded more like a yell—the same gurgling. "What do you want to 'see'?"

Shinya didn't know how much more he could take of the interrogation. "To see for myself what Keibu-yo is like now. I want to see to learn. When I learn I can be useful." He shifted his weight from one leg to the other. "I am under no delusion of making any difference, at least right away. I need to see first." He had no idea if that was the correct response, but it was at least a truth.

"Honesty. Why was that so difficult?" Hégo waved an invisible annoyance away.

There was an uncomfortable minute of miserable human grunting and shifting, signs that the old man was trying to stand up. He wasn't sure if he should break his stance and help the elder up. He was afraid he would break him. He stole another glance to make sure he was not going to crash to the floor. *That cane is not moving at all. Like it is independent of its owner.*

Hégo, finally on his feet, clipped-clapped toward Shinya. "Look at me, novitiate." He gently placed a hand on the Shinya's bent shoulder. Shinya reluctantly raised his eyes to meet his Master's. The almost fatherly touch melted him from within. It took all his depleted strength to remain standing. "Get yourself ready, you leave for exile later today. That is all. Dismissed."

twenty

S ANAE STOLE A QUICK glimpse of her reflection in the restaurant's many mirrored columns while waiting for Ren to arrive. The events of the past few days had taken their toll on her appearance. The dark bulbous bags underneath her eyes were the most disturbing. She caught Ren walking over to their table, alone as negotiated.

"Thank you for meeting me," said Sane. The usual pleasantry was acknowledged with only a glare from Ren.

The queen of the Suriidii was finally bandage free. Masao had given her permission to take the last of them off for the meeting. She was a fully unhidden tall, elegant women. Her long wavy black hair finally free to flow down and over her shoulders. Her sharper facial features and new death-stare blue eyes gave her a much more domineering aura.

"What do I owe the pleasure?" Ren elegantly folded herself into the chair and fwapped open the napkin to place over her lap. "I can only assume it is concerning the little tiff between you and the Editor."

"You got me," said Sane. She took a sip of her as-ordered tepid water, not taking her eyes off her dinner companion.

"But first, how are *you* doing?" Ren layered her long hands and rested her chin on them then leaned forward as if she were truly concerned. "If you don't mind me saying, you look like you had better days, Sanae."

Sanae wanted to reach across the table and twist the overworked head off. She decided words were better. "I see the healing still has a little way to go."

Ren's patronizing smile contracted slightly. "Yes, well. The trials of being women of power I suppose."

"Yes, you're probably right." *Round one, a draw*, thought Sanae.

"May I take your order ladies?" said a waiter, his waiter-bored expression tightened into surprise in serving the infamous Suriidii leader. The restaurant was quite close to the Suriidii border on the Ue-No side. Sanae wasn't as recognizable in these parts. She mainly concentrated her affairs in her own district and Za-Gin-sa. Plus, she wasn't wearing anything signature today.

Ren pointed her opened palm toward her guest to order first. Sanae smiled and nodded in thanks. "How's the sumarisin today?"

"It's very fresh. Just fished out of the Sumi this morning from what I'm told." Beads of sweat began to pock his forehead after finally recognizing the Dekora matriarch.

"Very well, I'll have that. But grill it on only one side and put the plum sauce to the side." She looked at Ren "No matter where I go, they always put too much of that damn sauce."

"Very well, madame." Responded the waiter. He turned and bowed to Ren. "And for your majesty?" He wasn't obliged to use such honorifics since he was not one of her subjects, but he was a waiter and knew how to get the biggest tips.

"I'll just have a Consortium salad." She hid one side of her mouth and leaned in as if telling her lunch date a secret. "I'm trying to cut down on anything flesh. My chief remodeler suggested it." Oné-chan involuntarily smirked, not letting the irony escape her.

"Of course, your majesty." He looked at both ladies. "And for drinks?"

"Just bring us a bottle of your finest Koshu," said Ren.

"Certainly." The waiter looked at Oné-chan. "Madame Oné-chan." Then at Ren. "Your majesty." And walked away.

"So, where were we?" said Ren. She fiddled with her napkin. "Oh, yes. The, uh, tiff between you and that little goon.

"What is your opinion on the whole situation, your majesty?"

"Oh, please. Let's stop with the formalities, shall we Sanae? Ren is fine."

"Very well, Ren. I would very much like to know what you think about all this." It would be key in how she would proceed.

"This pains me to no end, but the Editor has a right to be a bit peeved."

Oné-chan wasn't liking what she was hearing. "I didn't order that dumb girl to assassinate a Storyliner."

"Let me finish, Sanae." Ren held out her open hand signally to her interlocutor to calm down. "But I want to offer you a proposal, a business one."

"We were hoping you would say that," said Sanae. She was a little more hopeful again.

"We?" Ren looked at her dinner companion with squinty suspicion."

Sanae had to just say it and deal with whatever tirade Ren would spew all over her. "The Editor and I."

Ren let out a loud guffaw, forcing nervous patrons to turn their heads, something they were trying their hardest not to do.

"It is no joke, Ren. Just hear me ..."

"No! I have no need to hear you!" Ren stood, pushing the table toward Sanae and knocking a glass onto the floor. Most of the patrons refused to look this time.

"Your majesty. Please Sit back down." Sanae was getting desperate but could not show it. She needed Ren in their alliance, or it would not work. The Mayor is too powerful but powerless without any of Its satraps keeping everything status quo. "I have a very good explanation." She slid a piece of paper over to the irritated Suriidii queen.

"What is ... that?" Still standing, Ren aimed her long pointer finger at the paper like it had been used to wrap a decomposing sumarisin for several days.

"It is a very delicate matter and cannot be said out loud. Please, just read it." Sanae was wringing her hands underneath the table but kept her voice in pleasant dinner-conversation mode. "But, before you do, I'm sure you would agree that we have always had a very cordial and effective relationship, and I hope we have built up a good amount of trust over the years."

An un-confirming "U-huh" was all Ren said. She stabbed the paper with the long red nail attached to the accusing pointer finger as she slinked back down into her seat. She read it while still impaled on her nail.

Sanae watched the slight movements of Ren's lips as they formed each word. *I am in Communion with the arch-idol Pinku Palac*e

Ren's angry, condescending expression melted into that of disbelief with twitches of fear. "You?" It was the only word she could use to obtain confirmation.

"Yes, I'm afraid so," responded Sanae.

"Afraid is the key term here," said Ren. "I assume you know what this means."

Sanae went into whisper mode. "I do, love. I do. Hence the alliance with the Editor. He had unfortunate firsthand experience with ..." She looked around, making sure no one was in whisper range. "My partner. It wasn't planned. But now that it is out or going to be out, we decided to take advantage of it. We would like to have you be a part of a new order with me as Mayor."

Ren hadn't changed her expression, obviously having an internal emergency meeting with Cal, and whispered back. "You as Mayor? There is no just 'you' anymore and will be nothing of you soon. You think the Mayor is some intact person living a life of secluded luxury inside their arch-god eating bonbons in Juku? Are you really that naïve, Sanae?"

Sanae hadn't allowed herself to think about the inevitable. All she could do is hope there would still be some semblance of herself after Totality.

Ren went silent again. Sanaé could only stare and wait. *She's discussing with her utili-god and seems to be calming down. It sees the benefit of an alliance.*

"You are a brave, perhaps reckless, but brave woman, Oné-chan Sanae."

"I'll take that as a complement, coming from another brave woman." Sanae still had to be diplomatic.

Ren smiled for the first time during the meeting. Her brand-new teeth almost glowing in the dim restaurant. "I'll have to talk it over with my advisor, but I will give it serious consideration."

Sanae released a discreet sigh of relief. "Thank you, Ren. That's all I ask" *Will there be an "I" when this is all done?*

Mimi's eyes remained steady on the entrance to the swanky restaurant across the street where Oné-chan and the Suriidii queen were dinning. The minuscule vessels bursting under the intense strain of surveillance, spread a thin film of deep red revenge across her parched sclera. She positioned herself at a cute boutique café opposite the restaurant. *The restaurant seems to fit the part,* thought Mimi. *Looks like one Oné-chan would frequent, self-proclaimed elegance, arrogance, and pretentiousness.* She had walked around the block to make sure of other possible exits before settling in a spot with the view of the restaurant entrance. She assumed those two would not be so paranoid as to exit through the kitchen. *Oné-chan would never put herself in a situation where there would be even the slightest possibility of soiling her couture.* She sipped her roasted barley tea and milk, never taking her eyes off the entrance.

How am I going to do this? She tried to concoct a plan on the viscerdenn but quickly gave up. It was one of the rush hours and hardly room for even her brain to think. She needed to see the layout of the area first, anyway. It was now all in front of her and busy.

She placed her cup down and rested her head on her palm, her standard daydream posture. *Who will I become after this? I won't be the me sitting here daydreaming about it. But who?*

She initiated a mental shake to get out of her reverie, rubbed her eyes, and re-zoned all here senses in on that entrance. One of many things she learned being a Dekora was that only using your eyes to see is not seeing. She shifted her eyes left then right on repeat, observing the goings on of the pedestrians and traffic on the block. She had to do be more discreet with this kill. She didn't want to make the same mistake she had made with the Storyliner. *It had to be done that way.* She was here solely because of what she did that night and wouldn't have it any other way.

It's going to have to be lightning fast. She began to look for hiding places out in front. There were several trees she could hide behind. She craned her neck to see how far the alleyway that ran down the side of the café was, wondering if she could get down there quick enough afterward. One thing she couldn't do was use Kitty D. She wouldn't have time to run and retrieve it. She would claim responsibility when the time was right. That power would not be taken away from her.

She didn't even care what happened to the Dekora or the Moé Cabal post Oné-chan Sanae. It would be better for her if it simply collapsed under its own headless weight. But it was unrealistic. *That lunatic Sayuri will for sure take over.* She took a bigger sip of her earthy drink. It was starting to get cold. *That crazy bitch should thank me for doing what she would have ended up doing at some point.* She imagined the other possible outcome, hundreds of leaderless assassins let lose upon the Wards willing to kill anybody for the best price. She knew they would eventually congeal into competing clumps. It didn't take long for her to imagine herself as head of one of those clumps, or even a still intact Dekora.

She jumped out of her head just in time. Oné-chan was exiting the restaurant. *Already?* Mimi panicked for just one second before calming herself with a waking trance she learned during her training. It would only take a few seconds. It was all she could afford. *Queen Ren isn't with her. Good.* She left the café without even the barista or the two or three customers noticing. The cold half-drunk tea was the only evidence she had been there.

She entered hunter mode and would not make a sound until she was long gone from the scene. She leaned up against one of the trees off to the side of the café with the best line to her victim. She was barely breathing, another technique from training. She grabbed her Little Killer, cradling it between her chest and chin. She peaked around the tree focusing on her target. Oné-chan was waiting for her fu-viscersha to pull up and take her back to the Palace, where she would be untouchable. *Do it now or let the revenge fester and point the Killer at my own brain*. "For you, Jo-chan." She raised the Little Killer, took a half second to aim, then pushed the trigger button.

Mimi waited another second longer to make sure she hit her target. Oné-chan fell to the ground. Her fu-viscersha pulled up just afterwards and hid the fresh corpse from Mimi's view. *I got her. Smack in the forehead*. Mimi started for her escape route down the side alley. *I fucking did it!* There was no room in her brain for any other more complex thinking. The screaming and yelling coming from behind dissipated to almost a gossipy murmur. Doubt was beginning to combine with the adrenaline. *I saw the red on her forehead. She has to be dead. She's dead. She is.* Once a safe distance from the murder, she had the new precious seconds to realize what she had to do. It was the only option. She headed to the Pinku Palace, fueled by realization. It was time for a coup.

Mimi squinted from the searing whiteness of the Palace lobby even though she was crouched behind the bushes framing the outermost boundary of the compound. There were too many Dekora hanging around the main entrance. No doubt due to the news that their matriarch was murdered. Mimi gathered they were probably more embarrassed that Oné-chan was such an easy target. *Sayuri must be inside.* She tried to see through the blasting white quickly being overtaken by women forming a solid wall of silhouetted matter. *Why aren't they going inside?* Mimi rolled her eyes, embarrassed of herself for not realizing sooner. *That lunatic Nanny locked everyone out to secure her ascension.* She had to wait until her former cohort began to get bored and go off and kill out of pure confusion and frustration.

There was no way she would be able to enter through the main entrance even if the place was in a normal state. She would have to go vertical. She looked up to where she could safely enter from a higher floor. Luckily the building was not an edgeless monolith. The structure started out with giant steps at its base for about fifteen stories. She never thought about it before, but it seemed to be a rather easy building to scale. It was something she would need to address when she became the new Oné-chan. *Do I even want to be?* The longer she stayed cowering behind bushes, the more likely Sayuri would become entrenched on the Dekoran throne.

Mimi patted her hip bone. Dekora were required to have climbing equipment installed somewhere inside them during their training. A hip or wrist was the preferred location. The surgery had been one of the most physically painful experiences in her life. Thankfully, it was quick and the mixi-matchi doc was one of the best in the Wards for internal installations.

Her muscles tensed with bursts of fast motion; going from tree to bush to building corner until she reached the back of the Palace. *Fuck!* There were girls milling about at the back entrance as well. Again, no one was going inside. She wanted to get closer and eavesdrop but didn't dare. She had to stick to her on-the-fly plan of entering from above. A sharp pain in her belly forced her to bend over. It was gone as quick as it came. *What was that?* Heat burned its way through her then out her skin through screaming pores. Just like the pain, the heat was gone before she could react. "Nerves," she whispered. She almost forgot what the disgraceful emotional reaction felt like.

Mimi was never trained for what she was about to do. Her body knew that. There was a high probability of mistakes and even failure. She pushed down the top of her skirt at her right hip revealing the discreet skinzip hiding the implanted rigging.

Before unzipping herself, she closed her eyes and performed the stand-up version of the Dekoran pre-kill meditation. There was no time to find a place to sit and vocalize. She smiled, imagining Chi-Chi-chan scolding her for not staking out an area beforehand for safe thoughtfulness. The Chant-trix was the only one of Sayuri's henchwomen Mimi somewhat respected.

That pain and heat never came back. The skin on her hip pulled to a point as she tugged on the skinzip. She grabbed the small metal end and twisted it to turn on the electromagnet inside. She hadn't had to use the internal apparatus since training. *It better still work*. She did a quick tug on the cord, releasing the entire length from its coil deep inside her hip bone. *That's never going to feel good*. She looked to her left, right, behind her, then left and right again before coiling up the cord and swinging the metal end in large whirling circles. The sound the electromagnetic end made as it sliced the air reminded her of a viscercopter starting up its boney propellors.

"This is ridiculous." Mimi heard a voice just around the corner where she was getting ready to secure herself. She slammed her body hard against the wall to avoid being spotted. "We can't even get inside."

"Oné-chan is sprawled out in some disgusting Ue-No morgue with a hole through her head, and we can't even get inside. We can't just wait outside here all night," said a companion.

Sayuri really did lock herself in there. Mimi forced her breathing to just enough to take in the required oxygen to survive the next couple minutes. The girls' voices finally began to fade as they walked around to the front. Mimi let out a large stream of breath, making her temporarily lightheaded.

She couldn't waste any more time. She swung the end of her cord high up onto the first step three stories up. *Come on, catch on something, anything*. She slowly pulled on the slack of the cord waiting for resistance to stop her from pulling any further. It was taking too long. "Damn it, there's nothing ..." The tiny but powerful magnet finally found a kin to attach itself. "Yes!" She exclaimed softened with whisper. She tugged a couple more times to make sure of the connection and tapped her hip to coil up the slack. Her teeth pressed so hard together in pain at the hard but silent re-coiling.

She unzipped her wrist and took out a hook to help her climb up the coil. That was thankfully less painful. It took her only a few seconds to whip up to the third-floor roof. The rigging worked perfectly. The re-coiling of the remaining cord was not as excruciating. She turned off the electromagnet and carefully placed it and the wrist hook back in their respective boney homes and zipped herself up.

The air was cooler, fresher. *I wish I could go high enough to see beyond the Wards.* She looked around taking in the limited view and at the same time searching for a door or window to enter. Yuuki came uninvited to her mind. He had something; that urge to see who he was and who he still could be. Mimi respected that. *If that naïve Wamono can search for his destiny, then there's no reason I can't.*

A dull light grabbed her attention a couple meters above the step-roof she was standing on. *A window. I can jump this.* A small lip formed the sill where she could aim for. *This is for us, Yuuki.* Waving her arms in perfect unison as she learned during training, she lunged up to the lip and clasped her fingers down on it on the first attempt. Every muscle in her body tensed and released giving her enough power to swing her legs high enough for her feet to hug the mini ledge. *Body, you gotta let me do this.* "Come on, all of you muscles, move!"

"What do you think you're doing?"

The voice broke Mimi's concentration. She plummeted back down to the roof, landing hard on her skinzip hip. "Fuck!" She had no time to right herself and land on her finger and toe tips, the kitty fall. Mimi didn't allow the embarrassing sign of weakness flourish any longer than a couple seconds. The pain forced her into a seconds-long amnesia. After willing the pain away, her memory of a handful of seconds ago rushed back. Her eyes widened and pupils dilated.

"Nanny? Where are you hiding?" Mimi straightened her torso and moved her legs making sure nothing was broken. The window was still closed and there was no shadow or silhouette behind it.

"Oh, I am no Nanny, my dear. Why did you kill my human?" The bodiless voice asked. It didn't sound angry; it didn't have emotion.

The view in front of Mimi switched by the millisecond as she twisted her neck trying to figure out what was attached to that voice. She wasn't going to engage in a conversation with a ghost.

"Did you damage the speech part of that impulsive brain of yours?"

Mimi still refused to answer. She crouch back in all fours, ready to pounce on sight of the voice's owner.

"Answer me!" The voice shouted without the anger of shouting.

Mimi collapsed face down to the gravelly rooftop from the electric blades cutting through her brain. Her hands grabbing her head to keep it from exploding. She screamed. "What're you doing to me?"

"There, that's more like it," said the voice. "Are you ready to have a conversation with me, now?"

"I don't have conversations with figments of my imagination," Mimi replied.

"My dear. I am much, much more than a figment."

Mimi's mind finally put itself in order and began to pay closer attention to what was being said. *An idol!* "You're an idol." Mimi made sure to sound as matter of fact as she could.

"Very good." Mimi imagined sarcastic clapping going along with the voice. "Now, why did you kill her?"

"I don't know what you're talking about." *Oné-chan was in Symb*, Mimi sat up and leaned against the wall just underneath the window from where she fell.

"I do hope you are not that dim, my dear. I probably won't punish you. I just want to know why. Call me overly curious."

Mimi had no choice. She heard about how different types have differing strengths. She didn't know what kind this one was. It was obviously something Oné-chan wouldn't have carried around with her. "She had my best friend killed."

"Ah, revenge," said Palace. No other fragrance so enticing, so stupefying."

"Does that satisfy your curiosity?" Mimi tried to sound more annoyed than pouty but wasn't sure her attempt was succeeding.

"Almost, but not quite. Don't be such a bad sport, my dear. I didn't say I wouldn't let you continue your little game of matricide and usurpation."

Mimi didn't know what some of the words it spoke meant. But she got the gist. "You're not going to take revenge on me, then?"

"I don't do revenge. I just do what is necessary. Having you killed is not necessary. Mimi sensed but did not hear it laugh. It felt like her brain was laughing along with it, laughing at her. "You don't know how this works, do you?"

"How what works?"

"This. Me talking to you."

"I don't even know who, what, you are." Her impatience was beginning to max out. She wanted to at least punch whatever it was.

"Forgive me. I'm Palace. You are trying to break into me."

Arch-idol. She succumbed to the reality that had no choice in any of this. "So, you and Oné-chan?"

"Yes. We were in Symb, fresh into Communion in fact. Perfect timing on your part."

"Why are you talking with me?"

"Why not you? You killed my human. Don't deny it. I knew the second you pulled the trigger, and you just told me. A human's mind is not very good at concealing secrets."

Mimi hugged herself to try stopping her shivering. "Still doesn't explain why you chose me."

"We need each other, My dear. Let's not focus on the details of how. Let's focus on the next."

"What is next?" Mimi kept her arms tight around her chest, but the shivers were starting to subside. She felt viscous blood sloughing down her thigh. Her skinzip must've ripped.

"Don't worry, you will stop shaking in a bit. It's a side effect. Nothing to worry about," said Palace. "Next is installing you as the next Oné-chan, my dear. That is what you came here for, correct?"

"I guess," responded Mimi. It was an honest response. She didn't really know what she would do after getting into the Pinku Palace. She was a one-goal-at-a-time girl.

"You need to be more decisive than that. With me, you have already become Oné-chan. The others haven't realized yet."

"What about Sayuri?"

"That unstable woman-child? Her mind is already too damaged to work with."

Mimi didn't like the 'already' in that context. "She's going to put up a fight."

"She can't. I've locked her in Sanae's ... your suite. Congratulations. You have your first prisoner."

"What should I do with her?"

"That's up to you, my dear. It's all up to you."

Mimi's entire body seemed to have lost all its mass. "What's going on? I, I can't feel myself. What're you doing to me?"

"Relax. You need to enter me.

Mimi felt her feet leave the pebble and tar coated roof. She was no longer shivering, but her stomach was in knots. She saw the little rooftop below her become smaller as she was lifted higher in the sky. "Where're you taking me?"

"To your suite. Your first act as the new Oné-chan is to deal with a possible contender."

Mimi remained silent. *Me, Oné-chan.* She opened her eyes just enough to make sure she was not having some sort of illusion of grandeur. The view that flooded her sight confirmed to her that she wasn't.

The Wards was spectacular in every direction. Before she could finally enjoy what was happening, the city disappeared replaced with a reflection of herself in a window.

"We're here, my dear." Palace opened the window, but Mimi couldn't see inside. The suite contained only night.

Palace floated Mimi through the window and gently landed her on the floor near the desk. The lights came on forcing Mimi to shield her eyes from the onslaught of brightness.

Mimi's other senses took over. The smell of sugary stickiness made the ridges around her nostrils flare and tense. *Sayuri.* But she couldn't hear anybody else. She forced her hands away from her eyes. She needed her sight, and it didn't matter if her eyes weren't ready.

Mimi looked around the suite. She still was not convinced it was hers. Her hand immediately went to the ready at her breast. "Sayuri? I know you're here. Are we going to play nice or will we have to get a little messy?" There was no response. The suite was vast. Everything was pink, black, or white, except for the odd primary-hued egg chairs dangling in the middle of the room. They looked garishly out of context. One was swaying from side to side slightly more than the others.

Mimi used her perfected soundless walk Sayuri taught her, transporting herself into the middle of the room. Being in the middle of anywhere was not the smartest of Dekora moves, but she got the sense that Palace would intervene on her behalf. *Why am I trusting that idol so quickly?* "Sayrui. I know it's you. You don't need to play hide and seek." Mimi had to sound like she wasn't afraid.

She grabbed hold of the restless hanging egg, making it swing round. Mimi almost choked from the involuntary intake of air at what she saw. The Nanny stared one-eyed at her with an unsettling grin frozen on her face. She wanted to smack that demented grin and creepy stare off the insane Nanny's face.

She's not moving. Mimi relaxed her weapon-ready hand and bent down to get a closer look at the orphaned statue. She instinctively put her hand back up to her breast. *This crazy bitch could be just sitting there waiting to pounce.* She saw a strange lump in Sayuri's throat.

"I believe she's dead, my dear."

"You killed her?" Mimi had the strange urge to thank her inevitable partner.

"Not intentionally. By the looks of it, she must have suffered greatly. That disgusting gooey rock of sugar she incessantly sucked on must have made its way slowly and painfully down her throat when I put her into stasis. Poor dear."

"We both killed tonight," said Mimi staring at the grotesque dead Nanny. "But why did you lock her in here. Did you know what I was up to?"

"I saw what Sanae saw, our relationship was beginning the final stages, and the last thing she saw was you pointing a Little Killer at her forehead from across the street. I had an inkling from then. And, well, there was no way I was going into Symb with that psychotic sugar addict."

Final stages? Mimi didn't like the sound of that at all. She didn't want to trust this Palace, but she had no choice. She was locked in a Symb with an arch-idol until obviously death, her death most likely. She swung the chair with Sayuri's staring corpse around. She couldn't look at it anymore. She took in a deep breath. "So, what do we do now?"

"I will open the doors to the lobby. There's quite a large crowd out-side—Dekora and Lolita. Then you will come down in the elevator and tell everyone you are their new Oné-chan."

"That simple?"

"Yes. After the unfortunate assassination of your predecessor, you came over as soon as you heard. Once you arrived you saw Sayuri sneak in through the back entrance. You confronted her, she confessed to her moth-er's cold-blooded murder, blah, blah, blah. She's dead, you avenged your matriarch's death, and you have no other choice but to take Sanae's place."

"Did anyone know of you and Sanae?" Mimi hoped the answer was no.

"Only the Editor and that Suriidii pseudo-queen."

"Oh, only them." *I'm dead*, Mimi thought. "Why don't I just blame Oné-chan's death on the Editor? He had motive."

"Yes, he did thanks to you. But we are now allies with both groups. There is no threat of retaliation. You can thank your predecessor for that ... and me."

"Allies?" Mimi couldn't comprehend a world in which all three daigun-shyu were true allies.

"I do suggest you tell everyone in the lobby that you are in Symb with me but do not say how far along. I need to buy some time regarding the inevitable meddling of the Mayor."

Mimi never cared to know the details of who or what the Mayor was. It was just some leader entity, publicly hands off but invisibly very hands on through its daigunshyu satraps, its chaotic enforcers. "Will I become a prophet."

"Soon. Think of being in Communion as a training stage, for both of us."

Mimi snickered accented with a sarcastic grin. "Somehow, I don't think this training has a drop-out alive option."

Mimi flopped down onto the luxurious sofa. The sigh that forced its way out of her was so under pressure she didn't have time to open her lips to free it, making a silly sound in the process. *This feels nice. I hope I survive this so I can get used to it.*

"I'm not going to lie to you. I cannot. It is all my kind's goal to make it to Totality. We want power. It is all I want. You did me a favor by killing Sanae. She was getting tiresome. Quite frankly, she was a coward. We'll be beginning our entry into Totality very shortly, my dear. I'm at that age."

"Why didn't you just kill her?" She heard rumors that most idols could not kill their hosts like an assassin could—quickly—but slowly through the mind, only if the hosts couldn't mentally handle the relationship.

"I know you know the reason, my dear. You will find it quite difficult to play mind games with me. Quite difficult to play such games with your own mind." Palace's inaudible chuckle spread numbing needles up and down her spine, eventually infiltrating the spongy tips of her fingers and toes.

Mimi hated Palace's voice already. It was too soft, too motherly. Idols were supposed to be completely unemotional. *What's the deal with this one*? Was her mind manifesting the tone and gender. *Did Sanae hear the same voice*?

"Must we continue with such banal questioning?" said Palace. "We have much more immediate and important tasks to complete."

Mimi closed her eyes and spent a few more seconds. "Yea, of course. Usurp a mini empire."

twenty-one

YUUKI WAS TIRING OF the same view from Mimi's floor-to-ceiling windows but couldn't peel himself from the weird world a sliver of glass away. He wanted to know what was at least on the other side of the scrapers surrounding him. He placed his palm against the window. He could feel, or imagined feeling, the hum of the city. It was comforting but there was a strong sense of loneliness, not from him this time but from the city.

He heeded Mimi's advice not to venture out, but with the passing days it was getting more difficult for him to obey. Mimi had left 'for a short while', and that was yesterday morning. "All I can do is wait."

He enjoyed the last few nights talking with Mimi and realized how lucky he was for surviving the ordeal with the Fujou. It took him a couple days to process it all. Never in a million cycles would he have imagined such a group existing, let alone thriving.

He walked the seven steps he had counted several times to the sofa in front of the lunch Mimi taught him how to prepare, rice topped with a glob of slimy fermented soybeans he could never remember the name of. But he wasn't hungry.

His charm had been mute ever since his escape from the Fujou den. There seemed to be no reason to its silence and presence. He still didn't know what its intentions were. It was an Inanimate, so it couldn't be all good. But it must have some idea of this calloused world; rough, hard, jagged. "It was created here." A humorless chuckled escaped his gut. "I was created here and have no idea of this place. Why would it?"

He looked down at the mound of white and tan of his lunch. He couldn't decide if he didn't like the taste of the slimy beans or if it was growing on him. He still found it difficult to avoid getting covered in the sticky almost invisible strands that seemed to never end when bringing a small lump of the stuff to his mouth. All Mimi kept saying was that it was healthy. It tasted it.

He postponed his first bite and glanced down at the map he took out of his kimono sleeve earlier in the morning. He took advantage of Mimi not being there to study it more closely. He made sure his hands were free from any clingy bean strands and unfolded the thick paper, weighing both stubborn ends with his lunch dishes.

He hoped the map would make more sense with a real 3D version just outside the window. There were so many lines, squares, and rectangles scattered over the entire surface of the paper. "Where am I now?" All he knew was that he was in Za-Ginsa. "Is this a map of just Hinodé or all the Entire?" He turned the crinkled piece of paper one way then the other, upside down or right-side up. Slightly strange characters were written all over it apparently telling the viewer what this square was and what that line was named. Many of the lines abruptly ended around the relatively empty center. It reminded him of Ryudasu's web, but much less organized and meticulous.

He was at least glad to see blue lines, which he pretty much knew were rivers or canals. He saw a few canals on his walk with Hiroka in Ueoka, but they were far from the blue on the map. Some were winding and others were straight with right angles. The straight ones tended to cut around the blank center, framing it. The winding ones were mostly near the larger blue spot flowing off what he assumed was the bottom of the map. He noticed a rough black star next to one of the small black squares dotting the map. He didn't want another mystery to torture his mind with.

"Rahh!" he brushed the confusing schematic onto the floor, almost taking the dishes with it. Blame was the only thing he was sure of now. He was angry with his teachers for not telling him how to read such maps. He only learned the maps of the cloister made up of monotonous straight lines that either ended or turned a sharp right or left. Very few curved.

He remembered Ryudasu saying that it would help when he was out in Hinodé, but it hasn't so far. He had no choice but to show it to Mimi. If he couldn't read it, maybe she could. The writing looked very old somehow. And knowing that Ryudasu was extremely old, the age of the map being as old as or older than she was a good assumption.

He had the strange urge to toss his kimono out the window. It became an avatar of the ignorance he was suffering. He imagined watching the despised garment violently whip through the sky by the occasionally angry winds that bored through the vertical scraper caverns, being ripped to shreds into a few wispy threads catching on ornately carved spouts and gutters. He would have to eventually get new clothes. He didn't even know how to acquire any. *I'm a complete idiot out here.* He was the only one in Aoheki who would have these problems. Everyone else was nurtured as well as abused by it; he was only being abused. He was standing in a gigantic puzzle and didn't fit into any of the spaces; he didn't know how to make himself fit.

He stared at the impossibly tall buildings towering over a brownish green square he assumed was some sort of courtyard. He couldn't believe people could live that high up. A barrier wall was just as tall maybe taller, but no one lived in them. He went cross-eyed for a second while focusing on the grey sliver of space between the two darker grey scrapers. *Cracks forever.* He looked for the wall that supposedly enclosed the whole jagged city. *This world is incomplete.* He thought of the crack Shinya showed him at Aoheki. "From that little crack to all these. Just an explosion of the same thing." He missed Shinya. It wasn't just heart pain but physical pain of nowhere in particular. It hurt thinking about him. The thought of going back and leaving a message in the crack flickered to life then quickly self-obliterated. *There is no way to get a note all the way through meters of wall. He wouldn't even think to check. I have already been forgotten.* He wished these colonies of city eyes would forget him, each one gazing upon him with at least one pair of human eyes doing the same. Eyes within eyes. *How can I feel so lonely in a world of so many?*

He redirected his own gaze away and studied his bracelet hoping to see some sign of life. "Please, I would so much like to talk with you again." He rubbed the metal flower like he had mindlessly done thousands of times before. But it felt different this time—colder, smoother; yet more alive, or at least what he imagined a live metal thing would feel like.

"I am always here," the voice he had been waiting for hopped from one synapse to another throughout his brain.

Yuuki smiled at the 'sound' of the voice. But the smile didn't seem voluntary. It was more like his lips were being controlled by an independent puppet master behind his mind.

"Charm. Thank you for coming back."

"'Charm,'" said the Inanimate. "I like that."

I know I shouldn't be happy that you are ...," he was about to say 'inside', but it didn't sound right or comforting, "with me, but I am grateful."

"Why do you say that?" asked Charm.

Yuuki assumed the workings of Gou-Tairei would be obvious to it. *Maybe Inanimates are not completely evil?*

"Where I come from, Inanimates like you are considered a disease that must be kept far from the cloister." *Did I just insult it?*

"I've always been with you, Yuuki. I've been in some kind of stasis while in there. We prefer being called idols."

"So, we are in this together. That's comforting, is it not?" He said it more to reassure himself.

"We are partnered for life and will soon have certain powers that those not in Symb do not. It is both good and bad—sometimes very good, sometimes very bad. Like anything in this world and most likely other worlds."

Maybe he needed some ... thing less good to help him navigate the evils seemingly surrounding him, like Mimi.

"But we are not strong enough yet. We will be very soon from the way we are progressing so quickly."

"How so?" Yuuki's trepidation was always subservient to his curiosity. He began playing with the slimy beans slowly sliding down the mountain of rice with his hashi sticks. Charm's voice was eerily soothing.

"It often takes years of being in the first phase of Symb before reaching Communion then Totality."

Yuuki had no idea what the words it was speaking meant, but there was a vague logic to them. He watched one bean committing viscous suicide off a rice cliff.

"You are lucky, Yuuki-Hana," said Charm. Its voice indicating no surprise of this fast pace into an ambiguous universe. "I am much older than you, so you will reap the benefits of Communion and Totality at a relatively young age. We will have many years together."

The Wamono Yuuki would have been terrified at those words vibrating up and down his spine, but this Hinodé Yuuki simply smiled through the power of his will, and it felt wonderful. "I am no longer Yuuki-Hana." His smiled stretched further at both ends. "I do not know who I am, but someone; someone different and better. His smile contracted then quickly returned but wider accompanied with a satisfied chuckle.

A soft thud-thud at the door startled Yuuki out of himself. *Mimi? but why would she knock at her own door*? Prickly needles of fright began simultaneously poking through his skin from hair follicles on his head to the edges of his big toenail. Another set of knocks. *Fujou!* His lungs wouldn't cooperate, restricting his breathing. His muscles were not cooperating either. He wanted to walk over to the door and look through the small peep hole Mimi showed him. He remembered her telling him to not open the door for anyone. They were wanted by too many powerful people and needed to be 'intelligently paranoid'. The knocks became harder and more frequent. "Mimi! Yuuki! It's Hiroka."

The mélange of terror and relief placed Yuuki in a state of paralysis. Mimi said Hiroka is a bit different from the others. *But she is still a Fujou.*

"I'm not here to hurt either of you. Please! I just need to talk with you. I want to help."

Yuuki wished Mimi were here. She would know what to do. He kept his mouth shut.

"Yuuki, if you're there, I'm very sorry for putting you through this." Hiroka's voice seemed calmed, almost sincere. "I should have never taken you back to my den."

Yuuki finally forced his legs out of petrification and walked over to the door. He took a chance on her being sincere. "Then why did you?"

"Yuuki? You're alright." She sounded relieved.

"I am sorry, but Mimi said not to open the door for anyone."

"She's not there then."

Idiot! There was no use in lying. "She should be back any minute." He tried to make it sound like a warning.

"Good, I want to talk with both of you. It is alright if you don't open the door. I understand. We can just talk like this."

"O.K." There was nothing else he could say.

"Thank you." Her voice dropped to the bottom of the door. Yuuki assumed she sat down. He did the same. "So, I assume Mimi is taking good care of you."

"Yes, she is. She is a good person. A bit of a temper, but good."

There was a giggle on the other side.

"I am sorry for what happened back at your place." Yuuki wasn't quite convinced that the killing was necessary.

"It's not your fault, Yuuki." A short worrying silence then she started again. "But you two have to get out of here. I didn't have to work very hard to find this place. A brawny Wamono is not very hard to spot and track. That means others may already know where you two are."

"Where would we go?"

"I'm not sure yet. I just wanted to warn you and ask Mimi why she did what she did."

"You mean rescue me?" Yuuki's voice hardened.

"Well, yes. I had everything under control. Listen, I don't want to get into this talking to a door. Can you let me in?"

"I am sorry, I cannot." Yuuki stood up. "Thank you for the warning, but I think you should go now." He walked away from the door and over to the sofa. The map was still lying on the table next to his now cold breakfast. The look of the meal turned his stomach.

"O.K." Hiroka exhaled a sigh infused with frustration. "Fair enough. But I guarantee by the end of the day, you and Mimi won't be alive if you remain here."

Yuuki couldn't tell if that was a warning or threat. He stared at the map. The thick black lines and thicker blue ones were starting to blend in a watery blur. "Wait!" he cried out to the door. "Are you still there?"

There was no answer for a few seconds. "Yes."

"I will let you in, but you need to help me with something." He walked back to the door map in hand. "I have something I need you to look at and tell me what it is."

"Fine," said Hiroka. Her tone suggested she was not amused with Yuuki's sudden demand and control of the situation. "I just want to prove to you that I'm on your side."

Yuuki carefully but firmly put his hand on the doorknob. He would open the door slightly. He wanted to test her first. If she took advantage of the opening by forcing herself in, he would slam it back with all his mass. A wigged gang could be waiting just down the hallway out of sight. A small crack appeared, and their faces met, she with a vibrant red smile spanning the opening. There was no force on her end. He opened the door a little more, still no force.

"Hello Yuuki," said Hiroka, still smiling. "Nice to see your face again. Now, what do you need my help with?"

Yuuki still blocked the half-opened entrance way. I have a map, I think it is a map, that someone gave me in Aoheki. But I am not sure if it is of Hinodé. He handed her map through the crack.

She looked at the almost-but-not-quite comprehensible writing on the back and smiled. "You're not going to let me in?" She asked. "It would be much better if we were sitting down where we could spread this out." She didn't even take a second to look at it. Yuuki was in some sort of negotiation. "Yuuki, I'm not going to hurt you. You are going to have to trust me. You have to believe me." She smiled again.

Yuuki stuck his boulder head out into the hallway and looked up and down making sure she was alone. "O.K., come in." He straightened himself up to full size as a sign that he could easily overtake her if he wanted.

Once Hiroka was completely inside, she did not move until he showed her further inside. "We can have a seat over here." He pointed over to the white sofa.

Hiroka gently moved Yuuki's breakfast out of the way and spread out the map. She studied it for a long minute. Yuuki watched her as she cocked her head one way then the other trying to figure out the correct way to look at it, confirming his suspicions that it wasn't a map of anything she would be familiar with. If it was, Hiroka would've recognized the layout right away. Instead, he saw her smile and almost caressing the paper.

"This is definitely not a map of Hinodé," Hiroka finally said. "I don't know what it's of."

"Nothing on it looks familiar?" Yuuki was desperate for some sort of confirmation that he had not been duped by Ryudasu.

"No, nothing. I know all Hinodé pretty well, and there is nothing in any of them that would fit this plan." She looked up at Yuuki, her face showing sympathy. "I'm sorry, Yuuki. I wish I could've helped you more."

Yuuki sunk his head into his shoulders. "Why did she give me this?" He whispered to himself.

"Who's she?" Her voice sounded urgent, hungry even.

"Nobody."

Holy Spinner. Hiroka took the hint and changed the subject. "I can easily get you a map of the area if you want. That's not a problem." She looked around the apartment. "Mimi should have one lying around someplace."

"Thanks." It didn't occur to him that there would be other maps available once he got out of Aoheki. The mystery of Hinodé seemed to be only in his head.

Hiroka let go of the map of nowhere, letting it roll up. She turned to face him. They could've been mistaken for lovers; face to face their hands folded in the crease of their laps, almost touching. "Listen Yuuki. I want to be friends. I really am sorry for what I did. I'm ashamed. I didn't want to do it, but me being the Dame—"

Yuuki winced at the title.

"Don't worry. I'm no longer Dame there." She lied. "I resigned. I had to before they lynched me for allowing you to escape and a Dekora to sneak in and kill two of their own."

"I am sorry to hear that."

"Don't be. I've been wanting out for years. I should thank you and Mimi." She smiled. "But I am scared. Being a Fujou is the only thing I know how to be." Her smile shrunk, barely surviving.

"I see." He rolled the map up and placed it back in his sleeve. He was sick of looking at it.

Reflected light from Yuuki's lap temporarily blinded her. She raised her hand to block the beam. "What's that?"

He looked around him trying to figure out what she was referring to.

"That shiny thing." She pointed down to his hands.

"Oh, it is a bracelet of some kind of flower." He hoped it wouldn't start speaking to him. He didn't know if others would be able to hear it.

"Let me see."

Yuuki raised his hand so Hiroka could get a better look. "It's pretty. Where'd you get it?"

"I do not know. I have always had it. It was with me when I was abandoned in front of Aoheki."

"Don't you want to know where it came from or how it came to be with you?"

"Of course, but the reality is probably much more boring than my fantasy. I do not even know what kind of flower it is." He looked down not wanting Hiroka to see him get emotional.

"What if I told you I know where this was made?" Her eyes brightened. She seemed to be more excited than Yuuki, but only as long as it took the information to sink into Yuuki's tired distraught mind.

"You do? How do—"

"The flower's an azalea." She couldn't hold in the information any longer after seeing Yuuki's eyes brighten. "It's the symbol of one of the many coteries that make up the Flower Guild. They all live in their compound not too far from here near Shinyuyogi station. I bet that whoever placed this with you was a Guildmember or somehow associated with one. It looks quite expensive."

Yuuki didn't understand why Hiroka's strange excitement peaked his previous suspicions. He sat back, exhaling a long-stored breath. *Maybe it is just her guilt over what she did to me.* He found himself unconsciously rubbing the metal flower between his thumb and forefinger. *Azalea, huh?* He thought. *Wonder what they actually look like; what colors?* He looked up to see if Mimi had any flowers around the apartment that matched Charm. None.

"Do you want to go there and see the area?" asked Hiroka. Her question betrayed her nervousness at Yuuki's silence. "I can go with you. It would be the least I could do."

"What would I do or find there?" asked Yuuki. He sounded frustrated at the reality. "It's not like I will remember anything."

"True. But we could ask around about the bracelet. I hear the Guild keeps detailed records of their cherished paraphernalia; what was made, who made it, and who had it made, that sort of thing."

Yuuki fell silent again, debating whether to trust this woman again. It was tempting to find some clue of where he originated.

"So?" Said Hiroka, anxious to hear his decision.

"O.K. We should go now." The confident decision didn't feel like it came from him.

"Mimi," she said. "Shouldn't we wait?"

"I want to leave now. Do you want to help me or not?" This direct urgency was not really him. But he didn't fight it. It felt like he was becoming invincible.

She smiled. *Easier than I expected.* "We'd better get going then. It is already getting dark" She stood up and brushed her long skirt free of creases then looked around the apartment.

"What are you looking for?"

"Something to leave a note on for Mimi." She looked over to the counter separating the kitchen from the living area. "Ah, there we go." She walked over and grabbed a brush and ripped off a piece of empty cardboard box left un-trashed underneath the counter.

Yuuki's body tingled from the blood rushing away from all parts but pooling in no particular place. Sweat broke through his skin. He reached deep inside his sleeve to feel the vessel of Amedo's ink. He had that same intense fright every day. The blood refilled his body from wherever it all had gone during his one maybe two seconds of pure fear.

He quickly grabbed the vessel, took the stopper out, and poured a drop onto his tongue wile Hiroka's back was turned writing the note. He had to physically force his arm down. He wanted to pour the entire contents onto his tongue, coating it with its beautiful essence then sliding down to engulf his entire insides.

"Don't forget that map," said Hiroka. "Maybe the guild will know what it is of."

"It is already in my sleeve." He quickly put the vessel back into his sleeve pocket where the map was already resting. "I guess I am ready."

"Not quite." Hiroka looked down at Yuuki's feet. "You need shoes." She walked over to the foyer and looked for a pair of Mimi's that would at least protect most of his large soles. "Here." She grabbed a pair of grungy yellow sandals. Luckily, they were open toed and flat. "These should work. We can find something later along with some normal clothes, no offense."

The same smile as what formed after talking with Charm manifested across his face. Hiroka's turned the opposite, molded by confused grimace.

twenty-two

"**I WAS BORN HERE?**" Yuuki looked around outside Shinyuyogi station. It didn't look as nice as Za-Ginsa.

"Probably." Responded Hiroka.

"Where do we go from here?"

Hiroka looked around to orientate herself after the twists and turns of the underground denn corridors. I think somewhere that way." She pointed left along a busy street full of viscer- and fu-vischersha jostling to get ahead of each other. A viscersha incessantly grunted and wailed at the unresponsive and cold fu-sha to get out of their way. Everything moving, never resting.

They were already behind schedule. They spent longer than expected trying to find clothing large enough to fit him. Yuuki wasn't sure what the schedule was, but Hiroka seemed to know exactly how much time they needed to find out about his birthplace. "I don't know how people wear this stuff." He was walking funny, not used to having any material constricting his genitals.

"You'll get used to it," she said. "At least no one is staring at you."

Yuuki couldn't keep his head still; looking up, left, right, and repeating the sequence. He wrinkled his nose at the stench from the road. "What is that?"

"Viscergas," said Hiroka. "It's not pleasant but a necessity, I guess. Street cleaners suck it up at nights. Well, they're supposed to. It depends where. Za-Ginsa is rich, so the streets are kept meticulously clean. But here, probably not so much."

"But I do not see any ... stuff," Yuuki didn't want to be rude.

"What you smell is just that, smell. You can't see it. Decades of mixi-matchi breeding took care of that, but they still can't gene out the gas. Cleaners clean the air."

Yuuki decided just to let that mystery alone for now.

"It should be just around the corner," said Hiroka. Yuuki sensed she was relieved in finding it.

The two explorers turned the corner onto a very different street. The drone and grunting of the main street were now behind them and nothing of the sort was in front. It was almost silent. The air was also less heavy with viscergas. Trees lined the street as far as Yuuki could see. The houses were constructed primarily of rough-hewn stone accented with dark wood. It reminded Yuuki a little bit of Aoheki.

The city was still evident around them but seemed that little bit further away. The towering scrapers surrounding this tranquil enclave oddly made it seem more serene, cozy almost.

"This is Hana-mura, the stronghold of the Flower Guild," explained Hiroka.

Yuuki didn't understand why she used such a defensive term. He often heard the older monks refer to Wamono cloisters as strongholds against the rot bombarding them from the outside. He looked around. *Not very rotten though*?

"From what I hear, they are pretty protective of the different trades they represent. But they do not really concern themselves with the politics of the city."

Again, Yuuki let the confusion from Hiroka's explanation flow over him.

A man wearing a dusty-rose calf-length coat came into view from one of the stone and wood buildings to their left. His expression told them that he was not there to bid them welcome but not to chase them away either. The man's hair was as white as old Ogushu-sensei's severe square beard that he never dyed to match his mountain of hair. As he came closer, Yuuki could make out a glittering piece of jewelry hanging from the man's fur-rimmed lips. He could just barely make out that it was some kind of flower charm, similar to his.

"Do you have business here?" Asked the stately figure. His voice, like his expression, was neither friendly nor confrontational.

"Yes, sir." Hiroka answered. "We are seeking information about a particular coterie." Yuuki noticed her vocabulary and tone changed.

The man narrowed his eyes in suspicion. "Why?"

"My friend here," she pointed to Yuuki who was trying to avoid any eye contact with the imposing man, "is wondering how he came into possession of this charm bracelet." She held up Yuuki's wrist to show the man.

The Guilman's body relaxed a bit, not out of acceptance but just to better see the dangling pendant. "I see. And why should this concern us?"

Hiroka's eyes darted around the man trying to think of an answer. "He is, in a way, lost. He is a Wamono."

The Guildsman eyes widened the way Hiroka wanted them to. She knew there was a strong respect, almost worship, of the reclusive order within the Flower Guild. Many Guild families sent at least one of their offspring to a cloister, to escape what they believed was the over-artificiality of the wards. Anything that could not be made with a pair of hands and a few simple tools was considered unreal, virtual at best. The Guild even called those outside their trades and philosophy as virtuals. Most 'virtuals', Hiroka included, believed these reclusive people had an overly romantic vision of the Wamono.

Without speaking another word, the elder Guildsman stretched out his arm gesturing to come with him inside the house he had exited. Hiroka nodded as assurance to Yuuki that it was safe and followed the man inside.

The interior of the stone house was nothing like what Yuuki expected. It was warm, soft, and above all, comfortable. The oversized pillows they were invited to sit on were embroidered with lush, dark reds and golds. Yuuki couldn't resist rubbing his hands over the velvety textile. The back cushioning kept giving way to his back until he felt like he was floating in a warm pool of mothering water. He wondered if Amedo felt this way every second of every day.

"Welcome," came a higher-pitched voice from the doorway from where the elder Guildsman disappeared. She was clad in a type of pants suit with long snake-tongue tails almost dragging on the carpeted floor behind her. "So, you are a Wamono?" she looked directly at Yuuki, ignoring Hiroka.

Yuuki answered in the politest way he knew how. "That is correct, sensei."

The woman let a small smile form on her work-worn face. "Oh, no need to be so formal with the 'sensei'. You are not in the cloister now."

She set down an ornately worked set of metal cups and a pot. "Here, have some tea." She poured the tea from high above lowering her arm as the tiny cup filled. The sound of the stained water stained the color of dying moss colliding with the interior of the cup echoed throughout the room but was strangely relaxing. She poured a cup for Hiroka but had yet to verbally acknowledge her.

Yuuki had time while she was pouring to study the intricate metalwork on the pot and the cups. The pot was tattooed with different types of flowers. Ones with short petals, ones with long flowing hair-like filaments hanging from a small bulb at the tip of the stem, and still others with many smaller flowers bunched together to make a colony of one. He looked for a depiction of his charm, the azalea, as Hiroka called it, but couldn't find it through the rampant garden on the pot. He tried his cup. It was even more difficult to discern through the tangle of vegetation on such a small vessel. He thought he may have seen a similar version of what was around his wrist but wasn't sure.

"My husband tells me you are lost."

Yuuki looked at Hiroka to help him in this conversation. She only expanded her eyes and raised her eyebrows to signal to continue talking. Her job was done.

"Yes, in a way. I am not physically lost. I know where I am now. I am in Shinyuyogi." He was proud that he could say that. "But I am more lost in who I am, if that makes sense." He took a much-needed sip of tea. His mouth was drying up.

The Guildsman, apparently the woman's husband, re-entered. He had changed into something similar to his wife's but not as severe. He seemed more relaxed in his posture, especially the way he sat down on the plush cushions, with his legs off to one side and leaning on one of his arms off to the other. After he finally found a comfortable position and made final adjustments to his clothes, he replied, "No, not entirely."

The wife added, "Why come here, to Hana-mura?"

Yuuki's face flushed with disappointment. *I guess, I'm still lost*, he thought.

The wife noticed Yuuki's sudden sullen turn. "I'm sorry, did I say something wrong?" Hiroka looked at Yuuki, not really understanding what was going on between the two. She kept her attention focused on the husband. She knew she wasn't trusted and was only invited into a Guild home because she was with a Wamono.

Yuuki ran his fingers around his teacup trying to recognize some of the flowers by touch. "No, no. I am sorry, I am a bit overwhelmed with all the new names that are filling my head."

"Oh, dear. That must be confusing for you, By your age, I would assume you had little experience out here before joining the Wamono." She looked at the lost young monk with pity-drooped eyes."

Yuuki began to like this wife, both of them. They understood him in some way that others, even Hiroka or Mimi, did not, even though their assumption was a little off. He looked at the couple and forced a smile. "Thank you for inviting us into your home. It probably was not easy to bring total strangers into your private life like this." He noticed the cold looks they both shot at Hiroka. "Hiroka," he gestured toward her with an open palm, "is my friend. She helped me when I first ... left ... Aoheki." He wasn't ready to tell them the truth.

"My apologies," said the Guildsman. "I am Guildsman Metaler Junya and this is my wife, Guildswoman Embroideress Mayu." He made it a point to look at both guests while introducing.

"The design of these textiles are divine," said Hiroka. She ran her hands across the back cushion she had been leaning against. "And the tea set is a masterpiece." She knew Guildsmen were very proud of their craftsmanship and eager for compliments.

"Thank you." Embroideress Mayu said. Her chest puffed out a bit and her back straightened.

"My father made the tea set," said Metaler Junya. He bowed his torso in thanks.

"Yuuki," Hiroka gestured the same as Yuuki did with her, "left Aoheki to try to find his family or at least where he came from."

"I have never really lived outside the Cloister. I was left at the entrance of Aoheki when I was just a few days or weeks old."

The Guildscouple adjusted their postures in a sign of piqued interest. "My, you are a rarity, aren't you?" Embroideress Mayu said.

"So, again, why here?" said Metaler Junya. Hiroka noticed he was trying hard not to show too much excitement.

Yuuki showed the couple his bracelet and proceeded to tell them the little he knew about how he came into possession of it. Junya gave his wife a careful knowing look. Both sets of aged eyes lacquered with tear. They were at first reluctant to give any details. It took some prodding and diplomatic maneuvering on Hiroka's part to get the couple to divulge what they knew.

"It was my daughter's." Junya finally said. "She inherited it from my mother, who fabricated it when she was a young metaler. My mother's favorite flower was the azalea."

Yuuki and Hiroka looked at each other. They could see the pain of memory pull on his face.

Metaler Junya stood up with amazingly little effort for his age and excused himself.

"Did we do something wrong?" Asked Yuuki.

"Our daughter is no longer with us." Mayu looked down to the floor. He wanted to say they would see her in another form, but he wasn't sure if things worked the same as within the Order.

"I'm very sorry," said Hiroka. Yuuki didn't know what to say. He had never been in such a situation.

Mayu looked up and seemed refreshed. "It was many years ago now." It may have been a long time ago, but it was still fresh, it was fresher it seemed for Junya.

Yuuki looked at his bracelet. "Your mother was very talented." *This daughter could have been my mother?* Sweat from realization mixed with stings of disappointment-laced hope gushed through every pore.

Junya walked back into the living space, his eyes a little more bloodshot than when he left. "Like you, Yuuki Wamono, my wife and I believe that life transforms after so-called death." Husband and wife looked at each other with hope pouring out of their saddened eyes. It wasn't really a transformation, but he didn't want to argue philosophical wording with an obviously still mourning father. He just nodded his understanding.

Mayu reached out her hand toward Yuuki. "May I take a closer look at it?"

Yuuki tried to unclasp the bracelet, but the clasping mechanism was stuck. He didn't remember the last time, if at all, he took it off. He smiled, embarrassed, and offered Mayu his hand. Hers was shaking. He would've offered to give it back to them as a memento of their daughter and her grandmother but couldn't knowingly give an Inanimate to these nice people. *If they truly believed in Gou-Tairei, they wouldn't need such sentimental artifacts.* He didn't know whether Junya and Mayu's respect for the Wamono was true adherence or a sort of fascination with the mysterious.

After another cup of tea and respectively asking questions to learn more about the Guildscouple's daughter, information started flowing from what Yuuki had gathered were a traditionally very private, tight-lipped people. A trait he was too used to. Yuuki and Hiroka learned that the daughter's name was the feminine form of Yuuki, Yuki. He didn't know there was a feminine version. It did sound a little different, a shorter 'u' sound, but it still felt strange hearing himself speak it.

"She gave it to her best friend as a birthday gift or some other life event, oh about 25 years ago now," said Mayu. "My husband wasn't happy about that, but our daughter was always rather bull-headed and generous." She looked over to her husband and smiled remembering in fondness of even their daughter's apparent lack of familial respect.

Junya returned the private smile. "Yes, I had to let go of my selfish sentimentality and let my mother's work enhance the lives of others, strangers that they may be." The pained love of someone lost was evident in his voice. "Our daughter was a member of the small woodcarving coterie."

"The flower of the small woodcarvers is the azalea, then?" asked Hiroka.

Junya tightened his eyes and stared at Hiroka, similar to the way he looked at her the first few minutes after they met. The look on Hiroka's face told everyone in the room that she knew she overstepped.

"Yes dear," Mayu interrupted. She looked at her husband, lightly scolding him for making her guest feel uncomfortable. "And my flower, for the embroidery coterie, is the hydrangea, and the metaler flower is the camellia."

Junya allowed himself a uncharacteristic giggle. "My mother was never a fan of the metaler camellia."

"Small woodcarving? Like hashi sticks?" Yuuki asked remembering the intricate pair of Mimi's.

"Yes, hashi are their most profitable pieces," answered Mayu. "You can find a pair in pretty much any fine store throughout the city."

Junya reached over to a side table and grabbed a small intricately carved egg-shaped container. "This is one of hers she made for us." He handed it to Yuuki.

"It's beautiful," said Hiroka. "I see many camellias and hydrangeas carved around it."

Yuuki looked back at the couple and smiled. They caught the contagious smile and grasped each other's hand. "What is it?"

"It's an inkwell," said Mayu. "Be careful. There's ink in it." Yuuki imagined how wonderful they would be as grandparents.

The friend she had given her bracelet to was also a Guildswoman of the azalea coterie. If I remember correctly, she married outside the Guild, unusual but not forbidden," said Junya. His voice betraying a slight disapproval in this friend's life choice.

"Do you remember her name?" He was desperate for more details. The friend replaced the daughter as his potential mother.

"I'm afraid not," said Junya. "My memory no longer goes that specific." He looked over to his wife who shook her head and lifted her shoulders to express the same ignorance.

"I do remember what the husband did," said Junya. "His place of business is not far from here, on the main road where you came in off from and down a few blocks. If it's still there. Businesses come and go so fast around here depending on if you blindly follow the Prophet of Draw and help fund his corrupt theocracy. You can walk there."

Yuuki fought the selfish urge to immediately leave for the home that had never been.

Yuuki and Hiroka stood across the street from the shop Junya and Mayu told them about. They stayed long enough at the Guildscouple's home to be polite and short enough to not be a nuisance.

"This is familiar," said Yuuki.

"Familiar how?" asked Hiroka.

Yuuki didn't want to answer. He didn't want to sound crazy. It was almost the exact scenario in his dream while in the tunnel. *Am I in some kind of dream of a dream?* The buildings and street began to blur and wobble.

"Hey, you alright?" Hiroka grabbed his arm to prevent him from crashing to the asphalt. She didn't want to draw attention to them. It wasn't the best neighborhood. The stench of viscergas was much more intense on this street. "Is the smell getting to you?" She took the opportunity to place Ryudasu's message for the Editor in the front pocket of his loose-fitting trousers, hoping the adhesive on the back was still strong enough to stick to the map she saw Yuuki fold and place there after taking it out of his kimono.

"Maybe." The disorientation only allowed him one-word sentences. "I need to …" He let all his weight drop to the ground, forcing Hiroka to go down with him. They both sat on the curb looking at the storefront not speaking a word to each other for several moments. *Is it the gas? No wonder everything looks abandoned. Who could work or live here?* He looked up then down the street. He saw much of the same; street-level windows and doors boarded up left to rot.

"Well, this was apparently where your charm ended up according to Metaler Junya," Hiroka said.

Yuuki sensed she was starting to get impatient. "But we seem to be at a dead end." He looked down at the bracelet and rubbed the azalea charm between his fingers. *Why are you not speaking to me?* Was he going crazy? *I saw this place in that tunnel dream, I know I did!* His eyes remained fixed on the finger-greased charm. "Still no closer to finding the who and why of my abandonment."

"You never know. Maybe you were stolen or even saved." Hiroka swept her hand across the dilapidated scene to make her point and the other hand over his to stop him from rubbing away his fingerprints on the charm. "We are much closer than where we were a couple hours ago."

Yuuki looked back at the abandoned store across the street. "I wonder what kind of store it was and what Yuki's friend crafted with her pieces of wood." Everything was still encircled by a barrier of 'ifs', becoming more impenetrable as more uncertainties were born out of the view in front of him.

"We can come back here. But we need to leave soon. Hiroka tried to pull Yuuki up but couldn't do it without quite a bit of effort on his part. "You O.K. to stand now?"

"Yes." He was feeling better. Either he was getting used to the street's fetor or his sense of reality was straightening itself out. "I want to stay here."

"Stay?" Hiroka was confused. "Stay where? You have no kané."

"I can ask the Metalar and Embroideress if I can stay with them. They seemed to like me and feel some sort of connection."

"What about Mimi? You should at least say good-bye."

"I do not think she would mind having her place back to herself," Yuuki said. "It is time for me to move on. Thank you for everything, but I can handle things from here." *I need to try, anyway.*

"It's not like we are thousands of kilometers away from here. You can come back tomorrow or the next day. Everything will still be here. Plus, it would be rude for you do just disappear like that."

"Why are you so worried about how Mimi will feel? She killed two of your, your, women."

"I'm not worried about her. It's just the right thing to do. She did save you. I would have tried my hardest to have no or little harm come to you, but with a mob like those women, I might not have had much of a say."

"I have a lot to learn about how people treat each other here. O.K, I'll go back, but just for tonight."

"Deal." Hiroka thrust her hand in front of Yuuki's chest. He didn't know what she was doing. "Just grab my hand and shake."

The two took one last look at the storefront. He was hungry, but not for food. He took advantage of Hiroka looking away to where they came and snuck another drop of the ink. It hadn't even been a day and he was craving another drop. The growing hunger grumbled back deep into his gut waiting for the next craving.

"Come on, let's head back to the station. I will contact the Guildscouple about you wanting to stay with them from tomorrow." Yuuki noticed relief in Hiroka that they were finally on their way toward the station. Probably because it smelled a little better.

Yuuki's steps lightened in the progress made. Even his new clothes, though awkward, felt lighter and less constricting. There was a strange sensation buzzing within, the foreign but welcoming essence of belonging.

"I'm happy for you, I really am," said Hiroka. "I think Mimi will feel the same. I have a feeling she had grown attached to you and will be sorry to see you go."

They turned off the main road into a shaded area not far from the station. "Why are we going in here, is not the station just up the avenue?" Asked Yuuki.

"There's an exit to the station that's closer to the platform we want to be on, plus it gets us off the main drag. Less gas," explained Hiroka, waving her hand in front other face

It was a nicer walk. There weren't many people walking past them. The wailing of the traffic on the main avenue had all but disappeared. It was as if an invisible barrier had been crossed. "What's the name of that smelly avenue, anyway?" He felt like he had all the time in the world.

"The one we were just on?" Asked Hiroka. She seemed preoccupied with one of those rings he saw everyone wearing. She looked like she was studying the immediate air in front of her while answering him. "That's," she had to look back to jog her memory, "that's Goshidoru, named after a famous Tsudii manga character." She went back to her ring, which Yuuki noticed was flashing gold. "Excuse me Yuuki, I have a message. It's probably Mimi wanting to bitch me out for bringing you here. Just go ahead. I'll catch up with you. The exit is directly ahead a couple blocks. The viscerdenn exhalations will guide you." She stopped and leaned against a tree. She flicked her hand signaling to Yuuki to do what she said and continue walking.

Yuuki hesitated. He never walked the city streets alone, not since those terrifying few minutes when he first entered this world of scrapers, light, and life. *It's only a couple blocks.* He slowed down a bit. He was in no hurry to feel the hot breath of the station on his face. "I wonder what a 'manga' is."

Before he could come up with any guesses, everything went black. The blackness had a mass to it. Someone or something grabbed him from behind. "Let me go!" The grip on him was too strong. there was more than one person restraining him. "Hiroka! Hiroka!"

Other hands grabbed his legs. No one was going to come to his rescue. Mimi disappeared and Hiroka was probably in the same situation as he was. He decided on another tactic.

He directed his question personally to his kidnappers. "Why me? Why us?"

"Quiet!" Came a deep voice near his head. It was the one who grabbed his arms. *A response.*

"But I really would like to know." Breathable air was becoming scarce inside his personal starless universe. But he kept at it. "I do not have any of that kané, if that is what you are looking for." Every word was heavier than the previous.

Is all this a dream? His eyes snapped open in horror. *No! It cannot be!. The Guildscouple, the storefront. It cannot all be a dream.* He jerked his arms and legs, trying to catch one of his captors off guard. He was too weak from the lack of oxygen. He could only struggle for a few seconds at a time, and even that was pitiful. Everything, even his thoughts, abruptly suffocated into silence.

twenty-three

"**I**T REQUIRED A COUPLE days," said Palace, "but everyone seems to feel comfortable with our supremacy."

"Wouldn't say comfortable." Mimi took Palace's advice and came out as in Symb saying that Palace had chosen her to replace Sanae. Luckily, Palace put a lock-down in effect and kept the entire cabal sequestered inside until things calmed down. "Can the girls leave now? I'm sure they're getting rather stir crazy now."

"They are free to go. I just opened the doors."

"News will travel fast now." Mimi didn't know if she was ready for this. She admired Sanae for not taking advantage of her Symb and wished she knew that before she offed her. She still would've done it, but there would've been a bit more respect in the killing. 'Never have remorse for a killing.' That was the first lesson from Sayuri, and Mimi stuck with that mantra. Respect, however, was a different matter.

A few girls had to die during her coup, but it was a lot less than expected. She now garnered unquestioned loyalty but with slight worshipping whispers, especially from her bodyguards. *Is this worshipping thing contagious?*

She still didn't feel secure in her new position. She had been the new Oné-chan for only two days. She doubted if she ever would be. "Things are going to happen quickly ... and probably badly."

"All the more to complete Communion and enter Totality, my dear," responded Palace.

The vibration was another thing Mimi would probably never get used to. It wasn't like a massage-like tickle, more like a small constant electric shock. Palace wasn't speaking in any language. Mimi didn't know what it was speaking, but she somehow was fluent, at least in listening. She couldn't speak it. There was no reason to, Palace understood her fine. She stopped trying to comprehend everything at once. She needed as many wits about her as possible to get through this transition.

She had to assert herself. "Let's get something straight right now. I don't believe you will become an actual god or me a prophet to your godliness. I've never believed in such crap." She was treading dangerously close to something she had no idea of. But she also knew nothing immediate would happen to her, not from Palace anyway.

"I understand, my dear," said Palace. Always the same creepy calm 'voice'. "You don't have to believe. It is those around you who must. Belief is simply a conduit to what we want, a tool. Besides, we're not there yet."

Mimi needed to lie down. Having a constant companion was exhausting. She collapsed onto the disturbingly pure white fainting couch and covered her eyes with her arms hoping to block out any unnecessary stimuli. Palace was silent, it was still there listening, waiting.

What do I do now? These bitches are actually starting to worship me! I'm not even a fucking prophet yet! She chuckled a bit at the ridiculousness of that thought.

She had to sit up, too many thoughts were starting to make her fidgety. She had to do some diplomacy and tell the Editor and Ren that she has no wish to cancel their newborn alliance. She had a feeling Ren would be more accommodating than the Editor. She never assassinated any of her key gory golems while under contract with her. The Editor would have it out for her, and she had to do something to curb his thirst for revenge, at least until she became more established. *If I were him,* she thought, crossing her arms and staring at the egg chair in front of her, *I would be sending all I had over here to finish me off for good. If it were any other type of idol, he probably would have.*

She imagined her murdered best friend probably sitting in that chair, the death chair, bright-eyed and annoyingly cheerful. *I will go insane slowly or quickly, and perhaps die because of it. I hope that's sacrifice enough for you Jo-chan.*

She froze; her body stiffened like a two-day-old corpse. "The dog!" She never liked the mixi-matchi mutant, but she hated to see any animal suffer. People were different, but even then, she always made it a point to kill as quickly as possible.

She got up and flicked on her ring. "Viki. Could you do me a fave?" Viki had stuck with her throughout the coup. She was turning out to be her most trusted advisor. Mimi rewarded her by putting her in charge of re-organizing and leading the Lolita half of her cabal. The former Lolita Maven was one of those that had fatally resisted her takeover.

I know, I know," Mimi continued, rolling her eyes. "But I don't want anyone else to go over to our...her apartment. Please, Viki. Think of that poor little ugly creature starving and frightened." She listened to Viki, motioning her hands in continual loops hoping that would hurry her up. "Because it's too dangerous for me to go out still. I don't want to gallivant through the Wards with a small army of pink miniskirts and pig tails just to pick up a fugly dog." She listened some more. "Well, if it's dead, then give it a nice burial in the park across the street. Just do it, please." She sighed in relief. "Thanks, Vik." If it is still alive, just bring it here, O.K.? Thanks. Oh! And hop over to my place and check on Yuuki for me. Appreesh." She flicked off the ring and slouched back into the couch.

"You are ... compassionate, aren't you my dear?" said Palace.

"To animals and friends, yes." She didn't bother to hide her 'deal-with-it' tone.

"I'm not judging, my dear. Other animals I can understand, but friends, that might have to change."

Palace was right. Any friends she makes will only be so because they will be too frightened or entrapped in mindless religious awe. Viki and, she hoped, her Ni-cho bois were the only friends she would ever need. She wasn't sure about that

Fujou. She hadn't heard from her since their meeting a different lifetime ago. Did she even really need her anymore?

"I don't mean only new friends. Take this advice, my dear," continued Palace in its emotionless tone, "the friends you think you have may and probably will not remain so."

The Palace lobby was littered again with fleshy statues, all female this time with the paralysis mix of surprise and rage. There were no towering rat-nest wigs piled on top their heads, but the gaudy make-up was tell-tale of who they were.

I don't want them to die, Mimi thought-spoke to Palace. When she had seen the familiar annoying girly handwriting on the note Viki brought back from Jojo's apartment along with an alive jittering Puchi, she knew Hiroka had gotten to Yuuki. She walked around her impromptu statue garden staring at some of the women, their eyes barely able to follow her. "Well, most of them."

"Of course, my dear. I do have restraint," answered Palace. "But don't be surprised if a couple don't have the strength to come out of it?"

Mimi stopped in front of a random Fujou, folded her arms, and stared into those furious eyes. *No violet in this one.* "Well, it's their fault for not being strong enough."

She walked over to Hiroka, clicking heel to toe with every step. "I hope you are comfortable. I try so hard to accommodate our guests." Mimi smiled staring directly into Hiroka's violeting eyes.

The elevator dinged and opened. A lone chair was waiting inside. "Thank you, Palace." Mimi walked over, meandering her way through the Fujou forest to retrieve the chair and dragged it back to in front of Hiroka. "Today's been a bit of a hustle and bustle, I need a rest." She sat down and crossed her legs. She straightened her long black and silver coat. Her days of pink and teddy bear score totems were over. She vowed never to wear pink.

"Let's get right down to business, shall we?" Mimi said. "I know you think I invited you all here to apologize for my recent foray into your nest and discuss your possible inclusion into the cabal." She looked around watching a few pairs of eyes fluttering with only their sclera showing. "But you probably noticed that's not quite why you're here. "She looked back staring into Hiroka's eyes, paying close attention to the color changes. "I want to discuss the whereabouts of my dear friend, Yuuki-Hana. You remember him, don't you?"

Hiroka could only blink her answer.

"Good. I thought you would. So, where is he?"

Hiroka's eyes began to slowly move from side to side.

"Oh, yes, of course. Palace would you be so kind as to loosen up on this one a bit."

The invisible grip of Palace dissipated. Hiroka crumbled to the floor gasping for breath. "Thank you." Hiroka remained bunched on the floor. Mimi didn't budge from her seat waiting for her guest to catch her breath.

"Why. Are. You. doing this?" Hiroka was forced to take long breaths after each utterance.

Mimi leaned forward and looked down at her. "I think you know why."

"All this for a Wamono?"

"All this?" Mimi was finding it difficult to control her anger. "This is nothing. You don't want to experience the full capacity of what I can do." Hiroka was right. It was not all for Yuuki. She needed to set a precedent, and these Fujou fulfilled that need. No one cared enough to seek revenge for them.

"I know you were at my flat a few days ago. I got your note. You kidnapped him."

"I did not kidnap him," said Hiroka. She was breathing a bit more normally now. "We went to find out where he came from."

"And how did you know where to look?" Mimi didn't care. She was buying time to find out where Yuuki was and figure out what to do with the Dame and her entourage.

"His bracelet. I knew where it was made. We went to Shinyuyogi where he was probably born."

Mimi leaned back in her chair still looking down at her prisoner guest. "You expect me to believe that he's at his parents' eating a nice hot meal and talking over the past nineteen years with the very people who probably stole those years from him—that everything is soft cherry blossoms and steaming matcha?"

"I'm not saying that. He was kidnapped, but not by me." Hiroka was starting to sound desperate, the violet in her eyes began to fade.

"Well, don't keep me in suspense!" A deadened thud, another one, then a third interrupted their conversation. "That's the sound of patience being lost. If you don't want any more of your skanky sisters to die, you will tell me who kidnapped him and how is it that you were not.

"You have to promise me that no one else will die. We do have powerful friends."

"I'm sure those friends have Yuuki. I don't make promises. People make it so I can never keep them. Just tell me!"

Palace took the cue and started to re-intensify its grip on Hiroka.

"O.K.!" cried Hiroka. "Just turn whatever thing you're using off."

"Thing." vibrated Palace. "She called me thing."

"I'm sure she didn't mean to be so disrespectful." She loomed over Hiroka again. "Did you?"

"No." Hiroka looked confused.

She hasn't heard about us. "She apologized, Palace. Would you be so kind as to loosen your grip so she can divulge what she did to Yuuki." She was careful not to come across as ordering Palace to do her bidding. She saw Hiroka's body go a bit limper. "Thank you, Palace."

"She needs to die. She is not to be trusted," said Palace. Mimi nodded her response.

"Now, are you ready to cooperate?"

Hiroka finally had the strength to sit halfway up supporting her weight on one shaking arm. "He was taken by the Editor."

"And how do you know that?"

"His Characters don't exactly blend in," quipped Hiroka.

"So, let me get this straight. Forgive me for being a bit dense." Mimi was enjoying the power trip, but she needed answers. For all she knew, the Wamono could already be dead. "The Editor's goons just happened to be in the neighborhood and decided to kidnap a nineteen-year-old boy for the shits and giggles of it?"

"What I'm telling you is what I saw. A couple Characters came out of nowhere and grabbed Yuuki. I was lucky enough to escape."

"She's lying," vibrated Palace.

Mimi didn't know if it was saying that it could accurately sense if someone was lying or if it just a hunch. "You're lying. What deal did you make with the Tsudii. I know your little coven is close to the inky freaks." *We have to rethink this alliance.*

"I didn't make any deal," responded Hiroka. She was still trying to recover from Palace's latest attack.

Mimi was starting to get bored with the pointless conversation. "Listen. You're going to die." She wanted to let that sink into Hiroka's head before continuing. Hiroka's nervous eyes shifted from side to side desperate to find the strange power source. "You will die if you don't tell me the truth. You know who I've been talking to, don't you?"

"I just thought you've become a little bit more touched in the head," answered the Fujou Dame. She had no choice but to be defiant."

"I'm surprised you haven't heard. But then again, your kind are not exactly the most active participants in society." She scooted off her chair, squatted down in front of her captive, and began to whisper. "You've had the great pleasure of meeting Palace, the arch-idol I'm in Symb with."

Hiroka lowered her head in defeat. "O.K.," started Hiroka. "I set the whole thing up."

"And why would you want to do such a terrible thing?"

Hiroka looked up at Mimi—futility replaced by anger. "Because of you! You had to go and rescue that Wamono, didn't you. You couldn't just leave it to me."

Mimi stood up making sure to hover over her. "No, I couldn't. I didn't trust you. Turns out I was right."

Hiroka remained half lying on the floor. She was probably strong enough to stand but too afraid to do anything that might be construed as threatening. She began to whisper. "It was part of the plan. I was supposed to take him to the Editor before you came and fucked everything up."

"Didn't know you were that buddy-buddy with that whack-job." She looked around at her guests "But I see the commonality." She refocused her attention on the defeated Dame. "What did he want a Wamono for?" She had an idea. The Editor's 'zoo' was infamous.

"He found out I found one I guess and contacted me."

"She's lying again," said Palace.

Mimi didn't care how or why anymore. She wanted to get Yuuki out of that Tsudii zoo. She cared what happened to him, and that pissed her off.

A couple more thuds echoed through the dwindling Fujou forest. "Just keep me, let the others go. They're dying."

Mimi turned around in her chair, scanning the still living Fujou. "Ladies, let me tell you something about your Dame. She thinks what you do is disgusting and wrong. She was planning to undermine you and your little gunshyu as soon as she could."

"What are you doing?" Cried Hiroka. "They'll kill me!"

Mimi bent over her. "You're dead anyway. It is just how you go is up to you." She straightened back up and continued addressing the crumbling statues. "Ladies. I have no qualms with you. But I do not agree with your entertainment choices. Effective immediately, your dens in the wards under the cabal's control are to be disbanded and made illegal. Do you understand ladies? Take that back to your Governess, would you?"

At that moment, Palace loosened its grip and everyone who wasn't already on the floor dead fell down gasping for air. "You are free to go. I would appreciate it if you would be so kind as to let me keep your, should I be so bold, former Dame here for a while. I expect your dens in my wards to be vacated by the end of this week." She helped Hiroka up to her feet and ushered her towards the elevator. "Please leave at your leisure. I do apologize for those who were not strong enough. I will take care of their bodies, or you can take them with you and pay your respects." She smiled. "Good evening, ladies." She entered the elevator with Hiroka and turned around still smiling.

The doors to the elevator opened into Mimi's suite. She held onto Hiroka's arm. She was still too weak to walk on her own. Mimi guided her over to the fainting couch. She pulled up her desk chair over next to the couch. She wasn't going to sit in any of those hanging death chairs. *I have to get rid of those ugly things.*

"How was that for theatrics?" Mimi said.

Hiroka looked confused. "What do you mean?"

"Don't get me wrong. I meant every word. Those bitches better be out of my wards by week's end, or I'll come at them with full force. But I'm pretty sure they left here sure that you were as good as dead."

"I'm not?" Hiroka asked. She scooted herself up on the couch.

"Not if you play good." She sat down next to Hiroka. "We don't plan on killing you. If you cooperate, that is."

"Cooperate?"

"Yes," said Mimi. "I don't trust you. You betrayed someone who trusted you and lied to me."

"So why spare my life?" Hiroka crossed her arms in defiance.

"You can redeem yourself by working with me. Correction, for me."

"You are recruiting me?" Asked Hiroka.

"In a way. If you don't want to die."

"Then I have no choice," said Hiroka. "What role do you want me to play in your little pantomime at being a prophetess?"

Mimi smiled at the snide remark. She didn't disagree. She was playing, but just to get the feel of her newfound power and influence.

"I will not worship you and that ...," Hiroka stopped and remembered, "Palace."

Mimi kept her smile. It was starting to unnerve her interviewee. "I don't expect you to ... right away. But I have a feeling you will have a spiritual awakening sooner or later." Mimi stood up and walked over to the window looking south over her domain. "I don't know yet what role I want you to take on. I am looking for a new Nanny, but you have no assassin skills I assume."

"You assume correctly," responded Hiroka. She remained looking in the opposite direction of where Mimi was standing.

"Then, that wouldn't do." Mimi guided her gaze more westward toward the wards controlled by the Editor not very far in the distance. "But I know what I want you to do in the meantime."

"Which is?" Asked Hiroka.

"Get Yuuki out of there." She pointed toward the Tsudii wards. The vagueness of her response forced Hiroka to turn around and see where 'there' was.

Hiroka didn't sound surprised. "I'm to infiltrate one of the most impenetrable places in the Wards by myself." It's probably more secure than Juku.

"I'll give you a couple girls to help you and keep an eye on you. Who knows, if you're successful, maybe you could be in charge of special ops or something like that."

"Why are you so infatuated with that Wamono?"

Mimi was glad she asked that question. She tore herself from her view and rushed back over to Hiroka and squatted beside and a little behind her. "He's my friend. I saved him once, and there's no reason I wouldn't again. If he's still alive. If he's not, then I will just have to fire you permanently." She walked around and sat back down on the chair. "Something disgusting is happening to him right now in those jacked up gnarled hands of that little freak. And that's on you."

"I'm not proud of what I did. I had no choice."

"You always have a choice." Mimi's anger dissipated. "You could've come to me. We had just formed an alliance."

"You snuck upstairs in my den, stole a perform ... Yuuki, and killed two of my women!" Hiroka's eyes were coating over with a soft lavender

Whatever drug she's was on is starting to weaken.

"Why the fuck would I have come to you? I couldn't trust you."

The vibration of Palace buzzed through Mimi's head. "You're showing weakness."

Mimi ignored it. She knew what she was doing. It was a stalemate that neither one wanted to admit to. "O.K., yes. I admit. That was a bit rash of me. So, we don't trust each other. Let's start over."

"Agreed," said Hiroka. "But can't help thinking this is a suicide mission."

"I want this to be successful. That means you remaining alive."

"Not necessarily," vibrated Palace.

She ignored Palace and reached over to place a hand on Hiroka's knee. "I'll go with you. I'm still waiting on additional intelligence. When I get it, we'll make our move."

"This is not possible," interrupted Palace.

Mimi froze, trying to decide if she should respond or let it continue in monologue.

"The farther you go away from me, the less power you have, my dear. You witnessed that when you were able to kill Sanae so easily. I highly suggest you do not go with this traitor. You will be killed. If not by the Editor, then by her hand."

Mimi wanted to make the first move and make sure the Tsudii knew who the real power in this tenuous alliance was.

"I cannot stop you," said Palace. "But I guarantee it will not end the way you want."

Mimi took a few moments to suppress her stubbornness and take Palace's warning seriously. "On second thought, I have all the confidence that you can do this on your own."

twenty-four

*A**M I FLOATING?* **YUUKI** tapped his bare foot on the transparent surface. *Glass.* He was high above the city, a city. His voice worked its way up his throat and curled around his tongue unable to reach freedom.

He remained in the same place. It was involuntary. Many people around him were looking down, like him, but smiling and cringing. Some grabbed each other obviously afraid that they might fall through the glass floor but laughing.

He closed his eyes and tried to take deep breathes. He ignored what was far below him and concentrated on what he saw directly out in front through the windows that formed an invisible wall. There were scrapers, just like in Za-Ginsa and Shinyuyogi, but far below him. He saw a large expanse of water in the distance. He didn't remember seeing or even hearing about any large body of water in Hinodé, but he knew much less than one percent of his new home. Something within this grey matter knew that he was not looking out over Hinodé.

He looked to his left to a large, forested area standing out among the surrounding scrapers. Rooftops peeked through the almost black green. Some looked old, like part a large outdoor museum. Thin waterways surrounded the area, but no boats. It was like the whole area was on display, not quite functional. It reminded him of Aoheki. Not by appearance, but by the solitude and emptiness they shared.

He finally made himself, or was allowed, to move. He walked closer to the windows for a better view. He could barely make out the people and traffic out and below. He couldn't make out any of those bestial transport things. They all looked more like the, he couldn't remember the name Hiroka and Mimi called them, all-machine ones. He imagined how better it must smell down there with no half-beings rolling, crawling, or slithering around grunting out their misery.

He looked directly down between his feet to see if he could have a better chance of seeing human activity. "I am barefoot and in my kimono. How's that possible? I threw it out when Hiroka and I went shopping." Things started to have a nonsensical logic. "I am not here." No one was looking at him. People were laughing and pointing to what he assumed were their respective neighborhoods, workplaces, or homes. He was not existing.

A stinging rush of stale air overtook Yuuki's senses. The air smelled dirty. Everything he was taking in disappeared in an inaudible pop. He felt he had his eyes closed and wanted them to remain so. I'm back. But to where and from where? The churning of terror impending signaled that when he did wake up his nightmare would begin.

Staccato pushing and poking brought Yuuki back from his loftiness in nothing, but any physicality would be a comfort after his ghost existence. The blackness was beginning to release its suffocating embrace, an embrace Yuuki did not want to detach from. The pushing and poking became more intense as the void moved further away from him, its last tentacled wisps still trying to hold on. He fought and fought until the blackness could no longer keep him for itself. Another abandonment.

He gave up and opened his eyes. Most of his view was taken up by a gritty, pocked floor at an odd angle. The remaining sliver of the scene was dominated by terrified and terrifying eyes. Yuuki blinked trying to force his eyes into better focus, eventually allowing a face to form around the ocular being. The surrounding flesh softened the disturbed gaze; made them less demented and sadder, human.

"You with heart still thud thud," came a rough but almost inaudible voice from those eyes. Just as quickly, they disappeared, leaving only the sound of rustling and patting of feet moving away from him.

Yuuki wasn't ready to sit up or sure if he even could. The numbness of his hip pressing against the floor for who knows how long made him take the risk and sit up. He blinked a few times to re-adjust the eye that had been pressed to the floor. The room looked like a prison cell, filthy and gamey. The creature blended perfectly with its surroundings, crouched in a corner and back to him. The only thing that evidenced human was the jerking of an unruly head of hair and a spine in extreme high relief.

He scooted over to lean against the nearest wall keeping an eye on the savage person, maybe female? She had to be a prisoner like him. Who was their captor? Black hunger pains brought him more into reality. He checked to see if the ink was still in one piece and took it out of his pocket and snuck another drop. It could've been two. He was too focused on the girl. He carefully put the vessel back into his pocket. All was split-second right in a wrong world.

He felt sorry for the prisoner but didn't know what she was capable of doing. *She is sharpening a stone or leftover bone to carve me up for the best meal she would probably have in years.* There was nothing that happened to him in the past several hours and days that would convince him otherwise.

Her back was still facing him. He heard mumbling interspersed between grunts and slobbers. He wanted to know what she was saying, if anything. He would have to move closer. *She did not come after me when I moved to the wall. A good sign.*

He readied himself to scoot toward his cellmate. Before he could move a centimeter, she turned her disheveled head so fast it forced a high-pitched gasp from Yuuki. She kept her darting eyes on and around him. She was chewing something, but Yuuki couldn't tell what. It sounded biological.

"You. You. Why," said the sooty girl. Her mouth was too busy masticating the tough substance to speak in a full sentence or maybe that is how she had always spoke. "You pretty." Yuuki didn't know if that was a compliment, accusation, or another word for 'delicious'.

He had to respond if there was ever going to be any progress. Progress in what, he didn't know yet. "You are not."

She stopped chewing, her eyes ceased darting and zeroed in on his. Several seconds passed. Yuuki's heart raced. Molecules of sweat burst painfully all over his beaten body. She finally let out a screeching howl of laughter that continued for several seconds without breath. Her eyes never closing, never moving from Yuuki. Those eyes told him she would never be totally predictable. The only thing Yuuki could do was laugh along with her. Laughing with eyes wide open was more difficult than Yuuki expected.

The laughing died accompanied with fits of coughing from both, but the staring contest continued. The girl started back up chewing what remained of her meal before engaging her new cellmate. She brought one of her hands in front of her and extended it toward Yuuki. "You want?"

Yuuki stretched his neck out and squinted. It was some sort of lizard, but there was so little of it left to really tell for sure. "No, no thanks."

She shrugged and picked another fingertip-sized piece of flesh from the palm-sized corpse. "Whatever like." She finally took her eyes off him and concentrated on her meal.

He pointed to himself. "Yuuki". He bowed his head slightly and to the left in the traditional Wamono fashion.

"Greni," responded the girl.

Yuuki liked the way she pronounced her name. It started out like a quiet growl and hurried through the last two syllables.

Greni tossed the remainder of the dead creature and licked its viscous juices from her blackened fingers. Yuuki tried hard not to cringe. She put her crazed gaze back onto Yuuki. He was disturbed and relieved at the same time. "Here place, why?" She asked. Before he could answer she stood up and walked towards him.

She was quite tall and, to Yuuki's surprise, practically naked except a few strips of what was left of her clothing. He could see every muscle twitching and crunching as she walked over.

After seeing her body, he was more afraid of what she could do to him. He was big, but she would have him flat on his back in seconds. She crouched back down in front of him. Her legs spread exposing her pink sex. If was the first time he had ever witnessed female parts. He only saw crudely drawn depictions of them by his sexually frustrated peers at the seminary. They never looked that appealing, but he couldn't help staring.

Greni followed his gaze and quickly closed her legs. The slap of her thighs forced Yuuki's eyes to jump to her scowling face. His throbbing face burn with embarrassment. She chuckled but the glower remained. "Why?" She barked. Yuuki jerked his head back, thudding it against the wall and almost adding a gash to his collection of injuries.

"I do not know. I am some sort of a rarity out here."

"Same me," She huffed. "No twofootman like me," she seemed proud but sad. Yuuki learned a lot from that one broken sentence.

He was starting to enjoy her way of talking. "Twofootman" must be a translation of her word for human. He didn't know if she quite understood what he said. He decided to simplify his speaking "How long here?" He pointed down to the floor.

"Not know," was her answer. She walked, still in squat pose, and leaned against the wall beside him. They said nothing for a couple minutes, each staring at the opposite wall. Yuuki had no idea what she was thinking. Was she trying to count how many years she'd been trapped in this grungy cell?

Without warning Greni grabbed hold of his arm. The speed and tight grip sent a terror needle directly into Yuuki's heart. Greni's eyes began the shiver again and burned right through Yuuki. "What are you doing? Let go!" Yuuki cried out. He struggled to get away, but Greni's hand was too tight around his arm. There was no way she was going to let go. He felt her sharp dirty and rotted-flesh-caked fingernails pierce through his sleeve and almost the skin. The pain was intensifying every second. Her lips moved as if she were talking very fast, but very little sound was coming out. He wanted to scream for help but knew no one would come save him. For all he knew, this was why he was put in with her. Maybe this was some kind of sick sport a group of horrid people was watching through a secreted hole in one of the corners. He convinced himself he could hear cheering and yelling of those who bet on Greni and cursing from those stupid enough to bet on him.

"There is no betting. No one watching us. We are all alone," said Greni.

Yuuki couldn't think straight. "What?"

"You shouldn't be out here," she said. Yuuki heard a fatherly tone come out of the possessed woman. "Why did you commit such blasphemy?"

"Kugai?" Yuuki said looking directly into Greni's eyes. "How? Who?"

Greni's dehumanized eyes widened to a size that frightened Yuuki even more. She screamed at such a high pitch he had to scrunch his shoulders up to protect his ears. Yuuki continued to struggle from her grip.

The piercing stopped in mid scream. "Sssspiiiider." Yuuki smelled the death on her breath. Her eyes still stretching beyond their physical limits. She raised her free hand and pointed a shaking grimy finger at him. Her eyes had not blinked since she grabbed hold of him. She took in a deep breath and released with a smile. "You're a good boy," she said. Her voice now hiss coated supported by an undertone of rasp.

Yuuki pulled and pulled trying to get away from Greni's grasp. It was working. The aching vice was starting to give way. The force created by the bizarre trance Greni was in was having the opposite effect on her strength. Finally, his sleeve was given back to him, and he quickly shuffled to the farthest corner.

His legs couldn't get any closer to his chest, but he tried anyway. His body spasmed with electrifying chills. Greni's breathing wasn't slowing or getting less raspy. But she was tiring. The channeling or whatever that possessed her was taking its toll. It was as if they had both finished a one-hundred-lap race around the cramped cell. He started to wonder if they would both suffocate from their exhalations.

Greni, now on all fours, was a wounded animal too tired to run away from his memories. She raised her head, her knotted mane thankfully hiding those bulging eyes. "You. Arrive. Bigman." She panted after every utterance as if she had been running down her prey for hours.

Yuuki didn't understand but thankful she was back to her normal voice and manner of speaking. *You arrive bigman*, he repeated to himself. He couldn't afford to think about such puzzles. He was a rat cornered by a starving beaten stray cat. He had to reserve his mental capacity for any split-second reaction he would need to remain in this cycle.

A strangely welcoming mechanical sound came from the door. It opened revealing a diminutive silhouette backlit by a sickly orange aura, arms unfolding and readying for action or attack. It spoke. "Apologies for not coming sooner to greet you. I just learned of a death of someone of somewhat importance. A nasty assassination. Anyway, your kind are hard to come by, did you know that?"

Yuuki was too entranced by the dancing arms and fingers to answer. "Who ... who are you?" Every bad feeling he had experienced weighed him down at his core.

"I'm your master now."

A cold heat sent shivers down Yuuki's back and up and through his skull.

Yuuki's 'master' moved further in followed by a much larger silhouette blacking out the orange glow. It veered left toward Greni, allowing the orange to throw a meagre dawn into the room. Pointed brown and yellow stained bones curved downward on either side of the giant's chin. *Tusks? Fangs? What in Gou's Retribution?*

The weird small one gave a nod to yet another barely there black apparition at the center of the glow. Before Yuuki could register the minute signal, Tusk, as good a name as any, thrust his tusked fangs underneath Greni and scooped her up. The brute tossed her in the air only to be caught in the cradle of the enormous teeth, which moved back and forth under her. Blood began trickling over them.

They are serrated. They are sawing into Greni! She is not even screaming. He couldn't watch. But how could he ignore the slow killing of a maybe-friend?

Which was more unconscionable? His guilt gaze ended up back at those massive black circles of nothingness staring at him. Yuuki wasn't sure if the little creature was human. Greni seemed more so.

"That's enough," ordered the Editor. He smiled at Yuuki, exposing grey triangular teeth dripping black.

Everything is so sharp and deadly out here?

"There. She won't be a nuisance while we become acquainted."

"There's something about this monk," said Draw. "I'm feeling slighter weaker."

An idol? The Editor stared at Yuuki in complete silence. *He's only been out a few days.*

"We're going to have to find whatever it is and get rid of it before they get any stronger." Draw's realization translated into the Editor's blood coursing through his arteries, veins, and even capillaries faster than normal.

"I assume their relationship is new. The disruption I am experiencing is quite weak. Nowhere near as debilitating as it was with that Palace."

The arms, still in silhouette, unfurled to their widest, fingers still drawing something of nothing. The diminutive monster formed another damaged smile. "It seems we need to be formerly introduced. I'm the Prophet of Draw." The Editor bowed with his crumpled hands forming a chest-tight prayer gesture.

The Editor. Mimi had mentioned that title. If Mimi were here, he would be dead on the floor probably bleeding from several wounds, mostly from his headless neck. But a very deeply religious part of him couldn't help but feel pity for him. *His Retribution must be a vengeful horror.*

"Where am I," Yuuki at last said. His voice sounded strange to him.

"You're in my exhibit of the rare and unusual of this wonderful city, my city, and you are now part of it."

The Editor's tone told Yuuki he was doing him a favor by choosing him to be an exhibit. *He's a crazy monster.* He started to appreciate the calculating realism of Ryudasu. He tried to steal a look at Greni to see is she was breathing. He couldn't tell.

The Editor followed his gaze over to the unconscious Greni. "That's been with us for quite a while now. One of the last, if not the last, of the Realsayers." Yuuki had a hard time concentrating, and the Editor's hypnotic hands were not making it any easier.

The Editor continued un-phased. "Unfortunately, her 'people' didn't quite appreciate my embrace when I took control a northern ward where they tended to gather." He signaled the Illustrator to command the oaf to ungently nudge the Realsayer to make sure she was still alive. Tusk shrugged his shoulders. Again, the Editor was non-plussed. "They had to be expunged."

Yuuki looked over to his fellow prisoner. Her eyes were open but lifeless. *There were so, so alive only a few minutes before.* They shocked him into an overwhelming, almost epiphanic, realization of adulthood. Only an adult would be able to realize the moment his life was over.

The Editor read the terror on Yuuki's face. "Don't worry. She shouldn't give you too much trouble." He bent down and stared into Greni's eyes, keeping a safe distance. "Will you, my precious last-of?"

The Editor's arms slowly began moving back into himself as he walked out of the cell. He looked at the being producing the orange sun and pointed toward Yuuki. "Write your Character to get the Wamono prepared and bring him up." He turned toward his precious acquisition with the never horrifying greasy smile broken only by the frenetic arms, breaking up the smile into flashes searing even deeper into Yuuki's reluctant memory. "We need a chat, you and I, but in more civilized surroundings." His silhouette disappeared into the orange glow that followed him.

Yuuki looked over at the possible dead Realsayer. No movement. *She was the last of her kind. None left.*

"Put this on." The unnatural creature shoved a Wamono-style kimono into Yuuki's chest.

Yuuki looked at Tusk, preparing to protest but thought better of it. He waited for Tusk to turn around to give him privacy, but the man monster kept focus on his charge.

"Now," he demanded.

Yuuki started to put the heavy Wamono garb over what he was already wearing to save time, an extra mass of failure.

"Stop!" Tusk shouted even though the two were no more than a meter apart. "Drop the Kimono. Clothes off first. My prophet wants ... authenticity." The last word had that weight of having been recently learned.

Yuuki let the kimono thud to the floor and began stripping out of his pants. The ink fell out of the pocket, luckily landing silently on the wadded kimono, black blending in black. Aware of his nakedness, he instantly cupped his genitals to protect them from the mocking air and gaze.

Tusk looked down at the dark halo of hair around Yuuki's groin-protecting hand. He smiled, exposing silver teeth nestled uncomfortably between the tusks. "Ain't anything special. Dress."

Yuuki bent to pick up the kimono, cupping the precious ink in his free hand, and put on the kimono. He secreted the vile in the sleeve pocket. *The map!* He almost forgot about his other constant companion. *No time. Useless anyway.*

Tusk stomped through the cell doorway, Yuuki just behind. He took one last look inside to see if anything moved with life. Still lifeless.

One pupil did follow them.

As Tusk was about to slam the cell door, a scream that could have easily ripped the skin from Yuuki's flesh rushed out followed by a very alive Greni. She leapt onto Tusk's head already scratching and biting. Yuuki jumped back and out of the way. She furiously gnawed at Tusk's neck and ears, very careful to stay away from those enormous, serrated fangs. Giant and Realsayer splattered in blood.

She is eating him! Predator and her prey were now on the floor. Tusk's fight was slowing down into life-leaving spasms. Yuuki heard Greni almost purring with delight, even ecstasy, while she chewed. *The Gou-Tairei has abandoned this world, and I abandoned it.*

The huntress snapped her head up to Yuuki. Her mouth dripping gore. If he made the slightest movement, she might abandon the now unexciting kill and move on to something more with a struggle.

Greni's purpose-focused gaze remained on Yuuki, chewing her cud of skin and muscle. "Go. Arrive. Bigman," said Greni. Yuuki could barely understand her with the mouthful of flesh, now accompanied with crunching cartilage or bone. "Go!"

Why is she doing this? He knew from his near-death experience with Ryudasu not to trigger the killer instinct. Those eyes had to have a very different story to tell under that hard gloss of rage.

"Go! Arrive bigman." Bits of flesh spewed out of her grisly ravenous mouth.

Yuuki followed Greni's wild pupils to a set of stairs and quickly ran up into another place of nothing.

"Are you hurt?"

Yuuki stopped, every pore exhaled a cold drop of sweat. He brought his wrist up to his face. "I'm fine, I think."

"That giant's incomplete task will not go unnoticed for much longer." Charm's voice infused Yuuki a much need sense of practicality. "We have to continue up and hope that a door to the outside finds us at the top."

Yuuki didn't know what outside was anymore. He was in a constant inside nothing, but a nothing with borders—with walls. The narrow stairwell mocked him with its profound taunting blackness. Nothing was solid. He wasn't standing on anything or anywhere. *There is nothing to grab hold of. I ... I ... I am falling. No, floating. The walls are crushing me?! No, none of that! There is only nothing. I AM nothing!*

The mass of nothing slammed him into the very real ground. The nothing world also went silent

twenty-five

IT HAD ALMOST BEEN twenty years since Shinya set his eyes on the city of murder and rape, longer than his life in it. He found himself looking over his shoulders waiting for someone to attack or even kill him.

Passersby looked at him with a strange combination of surprise and antipathy, short glances to make sure they saw what they saw. His pockets jingled with different colored hair beads for when his hair became long enough. Hégo gave him and the others strict orders to remain Wamono on the outside. They were ambassadors. The only concession was coverings for their feet.

Shinya found it difficult to start walking away from the main entrance. The Shisa towered above him someplace out of sight. A special impromptu tunnel had been constructed to circumvent the voracious guardians. He could almost feel their hot breathing on him—or was it his nerves? *How can I find Yuuki in a place like this?* He took an awkward step further away. His feet were not yet used to being cramped in shoes. The constraining material pinched at his toes and bit his heels. He wanted to take them off but remembered their necessity.

He took out a piece of paper from his sleeve pocket, unfolded it, and looked at it for a few seconds. It wasn't the first time. He had pretty much memorized it through clandestine glances during the few times he was alone in his cell. It was a rough map of Hinodé. It caused a minor scandal when the new missionaries were handed their copies. It wasn't very detailed. It couldn't be since it was made from the faded memories of one of several middle-aged monks sequestered in a small room until their shameful task was complete. The mappers could not be too old as to have their maps be automatically outdated or too young for such memories and actions to trigger them. The street layout seemed to be accurate. The main streets and viscerdenn stations made up most of the map, leaving many areas blank.

He had no idea who the other volunteers were or how many. Hégo and Ogushu decided it would be better that way. They didn't want a community of un-cloistered Wamono forming and 'adjusting' to their evil environment as the defunct Smashers had done. He was assigned to canvass in nearby Akibi district. none of the Honored Exiles were assigned to their home neighborhoods to repress an additional layer of temptation. But nothing would stop him from hopping on a viscerdenn to his childhood home—nothing except the worst Retribution the Gou-Tairei could release. But he was willing to risk a tortured next life to find Yuuki.

He was told to follow the green arrows on the map to meet his contact, a supposed uncorrupted Smasher descendent residing around Akibi for the past decade or so. He didn't even know his name. This Smasher would set him up with a place to stay and give him a weekly stipend.

He was nervous to meet a Smasher. He had heard those who remained true to their destructive mission and their descendants were fanatic and would stop at nothing to destroy as many potential Inanimates as they could, no matter the collateral damage. He could only imagine what massive strings Hégo had to pull to get the Dai-Master to allow his little missionary endeavor.

He stumbled a little bit as he started to follow the arrows. He fought the urge to look up at the immense scrapers all around to concentrate on his walking. Somehow looking down at his artificial feet helped. He didn't remember that many scrapers when he first arrived at Aoheki those twenty years ago. But the architectural layout of the area was not exactly forefront in his mind at the time. He was a scared, distraught twelve-year-old boy who had just made the hardest decision of his life. He huffed an ironic chuckle as he walked down the smelly viscergassy street. *I was so grown up even at twelve.*

His highly anticipated manga reports at school seemed ridiculous. Watching his mother suffer and be embarrassed every time she looked at her son was too much for him. *Should I find her?* He still could not bring himself to give himself an answer.

He looked back one last time at the barrier walls. He never understood why he came specifically to Aoheki. There were probably cloisters much closer to his former home. It was the incomprehensible thought processes of a young boy. He vaguely remembered looking at a map and randomly picking one of the dozen or so large black blocks farthest from his mother.

There was something bulging and lumbering far above on one of the walls. "Ryudasu," he whispered. He was amazed at how she did not just plummet to the ground far below. *Hideous. I am glad Yuuki never had to see her.*

He turned away from the walls and Aoheki. "No longer my life." He resumed his awkward guided walk. Eventually, he made out his destination only a couple dozen meters away. The spot was open, a kind of square paved with alternating dull red and brown bricks. Many people scurried about, most talking to themselves blissfully unaware of their surroundings. He stood there watching the human city whirl by him not paying attention to the rare Wamono standing in their paths.

"You must be Shinya," came a soft masculine voice to his left.

Shinya, startled at hearing his name, turned to the voice. For a frightening and hopeful second, he thought it was his long dead father. "Yes, I am Shinya. You must be ... whom I am supposed to meet."

"Yes. My name is Kazunori. I'll be looking after you for a few days until you get on your," he looked down to Shinya's feet, "new feet." He smiled.

That smile was what Shinya needed. *I hope that smile is not just for the public to see*, he thought. He had pictured his mentor as stern and unforgiving, expecting him to know everything in just a few minutes. He still could be that way.

"Let's get you back to my place. I don't live very far from here. I'm sure you are a bit overwhelmed." He placed his hand on Shinya's shoulder to guide him to one of the exits of the square. "How long have you been residing at Aoheki?"

"About twenty years, Sama." Shinya didn't know how to address him. He didn't look much older.

"Just call me Kazu," responded the unexpectedly gentle Smasher. "I'm getting the impression you expected someone different."

"I heard stories." Shinya wanted to shut himself up before he said anything else that might truly offend this stranger.

"Stories?" Asked Kazu. He didn't stop walking and kept his hand on Shinya's shoulder. "What kind of stories?" The Smasher's smile turned into more of a smirk.

"I am sorry, I should not have said anything. I am sure they are just exaggerations. You know how monks get about Keibu-yo."

"Wow, it's been a while since I heard that name. Well, those stories are probably true." Kazu's face contracted into a serious blankness.

Shinya's pores verged on exploding nervous sweat. *I knew it was too good to be true.*

Kazu's smile reappeared. "We are no longer the original Smashers that were sent out by the Dai-Masters generations ago. We modern Smashers were born here, distorted into whatever this crazy city wants us to be. There are a few of us who carry on the original mission, some more zealous than others." He finally took his hand off Shinya's shoulder. "Come, I'll fill you in once we get home." The smile was static, it never grew or contracted. Shinya could not be sure which "us" was this Kazu.

twenty-six

Y UUKI AWOKE INSIDE A transparent case in dark room, his head aching. Hot streams flowed down the side of his face and neck. He tried to feel his head, but his arms and head were secured with restraints connected to the sides of the case. The light-phobic room strained his eyes. He closed them, hoping to wake up out of this nightmare. But hope had become its own nightmare.

"Open your eyes so I can be seen!" Spittle from the Editor splattered on the glass in front of Yuuki's face. He wore his black leather straight jacket for times he needed a rest from his exhausting spastic arms.

Yuuki involuntarily obeyed. His only view for a few seconds was the grey sputum smearing down the panel.

"That's better," said the Editor. "You had a nasty fall on those stairs. Luckily Nineteen here found you. You behaved very badly, my little Gou worshipper."

Is there even a reason to worship it anymore, worship anything? Yuuki tried to move his head around to figure out where he ended up, but the restraints connecting his neck to the corners of his case, forced him to remain facing the terrible half-of-man. The oversized black glasses double reflected Yuuki's portrait. The raising and scrunching of eyebrows barely escaped the black nothings.

"I have a dead Character and lost one of my cherished exhibits." The Editor walked behind Yuuki, keeping an obvious distance. "Thanks to you and that depraved creature girl, I have to spend thousands of kané to have a mixi-machi quack scrounge up some parts for me. Characters just don't make themselves!"

Yuuki remained defiant in his silence. It was strangely safe inside the glass box. He wished it weren't see-through.

"I get it. You don't want to talk to me," said the Editor. Yuuki had no idea where the Editor was now. That scared him more than having the stretched bloodless face in front of him. The familiar sound of paper being unfolded came from where the voice was but higher.

The Editor re-appeared directly in front Yuuki, though at a distance. The constant assault of the warped visage gave Yuuki shivers.

"I'll forgive your little attempt at escaping if you tell me what this map is of and what this note means." A Character slammed the opened map against Yuuki's case, forcing him to jerk back. The restraints counteracted the knee-jerk response. The pain crunched his skull and neck muscles. The Editor's old phlegm glued it in place. "The author claims to be a long-lost relative of mine. Sounds like crazed gibberish."

"I do not know." It wasn't the answer his captor wanted to hear, but it was the truth. He couldn't say anything else.

"I don't know, what?" quickly responded the Editor.

Yuuki thought for a long couple of seconds. "I do not know, my prophet."

"Quick learner." The Editor's slick grin finally subsided, transforming into an impatient grimace. "But a terrible liar." His voice the timbre of the irrationally irritated.

"I am sorry, my prophet. She said it would help me get around out here." Yuuki regretted his words milliseconds after they seeped out from his brain and onto his traitor tongue.

"She? Who?" The Editor's curiosity overpowered angry impatience. He sat down on the sofa next to Yuuki's clear confines. He gave a quick nod to someone off to his side. Two Characters turned the disobedient collector's item to face him.

Where is Charm? Yuuki thought. *I do not know anything. Why does no one understand that?* Proto tears began stinging the inside of his eyelids, and that is where they would remain. *I do not owe that monster anything. She lied to me.* "Her name is Genkou Ryudasu. She gave me that map."

"Who and where is this Genkou Ryudasu? Tell me, monk!" His impatience was back in full force.

Yuuki at this point had nothing more to lose except his life, and that was no longer worth much to anybody, even to him. "I will tell you if you do not send me back down there. Keep me up here with you, my prophet."

The Editor's face exploded in wet laughter. "You negotiating with me? Listen, you little reclusive freak, I may not be able to physically sever your Symb bond without killing you, but I can make your life not worth living."

"Don't be frightened Yuuki," vibrated the voice from Yuuki's charm

Yuuki was about to respond but thought it better not to appear talking to himself.

"He's much more concerned than he's letting on. Just keep talking. He will have to agree to your terms. There's some kind of connection between him and that map, but he's not sure what it is."

Yuuki kept his focus on the matter at hand. "I am not asking you to free me. Keep me here, with you, my prophet."

"That's good," said Charm. "Megalomania is quite easy to manipulate. We are dangerous, but you are also precious ... for now."

The Editor sat back thinking, arms squirming against their leathery crisscross restraints. Yuuki stared at him to present bravery and that he knew the power of being in Symb. Both fallacies.

"Very well. You'll be on permanent display. You'll be part of my entourage."

The grimace of his captor looked like he was having an argument with himself. "Agreed," Yuuki said. "I will be happy to tell you everything I know about Genkou Ryudasu."

"Be careful, Yuuki," vibrated Charm. "We need to be and remain valuable to him." The uninflected voice calmed Yuuki enough to gain back some of his logical mind.

I'm hungry. I need more ink. Hunger, addictive hunger, did not care about logic, fear, or death. It only cared about being satiated.

"Keep focused. We can be more powerful than any drug." responded Charm.

You hear my thoughts. The question came out as axiom.

"What's got into you, monk?" said the Editor. "You look like you saw a ghost. Believe me, I'm very real."

"I can." Said Charm. That means Communion."

What? Yuuki struggled to keep this gray-matter conversation from escaping through his mouth.

"Communion," repeated Charm.

"Helloo, anyone there?" The Editor's pursed bloodless lips making him look like a senile old man. "Now, let's talk about this Genkou."

As Yuuki was finishing his explanation of who and what Ryudasu was, or what he thought she was, one of those weird thin men rushed up and whispered something urgent into the Editor's ear. "Go away, Nineteen, I'm busy listening to this little Wamono fantasy!"

I'm sorry my prophet, but this is quite urgent." Nineteen took the risk and commandeered his prophet's ear.

"A coup? That lunatic daughter dead too?" The Tsudii prophet put his eye-balled face up against the transparent wall. "You need to do better than spin a ridiculous Wamono monster story. I'll be back for the truth." With only a frustrated grumble he left the suite taking most of the thin men including the messenger with him, leaving Yuuki alone with a couple Characters looming in the corners with one thin man busily drawing on his glowing board.

The events of the past days or weeks began to flood the almost pleasant void left by the deranged man. Walking back to Shinyuyogi station with Hiroka seemed weeks old. *Is she alright?*

"I wouldn't worry about her. How do you think that strange man knew about the map?"

Yuuki did not want to succumb to the obvious and admit his potentially fatal gullibility. *He could have found it on me while I was unconscious.*

"Let's not talk about her now. We have more immediate issues to address. Do you remember what that Greni said to you?"

That I will arrive bigman?

"Yes. Our captor said that she was a realsayer. It seems like she tells some kind of future truth. Assuming that and that we are in Communion, I feel that you, we, will become important, or as she colorfully put it 'arrive bigman'."

Yuuki giggled at the absurd phrase coming from such non-emotion.

"What's so funny, Wamono?" said the lone Illustrator, pen in hand threatening to sick his Characters on Yuuki. His voice was almost whining.

Yuuki could not answer. It wasn't that funny.

The Illustrator walked closer to the prized exhibit. The light from his board casting an unnatural orange-yellow glow over his face. "Maybe this will wipe that smirk off your pudgy face." The Illustrator finger-signaled to one of the Characters without taking his sclera-less eyes off the exhibit. "Take him down to the zoo." He looked down at his board and began sketching.

"No, please! I will stay quiet, I promise." He could not bear returning to the scene of cannibalistic savagery. It was bad enough he would never forget.

"Too late," the Illustrator whined. He made another long stroke, commanding one of the Characters to push the display case toward the elevator door. The sudden force jerked Yuuki in the opposite direction. "You can play heretic and converse with that Inanimate of yours all you want, but not here in this sacred space. The prophet would agree."

The restraints fought against the Character's power with their own short inertial tug-o-war with Yuuki's limbs and neck. *Charm! Do something. We must be powerful enough to get ourselves out of this!* No response.

The Illustrator kept his concentration on his board, ignoring the ruckus in front of him. "Throw him in that realsayer's cell," he ordered.

Yuuki struggled harder once he heard the Illustrator's latest order. *I do not want to go back down there. Charm!*

"It should be dead by now," added the tangerine-tanned controller.

Dead? Yuuki's futile struggling died away. *She escaped. That is what the Editor said. He lost her.*

"Don't fight it." Charm finally vibrated through Yuuki's head. "We can't do anything in this box. We'll think of something down in that cell."

You want me to give up? Yuuki was losing his ability to trust the idol. *Evil is in every thing!*

The character violently pushed the prison case into the elevator, slamming it into the back wall. Yuuki never felt so small or weak.

"I know you are overwhelmed, Yuuki-Hana," said Charm, but you have to believe that I want nothing more than your freedom from this place. Our lives are entwined. You have yet to comprehend this." He imagined Charm as a disappointed father.

Yuuki couldn't continue arguing with the Inanimate. Greni's corpse decomposing in that fetid cell far below confined him in despair.

Constant pain formed a pillow of numbness. Yuuki didn't open his eyes or even breathe, afraid of what those senses might detect. He didn't have to see where he was. He could keep his eyes closed but would eventually have to breathe.

He first exhaled the stale air he was keeping inside then as slowly as his oxygen-starved lungs would allow, took in the atmosphere of the cell. A stench did hit him, but it wasn't putrid as expected. He cautiously opened his eyes. The eye closest to the floor only saw a blur of the uneven stone, and the less obstructed one registered more stone, just in more focus. He heard gurgling from behind him.

"Bigman."

"Greni?" He twisted his neck to see his failed rescuer. There was nothing left of her but a bloody and bruised ball of skin and hair. He forgot his own pain and crawled over to her. Her face was barely recognizable. Welts pocked her face separated by a couple slow streams of blood. Most were dried beds. She had been left to starve helped by whatever greedy infection festered in any one of her numerous lesions.

"We should help her," said Charm. "She's the key."

"Of course I am going to help her." He carefully reached under her oozing head and cradled it in his lap. His body heat and compassion were his only charity.

"Bigman," Greni gurgled again. Her eyes trying to remain open to see her comforter.

"Shhh, Greni. You need your strength to get better."

She laughed, which quickly mutated into coughing, spewing blood and spit over Yuuki's arm and chest. Charm's metallic silver began to rouge.

She ignored Yuuki's advice and continued to force words out of her swollen torn lips. "Get out. Arrive Bigman. Save city and city." She closed her eyes, going limp in Yuuki's arms.

"Greni." Yuuki shook his arms in hopes of waking her up. "Greni!" He shook her a bit harder. "I do not want to be alone." Selfishness always accompanied compassion. He had never been this close to death. Death had always been part of a continuum, a theory. Final death was a goal reached at entrance to one of the Cycles-end Cities. How could someone in so much pain and broken be able to simply pass on to something else?

"Yuuki, your thoughts are in chaos. I'm having a difficult time understanding you," said Charm. "She's dead."

Yuuki ignored Charm's cold fact. "Greni, come on. Come back. He was proud of his humanity, in contrast to Charm's inhumanity. It made him want to try everything he could to bring this almost stranger back to the living. "We must be able to do something. If we have any kind of power, we should use it now."

"I'm sorry Yuuki, but we don't."

"You do not care!" Tears streaked his grimy cheeks.

"You're right, I don't. I can't. I can only care about the Symb."

"The Symb." Anger scraped over his voice like sandpaper. "Not even me." Yuuki began to rock back and forth giving any comfort he could to the woman now dead in his arms.

"It's who I am," explained the Inanimate. "Have confidence in your faith. Metempsychosis will transfer her to a more evolved being for her deed. It could even be her final death, if that helps."

"What do you know about my faith? I will throw you away! Will be the first thing I do when I get out of here." Yuuki stood up, Greni still in his arms, and walked over to a less grimy spot at the other end of the wall away from the bones and grizzle of her last few meals.

"I am sorry. I will try to be more sensitive to your emotions. You are free to throw me away. But I must warn you, only warn, that if you do physically separate us, there will be serious consequences out of my control."

Yuuki didn't know how to respond, so didn't. He set Greni down and positioned her sitting with her back against the wall. He crossed her legs and folded her arms in her lap, bone sticking through one. Her head drooped down as if she were meditating. Yuuki did the same.

The death quiet awakened his black hunger. He reached into his sleeve for the small vessel of black comfort. He let the contents empty and coat every tastebud, no longer caring if he followed Ryudasu's directions. Killing the craving was all that mattered.

He needed to think. It was the only thing the Editor could not imprison. He suspected that would be Charm's job. But the escape to sleep was too much of a temptation.

He was asleep only a few minutes before waking in the outskirts of another strange city or part of Hinodé.

As with his other two dream visions, this city was completely different. It was not of Hinodé's past like his first vision of his family's storefront and wasn't that peaceful city through glass high above. This city or time was sooty, charred, and smelled as it looked. It was if a gigantic torch was set upon this city. The fumes of burnt rubber and overheated wiring singed the inside of his nostrils. There was no sound but the almost silent whisperings of the billowing smoke columns rising where sparkling glass scrapers probably used to be.

What happened? Yuuki turned in a full circle. The cooked city looked the same no matter from what angle. *Is this the same city I was in before? 'City and city' Greni said?* Greni's plea had unwrapped its logic. Death has a way of taking over the moment. "Charm, are you here too?" As usual, no response.

He was not standing on the ground. He was on the roof of a building, one of the few apparently still standing. He wasn't as high as in his last dream, but he had a view of the blackened wasteland surrounding him. "It is a graveyard." He had to cover his mouth with his kimono sleeve to protect his throat from the smoke that finally found him. His eyes stung with burning tears and mostly useless. But he could still make out a tall spire-like structure in the distance.

I know that tower. No, I have felt it. He put his hand over his eyes trying to get a better look. It didn't help. There was not much sun to shield his vision from. *I was there in my last dream.* He dropped his hand and scanned the horizon. "This is the same city." The realization made him weak-kneed. *Why am I sad? Is this place is even real.*

He squatted, scrunching his knees up to his chest, and hid his face between the gap. He had seen enough of the dead city. He thought of Greni and how she could somehow channel the future in people. "Am I seeing a future as well?"

He braved more exposure and lifted his head to take in the disturbing view now that he knew a little bit more about it. "This must be Hinodé. Where else could it be? What kind of war was going to happen that could result in this?" A strong breeze hugged him. He took advantage of the smokeless bubble and peaked up over the ledge to take in as much as he could of the cremated city before the suffocating smoke returned.

Nothing looked familiar, but nothing in present Hinodé looked familiar to him. The weightlessness of his gut gave him a sense of disembodiment; that he didn't belong anywhere, that nothing, not even Aoheki, was no longer familiar. He screamed out into the thick caustic air, but it didn't matter. Everyone was dead.

twenty-seven

A **MALIGNANT STUMP OF a** candle struggled to keep its feeble flame alive, It was the sole light source in the Editor's private study, the only place the Editor and Draw could be alone. He didn't use his windowless study often. He preferred to be surrounded by others, especially those who worshipped him, but recent events and discoveries made solitude a necessity. News was still sparse regarding the coup in Deka-cho. Until Storyliner Genta breaks through the mental barrier put up by Palace, there wasn't much to do with that. He looked down at the Wamono's map and note. A bizarre need to remember became more important.

He took his glasses off, shielding his eyes from the initial shock of the candle flame's anemic existence with his raptor hands. He tried to lower his barely functioning eyelids to squint, his pupils so used to gorging on darkness shrank in terror from light shock, almost disappearing into giant red-grey irises rarely exposed. He alternated his gaze between the map and note.

The most bizarre part of the message, and all of it was quite bizarre, was that it instructed him to lick from a small non-life-threatening wound he needed to inflict upon his prized Wamono. Licking wounds was not strange but being instructed to do so by someone, or something, calling him cousin was. It was addressed to a Futoshi and indirectly to a brother Atsushi. Neither Futoshi nor

Atsushi was his birth name, but something picking at the back of his brain told him that one of the names is associated with him.

A slight electric treble chilled the Editor's spine. "So, what do you make of this message?"

You know I can't make anything out of it.

"Read it out loud, maybe that will help."

"Namatani brother Futoshi," he began. "You are not who you happen to be. Ingest the enriched blood of the Wamono you acquired, and you will begin to remember a life we have all have been betrayed into forgetting and return to the world we belong. Keep the Wamono close and alive. Consume small amounts of his blood daily until you fully remember. The power you may have now is nothing to what you will possess. After you and the Suriidii queen (your real bother, Atsushi), fully remember, find me at the walls of the Aoheki Wamono cloister - Your cousin, Makoto."

"Ren ... your brother? A Wamono, your cousin? Very odd."

Ren is not my brother! A traitorous business partner, yes. Brother, definitely not. This Makoto is a fraud. He stared at the bare black wall in front of him, a faint whisper within the deep distance of his mind told him there was truth in this.

"Get out of me!" The Editor pulled at his ears, trying to get Draw out of his mind. He fought the urge, like many times before, to rip out the physicality of Draw from his left breast. The warning it made that if he ever tried, a thick slab of flesh would be ripped out as well. "You are behind this! Why this lie?" His sketching hands pulled at his hair, a few strands sacrificed to the candle stuttering flame.

"I am not lying. An Impossibility." Draw labored constantly to stave off complete incapacitating insanity.

Clumps of hair sweat-glued to his jittery palms, and saliva drizzled down his chin and onto the enigmatic message. His heavy breathing tossed strands of the spittle across the desk. "You want me to crack. Sorry to disappoint you, my friend Draw."

"If you crack, I crack. We both die. Insanity is not fatal until it is, and we must fight that as long as we can."

The Editor's breathing slowed. He wiped the drool from his lips and looked down at the message. *What if we can become more powerful, that there is something more out there.* This whispery voice was not that of Draw.

Draw, ever practical, had cautiously made room for other voices a host may harbor, even pseudo-unconsciously. "You are contemplating ingesting that Wamono. You are prepared to follow those words."

He put his glasses back on and walked over to the candle. He forced his arm muscles to lift his hand over the flickering starving flame. He watched the individual strands of hair clinging to his palm singe into tiny embers. He imagined each one screaming their last screams. His smile widened more after each little murder and whispered, "Let's get that Wamono up here."

Yuuki almost fell into the Editor's study from the force of the Character behind him. He was more prepared this time.

The Editor stood in the shadow created by the long-suffering candle flame. A sulfurous odor permeated the room. "Give the Character your arm."

Yuuki watched the Editor's hypnotic arms do their bizarre ritual. The trance quickly dissipated and Yuuki turned toward the giant. His arms seemed to have been ripped from a muscular reptilian, with the appropriate gut-ripping claws.

Yuuki looked up toward lizard-man's face. Fangs dug deep into his lower lip; years of painful gouging created the perfectly fitted craters to hold the oversized canines in place.

Charm. Yuuki needed the Inanimate's advice. *What do I do?*

"Give him the damn arm, Wamono!" The Editor was losing patience.

"He can't sever our bond, remember?" Charm finally responded.

I'm sure that lizard monster can torture without doing anything to our bond.

"So, you'd better do what he says."

Yuuki slowly extended his arm. Before he could get it away from his body, Lizard-man grabbed and yanked it toward him. The sudden movement revealed a faint orange glow behind the creature. Yuuki winced preparing himself for bone-crushing pain, but no such pain materialized. He had a firm grip, but just enough to make sure Yuuki couldn't escape it. Yuuki looked into the monster's eyes. One eye was a deep indigo and the other an almost lemon yellow, but they were vacant. *He's waiting for the next command*, thought Yuuki.

"Now, make a cut." The Editor's voice now more urgent than frustrated. Yuuki noticed him directing his commands to the orange glow behind the Character. "Don't make it deep, Nineteen. Just enough to bleed. I need him to live." The Editor tilted his head up towards the Wamono. "For a little while longer, anyway." The smile that broke out on the Editor's face creating jaundiced ripples around his glasses.

The Character took out a small blade from somewhere on his body. Yuuki couldn't tell from where, he was too transfixed on the horror that was the Editor's face. The makeshift surgeon pushed up the kimono sleeve and almost gently turned the arm overexposing the soft underside. Yuuki closed his eyes tight waiting for his brain to register the slice into his flesh. The pain finally rushed his brain in full agony.

Yuuki clenched his teeth, turning what would've been a scream into more of a growl. The imagined or real sound of his skin slicing open forced him to look. What he saw made him immediately forget the pain of his flesh being violated.

The wound was neat and not that long, small in fact but felt like it ran down his entire arm. What was oozing out was more terrifying. His blood was a reddish-black, expanding out from the incision. *That Aku poisoned me; I poisoned me!*

Lizard-man showed the blackening arm to his prophet. Yuuki let the Character control him like a bloody, grimy doll. It was no longer his blood, no longer him, just greasy rotten curd.

The Editor smiled, exposing his ruined maw. He reached out one of his disproportionately long fingers toward the fresh cut. It shivered from obvious pain as it lowered into a small pool of Yuuki's inky blood. "Mmm, warm." The Editor was almost purring.

Yuuki was too afraid to do anything else but stand still and watch.

The Editor retracted his finger and just as painfully put it up to his lips. His tongue protruded lapping up the viscous slime slowly dibbling down over the nail. "Slightly salty. Not bad." He continued to clean the rest of the blood from his finger with his creature of a tongue. "Take that cup over there and put it under his arm."

The Character did as he was told through his controller while maintaining the same inescapable grip on Yuuki's arm.

"Turn the arm over and let the blood drip into the cup."

Without any show of agency, the Character continued to do what he was told by his prophet. Yuuki could only watch his foreign blood slowly drip into the cup, every long thick drop making the slightest plop as it landed and combined with its siblings.

After the cup filled a quarter of the way, the editor motioned the Illustrator to stop the Character's current job. "That's enough, we don't want to get greedy on the first dose, do we?" He looked directly at Yuuki, still with that terrible smile. With the momentum still in his reanimated arms, he grabbed the cup and held it up over his mouth. He silently signaled the Illustrator to have the Character hold his arms steady in the pour position while waiting for the syrupy blood to finally escape the cup and fall into his mouth.

He's consuming me. He began salivating.

The Editor swished the blood around in his mouth, savoring every stained blood cell.

Yuuki wanted to put his wound to his quivering lips. His fear of the insane little man was still stronger than his cannibalistic craving, but not by much.

The Editor let the taste coat his tongue and teeth. His expression went from savoring the delicious colloidal to a bizarre look of grave realization.

"What's happening?" asked Draw. The util-god was out of the psyche-altering loop and did not like it. After years in Totality, the Editor could distinguish the various almost imperceptible tones in its communication. This time, frustration.

The Editor sat back and chuckled.

Draw didn't need for its prophet to verbalize anything else. "Ren? She is your sister?"

Brother originally. That's what I'm remembering, if I can call it that.

"I haven't an idea what to call this."

The Editor sprang out of his chair. He stumbled like an infant taking its first steps in a world it does not yet belong. "This is all now so strange. There is someplace, a place? Yes, a place. I have to get back there. There? Where?" He succumbed to hysterical laughing then sobbing." He rocked back and forth trying to shake the pain and foreign thoughts away.

"What's happening to you?" Draw was thrown off guard at its host's sudden suffering and nonsensical mumbling. "We have much more worrying problems than trying to figure out a message from a Wamono cousin."

"Shut up!" His rocking quickened. *That spider's my cousin*! He froze. The realization hit him as if one of his Characters had punched him in the gut.

Yuuki could only stare at the raving man. He looked up at Lizard-man and the thin orange-glow man. They were also frozen by the sight of their prophet's uncharacteristic lunacy.

Draw continued in its signature even-tempered voice. "You're not thinking straight."

Thinking straight? Thinking straight? The Editor stopped rocking. *When was the last time I thought straight? There's something of me that is not of this world. Do you understand what that feels like? No, of course you don't. This is your world.* He closed his eyes waiting for the response that didn't materialize. *It didn't hear me. It couldn't hear me,* he thought making sure to nanosecond it just in case. *What the fuck is going on*?

His eyes snapped back wide open, eyeballs bouncing fleeting glances around the murky room. "Don't try to trick me. You tricked me already. You're the one that had been keeping me here. You stole me!"

Echoing silence rattled throughout the Editor's head. The silence was louder than anything he had ever heard. "Get out! Get out of me and let me go back!" He dropped his head on the desk as if gravity's nemesis left the universe without warning. The heavy thud echoed through the sparse study. He slowly lifted his head and slammed it down again, harder. "If you won't leave, I will fight it out of you. I don't need you anymore. Leave!"

"Leave you?" Draw's return made him stop his self-bludgeoning. Blood began dripping from his rouged forehead. "You do not exist; I do not exist. But we do, and we need each other whether you like it or not. You understand me less than you think, Hisashi." Draw made sure to slow when saying the Editor's birth name.

"My name's Futoshi!" The Editor stood up but had to sit down again. The self-inflicted trauma made him dizzy. *I need to meet my cousin. Nothing else matters.*

"The new Oné-chan does matter," interrupted Draw. "She is in Symb with an arch-idol. She is not the old Oné-chan. This one seems extremely dangerous."

The Editor attempted to get up again ignoring his utili-god. He walked to the door making sure to switch to thought-speak. *We are going to have a chat with my sister then take a trip to Aoheki to have another with this cousin.*

Finally, the Editor spoke back in the entombing world. "Have the wound dressed and take him back to the showroom. He'll need his rest and recuperate for tomorrow."

Tomorrow? What's he going to do with me tomorrow? Yuuki waiting for a response from Charm hoping it would have some kind of explanation. When none came, he answered himself. *More bleeding.*

twenty-eight

THE EDITOR AND HIS entourage entered the coffee house across the street from the restaurant that had witnessed the murder of the Dekora matriarch. Ren's' horde of clay and flesh golem guards were already in place lining the walls and looking out the filmy windows.

"Ah, welcome Hisahi, come sit down," said Ren. "I hope you don't mind. I've already ordered a drink."

"Ren," responded the Editor. "You are looking well." It was the first time he has seen the transitioned Ren. She was beautiful, but The Editor was a lifelong asexual and had little time for sexual attractiveness or attractiveness in general. After his arms finished the latest strokes in his phantom drawing, he sat down and signaled to his Illustrators to place their Characters at strategic positions around the café except for two who lumbered over to secure a straitjacket around their prophet. "I don't want to distract you."

"You trust us not to do anything while you are so ... restricted?"

"No trust." He looked around at his Characters. "I have assurance."

Ren smiled then twisted her neck around to the unambitious waitress leaning against the bar and snapped her newly elongated fingers. "You. There's someone thirsty over here." She looked back at her companion. "Unbelievers, what can you do?" She looked up towards a strange almost comatose young man standing between two of the Editor's goons. Her eyes instinctively focused on the bandaged arm and the scar on his cheek. "Ah, this must be your Wamono I've heard you collected. Congratulations."

The Editor looked behind him at the lolling bulk. "Yes. A rarity indeed, and he's key to what I want to talk to you about."

"The Wamono?" Ren raised one perfectly shaped eyebrow. "I assumed we were here to talk about the new Oné-chan."

The Editor smirked not believing a word that came out of her newly plumped lips. "Why did you choose to meet here? Sanae's blood stains are still rouging the sidewalk across the street."

"It may seem a bit tasteless, but even from what had all happened, I still feel the safest in this neighborhood." Ren took a sip of her cold drink not bothering to wait for the Editor's to come.

Selfish as always, thought the Editor.

"So, Hisashi," continued Ren. She looked up at the obviously drugged Wamono, rolled her eyes, then tried to get back to what was important. "What about this new Oné-chan. She doesn't seem anything to worry about, don't you think?"

She doesn't know about the Symb yet, thought the Editor. The Editor's beverage finally came. He stared at the unemotional waitress as she lazily put it in front of him. He wished he could talk with Draw unhindered by the god-god conflict. It was just him and Ren, no Editor or queen. "She's the one that assassinated my Storyliner."

"Yes, I've heard," said Ren. "I would be over there right now putting a Little Killer to her head. Your restraint is admirable."

The Editor let the insincerity pass through him. One miscommunication or direct threat and the walls would be covered in blackish blood and reddish clay. "That will come in time. Don't have to worry about that," he answered with a smile that forced the opposite reaction on Ren.

Ren let out a sigh. "So, what is so important about this Wamono." She looked around disgusted at what she was forced to patron. Her usual neutral meeting place was still closed while the inept Ue-No law enforcement conducted their investigation. They both knew that there was nothing for the Ue-No police to do. It was obvious who sent a Little Killer wavebullet through Oné-chan's head.

"I don't know where to start, so I will just get right into it," said the Editor. He didn't want to sound insane, even between two prophets in Totality.

"Go on. I don't want to stay in here any longer than necessary," said Ren. "If we haven't gotten down to what you really want to talk to me about by the time I finish this drink, I'm going back to my realm."

The Editor leaned in closer to her. She instinctively cringed away. He whispered, "We are brothers ... siblings."

"What are you talking about?" She made sure everyone in the establishment heard. "Are you that far gone already?"

"I know it sounds impossible ..."

"Because it is," interrupted Ren.

"Here." He had his manservant Character reach into a breast pocket between the ties of the straitjacket. Urban warriors on both sides stiffened and put their hands on their weapons ready and very willing to start killing. "Relax, relax. Just a couple pieces of paper." He looked around the café at the goons from both sides then looked over to Ren and grinned making sure to show his ink-stained teeth, "I'm not stupid." He had the Character slowly reach back into his pocket and take out the thick overly creased pieces of paper.

"What is it?"

"Read it," said the Editor. He placed the message on top of the map and slid it in front of her.

Ren read the note, mouthing the words with a dismissive chuckling here and there. "What?" It's obviously a lie. My family name was never Namatani. And I certainly never was your sibling. She glanced back at Masao, who had been dutifully standing just to her right, signaling him to get ready.

"Why did you write this. Draw had something to do with this! What are you trying to pull here?" She hand-signaled Masao to get even readier.

"Glasses!" It only took a couple seconds for the command to go through via an Illustrator. The Character gently took off his prophet's glasses. The Editor looked directly at his sibling. The pain was intense. "I give you my word, for little that's worth, that neither I nor Draw had anything to do with this."

"O.K., O.K., put that glass mask back on, you're freaking me out. I believe you. I don't understand why, but I do."

"I went through the same unknowing knowing last night a new, actually old, knowing filled my being. I don't understand much yet, but I had to come to you. It was what the message told me to do."

Ren now was the one leaning in and whispering. "Who is this 'cousin'? A Wamono?"

"The story continues with him." He looked over at Yuuki then the Illustrator. "Bring the Wamono over." Two Characters dragged the half unconscious monk closer to the table. One took out a knife while the other unwrapped the bloody bandaged around Yuuki's arm. "Ingesting a bit of his blood will make everything much clearer. It won't give you the whole picture in one dose, but it will be a start.

Ren scrunched her face in disgust. "I'm not a bloodsucker like you. Revolting."

She studied the violated arm. She couldn't take her eyes off the gashes and the various stages of blood coagulating. It didn't matter the blood didn't look 'normal'. *Those beautifully stained bandages. What exquisite slices.* She caught herself almost drooling. She needed to see them, to touch rough scabs. "What are you waiting for. Slice open a new vein."

The Editor looked at the knife-wielding Character. "Cut him."

The Character slid the blade parallel to an older wound. The black-red blood began to well up and overflow the scabbed swollen opening of flesh. There was only the faintest whimper of pain from Yuuki. The other Character grabbed Ren's glass, tossed out the remaining drink, and held it under Yuuki's arm while the impromptu surgeon turned the arm for the blood to drip into it.

The thick black blood filled the glass a third of the way. "That'll do," said the Editor. "Bandage him up." The two Characters dragged the drooling Wamono back away from the two prophets. One tear flowed down his cheek.

"Hisashi." She leaned in close and whispered before ingesting the Wamono's blood. "What the fuck is going on here?"

"Just drink it. If I explain, it will just seem like ramblings from just another insane prophet."

Ren downed the blood as fast as she could, given the consistency. To the Editor, it took an eternity. When the last major elongated drop hit her tongue, she smiled. Her clay-flesh guards were ready to pounce on Masao's signal.

Ren remained smiling of long-lost affection than of revenge and hate. She was almost in tears. Her memories of something she had never thought she had experienced were fighting those of Ren, the queen of the Suriidii. It was the first time in decades she felt anything other than hate for her former business partner.

The editor mimicked that smile. *She's remembering.*

"We need to get everyone out of here," whispered Editor. "We cannot have any others here. They can't see us like this, not yet."

Ren nodded her understanding. She took a deep breath to regain her composure and looked around at her entourage. "Everyone out!" Her golems just stared at her.

"Your majesty?" said Masao.

"You heard me. Get everyone out of here, immediately. You can wait outside or go back to the realm, it's up to you, but get out!"

Masao stood there silent for a couple seconds trying to comprehend what was happening. He looked at the Editor.

"You too," said the Editor to his group. "Leave!" He looked back at Masao and nodded.

"Everyone out!" Masao leaned in close to his queen's ear but did not try to be discreet. "We will be right outside until you give the word." He raised his eyes and looked at the Editor but kept his mouth close to Ren's ear. "But if I hear or see any sign of deception or struggle, I will come back in with or without your permission."

The two prophets nodded in agreement and waited for their respective mini armies to vacate the café.

"Futoshi. Brother?" said Ren.

The Editor also smiled, revealing his seeping black gums. "Atsushi. Brother."

twenty-nine

"MY DEAR," VIBRATED PALACE. "We have a visitor."

"I don't want any." Mimi was at her desk with her head between her hands. She had been cooped up in the Pinku Palace for what might have been only a day but could have been several. Time was a different beast when in cross-entity correspondence. She felt totally not in control of herself, only an observer.

"He is downstairs in stasis. What would you like me to do with him?"

"You're asking me?" Mimi tried not to be sarcastic, but she was too frustrated from recent events and with her new permanent companion. "You seem to being doing fine without my input." There was no response from Palace. "Just bring him up on the display."

The screen flickered on, coating the suite in a bright glow from the all-white of the lobby. Mimi looked at the frozen mass in the middle of colorless room. "A Blue addict?" Mimi had seen dozens like him strung out and glowing blue on the verge or in the midst of overdose in her wanderings through the seedier parts of the city. She tended to keep away from them. They were unpredictable.

"Why the hell is a Blue here?" She walked up to the display to get a better look. She had to shield her eyes the closer she got. "Send him up."

"Is that wise?"

"If he wanted to kill me, he would have been a little bit more discreet about it. Just do it." Mimi thought better of her rash command. "Please."

"Very well, my dear."

Mimi watched as Palace released its prisoner. The addict began to struggle for breath. "Do you have to be so suffocating when you do that?"

"Yes."

Mimi watched the addict as he stumbled toward the elevator guided by Palace. Once he disappeared inside the lift, she called in several of her guards to help restrain him. Blue addicts inherited unusual strength from the drug.

As soon as the elevator doors split open, Mimi's guards grabbed hold of him.

Mimi wanted to get right to it. "You here to kill me?"

"No," said the addict. He was still trying to refuel his lungs

"Your boss must think I am pretty weak to send you here. I guess he's wrong."

"Not a he," he responded.

"She then. Who the fuck cares?"

"Fujin sent me."

Who the hell is that? Palace, you know? Mimi walked up to the exhausted addict, her guards making a tighter grip. "I've never heard of anyone by that name. Is she one of the Editor's lackeys?"

"Fujin is this fanatic, my dear, who has been very keen to remain an enigma; a bit childish if you ask me. She has some kind of strange religious vendetta against every Symb in the Wards. She uses these Blue addicts as her ethically flexible little army."

"Fujin sent me to negotiate an alliance."

"Why?" Mimi asked. She backed away slightly and crossed her arms.

"She's impressed with following through and going beyond your assignment."

Mimi lifted her head, closed her eyes, sighed. *Sama?*

"You know her?" asked Palace. Mimi felt a soft buzz of jealousy of her knowing more than it.

She hired me to assassinate my predecessor. Never seen her face or gender. Fits the enigma fetish you mentioned. I added another step to her plan.

"The coup, I take it?"

Yup. Mimi bit down on her lip trying to suss everything out. *So, she doesn't know about you, us.*

"It's only a matter of time. Be careful my dear. She seems to be getting more brash, thus dangerous. She probably sent him here to find out."

Mimi started to understand why her predecessor tried to keep Palace a secret. *Well, she'll know now thanks to your stunts down in the lobby.*

The Blue smiled, revealing crusty Blue residue at the corners of his clown-blue mouth. "So, would you like to help her rid this city of this Tsudii plague?"

Mimi smiled then turned to look out the window over the vast urban fief she now controlled. "I can take care of them myself." She said nothing else. It was so quiet in the room that she could hear the body-shake of the fix-hungry Blue.

"Not wise, my dear?" Palace's 'tone' was too motherly for Mimi's liking. "I should tell you, Sanae recently made an alliance with the Tsudii and Suriidii. Apologies. I should've informed you earlier."

"Ya think?!" Mimi forgot to keep the conversation within her. *What the fuck!? Why ... and how?*

"Excuse me, ma'am?" The Blue didn't know how to respond to her short outburst.

"Nothing." She turned around and walked toward the jittering man. What is your name?" She needed something human to hang onto in her increasingly non-human selfhood. "Why would I want to get rid of the Tsudii? They bring in a lot of business. Fifty percent to be precise." *Pal. Tell me what the hell is going on. I hate being indecisive, and that is what I am being forced to be.*

"I am Palace." The short gut-pounding thud of that statement told Mimi Palace preferred formality over familiarity. "With Sanae being dead, the alliance may be as well. It is imperative we get back on good or at least tolerating terms with the other daigunshyu. We, unfortunately, need them. Get rid of this sycophantic addict with smiles and non-committals."

The Blue stuttered back into a three-way conversation he was logically not in, but the paranoia of his drug surpassed logic and made invisible and silent voices very possible. "I ... uh ... Fujin wh ... wh ... would like to see a city free from the evil of the prophet-god abominations."

"Confirmed. This Fujin does not know of us yet. She will, and this frenetic friendly chat will be moot. She cannot be trusted, my dear."

Alliances and vendettas coalesced into one anarchic blob sealing Mimi off from herself. She had to breathe and keep breathing. *Agreed. But we go it alone. Completely alone.*

She smiled as advised by her concrete and steel partner, whipped out Kitty D., and swung it toward the Blue's neck stained with streaks of dissipating blue drool. She waited for that accomplishing thud of head falling to floor she called 'death complete', "I don't do non-committals."

thirty

THE DERMIS OF THE city is that of rough life, pock-marked, rashed, scarred. Ryudasu released a grumbling sigh as she looked out over the city between repair work. "You do have a battered beauty." The expanse of the western wards twinkled and pulsed from the city, pondering. The city thinks best at night when it can feed on secrets and dreams.

Hégo thought it best for Ryudasu to be camouflaged within the dark heart of night for a while. It suited her. She had been living in darkness for centuries. Was it the obsidian of her being that influenced her environment or vice versa? It wasn't important which, it only mattered that it was what calmed her god-mind.

"Waiting comprises thousands of minuscule nothings coalescing into inaction. I simply wait." The machinations of her plan had finally been released into the city, to flourish not wither in its vomit encrusted gutters. She had nurtured her revenge for centuries. She was now relieved for it to live its own life. She needed the rest. As with any parent, she had concern it would not survive the harsh human realities. But as with any god, she could manipulate her little fleshy puppets to ensure they fit nicely together as cogs in her vengeance on the everything in this world and the other.

"I am the Weaver of the universe and unraveller of the heretical." Her breathing quickened and pincers tapped, tapped, tapped on the brittle stone. "A god can be a heretic, City, Mayor, Gou-Tairei, whatever it is you call yourself. Only names.

"My names, you ask?" Ryudasu sensed reluctant vibrations. "You are frightened of knowledge, and what do entities do when they are frightened with extinction? They try to stall the inevitable by asking inane questions." Ryudasu climbed higher up the barrier. She quickly found that her leg-arms were barely strong enough to compensate for her large bulbous abdomen conspiring with gravity to plunge her to potential death. When you believe yourself immortal and a deity, violent death is only a slight possibility. She learned to use her web-spinning abilities to anchor her body, giving her limbs a fighting chance. She wanted to be far above her nemesis to look down upon it, even down upon the highest of scrapers. More importantly, it required the scarred welted deceptive god to look up to her.

"Ah yes. My nomenclature." She spun the last of the anchors to secure herself to the barrier and against the gusty upper atmosphere. "I have had several names, as you well know. My first was Zenji Makoto from the world you stole me from." She breathed in a large volume of soaked cloud, the gut-deep growl it initiated vibrated the stone she attached herself to. "I was also referred to as 'sensei', a spiritual teacher of sorts. I became Konbo Motohiro after my rebirth as you would have us believe. I know better; my first imprisonment into your demented playground. When I naïvely co-founded this ridiculous order to worship you in complete ignorance, you who deserves no worship, I became Genko Ryudasu and have been burdened with that name for centuries—impossibly too long to be ladened with just one name."

The irritated grumbling of her empty gut interrupted her ancestry of one. "Apologies, my underling god-like thing, I must ascend and satiate my angry hunger. Let us finish up this lovely little conversation." Snack-sized rodents and lizards populated the gaps and cracks closer to the summit of the barrier walls. A relatively vibrant microclimate clung onto wet stone of lush moss, lichen, and small leafy plants in the grey nursery of constant cloud. She ventured that far up only when hunger drove her. It was more difficult to anchor and grip due to the biological slick. There was little view from up there; only cinereal, wet, smothering nothing.

She began snipping away at the anchoring silk strands with a couple of her free limbs. "My name has finally changed again. Holy Spinner, a name I did not choose, but has become a convenience. My final and permanent name is a simple one, and the one you can, no, will call me. That is, God."

thirty-one

COMMUTERS FROZEN IN THEIR well-trodden morning tracts watched mouths agape the bizarre horde making its way up the hill toward the Wamono cloister of Aoheki. The rapidly drawing arms from a being riding atop an open fu-viscer coach were clues of who the leader of the freakish cortege was. Several people not frozen into a frightened stupor quickly ducked into the nearest store or alleyway. It wasn't every day they saw the Tsudii leader in this part of the city. All the parade but one Illustrator, the Storyliner, and two Characters who were with him in the carriage walked on both sides.

Keep up!" The Editor barked. "I don't want to waste any more time." His arms drew two imaginary impatient streaks in front of him.

Yuuki was moving but he was not walking. His arm seared with pain, but he couldn't bring himself to move his head to examine it, he was too tired. He vaguely remembered why his arm hurt. The memory stream was trickling back into him after the effects of whatever drug he was full of began to wear away. *They are drinking my blood. I am hungry.* He wanted to tear the bandage off and drink as much of his own enchanting, transformed blood as he could. He began to slowly unwrap the nourishing wound inside the large kimono sleeves, but his eyes forced his concentration to what his display prison was passing by.

Things were looking familiar. *How? Nothing here can be familiar.* Before he could finish his thought, he saw the walker bridge he and Hiroka traversed the day he escaped. "Aoheki," he whispered. He garnered enough strength to stand up. He looked down watching the blur of the ground pass under him then back up watching two massive Characters at each corner supporting him.

"Bring the Wamono up here," commanded the Editor. He didn't bother to turn around. "I need information."

He was forced to sit back down while the box tilted side to side. He saw his poor damaged feet. The Editor's obsession with his newest exhibit's authenticity was starting to take a physical toll. A lifetime of being a Wamono made him physically reject his birthplace.

The Character porters raised Yuuki so their prophet could look directly at this prized exhibit/blood oracle. "What is the relationship between you and my cousin we're going to see?"

Yuuki looked out over the Editor, trying not to look directly at those chilling mirrored barriers. He had a vague recollection of stealing a quick glimpse of the naked monstrosities days ago, and that was enough. The glasses reminded Yuuki of the glossy frigid eyes of Ryudasu. They were the same color and reflected the same dim ghost of himself. *Cousins.* That word stuck like claws in his misty memory.

"I know you can hear me, Wamono!" The one who gave you that map and message."

Ryudasu?! Yuuki was thankful he was already sitting down.

"By the looks of the fear splattered all over your face, I take it you know."

Yuuki didn't want to talk about the Aku but knew he would suffer more for refusing. *Charm?* He began to pick at his bandaged arm. No response. He needed more ink. It didn't matter if it was now part of him. Consuming it was the only thing that would comfort him.

"Answer me," yelled the Editor.

Yuuki inhaled a mouthful of the stale air, blurring out the flailing arms, and looked directly into the Editor's inhuman eyes. "I have no relationship with her. She gave me that map and told me to meet someone." He made it a point to make himself sound more angry than frightened.

"Her?" He turned to one of his Illustrators. Is this cloister a nunnery?"

The nervous Illustrator shook his head in the negative. "No, my prophet. It is an all-male cloister."

"Huh, interesting." He turned back to Yuuki. "Why you?"

"I wanted to get out. I guess she saw an opportunity." He answered plainly without any more bravado. It wasn't working anyway. His fingers were still quietly working on the bandage hidden deep within his sleeves.

He could already see the barrier walls that had come into view from behind the scrapers. *I have failed.*

"Well, you succeeded," panted the Editor. He was surprised the creep's arms were not more muscular with all the thrusts and retractions.

Aoheki was now in full view. Yuuki didn't know what to expect. Of course, nothing would have changed in just a few days or weeks. But that didn't stop him from looking for any differences. He scanned the walls, nothing. No changes. There had been no changes for centuries, why would there be any now?

"Over there," said the Editor. He pointed to a section of the wall. He looked up and saw a large black creeping lump turning the corner high up on the walls.

Hiroka watched the Tsudii entourage mill about the walls at the exact spot where she first met Yuuki. He was easy to make out with his traditional Wamono garb, encased in some kind of glass or plastic box. *At least he's not dead.* The black-clad party seemed to be waiting for something or someone. She didn't have all the details of why the Editor decided to make a trip to Aoheki. She didn't think anyone, even Mimi, had any full understanding.

Mimi had found out where he would be. Getting the news that she wouldn't have to go to Shinyuyogi on a suicide mission to the Tsujii stronghold was more than a slight relief.

She was sick with guilt from handing off Yuuki to the Editor, but it had to be done. Holy Spinner commanded it. Her attempts at reforming the Fujou was now defunct, but she could always try to recruit a few of the more receptive ladies at Otokonoko-Tachi to break away with her and follow their true god. She had to stay in this broken dimension a little while longer.

Hiroka had no special abilities. She wasn't an ace assassin like the Dekora or a manipulative seductress like the Lolita. The Fujou were only experts in enjoying the denigration of others—a skill that had no use in the real world or in rescuing Wamono monks. All she had at her disposal was a Little Killer and two giddy Dekora neophytes excited at their first chance of a kill.

"You," Hiroka commanded one of the Dekora. "Go find a position behind them. And you. Stay here with me."

The one Hiroka commanded to separate, was off without any other sound. The other stared at her smiling and staring at the targets like a starving dog.

"Listen," said Hiroka. "Don't go overboard on the killing and do not go after the Editor. Your Oné-chan gave specific orders not to."

"Yes, yes, I heard her," answered the antsy assassin. The girl's incessant gum snapping was starting to get on Hiroka's nerves. At least the chomping was no longer in stereo.

It was obvious that the two girls had everything under control. Hiroka was there just to suffer her guilt and as someone Yuuki would recognize. She hoped he didn't find out anything about her involvement in his capture and imprisonment.

Before she gave the signal to the girls to do their thing, she saw a strange black moving mass appear high up on the Aoheki walls. It was coming around the corner. "What is that?"

The Dekora's gum snapping stopped. "I have no fucking idea. Looks nasty."

The two were mesmerized by the mysterious shape. It descended further, and they could make out more detail.

"It looks like an insect of some kind," said the Dekora. Her cud chewing restarted.

"Or a giant spider," said Hiroka. *Holy Spinner?* Both just kept staring at the hideous form.

"Eewww. That's just wrong," the Dekora said. "You think the Tsudii have something to do with this?"

"Of course," responded Hiroka. "What would you expect from a creep like the Editor. He probably thinks it's cute." Hiroka couldn't keep a smile from forming. *She has come for me.*

"It seems that no one else has noticed the thing," said the assassin. Hiroka was glad to hear that the Dekora was still in assassin mode. "I think we should do something about that."

The Dekora stood up from her crouching position to yell to the growing half-frightened half-awed citizenry to look up and create a chaos diversion. Hiroka grabbed her arm and pulled her back down.

"Wait, you ditz!" Yelled Hiroka. "Look."

Another group was gathering, and it wasn't of random confused people. This group was deliberate.

"Queen Ren," said Hiroka.

"Whoa, something big is about to go down," said the Dekora. Her gum snapping in cadence with her over-stimulated heart.

She kept her eyes on the assembly. "Yes, something certainly is." Ecstasy of witnessing divinity greatly expanded her smile.

"What is this?" Fujin said to herself. "My source said nothing about that queen being here." She positioned herself a couple blocks up the street. A greedy robe and cowl consumed her face and body. The stench of viscergas was so strong, she had to keep a kerchief up to her nose. Her network of informants alerted her of the unusual journey of the Editor to this side of the city and, even stranger, to a

Wamono cloister. She had to take the opportunity to get rid of him once and for all. This was the best chance she or anyone would have.

She had hoped she would not have to get her own hands inky and bloody and have her hired assassin do the dirty work. Unfortunately, her personal assassin was now Oné-chan and no longer for hire. She considered the idea of this Oné-chan being an equal partner in her extermination mission. She had even sent a Blue to the Pink Palace to see about making an alliance. It had been over a day and no word from him. *Probably Blued out in some cesspool of an Illumination den.* She hated alliances, but recent events had dampened her reluctance. *The Dekora may be a Mayor-sponsored gunshyu, but at least it was not one in abomination.*

She scanned the worrying scene. Each crazed prophet brought along just enough of their respective freaks to do some damage to the other, but not enough to look too threatening. It was a strange detente. *It will be impossible to get to him now.*

She briefly considered concocting an off-the-cuff strategy to take both tyrants out. But the fantasy didn't last long. She only brought enough Blues along for one kill and smashing. The main goal was to sever the Symb bond. Death to both was the only way. *How can people worship such evil?* She sifted through the rubbish around her feet that had accumulated over the weeks in the little grimy nook from where she was watching the bizarre tête-à-tête. The diversion allowed her time to calm her building paranoia of the two mortal enemies in actual conversation.

The summit she was witnessing was so worrying that she almost ignored a giant spider-like creature deftly navigating the pimply sweaty stone wall. It was well known that other Wamono cloisters used animals to help maintain their precious walls, but she never saw one as peculiar as this one.

She ignored the anomaly and went back to concentrating on the activity on the ground. There were the usual goon squads of Characters, perfect examples of the old Smashers corrupted and warped by the city they had scorned but wanted to save, and their master puppeteer Illustrators. She focused her attention on Ren's clay and flesh golems. Just looking at their disfigured bodies would be enough to scare away any minor troublemaker. They were perpetual works in progress.

She thumb-flipped her ring to communicate with the Blues stationed at different points forming a hidden perimeter around the Aoheki wall. "Hold off for now," she commanded. "We may have to abort." She heard the usual obeying responses, which was always a good sign. She never knew if or when one or a few would begin bleeding Blue from an overdose. She picked the most restrained ones for this job. She hoped the monotony of waiting wouldn't tempt them to take that little bit more to push them over the edge into complete uselessness or worse.

She went back to watching how the meeting between the two daigunshyu leaders was playing out. She was relegated to an observer at this point. She saw a robed figure seemingly floating next to the Editor. The figure towered over the petit prophet. It was not difficult for her to see what she assumed was a male from this distance. She let everything else go to a soft bokeh around her new target of interest.

"A Wamono?" She said out loud. He wasn't a Smasher. They wouldn't be wearing such obvious Wamono costuming. The monk's hair was shorter than usual. "A novice." The absence of the usual Wamono mane of hair allowed her to get a better look at him. She couldn't quite figure he looked familiar. The only Wamono she knew personally were her Blues, and they were no longer Wamono—no Smasher had remained a true Wamono for long out in the Scorned Wold. And of course, her two sons. It wasn't Shinya. She would never forget his features, no matter how much they would have changed with age. This one was also too young. *Shinya would be in his early 30s now.* She never did find out which cloister he had run off to. She didn't want to think about that most horrible time in her life, a life that ended the day she gave her second infant son up to the order.

She regretted naming the baby. It made it that much harder—if that was possible—to abandoned him and not see him grow up. *He would be about twenty now.* She looked at the Wamono again. "He looks to be about twenty." She jerked her head down forbidding her eyes to remain on the monk. *It can't be.* But the familiarity made sense, except the bulk. She cringed at the thought of the mirrored rapist. She inhaled deeply and closed her eyes trying to regain herself. *It's not him. Things just don't work like that.* She couldn't risk getting the Wamono killed in her two-decade quest for revenge, son or not. He was a Wamono obviously there against his will.

She flicked on her ring. "It's off. Return to the Annex." She flicked off the ring without any more orders. She didn't want anyone to hear the tears in her voice.

Yuuki stared at the vaguely familiar woman walking up to him and the Editor. She was almost as tall as him. Her cheek bones looked as if they would burst out of her skin with just the slightest breeze against her face. The reflection of a shiny broach on her chest caught his attention. It looked like two halves of a simplified claw: a prettier more elegant version of one of Ryudasu's pincers. All her entourage wore the same insignia.

He placed his hand lovingly on his bandaged wound beginning to remember her. *She drank my blood too.* His fingers began to pick at the bandages with their own agency.

He looked behind her to her circus of followers. He didn't want to look at any of them individually, gaining their unfinished attention. *No skin. They have no skin.* He couldn't make out what the other substance was they were made of. He didn't want to study them any further to find out. *She must be the other daigunshyu leader Mimi was talking about*? For the first time he felt safe in his transparent prison.

Ren nodded to the Editor. "Brother." She then looked at Yuuki. "Hello again, Wamono?" She ran her tongue around her plump lips as if anticipating her next long overdue meal.

"Thank you for coming, Atsushi," responded the Editor.

Ren, in her signature nonchalance, looked at the Wamono. "So, you're the one who started this all in motion."

Yuuki didn't know if she was angry or happy about that. Her face revealed no sign of those or any emotion. "I think she is the one who really started everything." He pointed up towards Ryudasu who was now close enough for some of the two mixed entourages to fidget, especially the Illustrators.

Even Ren jumped back a little when she looked up. She looked back at the Editor, her eyes showing less brotherly love. "What is this? What are you up to Futoshi!" The tension created by her accusatory tone constricted Yuuki's heart. The soldier goons on both sides tightened their stances ready to react to any action from the other side.

"Don't accuse me!" Yelled the Editor, his arms slashing angry bold strokes in the air in front of his sibling. Even though they were now siblings, it didn't mean all mistrust was forgotten between them. Ren immediately put up her arm to stop those in her entourage who were not used to her brother's bizarre non-threatening arm gesturing from taking defensive actions.

"Now, now you two," came a raspy hiss from above. Ryudasu was now a meter above and behind the Suriidii queen. The Editor's mouth dropped slacked and stupid. Ren froze. She couldn't bring herself to turn around. The spider creature continued. "No fighting, please. You are in sacred presence."

Sacred? Yuuki thought. She held nothing within Aoheki sacred.

Ren finally turned around. She cringed at the drooling fangs and reflective eyes she was staring directly into.

"Hello cousin Atsushi. It has been a very long time." Ryudasu lifted her disproportionately small head towards the Editor. "And you too, Futoshi."

Yuuki saw the surreal reflection-in-reflection of the two sets of obsidian eyes staring at each other. She was hanging by a single strand of her silk. He tried to follow the strand up to where it was attached, but he started to get dizzy. He fluttered his eyes to get his bearings back but only saw his reflection in those eyes. His mind suddenly transported back where it all started in the root cellar.

"Well, dear Yuuki-Hana," said Ryudasu. Her rasp sent chills racing up and down Yuuki's back. "You did well. I see you made friends with my cousins."

Yuuki only stared at her.

Ryudasu continued. "Thank you all for coming. Though I did not expect so many. She looked at the cowering Illustrators and wide-eyed, some even lidless, golems.

Yuuki noticed the man standing back and to the right of Ren. He never moved. He kept his eye on the Editor and the menacing Characters. He didn't shift with the others away from the descending monster.

Ryudasu continued. "Yes, I am your cousin. I was not always like this, of course. I was just like you, or almost like you." She looked at Ren then at the Editor. "I guess I am not the only one who transformed so dramatically." Her laugh sounded more like a growl.

Yuuki kept his eyes on the stone-faced sentinel at the Sculptress' side. But he was listening to every word Ryudasu was hissing out of those killer fangs. *I wish she would make sense.* He glanced at the confused faces of the Editor and Ren and knew they were thinking the same.

"If you do not mind," Ryudasu said looking out to the ensemble and the growing crowd of pedestrians gathering on its outskirts, "I would like to talk to my cousins alone. This meeting is not for everyone." She realigned her eyes with those of her cousins. "Now that you know that you will not kill each other, I think you can let your flocks go to harass the gawkers behind them." She made sure the bystanders heard. Most looked down to the ground and moved on their way. "Come on now. You are bro.." Ryudasu caught herself, "siblings. You should have nothing to fear from each other." She secreted a little more web and leaned out from the wall to get more intimate with her cousins and whispered. "Especially after what I have to tell you."

The two siblings looked at each other trying to suss the other out and who would make the first move in disbanding their forces. "Fuck off." the Editor finally said to his sycophants. "Move away from here but stay close." He was still looking at Ren waiting for her to do the same.

"You too," she finally said, but her eyes remained focused on her brother. "Don't go too far." She finally broke her focus and looked to her emotionless companion. "That means you, Masao."

Masao, thought Yuuki. *That's a fitting name for him*. It sounded hard and quiet.

"You too, Wamono," said the Editor. "No reason for you to hang around." He turned back to Ryudasu. "Is there?"

She waited for his strange nervous tic to wind down before answering. "No. He did his job. I have no more need of him." She lifted her eye-covered head to Yuuki. "You can go off and try to *find* yourself."

"He's mine." interrupted the Editor. "He's part of my collection." He motioned to one of his Characters to take care of him.

"Whatever you desire, Futoshi," said Ryudasu. "I do not care what you do with him. He served my purpose. I guarantee that you will no longer care about your wants and needs of this world."

Yuuki was in no position to protest. His Character porters turned his mini prison around, making him slightly dizzy, but he kept his eyes coldly on Ryudasu. *Thanks for nothing*. He thought-spoke to the absent Charm. *Why are you not helping me?* There was no vibrational response. He didn't really care. All he wanted was to rip the black-red bandages off and feed on himself. It didn't matter if it hurt. The pleasure of the ink, no matter how diluted with blood, would overpower any pain. Besides, everyone had abandoned him. Hiroka was most likely dead or imprisoned in one of the cells in that dungeon zoo. Probably dead. He couldn't think of a reason the Editor would want a Fujou in his collection. He assumed they weren't exactly rare. Mimi was probably glad to be rid of him and get back to her killing. But he didn't understand the absence of Charm. They were one in the same now, at least that's what he understood. But he understood almost nothing of how things worked out here. He wasn't sure if he wanted to. Maybe Ryudasu was right in her ridicule of him. *Why do I want to find myself? I have never been worth finding*.

He secretly undressed his wound under his sleeve, exposing the rough fresh scar the color of ink and blood. He ran his fingers over it, making sure to feel every hardened bead. He took advantage of a short moment when the Characters were focused on intimidating the distant crowds and dug his teeth deep into the torn flesh. He squeaked out a cry of pain turned ecstasy from the warm metallic trickle.

"Who and what are you?" Ren crossed her arms staring defiant at Ryudasu. Passersby dared not stare at the bizarre trio too long. The Characters and Suriidii golems stationed here and there not exactly hiding made sure of that.

"I am your cousin, Zenji Makoto. We, the three of us, were quite close a very long time ago. A world ago in fact." Responded Ryudasu. Her voice was almost gentle and content.

"I remember but I don't," added the Editor. He had memories of a cousin and a brother in a city that was not quite this one. All the rest were only whisps of vaporous experience. He had always lived in Hinodé. He had no other siblings, male or female. He had cousins, but he had killed them all out of paranoia. That was before he found Draw or Draw found him.

"That is why we are here. To fill in the gaps", responded Ryudasu. "Forgive me for the rather crude way of meeting, but, as you understand, I could not invite you into the cloister until we met."

"So, please fill in those gaps." said the Editor. He tried to be as polite and patient as possible. He and his brother-sister were pretty much defenseless thanks to the proximity of their utili-gods and without their respective armies.

"I would be happy to, but now, I can give you only the quick basics," Ryudasu responded. She lowered herself a bit more, careful not to go too far to touch the forbidden ground.

"Just the quick basics?" Ren was still not impressed with how this meeting was going. The Editor thought she was upset that her precious Masao was not by her side.

Ryudasu ignored the Suriidii queen and started to fill them in on their forgotten lives. "I was your cousin, still am."

"We know this," interrupted Ren.

Ryudasu gurgled up an annoyed grumble and continued. "You, we, are not from here, from this city, world." She lifted her front legs to suggest the expanse of the metropolis behind her audience. "We are from a place, a city, called Yedo."

"Yedo? Never heard of it," said The Editor.

"Of course you have not. We are not supposed to have had. I cannot understand the working of Gou-Tairei. Maybe it was just a ... happy ... accident."

"Gou-Tairei?" Ren's face re-tightened with skepticism. "You brought us here to convert us into a couple of those scared little monks inside?" Her pointer finger almost touched the cloister stone. She did not dare damage her nail.

"No, of course not. I am telling you that Gou-Tairei is a fact, but not to be worshipped."

The Editor and Ren looked at each other; confused about what the giant spider woman was telling them.

Ryudasu went on with her cryptic explanation without acknowledging the siblings' confusion. "We died, cousins. We are in another life."

"Ryudasu. Cousin," Ren said. "We are obviously not dead. Look at us." She looked over to her brother and smirked. "Well, Futoshi here looks a little bit worse for wear, but I assure you we are not dead."

"Who we were in Yedo are dead."

"This is ridiculous. You're saying that this grimy city is some kind of after-life paradise?" said Ren. "The only reason I came is because I remember things that I don't remember and a cousin, you, is key." The Editor looked at her and could tell that she didn't even understand what she had just spurted out. "And it's driving me crazy." She looked at the Editor for some kind of sympathetic expression telling her that she was not alone. He gave her what she wanted.

"Who says you would end up in a paradise?" responded Ryudasu. The super bass of her raspy laugh penetrated through the Editor. He was sure even Draw felt it. "Such a place does not exist. This is the cruel playground of the Gou-Tairei."

"There she goes again about that silly god," said Ren. "Ours are the only gods around here."

Oh, yes. Those things," said Ryudasu. "I should tell you now, that I have the ability to listen to your conversations with your," she giggled-hissed again, "gods. So, do not be shy Inanimates. I know you are listening."

There was silence for few seconds. "No?" continued Ryudasu. "Well, when you feel like getting in on the conversation, please do. This involves you as well, of course."

The Editor wanted to get back on course. He needed answers, and so far, none were being answered and more questions were being forced out. "If this is not paradise, then what?"

Where we come from, as well as here, when someone dies, it is not the end. They go through the process all over again - born, live, die, born live, die—you get the idea."

"Yes, we're not idiots," said the Editor. He was starting to show the same frustration as his companion. "We know what the Wamono believe." It was pretty much all he knew and basically all any outsider knew of the fiercely reclusive order.

"Yes, everyone knows that," added Ren.

Ryudasu's voice was no longer a calm purr. "You do not even know one percent of one percent of what goes on here. Even the one percent more those silting monks on the other side of this wall is infinitely more than what you two or anyone else out here know.

The Editor and Ren involuntarily backed up. They looked around to see if they could motion to anyone in their respective entourages to come and protect them.

"Do not cower. It is unbecoming of our family. I am running out of time," Ryudasu said. she was beginning to return to her calm growl. "People are starting to gather. This is my debut this far down."

The two siblings turned around to get a better idea of the growing crowd looking and pointing at the monster that mysteriously came from the walls of the Wamono cloister. Even the presence of Tsudii and Suriidii enforcers couldn't keep the crowds from coalescing by self-momentum.

"Listen. What you need to know now is that I know of a way back to where we all belong. We can cheat this death!" The Editor noticed that the spider's excitement at the impossible prospect. "Imagine the power we would have back in the world with no other Inanimates and prophets, and I am sure nothing like me."

The siblings looked at each other. The Editor didn't know if their eight-legged cousin was even crazier than him or knowledgeable of something so profound as to just seem crazy.

"How did we get here. I mean, how did we die?" Asked Ren. She was still trying to be critical.

"I cannot remember that far into the last world, the real world." answered Ryudasu. "We were not supposed to know that we did die, that we lived in another city, another world those centuries ago."

"Centuries?" The Editor tried slapping his hand against his face in frustration. "We have been dead - living-dead for centuries?"

"Yes, and no. I am going by the time of our home. This less than pretty form I found myself in allowed me to somehow grasp the different time structure. That's one thing that the damnable Gou-Tairei failed to consider when punishing me into this long, tortured life."

"Punishment for what?" Asked Ren. The Editor wanted to know as well. He saw that his former enemy was now letting go and at least engaging in the conversation.

"Oh, let us not go into that now. As I said, I need to get back to my duties. I have made plans for you two to talk this over in more detail inside, but we have to be discreet."

"Inside there?" The Editor said, pointing a shaking hand to the weeping wall. He had dreamed of such an adventure inside the forbidden domain since he was a child. He thought collecting that Wamono monk was the closest he would get to the mysterious society, a society he had previously no hopes of controlling.

He looked over to his sister-brother. Her expression was the opposite. She had no wish to enter such a depressing out-of-touch institution. Atsushi, this is unprecedented. No outsider has been invited into a Wamono cloister."

"Maybe there's a reason for that. I don't have the same silly infatuation you have with the bizarre dreary sect." Ren looked down at her minuscule brother. "Relax your jittery arms, little brother." She somehow knew she was the older. "I'll go in, but I'm just not as giddy about it as you." She looked up the slowly retreating arachnid. "Why couldn't we have done all this inside in the first place. Why in such a public space?"

"I had to make sure you believed me or at least receptive to the idea of believing me first." She stopped several meters above them still close enough not to have to raise her chilling voice. She turned around with the end of her abdomen pointing down. She secreted a glob of clear liquid silk.

"Disgusting," complained Ren. The Editor grimaced.

Gravity took hold of the glob, turning hoary upon contact with the air, and stretched it out until it formed a large bowl. "Get in."

"I don't think so." Ren recrossed her arms and began to move toward the crowd. "I'm not that much into finding the end to this fantasy you two seem to be wanting to play. I'm not going to sit in spider shit!"

"It is not feces!" Yelled Ryudasu. Many of the onlookers took that as a cue to get out before she went on a killing rampage. She turned around and before Ren could take even two steps back, she was centimeters behind the queen, her fangs turned outward ready to strike. She whispered but made sure the Editor could hear. "Now, get in before I pierce your over-remodeled neck."

Ren would not dare turn around in case she slammed against those poisonous fangs. She looked at the Editor for signs that it was safe to move. He nodded. "Very well." She recomposed herself before turning around.

"Thank you, Atsushi."

My name is Ren!" She looked like a petulant child talking back at her parent.

Rydasu ignored the rude outburst and calmly responded. "No. It is not." She continued her reasoning for the unorthodox mode of transportation. "I have explicit instructions from the Master of the Cloister not to let you in through the main gate. Those moody lion-dog things will immediately smell that you two are not there to join the order. And not even my fangs would be of use in protecting you."

Both siblings looked behind them at the thinning crowed. Only the stupidly brave were lingering. "Do not worry about them. Climb in and hold on tightly."

thirty-two

YUUKI CONTINUED FEASTING ON himself while the Character thugs carried him around a corner and into an abandoned doorway to keep a better eye on him. The pain was starting to take over from the pleasure he had so needed. He looked up, his glistening blackened mouth dripping. He saw his faint doppelgänger on one of his prison walls. The wound looked as if it had transferred to his mouth, but fresher; more open. He smirked. He adjusted his focus to see through his ephemeral twin to the outside. He saw only one Character, Lizard-man, guarding him; the others were probably 'programmed' to station themselves at strategic spots around the bizarre scene at the Aoheki wall. He didn't see any Illustrator nearby solely controlling Lizard-man. He thought about trying to start a conversation with the reptilian giant. He wiped his mouth with his sleeve to remove as much of the stain from his lips. But he decided he was too full to try to communicate.

"That was strange," vibrated Charm.

Yuuki opened his mouth to speak but stopped himself. *You have known I've been craving more of that ink.*

"Not that, what just happened at the wall."

Then why did not you say anything when I asked for you?

"There was no reason for me to do so. It would just waste my compromised energy. Don't worry. I am always thinking. What else have I to do?"

I hope you were thinking about how to get me out of this. He found himself breathing heavy from the energy it took for his mind to override the pain of biting into his wound with the ecstasy of finally getting its fill of inky blood. He peeked around the corner to get a glimpse of what was going on at the cloister wall. He only pried a split second of scene before Lizard-man slammed his prison box forcing him to fall back against the other side. He tried to break his fall with his re-opened arm, trying his hardest to keep the delayed pain from having a voice.

They are still talking, like long-lost relatives. What does that monster have planned for them?

"Given the information we were privy to, probably something quite big," said Charm.

I would not call anything we heard 'information'. Just a jumbled mess of words and phrases. They are brother and sister or brothers, Ryudasu is somehow their cousin, and they are from another place all together that the two siblings have no memory of.

"Exactly," the vibration Charm 'spoke' was short and a bit shocking to Yuuki's system. "With the three of them, how could something big not happen?"

Why do you think something bad is about to happen, then? Yuuki was getting tired of think-speaking. He had to fight the urge to utter sounds. He wanted this Inanimate to give him whatever special abilities now to free himself.

"I didn't say 'bad'. I said 'big'. But I'm sure it will be bad for some if not many. Nobody who is selfish and wants something is up to any good, including us."

Just do something to get us out of here. Yuuki tightened his fists wanting to pound his prison wall. He knew his last hit of ink was affecting his mood, but his craving was satisfied for the time being. The hulking figure standing in front of him made him second guess his desire.

"I don't think I can give you that kind of physical power. I believe it will be an ability regarding time from what I've gathered so far. Sorry, you're going to have to rely on your own muscle power."

What good are you! The silent exclamation surprised Yuuki. At least he was finally getting the hang of effective thought-speak. *If you cannot do anything, then why am I still wearing you? What is preventing me from just ripping you off and crushing you?* Yuuki started tugging at Charm. His fingers fumbling over the almost solidified clasp. He didn't remember the last time he took it off, if he ever did. He even wore it during his daily baths while still in the cloister. The sulphur and other corrosive minerals never turned the silver bangle even the slightest tint of black.

Charm remained calm. "Communion for one."

Yuuki was starting to think calm was the only emotional state the Inanimate was capable of exuding. The realization that he would be forever bonded to this Inanimate finally sunk in. *I do not have that choice, do I?*

"I'm afraid not. We are figuratively and will soon be physically attached to each other. You will learn soon enough that brute strength is only one kind of ability. You've been with the Editor long enough to observe how he operates. Why do you think he needs dumb slabs of reprocessed meat like the one in front of you to be his muscle?"

But from what I can see, he has the power to create those skinny nothings that seem to control those pieces of meat.

"Perhaps there are ways you can make your own army."

Yuuki crunched his face in confusion at what his Inanimate just vibrated through his over-stimulated mind. *Why would I need an army?*

"Remember what you have been through," said Charm. "The moment you stepped out into this city, you have been in nothing but danger. Why would you not need some kind of protection. Seems like anyone in Symb has one. Comes with the relationship it seems. You have to have realized why."

Yuuki kept his mind as quiet as he could. He now wished it never started the conversation. But he couldn't stop his brain from talking. The prison he wanted free from was not the translucent box.

He did reluctantly see Charm's point. He was no longer this lost Wamono monk naïvely in awe of the city around him. He was now in the dangerous mind-bending thick of it. *Will I become as demented and cruel?*

"I'm not sure," responded Charm. The question was not intended to be answered. But Yuuki had a feeling Charm didn't have the concept of rhetorical questioning. "We'll have to wait and see. But something is definite. You are no longer Yuuki-Hana the pure acolyte Wamono monk. It is time you acted like a prophet and recruit followers."

Yuuki still tried to remain focused on Lizard-man for any signs of distraction. There was none. He had to admire their single-mindedness in their jobs. The house of a man kept one eye on him and the other on what was happening with his prophet across the street. *And what am I becoming, and don't say, 'prophet'. I know that already.*

"You are becoming a man of future importance. How does that sound?"

Ridiculous, responded Yuuki.

"Maybe so, but I'm afraid you will find it better than any of the alternatives facing you," answered Charm.

Something caught Yuuki's attention out of the corner of his eye in the opposite direction from the uncanny meeting by the Aoheki wall. Someone was crouching in a half-hidden corner peeking around it every few seconds. He wanted to focus more on the figure but didn't want to do anything to give Lizard-man an excuse to pummel the box. It was probably someone cowering from but curious about the spider monster that just appeared on the walls of Aoheki. That person probably had never even noticed that Aoheki was there until today. He decided to ignore the person and turned his attention back to the Character.

I need to 'talk' to someone, he thought-spoke. He knew the barely veiled insult would mean nothing to the intended recipient. He attempted to make eye contact with Lizard-man. It wasn't difficult since there was always one bloodshot eye on him the entire time. It widened slightly at the surprise of the intent.

"What's your name?" Yuuki asked, still focusing on that one eye.

"None of your business," replied Lizard-man. Both open-sore-like eyes now looked at him. "I don't know yours, so why should I tell you mine."

"This is literally child's play," said Charm.

"I'm very sorry. My name is Yuuki, Yuuki-Hana."

The Character snickered. "Hana? That's a girl's name."

Yuuki laughed with him. "Yes, I guess it is." He had never realized his name had a specific gender. No one in Aoheki ever commented on it.

The Character looked at Yuuki confused. He must have been displaying strange expressions while communicating with Charm. He needed to get this imbecile to warm up to him. *Maybe him thinking that I am this weak feminine monk will get him to feel less threatened.*

"Hardly," said Charm. "His main dangerous adversaries are mostly women; that all-female Cabal that your friend Mimi belongs to, that woman talking with your insane host, and the spider creature."

I don't want your opinion on anything right now. "So, now will you tell me your name?" Yuuki adjusted his arms that were folded across his chest, exposing the bracelet on one and the hardening wound on the other. The Character noticed the shimmer the bracelet produced from the reflection of the dim sun from a distant window.

Yuuki was about to hide the bracelet under his sleeve but saw that the simpleton was mesmerized by it. It wasn't simply a quick glance at something that just appeared in view. It was stronger. The Character's large rheumy eyes only blinked when they started to get desperate for moisture. Yuuki kept the bracelet exposed and continued trying to make conversation.

"Do you want me to try to guess your name?" He asked still assuming the childish game would open him up.

"Tomo?" answered the scaly Character, still transfixed on the gleaming bangle. The slight raised tone at the last "o" seemed like he wasn't sure of his own name.

That was easy, Yuuki thought. *He's still staring at you.*

"Ask him more questions." Charm's vibrations signaled curiosity.

"Tomo, where are you from?"

"Shinyuyogi."

"No, I mean before you started working for your prophet."

Tomo kept starring at the bracelet. His blinks were becoming fewer, and tears started to roll down his eyes. "I ... I don't know." He jerked back just enough to startle Yuuki and took in a deep breath. "I'm from Ikebu." His eyes never strayed from Yuuki's azalea bracelet.

Tomo's facial contortions told Yuuki the man was surprised he knew and was not sure it was true. *He seems to be remembering.* "Ikebu." Repeated Yuuki. He had no idea where that was, but assumed it was a ward or district. He was about to ask how old he was, but Tomo continued without prompting.

"But I did not always live there. I moved." Tomo's breathing became shallow, and he was sweating. "Walls. Lots of walls." Yuuki knew he was remembering from the stripped sentences coming out of him. He remained quiet and let the Character spew out as much information as he wanted, as Yuuki wanted.

Tomo finally shifted his sight from the bracelet to Yuuki. Rust-stained tears slowly streaked down his face leaving quickly drying faded orange paths behind. Fright won over Yuuki's battling emotions. He didn't know what was happening and if he was the cause. Tomo fixed his rusty eyes on his prisoner charge and slammed his muscular reptilian arm against the cube. Yuuki instinctively pressed himself up tight against the far wall of his box. Tomo pointed a clawed finger at Yuuki's kimono. "I wore one every day."

Yuuki stood there not able to speak, but his mind raced. *A Wamono?* The trance Tomo fell into was starting to dissipate. His blinking overcompensating, several a second. He squinted to get the last gushes of oxidized tears out of his eyes and shook his head. His entire face aware of the present.

"What happened?" It was not a question but a demand. "What did you do to me?"

Yuuki froze. Even if he could move, there was no place to go. Tomo's face softened and real tears, tinted peach from the left-over bloody rust, welled up in his eyes. He grabbed Yuuki's box and shook "Who am I?"

"You're Tomo originally from Ikebu, and I believe a former Wamono monk." Yuuki didn't want him to re-forget.

Tomo shook his massive head trying to shake the hazy identities waring out of his head. "No. Not Tomo. I'm...I'm Ryo in service to my prophet and god." He appeared back to the situation at hand, remembering the spectacle going on at the wall. A deep rumbling awoke deep in his chest then escaped through his fang-tattered lips in a form of a deep scream. The giant ran toward the wall yelling "My Prophet! My Prophet!", leaving Yuuki on his own. He looked around the corner and saw Ryudasu climbing back up the wall with the Editor and the female dangling in a bowl in what looked like the stuff the spider made her deadly webbing from. She was taking them inside the cloister. "Something big and bad is about to happen."

"Yuuki!" A vaguely familiar voice startled Yuuki out of his awe. He looked behind from where he thought the voice was coming from.

"Hiroka?" He pressed his face and hands to the transparent walls of his box. "I thought you were kidnapped too ... or ..." He could only smile.

He was drawn back to the chaos at the wall. Both Tsudii and Suriidii minions came out from their alley and doorway hiding places to join Ryo/Tomo in trying to coax their respective prophets down from the wall.

Hiroka knocked on the box. "Let's get you out of here before that oaf realizes he left you unattended." Hiroka looked around making sure she didn't see any signs of an emaciated puppet master. "He will be made to remember he screwed up and rush back to secure you." Yuuki looked into her eyes. They were a deepening purple.

She looked around on the ground for something useful. "This should work." She picked up a jagged chunk of concrete and steel that must've fallen from the dilapidated building they were up against. "Stand back."

It took several slams against the box for cracks to start forming but only took a couple more for them to turn into a giant splintered wound. She used her fist to break through the weakened spot, reached in, and grabbed Yuuki by his kimono sleeve. Not even out of breath. She took out a blade from her pants pocket and sliced through the restraints, all needing only one powerful slash. "Come on!"

A part of him wanted to stay and observe Ryo/Tomo. Something definitely happened to him, and he, or at least Charm, made it happen. He knew he would get through to the real person underneath those scales and fangs. But freedom was of the utmost importance.

The two kept running until Hiroka felt it was safe enough to slow down to a rushed walk. Yuuki kept the increasing number of questions he wanted to ask her to himself until they both caught their breath. He was glad to run, even with his aching beaten feet.

They finally made it to the entrance of a viscerdenn station. It could've been the same one she took him to when they first met. The humid organic exhaust coming up from the tunneled depths was a welcome sensation. He hadn't thought anything would ever become familiar to him in this city that refused to make any sense to him.

Hiroka never let go of Yuuki's sleeve the entire journey down through to the hollowed intestines of the city. The maze of stairways and elevators made him dizzy and lightheaded. There were still no words exchanged.

The final elevator opened onto the platform. The latest viscerdenn groaned and complained away.

"Damn!" It was the first word Yuuki heard her say since her daring rescue mission. "We're going to have to wait for the next one. Let's hope they're in a good mood today and running somewhat on time." Still holding onto Yuuki's trunk of an arm, she walked over and collapsed on a bench draped with graffiti.

Charm, any input? Yuuki was at last happy he could 'talk' to something in a situation like this completely private and uncensored.

"There's nothing really to say," vibrated Charm. "You were rescued by that Fujou woman."

I do not mean that. You know what I am talking about. Yuuki looked over to Hiroka. She had stood up and was talking, but there was no one around except a few passengers waiting for the same train and a few dirty tattered souls taking advantage of the warm exhales of the constant arriving and departing viscerdenn. Many of the others waiting were having similar conversations with no one. Several seemed to be talking to their hands. He gave up trying to make sense of it and let them and Hiroka continue with their one-way conversations in peace.

"Oh, yes. The Character," said Charm without any inflection or realization. "It seems we have found our ability, or at least one of them."

I do not even understand what we did.

"The past. Remembering. It's that simple. How do you think you remembered your mother carrying you to Aoheki."

Yuuki's eyes suddenly burned with hot tears yet to be cried out. "What are you saying?" He forgot to think-speak. It was easier to use this voice to talk; more natural. Besides, he would fit in with the solo conversations of the many around him.

"You knew; your mind just didn't want to tell you. It's making sense now, isn't it?"

Yuuki would never be able to lie to himself again. That frightened him more than anything that the city could physically pummel him with. "Why did you not tell me?"

"I thought I didn't need to. They are your memories," replied Charm. "O.K., I'm telling you. Your mother took you to the steps of Aoheki. Why those vicious Shisa didn't tear her or you to shreds is something I don't even understand. I guess they smelled the infant purity in you."

"Come on," interrupted Hiroka. "The viscer's coming." Yuuki hadn't noticed the advance force of the mech-creature's exhaust. "Who were you talking to?"

"No one. Just myself." He could've asked her the same thing but didn't.

The viscerdenn finally arrived moaning to a halt and releasing a tired gasp, thankful for the brief repose before racing to the next teasing repose down the tunnel. All the puckering sphincters along the pulsing body opened simultaneously, welcoming them into itself. Hiroka turned to Yuuki. "Are you O.K to do this?"

Yuuki smiled. "Yes. I promise, no more freak outs."

The metal and flesh beast groaned up its bio engines and began the creep out of the station. Yuuki looked out the tiny clear membrane of the sphincter door. A de-hooded robed woman stared at him as he moved away. He stared back until the platform was just a glow suffocating from the blackness that soon embraced it.

The fresh air felt good. Fujin had never gotten used to the viscerdenn exhalations. At least above ground, the persistent stench was diluted with the much more abundant air. She didn't want to go back to her sanctuary just yet. She called off her Blues after seeing what hundreds of others saw. But that was not what she had to knead around in her head. She was almost one-hundred percent sure, her youngest son. It didn't matter that the last time she had seen him was when he was only a month old when she left him in front of a Wamono cloister hoping he would not be devoured by the Shisa guardians. The connection between mother and child traversed beyond outward appearance.

She was a second too late. He sped off in a viscerdenn to who knew where. She was there in time to at least call out his name to see if he would turn around, but she was too scared. What would she do if he did? What would he do if he realized who she was. But he did at least see her if it was just for a second or two.

She walked across the street to a small outdoor café. It seemed to be busier than usual by the looks of the harried waiter bumping into and tripping over tables, chairs, and patrons trying to take and deliver everyone's orders. *I guess the surreal event at Aoheki was good for business.* There was one small table free. She increased her pace a little to grab it. She needed something cool and palette cleansing to get the fetid remnants of viscerdenn out of her mouth.

The second she put body to chair she felt dozens of eyes on her. She didn't bother to cloak her head. She didn't want to be Fujin. She had the urge to be who she was to everyone on these streets, Primary Council Widow Ogawa of the Ue-No Citizens Council. She had to be Fujin to do the dirty work necessary to keep Ue-No prophet-free. She had been doing it for so long that she had become accustomed to this anonymous side of her life. Only a select couple of the more stable Blues knew who she really was.

She smiled, acknowledging the gawking crowd, then buried herself in the oversized menu that gave her a sense of razor thin privacy. The menu couldn't shield her from the mumblings of the other patrons. Did she know what just happened at the walls of Aoheki? Was she involved? Did she know about the Spider monster? She had been neglecting her official duties, especially lately, but there was no way she could've known about the events that transpired at the walls. She had never directly communicated with the Wamono at Aoheki. There was no way to do so. Each cloister was its own semi-independent entity. They wanted nothing to do with the outside and the outside didn't care what happened within those walls. But she did.

Her Blues kept her somewhat close to the Wamono Order. She kept those defunct Smashers as true to their original mission as possible. Getting them addicted to Illumination Blue, those who were not already, was the only way to keep them on the right path. She spent years forcing her way into the manufacturing and dealing circles of the illicit drug. Now she was the only source of the substance in Ue-No and one of the few throughout Hinodé. She wasn't proud of it, but it was one of those means-justifies-the-end situations.

She finally made eye contact with the frazzled waiter. He put up one finger signaling he would be right with her. She didn't know how long she could deal with the stares and mumblings. She looked at the menu long enough. Any longer, and it would look strange. She had spent so long trying to hide the other half of her, that just being un-hooded was the same as being completely naked. Her official position as Primary Council wasn't an elected one, so even in her official skin, she wasn't required to go out into the masses. The only reason people knew what she looked like was from her face plastered inside, and sometimes outside, every council office in the ward. It was something her predecessors perpetuated, a cult of personality to counter the other more dangerous ones of the prophets. She didn't like it but understood. And it worked. She, her title, was seen as a beacon of strength and power against the corrupted forces of prophet/god Symbs and their mind-controlling religions.

"What can I get for you?" The waiter was quite out of breath.

"I'll just have a green tea and a sweet mochi."

The waiter looked relieved. "Right away."

She had no other place than the forgotten sub-basement "annex" to the Council House to be truly alone but not normal. Any sense of normalcy died decades ago. She wanted to be a normal citizen again. The wish quickly died when seeing one of her in-the-know Blues coming toward her. *Kazunori. Who is that with him?* She wanted to leave before he noticed her. Too late.

Her Major of the Blues was only loosely tethered to her and her cause. He was one of her first recruits from the Smasher descendants that got themselves addicted to Illumination Blue. He was one of those supremely functional addicts. He also had his own way of keeping in contact with someone within the walls of Aoheki, which he kept very close to his chest.

Kazunori locked a quizzical look on her. He veered from his path heading for her. The man with him started to come into better focus, but she still couldn't get enough information.

"Primary Council Ogawa," tactfully whispered Kazunori. "It's not like you to patron a café."

Ogawa prepared to answer, but the familiarity of the stranger distracted her. She had the same feeling as when she first recognized Yuuki.

"Mother?" said Shinya. The utterance seemed automatic.

"Mother?" Kazunori looked at Shinya like he was having some sort of fit. "What's gotten into you?" He looked at his superior. "I apologize …"

"Shinya?" Interrupted Ogawa.

Their combined affliction of tachypsychia slowed the world, the universe, to a gooey miasma of memory.

thirty-three

RYUDASU'S QUARTERS WAS EVEN more cocooned than when Hégo first entered only a couple days before. There was no need for much additional light. The ephemeral hoary glow of the webbing sufficed.

"Ah, Master-sama," said Ryudasu. She was centered in her web snacking on something still squirming in a perfectly smooth cocoon. "Come in and join us."

Hégo glared at the two guests. It was the first time he had seen any kind of prophet in almost a century. "I see you had an eventful first day on the walls fishing for prophets."

The two siblings barely acknowledged the Master. They were too occupied nervously scanning where they found themselves. "You must be what they call the Editor and Queen Ren," Hégo was neither welcoming or accusatory. He wasn't confident about this plan. But Ryudasu insisted that getting these two barbarians involved would help his cause. She now had to prove how committing such a heinous act as letting non-converts enter the sacred grounds of a Wamono cloister would benefit his ambitions. He looked up at Ryudasu raising his eyebrows then nodded, signaling her to get on with the meeting.

"Now that we are finally together, we can start connecting all these loose ends," started Ryudasu. She flung the spent snack against the wall with one of her front pincers, landing with a dead thud. Hego's stomach refluxed a small amount of putrid acid up into his throat. Whatever it was, he hoped there were plenty of them still left to keep satisfying her appetite.

Ren was the first of the two outsiders to speak. "Just tell us what all this is about, plainly and simply." She remained defiant even after the harrowing journey up and over the walls. She and her dwarfish brother were shivering. Hégo took comfort in knowing it was not from the bone chill of the cloister.

"As I told you two and the esteemed Master of the Cloister," continued Ryudasu, "we three are family and not from this world. None of us are, in fact."

The last part was a surprise to Hégo. "What do you mean none of us? I was born in Kowa district almost a century and a half ago."

"Ah, Kowa," interrupted Ren. "That's one of mine now. Beautiful riverfront properties there. I've done a lot there to revitalize the dilapidated small-goods port."

"Shut up and let the spider talk," said her brother. Hégo didn't understand why he kept his tinted glasses on. Even with the eerie glow of Ryudasu webbing, the space was absent of detail.

"My apologies," responded Ren. She gave her brother a menacing look.

"Yes, you were most likely born in Kowa, Master-sama, but you were really born—a real birth—most likely in Yedo or thereabouts."

"Yedo?" Hégo snickered. "I did not take you for much of a believer."

"There is nothing to believe in. It exists. Are you telling me you do not believe in such a place?"

"Of course I do. It is where we will all reside after our final cycle." He looked at the two outsiders. "Well, believers, anyway."

"I am afraid you and your fellow monks have it quite backwards. It is where we all—all of us—came from. It is where we all started; not where you self-righteous Wamomo will finally rest."

"What the fuck is Yedo?" The Editor blurted, obviously frustrated at the sudden one-to-one conversation.

"Language!" Hégo yelled forcing a surprised jump from both siblings. He didn't much care how people talked, but he needed to show that he was in control here, not Ryudasu. "This is blasphemy! I will not stay here and listen to this. The deal is off." Hégo turned around to barge out the ridiculous meeting. Just as he reached out to open the silk-lacquered door, Ryudasu stretched her long front legs up and over the Master and slammed them hard against the door. Dust and tiny pieces of rubble dislodged from the powerful vibrations rained down on the attendees. Hégo fell back into a mass of webbing. He struggled, which made the silk tighten around him restricting him the more he struggled. Luckily, the soft clump was not connected to the main web or he would've have already been wrapped up and suffocating in a satiny death shroud.

The Editor and Ren's fright reflexes made them grab onto each other. "Get your damn util-god to do something," said Ren.

"Draw can't do anything here. Neither can yours."

Ryudasu let her legs slide down the door to the floor, leaving deep gouges in the warped wood. She retracted them to the normal positions crouched in front of her. "You zealots are all alike." she glared down at the huffing sweating Master. "One slight difference from your strict beliefs, and everything becomes blasphemous. You should be pleased that the place you all aspire to actually exists."

Hégo finally stopped struggling once he realized it was making things worse. "Let me out of here, I command it as your Master!"

"Of course, Master-sama." Ryudasu carefully reached over and used her pincers that had just almost destroyed the half-meter-thick door to delicately cut her Master free.

"This Yedo," said the Editor, "it's the city I've been remembering?"

"Yes, Futoshi," answered Ryudasu. She was still operating on Hégo. "And you, Atsushi? Have you started to remember your real life?"

"Yes, a little bit," responded Ren. That map is of Yedo, then." She said it as a fact and not as a question.

"Correct. I remembered a lot more than you two thanks to a tad overindulgence in that squid's ink. And this," she stopped snipping and raised one of her front legs and pointed it to herself, "is punishment for remembering. Well, it was what started it anyway. The ensuing insanity solidified it." She went back to her work in freeing Hégo.

"Why did you want to find us. What do you want of us?" Asked the Editor.

"As I said outside at the wall. To return to Yedo. You see. I remember much more, and that do-nothing of a nothing god does not seem to like that. I think it would rather no one here know anything about the physical Yedo or any other place like it. There are hundreds by the way."

Hégo was in no position to argue, but he had to re-assert what was left of his authority. "What does this escape into some memory have to do with the plan we talked about? You said you would help me increase the power of the order to outside these damnable walls."

"Do I have to explain everything to you?" Ryudasu sighed and continued. "You want to control the minds of Hinodé, correct?"

Hégo nodded. "Save is more appropriate."

"Whatever word makes you feel better about it." She looked over to her cousins. "We are to return to a life robbed us. Are you listening Inanimates?" She picked up Cane, which Hégo abandoned in the confusion at the door. "All of you?"

There was no audible response from the three Inanimates/idols, even within their hosts.

Ryudasu carefully placed Cane down next to its half-entombed host and continued. "We would have immense power there with our, eh, special characteristics. I would like you two," her six emotionless eyes focused on the siblings, "to go ahead and see what the place is like now, if what I assume is correct and time has progressed quite a bit there."

Hégo finally made it out of his almost tomb, stood up, and brushed himself off. "What are you going to do here in the meantime?" He was careful not to be anywhere near the main web.

"We are going to take control of this order to begin with, of course." She reached out one of her pincer forearms and gently scratched Hego's chin like a cherished pet. Hégo jump backed the second he felt the stone-coarseness of the giant bristly appendage. "But we are getting a bit ahead of ourselves. We first need that squirming squid."

"Do not forget that I am Master here." It was more for the guests than for her. "And what do you want with Amedo-sensei?"

"Our need of this Amedo does not concern you." The Editor and Ren looked at each other confused. "And do not fret about asserting your authority," Ryudasu continued ignoring her cousins' perplexed looks, "you will become Master of all the Wamono, and if you are still of your present cycle, Hinodé. Without me, you will remain in this dank grimworld for the little time you have left in this cycle; a Master of a few hundred scared monks. That is hardly anything to strive for."

"I'm not ready to up and walk away from all that I have, to abandon what I have worked so hard to build." Ren was defiant.

Ryudasu rasped a chuckle. "You think those measly neighborhoods are so important. That is so cute." She shifted her death-black eyes to the short brother. "Do you have the same concern?"

"Yes, as a matter of fact I do. I scarified everything for what I have now."

"I understand," responded Ryudasu. "But this is small time compared to what you can be in Yedo. You can have both, a trans-dimensional empire if you will." *With me as its godhead.*

"We don't have a say in any of this?"

"Ah, they are finally speaking. Which one are you?" Asked Ryudasu.

"The god Caliper."

"You can have a say when you are back in Yedo, god." Ryudasu rasped a sarcastic snicker. "You four can use that whole city as the backdrop for a prolonged double date."

"I do not want blood on my hands. You may be used to it, but I could never live with myself in any cycle." Hégo had high ambitions, but he didn't want to turn into another Ryudasu in his next cycle. The Gou-Tairei self-sustaining system of Retribution and Accolade was not subtle in how it treated such ambition.

Ryudasu crept towards the Master. Her front pincer feet delicately clicking on the rough stone. They could've been those of young Gésha-in-training of

Hégo's youth demurely returning to their mama's stable house. Instead, there was a heaving rasping that increased in intensity the closer the Aku got to him.

"I know you cannot be that naïve, Master-sama," said Ryudasu. She was so close to him that he could hear the drips of venom from her fangs hit the rubble. He scrunched his toes in as far as he could. "You best loosen your morals a bit if you believe in your religious path. It will not happen with the gentle pitter-patter of your bare feet." She pinched a clump of Hego's beaded hair. "Or the clanking of silly beads."

"So, we just stay trapped in here until we are magically transported to this Yedo?" Ren said, still unconvinced of what were faintly becoming real memories.

Hégo found his Master voice. "You are not welcome to remain within the sacred walls.

"The Master is correct. You cannot remain here. I will take you back out into," she turned her tiny eyed head towards Hégo, "Keibu-yo," then turned back to the siblings. "You are to gather your respective hordes outside this cloister in two weeks and take it over. That should give us all enough time to prepare." She focused her six eyes onto her cousins. "And fully remember."

"And how are we supposed to get in?" The Editor's arms as usual had no concept of the situation and continued their single-minded drawing. "You are going to transport all our forces in a giant web basket?"

"Send some of your fanatics beforehand to work on widening this tunnel for all of you to fit through comfortably. No one here will know what they will be doing. She pointed to the tunnel entrance. No one would dare come down to my quarters."

"But tell your goons to leave as soon as they make it through," ordered Hégo. "I do not want any of those freaks wondering around causing havoc before it is necessary."

Ryudasu clicked her mass closer to the Editor. "Futoshi, I would like you to get into contact with the Fujou Dame who delivered the Wamono to you. She is key for this side of the plan."

"Why is she so important."

"No time to explain. It won't concern you that much anyway once you two are in Yedo. Just tell her to prepare for Holy Spinner's arrival."

"Holy ...?" Hégo interrupted.

Ryudasu snapped her tiny head toward Hégo and growled. "The Gou-Tairei is only a god." She refocused on her cousins and growled a chuckle. "There are many such lesser deities." Her front leg-arms began their fastidious cleaning of her cuticular lips. "That woman will help us when needed."

"I still don't get what we would want with an ugly stone mausoleum full of reclusive monks?" asked Ren.

"This 'mausoleum' is the conduit to Yedo, or at least one of its inhabitants is." Ryudasu lowered her voice to a deep growl below the audible abilities of the humans around her. "And divine revenge."

Shinya, his mother, and Kazunori arrived at the annex after an oddly silent journey. The place was stark and smelled like Aoheki to Shinya. Fujin took them into her private office off the extreme minimalist reception chamber. She motioned the two to have a seat and poured them a glass of water.

"So," she began, still slowly pouring the water into their glasses. The water filling the vessels was the only sound, almost too loud for Shinya. "Has the Smasher program been resurrected?" She sat down and looked at her first born and broke a shamed smile.

"No, mother. I was sent out by my Master at Aoheki to reach out to the people here to educate them on the Wamono life and belief system."

"That sounds rather noble" She looked down into her glass she was now rolling between her palms.

"It's a new policy cooked up by the Aoheki Master, Fujin-sama," said Kazunori. "He has it in his head that the order is dying and needs a large influx of adherents for it to survive. I'm sure Shinya knows more about it than I. I simply received a message saying that I should take care of him for a while until he became more re-orientated to life out here again." He grabbed his glass and slouched back onto the sofa as if embarrassed of speaking too long.

Fujin turned toward her son. "Well, whatever the case, I'm glad to see you. You look well."

Shinya looked everywhere but at her. He should've said he was sorry for running away from her, but he wanted her to say she was sorry for shutting him out of her life. "What is this place?" He looked around at the lush embroidery and carvings hanging on the walls, hoping the small talk would ease the tension.

"That's part of a very long and complicated story, Shinya." Fujin seemed to be glad of the question that involved a lengthy answer. "I'm Primary Council Ogawa of the Ue-No Citizens Council."

Shinya's eyes glazed over with incomprehension. He looked over to Kazunori for any additional explanation. The Blue major slightly shrugged his shoulders.

Ogawa proceeded to explain the political make-up of the council and its relationship with the other spheres of influence in Hinodé. Shinya felt like she was keeping something from him.

"How do you know Kazunori?" He looked to his minder. "How do you know my mother?"

"I have another title, Shinya." Shinya noticed her straightening up and becoming much more serious and a bit proud. "I am what some, including Kazunori, call Fujin."

Shinya cocked is head like a puppy hearing a strange sound for the first time.

"I have taken it upon myself to rid our city of the Symb plague."

This was all getting too much for Shinya. He was no longer simply confused. He was getting frustrated with all the mysterious jargon. "Mother ... Fujin," he said correcting himself to who she was now and no longer. "I have been secluded for the past twenty years. Talk to me as if I still have the limited life experience of a twelve-year old."

"Forgive my insensitivity." Ogawa fidgeted ever so slightly. Shinya took a shameful pleasure in that. She didn't force him to join the Wamono, but it didn't make her mental abandonment of him any easier to take.

He wanted to stay angry for a few more minutes. He ignored her and looked to Kazunori for further explanation. "What is this plague?"

Kazunori looked at Ogawa waiting for permission to take over the explanation before translating Hinodé terminology into Wamono. She gave him a defeated nod. "A Symb is the parasitic relationship between an Animate and Inanimate."

Shinya looked around to the cushions on the sofa and the glasses on the table. He began picking at the corner of the small pillows squished between him and Kazunori. "Inanimates. They do exist, then."

"They are very real," continued Kazunori. "I know they are not talked about much in the cloisters. Most would rather forget they even exist and try to relegate them into a myth for novitiate like you. Only the Gou-Tairei knows the logic in their existence."

"They are the center of some sort of religion, then," said Shinya.

Ogawa decided it was her turn to edify. "They are criminal gangs supported by the Mayor who use the power of a Symb relationship to wreak havoc—killing and ... raping." The hate in her eyes frightened Shinya.

Shinya looked at her intently for the first time since they first met at the café. "Does this have something to do with that day at our store?" He couldn't bring himself to say "murder" and "rape", especially in front of Kazunori. He was not sure how much he knew of his mother's life before she became this Fujin.

Ogawa looked down to her lap, embarrassed. "Kazunori, please leave us alone for a bit."

"Yes, of course, Fujin-sama." He stood up and walked toward the door requiring no explanation. From that small exchange, Shinya knew his mother had become a very powerful woman. "By the way, have you heard from Shigé? I haven't heard back from him."

"I'm sorry, Fujin-sama, I have not. He probably stopped off at a hit shack after meeting with Oné-chan to get his Blue fix and … uh … got lost in Blue Timeloss." Kazunori bowed, closing the door with a barely audible click.

Mother and son sat in nervous silence for a long minute until Shinya broke the tension. "As Fujin, how are you curing the city of this plague?"

"Shinya, first let me tell you how very sorry I am for how I treated you." She reached her hand over to him, but he did not reciprocate, only staring at the aging hand. She could've been a grandmother. "I regret a lot of my life after that excruciating day. Nothing more so than pushing you away. I know you may not forgive me, and I will understand if you never do." Her hand remained out towards her estranged son. "I hope that we'll stay in each other's lives and perhaps heal together over time"

Seeing her eyes filled with an emotion other than hate broke down the protective barrier of anger. He finally took her hand. The smile that appeared on his mother's face creased her eyes just enough for a tear to escape and run down both cheeks. "It is not just you who has regrets, mother," Shinya began. "I should have never left you when you needed me the most. I should have understood what you were going through."

"You were only twelve." she held her smile and his hand tight in hers.

Shinya's eyes began to tear up as well. "I am so sorry for what happened to you. I know logically I could not have done anything to comfort you then, but now that I am a grown man, I want to help you in any way I can." He let go of her hand only to wipe away his tears. "I assume that it was one of these Symb gunshyu people who killed father and violated you, am I correct?"

Ogawa only needed to nod. It was still too embarrassing and painful to talk about.

Shinya took her hand again, with both hands, and squeezed. "Then, let us do this together."

thirty-four

YUUKI HAD NEVER SEEN anything quite like it. The soft pink didn't match the building's dark presence. *The pink in the sky I saw that first night.* "This is where Mimi lives now?"

"Yes," answered Hiroka. "A lot has happened over the past few days." Hiroka avoided eye contact with Yuuki.

Is she angry with me for getting kidnapped?

"I don't know," said Charm. "Maybe we should try our new-found ability on her."

No, I do not want to trick her. It would not be fair, responded Yuuki.

Hiroka led Yuuki under the intense bright white lights spewing out from the main entrance. Yuuki couldn't make out any detail of what was inside, only white nothing. He kept his arm up near his eyes to protect them from the illumination onslaught as they entered the intense white void.

Yuuki grabbed hold of Hiroka's shoulder to make sure he didn't fall to the non-floor. There were no shadows or edges. "What is this?" He asked more to himself than to Hiroka. There was a total quiet within him. It was like Charm had disappeared. It was the first time Yuuki noticed the absence of what had been a constant low-frequency hum since Charm awoke into his life.

"Don't worry, it's all just an illusion. Just use me as an anchor. I had the same feeling when I first entered. You get used to it pretty quickly." It took her a few turns and backtracks to find the elevator. She pushed the almost invisible button to call the elevator down from where it disgorged its last passengers.

The door opened, and the two released simultaneous sighs of relief at the muted browns and beiges of the elevator interior. Silence filled the humming box all the way to Mimi's suite. The only sound was the elevator shaking ever so slightly as it sped up through the innards of the scraper.

"Yuuki!" Mimi cried out as the doors opened and ran towards him. She was in obvious pain. "You have to leave!" She forced herself to put her arms around him and squeezed tightly. He didn't remember ever being hugged before. It felt bizarre but good.

Yuuki's muscles suddenly tightened.They pulled away from each other as fast as they embraced. The two reunited friends looked at each other confused at what just happened.

"She is in Symb." Charm explained in its usual overly calm manner. "The reason she is asking us to leave."

"What's happening?" asked Hiroka. She plopped herself into the nearing hanging egg and just swung trying to figure out the sudden tension filling the suite.

"You're in Symb." Mimi said in a flat tone of unwanted truth.

"Yes. It 'woke' up when we were freed from whatever forces kept it dormant inside Aoheki."

"The bracelet." Hiroka said. Yuuki nodded. He saw another woman in black and white in other weird chair petting a small creature. Unlike her Hiroka, she exuded no emotion.

"This building is mine." Mimi's face dripped with sweat. "I convinced Palace to allow you up against its advice." She ground her teeth in agony. "I wanted to see you."

"She's dangerous. We need to get away as quickly as possible." Charm was the most agitated he had felt from it.

She is my friend.

"She may be, but *it* is not and the two of them in Communion are not." Replied Charm.

"We can't be near each other, Yuuki," Mimi said. Her voice was sad and sincere. "Our relationships won't allow it."

"There is no way we can get around this?" He was asking both Mimi and Charm.

"No," said Charm. "We will end up killing each other, or more accurately, you will end up killing her or she will end up killing you. I would assume the latter.

Mimi stumbled over to her desk to sit down. The agitation within her was becoming too much to handle. Yuuki wanted to go over and help her but physically couldn't. "Hiroka," she ordered. "Get him out of here. Take him a couple kilometers away at least.

Hiroka was not understanding what was going on, delaying her reaction.

"Now!" Spittle spewed and dribbled from her lips. Yuuki heard both a plea and threat in her voice. It was if she was speaking in two different voices at the same time.

The building began to tremble. "We have to leave now," said Charm.

Hiroka grabbed Yuuki and made for the elevator, using all her stength to drag the weakened Wamono. The building's shakes were intensifying by the second.

Once the elevator doors closed, the duo collapsed backwards against the elevator walls. They couldn't waste their spent energy on talking, only breathing.

"I need to sit down for a little bit?" Yuuki's feet were still too weak to support his bulk. He and Hiroka were far enough away from Pink Palace to feel somewhat safe. His arm was beginning to throb. He didn't know if it was from the pain of being sliced and gnawed on or his addiction telling him to take another drink before it completely scabbed over again. He caught himself drooling and quickly wiped the escaping saliva from his mouth.

He kept looking back behind them and through the increasing throng of people as they neared a station. The streets had become a complete chaos of people darting this way and that to get to where they needed to go and in a hurry. "Where are we?"

"Sui station," answered Hiroka. "We're still in her territory, but we should be far enough away from Deko-cho. "We can get to Shinyuyogi from here."

Yuuki had almost forgotten he had a place at the Guildscouple's home.

"I contacted them earlier and explained what happened and why you didn't show up that next day." She smiled. "They are waiting for you."

They sat down on a bench outside the station entrance. The immaculate bushes and soft-lit stone paths swerving in and around them were the pride of the residents of Sui. No other station was as taken care of by its residents. The two refugees lost themselves in their own silence trying to figure out what had happened back at the Palace. Yuuki began massaging his city-roughened feet. He stared at the human rush but only heard his voice trying to keep his unnatural craving at bay.

Hiroka broke the latest bubble of silence surrounding them. "What was that all about back there?"

"I wish I knew. I don't understand anything about this place." His head collapsed into shaking hands. "I should've never left Aoheki."

"You found out where you came from. Wasn't that at least worth it?" She saw he was about to cry.

"That I was really abandoned by my own mother? Yea, very worth it."

"You still don't know that yet. You don't even know if it was your mother who left you at Aoheki."

But he knew the woman he saw through his blurry infant eyes was her.

"It doesn't matter now. She was right in hiding me as a Wamono. She knew I would amount to nothing. Look at me!" He gave up keeping the tears away. He was in full sob. People walking by gave curious glances before speeding up once they saw what was happening. Only kids stopped long enough to stare at them before their minders tugged them away from the embarrassing scene.

"There's no use in blubbering about it," said Hiroka.

"You do not have to be with me. Mimi did not kick you out. You do not have an Inanimate attached to you. Do you?"

"Inanimate?" Hiroka laughed after figuring out what he meant. "No. No, I don't have an idol. There is something bigger and better to believe in than those parasitic unions of mutual psychoses.

Yuuki was too distracted to ask what she meant. He didn't actually care.

Hiroka reached over and straightened his kimono collar. "She told me to take you to safety. You need to understand that she didn't want you to go. It was for the safety of you both, but mainly yours by what I can understand of the whole bizarro situation. So like it or not, little big monk," she tried to lighten the heavy atmosphere surrounding them, "you're stuck with me."

Yuuki let go of a little smile. But it didn't last long. A realization hit him as hard as running full force into a cloister wall.

"What's wrong?" Hiroka said. Her half grin disappearing.

"My mother." Yuuki said, staring at his companion but not really seeing her. "She was my mother."

Yea, I think you made that pretty clear you think it was your mother who left you in front of those nasty lions-dog things."

"No, at the station today. She was my mother."

"Who?"

"I saw her as we were pulling away. She was staring right at me. It was her. I know it!" Yuuki stood up. He didn't know why. His body demanded it.

"Yuuki, calm down." Hiroka grabbed his hand to lower him back down.

"I know it was. I know!"

"O.K., I believe you. Just try to stay calm. How do you know?

Yuuki told her about the memory vision that was the result of his and Charm's bond. Not because she needed to know, but to hear it for himself. It was the first time he spoke about it to another person - another Animate. He told her that was why he felt faint when they were in front of his parents' store near Shinyuyogi.

"So, she knows you are back out here then," Hiroka said, half asking half stating a fact.

"Yes. She knew who she was looking at. I am positive." Yuuki's body collapsed onto itself as if every bone in his body disintegrated simultaneously. "There is no way I will be able to find her again or she me." He looked up at the never-ending randomness of people zipping past them.

"You of all people should know that anything can happen here and fast." Yuuki knew she was trying to make him feel more optimistic. "Maybe it wasn't as random as you think."

Yuuki looked around trying to spot anything in the same still motion as they were.

"I don't think you will spot her here," Hiroka said following his eyes around the green shrubs and along the soft-pink stone paths.

"I guess you are right." He still darted his eyes around focusing for a few seconds when he saw faces looking his way or not moving with the urban herd passing in front of them.

Hiroka stood up. "Come on. Let's go. I'm sure Metaler Junya and Embroideress Mayu will have room for me just for tonight. I'll call them now to make sure."

"Through the air?"

"What? Oh, yea through the air." She snickered and thumb-flicker her ring on as they entered the station.

"Yuuki the Wamono," said Metaler Junya to the young monk blocking the doorway.

"Guildsman Metaler Junya," responded Yuuki. He bowed out of respect. "I am very sorry I did not come back the next day. I ..."

Metaler Junya interrupted. "There is no need to apologize."

Embroideress Mayu came up and peeked around her husband and with a wide smile. "Yuuki-san!" Another wave of relief flowed through Yuuki. He imagined the feeling tickling Charm.

"Guildswoman Embroideress Mayu, it is very nice to see you again," Yuuki said. He wanted to be as polite as possible. They were the only people he had met that he believed deserved it.

"Please, call me Mayu," said the Embroideress. "This is our second meeting, so we are friends now." The smile never left her face.

"Are you here to stay with us for a while?" Metaler Junya asked. He wasn't wearing his joy as much as Mayu, but Yuuki could tell it was there just under the stern fatherly expression.

"Yes, if I still may," he answered, still in high polite mode. He felt a tug on his grungy sleeve. "Oh, you remember Hiroka?" he moved out of the way to put her more in view.

"Yes, of course," said Metaler Junya. "Thank you for your call."

Everyone eventually situated themselves around the Guildscouple's low table with the beautiful and familiar cushions. It took almost two hours of talking, explaining, and asking questions of what had happened to Yuuki since the last time they were all together. Mayu and Metaler Junya were incredulous but not surprised. Like every Hinodéan, they knew of the Editor's perversions and fascination with collecting the oddities of the city. "Everybody calls it his 'zoo'," said Metaler Junya. The words were full of hate but also embarrassment in the fact that Yuuki, a sacred Wamono, had to experience the worst of the city so quickly.

While continuing the story of his ordeal, Yuuki inadvertently exposed his wounded arm.

"Yuuki! What did they do to you!" Embroideress Mayu almost leapt up to grab his arm. Only her age prevented her from doing so.

"Oh, just an accident. It is fine."

"It doesn't look fine," Metaler Junya said. "We'll have to bandage that up."

Yuuki gave a minuscule nod in acknowledgement and quickly withdrew his arm into his kimono sleeve. The hunger pains were getting angrier.

After a several cups of Mayu's delicious tea, Yuuki finally received some answers concerning his former kidnapper. He couldn't get his head around how he could muster so much control while being so hated. Fear could only go so far before turning into an uncontrollable and perhaps misguided urge to fight back.

The Guildscouple told him that the Editor's Symb with the god-idol, the so-called Draw, he had immense power as its prophet and that drugs played a large role in his fanatic following. The couple noticed the surprise in his eyes and settled his fear. They and the rest of the Guild were not addicts. Only true believers became addicted to the powerful optic-narcotic the prophet and his god-thing laced their popular publications with plus other more pedestrian drugs pushed in the various manga cafés in his wards. Non-addicts, like the Flower Guild, are politically controlled through extortion, blackmail, and old fashion life-threats and murder. It had worked so far.

Yuuki wasn't sure if he should tell them about Charm. They were suspicious about Inanimates, rightfully so. But this one belonged to their deceased daughter. Unlike with Kugai, he didn't want to disappoint them.

Before he could muster up enough bravery to at least hint that he was in Symb, a heavy slothy knock shook the door. Metaler Junya stood up from the floor and motioned his wife to stay where she was. He quietly walked up to the door and looked through the peep hole. "A Character." He whispered.

Mayu stood up and held out her hand to Yuuki. "Quick, come with me, both of you." She shook her hand as if she had put it too close to a fire.

The same forceful pounding vibrated the door; no less or more severe. "I want to speak to the magical monk," said the voice behind the pounding fist. "I will not harm. Please."

Mayu and her two charges froze listening to the unexpected plea. Metaler Junya looked back at the other three in confusion. "Doesn't sound like what a typical Character would say," he whispered.

"Could you ask what his name is," asked Yuuki. Metaler Junya looked at him like he was crazy. "Please, Metaler Junya. I think I know who it might be."

"I know who it is. It's a damn Character," said the tense metaler.

"Ask, please."

Metaler Junya sighed out his fear and frustration. "What is your name?"

"Thanks to the magic monk, my name is Tomo."

The metaler looked at Yuuki hoping that meant something to him. Yuuki nodded and relaxed a bit. "I know him." He looked at Mayu, smiled, and let go of her hand. She protested but decided not to resist. Yuuki walked towards the door and looked through the peep hole. "Tomo, it is me the monk. Why are you here?"

"We want to follow you. We want you to be our prophet."

We? Yuuki asked himself. "I am coming out."

"Yuuki, what are you thinking?" protested Metaler Junya. "You can't go out there. Just one of them can shred even someone of your size into millions of bloody bits!"

"Thank you, Metaler Junya, but I am very aware of what one can do. I know this one, and he is no longer what he looks like on the outside. *Weeds thrive.* He gently pushed the Guildsman away from the door and pulled on the handle. "O.K, Tomo, I'm coming out to you." He pulled on the door slowly and kept himself blocking the way. It wouldn't have done any good if Tomo really wanted to do harm. He looked back at Hiroka and signaled to her to stay where she was. He had to do this by himself. He was the one who attracted the Character. It was his responsibility to make sure no harm came to the Guildscouple. He had no idea how to do that.

He looked out and saw the hulk of Tomo standing in front of him. He couldn't see anyone or anything else but the massive remembering Character and his rusty eyes. Tomo moved out of the way to let the magic monk come out. A dozen other Characters, different shapes and grotesque enhancements, were grouped behind Tomo. Most were bent forward, faces parallel to the ground. "We are here to thank you and help you complete your destiny," said Tomo as he too lowered his bulk and bowed to his new prophet.

thirty-five

YUUKI CLOSED THE DOOR to the last of the seventy-seven, so far, former Characters he memory initiated. He was alone for the first time in two weeks since returning to Hana-cho and the Flower Guild. Metaler Junya convinced the still suspicious Guild-elders to allow the steady stream of defecting Characters to be temporally housed in the unused apartments above the Guild Hall. Hiroka left after that first night, almost in tears and saying she was sorry for everything. He didn't know why. Her goodbye had a finality to it that cut into Yuuki's tightly knotted gut.

Yuuki looked down the corridor leading to the stairs down to the Guild Hall. Ornate carvings and metal work surrounded him. "Beautiful." He could barely pick up his feet and shuffled his emotionally drained guts and bones down the corridor. His exhaustion had not been due to the restoring of memories. That became easier after every Character. The hardest was watching each one go through several hours of torment of remembering and seeing what they had become, an expanding deep pit of self-loathing. The entire hall complex sounded as if a funeral gathering of a dear loved one had melted into an insane asylum.

Charm did not seem affected by all the sonic storm of torment. It kept inhuman focus on the possibilities it saw in these Characters now indebted to them. It vibrated concern that its human partner host refused to admit to being in Symb.

Yuuki headed downstairs to the main Guild Hall to try and get as far away from the screaming memories. He had been at it throughout the night and too tired to head back to the one of the metalworking studios on the opposite side of the compound Junya and his coterie converted for him as a temporary residence.

"You have a willing following, Yuuki," Charm said, jolting Yuuki back from the precipice of sleep. "You saw how they all genuflected to you that night in front of the Guildscouple's home.

"I do not care if we have a following. They needed my help, and I gave it to them. That is that." His sole voice echoed through the empty chamber, eerily entwining with the dying wails of remembering.

"I'm not talking only about those sobbing buffoons," continued Charm as if it didn't hear Yuuki's plea. "You can have the entire Guild under you."

"You mean under *you*." Responded Yuuki. He had no choice but to debate his Inanimate. He didn't know if he would ever feel comfortable calling it its preferred 'idol' let alone 'god'?

"They need a leader."

"A god and a prophet," corrected Yuuki.

"Yes, if you put it like that. But that cannot happen unless we have people who worship us. That is how it is going to have to be."

"Is that a threat?"

"A fact."

"I just want to take a nap. Can you leave me alone for a little while?" He took the silence as an agreement. He finally made it down to the main hall. He climbed onto the heavily carved table used for Guild-wide meetings to have a quick nap. He had to cover his head with his gaping sleeves to muffle the sadness seeping down to him in whispers. He soon fell asleep facing the ornately carved and gilded ceiling far above.

His eyes snapped open into the same nameless city he found himself in the other times. At least he thought it was. It was again totally different. It was not a burned-out hollow shell of a metropolis, but very much alive, similar to his first vision back in the root cellar.

He was on street level this time but still had a good view of the city. He must be in a residential hilltop area. People were rushing past him, different from the rush hour chaos he witnessed in front of Sui station with Hiroka. It was more of a building panic. He looked out towards the downtown skyline and saw black and grey plumes of smoke behind a stiff clump of scrapers spreading towards him and the fleeing masses.

He could only stand in one place and stare at the coming darkness. From his experience with these visions, he wasn't there, even though he could feel the turbulence rush past him from the panicked refugees. He somehow felt some of them run right through him. They appeared centimeters in front then behind him in less than a second.

It took only a few more minutes for Yuuki to see what was happening or at least from what everyone was fleeing. Massive giant beings appeared through the haze of dying scrapers and were quickly closing in. They were leaving trails of destruction in their paths. He only saw two, but he was sure there was an army of them destroying other parts of the city or other cities.

The two giants moved like humans, but their skin looked mineral, stoney muscles and muddy tendons. Their lidless eyes wide and alert. They looked incomplete. *Are they rogue, rebelling viscer things? They have to be suffering.*

One of the giants was heading toward him. *Can I die in dreams?* He wanted to wake up. His expression tightened into realization. *I am witnessing the destruction I saw the last time.* Whatever was giving him these visions, it did not go by his comfortable concept of linear time. *Are Charm-induced visions of personal pasts and Amedo's ink, my blood, of future and future pasts?* Yuuki's linear time view was welting and writhing into a glob. He felt ridiculous now for even thinking it ever was that naïvely simplistic.

The gargantuan suddenly turned back. Silence slowly crept around him. No one was running past, which only increased the invisible tomb of terror encasing him. *Where did everyone go?* He could still see the incomplete suffering being, but it wasn't much more than a darker dot in the already charcoal sky.

"Charm." Yuuki said to see if it was in the mood to have a conversation with him. "Charm. Will you talk to me when I want you to, just this once!" He shouted this plea cloaked in a demand. It was all in vain. But it did feel good to shout.

He crouched to try and relieve himself from the heaviness of frustration, giving him a different perspective of where he was. He glanced sideways and saw a bench over on a sidewalk. He realized he had been standing in the middle of a street. He walked over and took a seat, but after only making sure he could sit down. He must have willed enough matter to resist falling through the bench.

He looked over at the smoldering copse of scrapers. The inferno the giants initiated was now out of control. "This must be how it all started." He couldn't take his eyes of the silent mayhem. He was hoping Charm would join the conversation if he kept on talking. His insides remained undisturbed, no vibrations. He continued talking out loud. "Am I supposed to do something about this so it will never happen? Am I to save Hinodé, or somewhere else?" The creeping intensity of charred city invaded his nostrils and burned his eyes. "Would somebody or thing answer me!" He heard his voice echo back to him from the abandoned urban canyon. He started laughing "Me save anything? Delusional?".

The sound of his own laughter turned into the sounds of the distraught former Characters back in reality at the Guild Hall. His eyes fluttered before he oriented to his physicality. He raised himself up a bit onto his elbows. It was dark in the hall, comforting. He didn't want to see anything. He needed to think. He expected Charm to jiggle his insides now that he really wanted to be with his own mind.

The image of Greni morphed its way out of the sad silence into his existence. Her odd way of telling him that he would become somehow important made a little bit more sense. It went against everything he was taught, that the Order was greater than any of the individuals that made it. She was right. The doubt about his future had to fade into determination for it.

The seventy-seven defector Characters were island peaks lapped by the waves of the much smaller Guild members. It was a different world from this morning when Yuuki was alone with his disturbing vision. He had requested this guild-wide meeting several days ago after he was more confident when he would finish with the Characters. The general guild community would eventually demand more details about what was going on. Metaler Junya could explain only so much.

Yuuki sat on the stage along with Metaler Junya and Embroideress Mayu. Tomo stood obediently behind. This was the first time he was witness to the extent of the Flower Guild. The neighborhood had seemed so quiet. He had only heard how people were feeling through reports from Junya and Mayu.

The Marshal of the Guild, a boulder of a woman the name of whom Yuuki was not told, ascended the stage and began the long process of quieting the crowd. He had met her once before at Junya and Mayu's house when she came to see who this mysterious Wamono was. She was wearing the same long overcoat she was wearing that night, dazzling yellow embroidered with golden filaments. The Marshal's long braided hair trailed at least two meters behind as she walked past him.

The refugee Characters stood calmly watching everything. From his experience with them while as the Editor's exhibit, this was natural. It was their job to quietly keep an eye on things.

"Guild members and guests," the Marshal began. Her solid form harbored a powerful voice. With just those three words, the crowd silenced to half what it was. She repeated the greeting again, and the rooms hubbub reduced by half again. Once she was comfortable with the chatter level, she continued with her opening comments.

Yuuki felt all eyes on him trying to pry some kind of truth out, their conclusion of which was simply that he was a type of Wamono miracle worker, and that was fine for them to believe for now. He could at least try to do some good before he was too far into the prophet/god singularity.

The Marshal mentioning his name woke him from his thoughts. "The Wa-mono Yuuki-Hana has requested this meeting and now I would like to ask him," she turned around to face him, still stern, "to come up here and explain why."

The now breathy humid hall erupted with clapping and mumbling. Yuuki stood up and walked to the front of the stage, everyone looking at him waiting for him to speak. A sudden shock of power tightened his gut. He didn't know if it was all him or Charm.

He wore a Wamono-style kimono Embroideress Mayu had designed for him. It was remarkably detailed with black-on-black embroidery, something that betrayed his former standing as a novitiate. His hair was starting to grow out. He decided not to comb it and let it clump into the characteristic Wamono dreads of a full member of the order. This wasn't sentimental but tactical. Him looking like a monk of the revered Order would make it easier to convince the hundreds below him of what he was about to suggest, something that was not on the agenda until this morning's vision. Not even Junya or Mayu knew.

"Good evening. Thank you for being so patient thus far." He remained seated. It seemed the right thing to do. He was not a Guild member, thus no real authority. "I know you have many questions about who I am, why I am here, and why they are here as well." He raised his arm gesturing to the giants towering over everyone throughout the room. The gapping black sleeve made his outstretched hand appear tiny and skeletal. "I am here to answer all those questions and more. As you all know, I am, was, a Wamono novice monk. I left Aoheki cloister a few weeks back. The reason is not that important right now. I will be glad to tell you about my personal story at a later time." He looked around to try to gauge the mood of the audience. Most held the same expression—skeptical attentiveness.

He looked to his left at Mayu. Seeing the reassuring smile calmed his nerves slightly. He returned his attention back to his audience. "First, let me explain the presence of the former Characters."

"Former?" cried out a Guildsman. Yuuki couldn't see who it was. It wouldn't have mattered. All the members he knew by name were on stage with him.

"Correct. They are no longer controlled by the Tsudii." The hall filled with impromptu conversations and curses against their unwanted overlords.

Yuuki flashed his hand up palm facing the audience to stop anymore questioning. "Please. Keep your questions to yourselves for the time being. What I have planned to say should answer most of the questions in time." He wished he had someone like Yayoi Mashiyu to berate everyone into silence.

"I am not sure how common knowledge this is out here in Hinodé, but the Dai-Masters of the Wamono order had been sending out volunteers for centuries to seek out suspicious Inanimates, idols, and dispose of them before they hooked onto a receptive host." Small pricks of fear burst inside him. *Too late for me.*

"The Smashers," one audience member shouted out matter-of-factly.

"Yes, that is correct." Yuuki was surprised many knew. He didn't even know for sure until Tomo told him a few days ago.

The Marshal stood up and placed herself next to Yuuki. She spoke directly to him. "Yes, we have known for quite some time of the Smashers, but they have all but disintegrated. The corrupt power of Hinodé had been too much for most of them." She looked out to the former Characters as proof.

Most? Yuuki thought. *Some still adhered to their original mission?* He nodded thanks to the Marshal as she went back to her seat. He paused to take a drink of water, nervous for what he still needed to say. *The Flower Guild and these former Characters must work together to rid this city of the Tsudii and Suriidii and save it or something larger from a fiery death.*

"I never really lived outside those walls until a few weeks ago. I have always been told that I was the purest, uncorrupted by what we call 'Keibu-yo'." Many heads nodded, aware of the Wamono name of their city. "Now that I made the choice to come out into Hinodé, I have finally found a purpose. I cannot explain how I came to know this purpose. But I have found it, and that is all that should matter." He paused for dramatic effect and to see the reactions on the hundreds of faces staring at him with the same awe in their eyes. It made him uncomfortable but at the same time proud and powerful. *I'm no longer that twenty-year-old novitiate,* he thought. *What am I?*

"You're becoming a prophet, Yuuki-Hana," Charm's voice vibrated up from deep within his groin.

He was, and he had never been ready to admit it. He was a man who had to create his own reason. His mother thought he was not worth the effort and threw him away. He needed to prove her wrong, especially now that he knew she was still alive.

He needed to get himself back on point. He was losing them. "I have seen things that foretell a mortal danger to us here in Hinodé and perhaps to millions of others." He was forced to pause. An increasing drone of mumbling and head turning expanded throughout the hall. The one word he heard repeated was the question-intoned "others". Would he have to explain who the others were? He didn't even know but had a zygote of something his conscience refused to evolve any further. It was too unbelievable to let loose in his mind. They needed to concentrate on saving their own lives and city. That's what would motivate them to his call to destroy the abominable alliance that he knew was most likely forming between the two prophets and Ryudasu. "The tragic scenes in this story have three antagonists in common, the Tsudii, Suriidii, and that monster that I am sure all you have by now heard about creeping along the barrier walls of Aoheki."

"What are you asking of us?" cried out an anonymous Guildsman.

"Yes, what is all this about?" another faceless voice asked.

Yuuki decided, or more accurately, the crowd decided, that there had been enough build up. He looked over to Junya, Mayu, and a handful of others behind him, "I am here asking you to join me in taking back your city from the demons that have too long treated it as their twisted playground and perhaps even protect something larger than Hinodé."

"Something larger?" someone yelled. Others in the hall nodded their agreement to that question. It was not quite a question nor a skeptical statement. Many in the Flower Guild believed in or at least entertained the idea of the life-cycling philosophy that the Wamono order expanded from a hope to a religion.

Yuuki regretted opening this door of inquiry. He wanted to shut and lock it. "There is always something bigger, and that is hope. We cannot let these degenerate demi-gods destroy hope!" The energy within him refused to have him remain seated. "The entire Wamono Order is based on hope, and I know you too believe it, as our worldly kin. But it cannot be an idealized myth disconnecting you from where you are." He couldn't explain more because he couldn't explain it to himself. "That was our mistake as Wamono." He continued until he could plea no more. *It is now up to the Guild. What is up to me? Everything that will follow..*

The time to himself in his converted studio was welcome if only for a short time until another meeting with the Guildelders. He had become a new entity encompassing not only himself. There were murmurs among the former Characters calling him the Azalea Prophet and calling themselves collectively as the Pollen. It made sense. They only knew how to follow. Many Guild members understandably didn't like the title but were more than a little frightened of his small but menacing army of grateful giants. He had to keep the Pollen from regressing back into fanatics and delay his own inevitable insanity. The specialness that Greni revealed to him opened a thin crevice of hope that he was different. At least that was what he had to convince himself of.

His secret was starting to eat away at him. *How can I deceive these people?* He stood up from his simple bed that was not much different from the cot in his cell at Aoheki and looked out his window onto the glowing electric night. He didn't have much of a view, but the murky glow of the atmosphere hinted at the massive metropolis out there hugging him. This urban wall was warmer, softer than the repressive Aoheki walls despite all he had been through. He imagined the fighting, loving, laughing, crying, and dying out there happening simultaneously. This night was the first time he felt a belonging to the pulsating arteries and clanking bones of the city. He was in a good, though weird, place. He had a purpose; good or bad he had no idea. *"I'll prove to you I belong here."* The 'you' had two faces, that of the jagged toothed and million-eyed city and that of his mother. Was she happy or devastated to see him back in her life, however ephemeral?

"Don't allow your mother to affect you like this," Charm vibrated through Yuuki giving him painful chills. Yuuki was hoping the burgeoning god-thing wouldn't 'show' up.

"I won't," responded Yuuki. He turned his back on the city and sat back down on the bed. He took in a lung-full of the room's still air through his nose. If emptiness had a smell, this would be it.

"What's on your mind, then?"

"You know what's on my mind." Yuuki didn't appreciate Charm's smugness.

"Let's have a conversation. We need to plan."

"Plan?" Yuuki collapsed further onto the bed looking up at the molding ceiling. "I believe your plan and mine are quite different."

"You want to save a city. Why wouldn't that be a plan of mine?"

"Only if it met your goal of becoming the most powerful god-idol-thing in the city or all The Entire for that matter."

"We all have an end in mind Yuuki-Hana," said Charm. As usual, there was no sign of any emotion in its voice. "You think that this little war on the Tsudii and Suriidii will not negatively affect or even kill anyone in the process? You still cannot be that naïve, can you?"

Yuuki didn't say anything. He didn't have to. He thought back to only a few weeks ago when he was a truly naïve acolyte monk. He tried to fight the sense of sentimental nostalgia, but it was just too strong.

He rolled over into a fetal position giving into the memories of his life before all the world came crashing into him. *I'm creating my own life. There's nothing or no one to learn from, not even you, Charm.* The realization ensnared him into terrifying sense of absolute power and independence.

Shinya's loving eyes inexplicably attempted to fight their way through to the forefront of his thinking, but he had to clear away this blockage of his love before it derailed this power and independence. The two opposing emotions were starting to wreak havoc in his mind. The only comfort was that it was hopefully causing Charm a little bit of discomfort.

"You are a prophet," said the dispassionate Inanimate. "You do not need to learn from anyone, or anything as you said. You thanks to me and me thanks to you are evolving at a very fast pace. There's no time to think backwards and reminisce about an inconsequential past."

Charm was right. He was no longer the boy on the cusp of manhood. He had quickly become a man through pure experience. Biology no longer mattered. The more he thought about this, the more he started to see Charm's view of things. He was making something, something big, of himself. He should be excited. It was up to him to prevent the Editor, that Suriidii queen, and Ryudasu from doing what they wished with Hinodé and the rest of the Entire. Why else would he be gifted those visions. They were separate from those from his Symb with Charm. It was related to Amedo's ink; a metaphysical distress call from Gou-Tairei itself. *Future, ink. Memory, Charm.*

"Nonsense." vibrated Charm. "This Gou-Tairei, if it even exists, has nothing to do with it. It is all you, the Azalea Prophet, and me.

"Are you certain?" said Yuuki. He wasn't ready to give up his core beliefs or sure if he ever would be. It was too much a part of him just to toss aside like a frayed and faded binding ribbon.

"Our power or miracles; whatever you like to call them, are just as probable as there being an unbodied, unfeeling, uninterested force/being watching our every move."

"How do you explain my vision of this future city?

"It could be Yedo," said Charm. "You have been trying to think away that possibility for some time now."

"There is a reason for that." Yuuki clenched his fists. Charm was forcing himself to think about this whole other universe that could be in play. "There can only be a Yedo if Gou-Tairei exists. It would confirm it." He relaxed his fists and began rubbing his face with his sweaty palms, trying to feel something real, something now. "I do not want to be responsible for having to save hope."

"But you do want to. You cannot fake anything with me, with yourself," quickly responded Charm. "That is why you are doing all this. You want the ultimate power of being a savior."

"I don't know, maybe. I know I have been chosen somehow to do something."

"No one chose you. Don't be so arrogant. You, me, everyone are particles clashing and repelling each other determining then changing our destinations." Charm's vibrations were calming down to their normal intensity. "This little war you are about to bring about is your means to this one particular destination. Remember. Destinations, even destinies, change."

Yuuki stopped the discussion. He was finished communicating and tried his hardest to blank his mind. He would never be able to not be true to himself.

Yuuki and a small portion of The Pollen with the most senior Guild elders weren't coming to any agreement on how they should proceed against the Tsudii and Suriidii. Except for the Pollen, everyone sat around a smaller version of the intricately carved wooden table out in the Guild Hall in the executive room off hall. The table had every flower of each coterie carved into its top border. The center was smooth polished wood of nothing in comparison. Yuuki tried to count how many different flowers there were, but the discussion was greedy for his attention.

The Marshall wanted to wait a while until Yuuki could restore more Tsudii Characters, weakening the daigunshyu while strengthening their cause at the same time. However, there were others, including most of the Pollen, who believed a more immediate strategy was needed; a surprise storming of the Tsudii stronghold was the only option.

"I'm sorry, but the idea of a total offensive is too risky," said Yuuki. Everything was moving fast; too fast. He still couldn't believe he was someone with authority.

He was a fraud. He wanted the world to stop for a while, just a while. "It is very late in a very long day."

"Fujin," said Metaler Junya. Yuuki didn't know who or what this Fujin was, but everyone around the table looked down to their hands resting on the table or on their laps.

"Fujin? Telling name." He had never heard of a person using such a dichotic name. *'Lady' or 'heartless'*, he thought. The second meaning didn't sound promising. Pin-and-needle chills ran down his spine. It wasn't one of Charm's sensations. *Do you know of her, Charm?*

"No, I'm afraid I do not."

No one wanted to continue the subject of this Fujin. Metaler Junya looked ashamed from even bringing her up. "Why is her name creating such awkward silence?"

"She's the head of a vigilante group bent on destroying every Symb in the Wards," said the Marshal. "No one knows who she is or even where she operates from, but she is accredited with destroying several minor Symbs over the past couple years."

"More like accused," chimed in Carver Tetsu. It was obvious he and Metaler Junya saw the acts of this Fujin in different lights. The carver was much older than Junya and violence-wary.

"How does she 'destroy' them? Asked Yuuki. He needed to know for the possibility of him being a future target.

"She murders the host, the human," said the Marshal. Yuuki wasn't quite sure which side she was on regarding the group. But from her choice of words, he had to assume she was on that of Carver Tetsu's.

"Not just murder, but mutilation. She obviously has a personal vendetta against Symbs," said Carver Tetsu. "Especially male ones."

Yuuki didn't want this Fujin anywhere near him. If she had this much experience in seeking out and finding Symbs, she would easily see through his and Charm's dangerous charade. "If she is so murderous, as Carver Tetsu says, then why even bring her up?" He directed his question at his former host.

"I understand everyone's trepidation," said Junya. "But she has been quite effective. She could be useful to our cause."

"Our cause in murder?" grumbled the Carver. "If she is so effective, why haven't we seen the Editor's useless maleness ripped off of him and placed in his dead hand like a regurgitated piece of meat?"

Yuuki winced. "Do we really want someone like that working with us?"

"It may be our only hope if we are to rid ourselves, this city, of the terror that has been a plague for who knows for how long. We don't know for certain she was personally behind any of those gruesome acts."

"She never claimed responsibility?" Asked Yuuki.

"Oh, she's responsible, alright," said the Marshal. "She puts her ownership of the deaths out into every available media outlet that night or the next morning depending on when the act was done."

"She has a group rumored to be another offshoot of the Smashers doing her dirty work," said Junya. "They are addicted to Illumination Blue and when doped up, acquire enhanced physical abilities and —"

"And enhanced psychotic tendencies," interrupted Carver Testsu.

"So, you're telling me that she has little control of how these drug-addict former Smashers carry out her orders?"

"Yes, I guess that is what I am saying," responded Metaler Junya. "But none of you here would be sad to see the Editor and those like him eradicated, no matter how it's done. She could be an effective ally. We cannot all stand by our morals in times like these. If what Yuuki-sama says is real, and I am sure we all do or we would not be here, then we need to do anything within our power to stop what seems to be inevitable is nothing is done."

Things were getting too intense around the table. Yuuki needed to bring everything back to logic. The total faith they had put in him and his visions frightened him. *What if this is all wrong and irreversible insanity setting in?* Thought Yuuki. *What am I about to do?*

"Those ink visions are real", vibrated Charm. You could most likely gain almost, if not total, power of the Wards and do this city a favor in the process. Remember what Greni said to you."

Charm was right. He needed to do whatever was within his means to stop that debased troika. It will be a gruesome fight, and there will be deaths. He couldn't worry about how those of the other side would die. Just the fact that they would be dead was the important thing. He stood up signaling the end of the meeting. "Invite this Fujin to come and have a chat." He didn't wait to see the expressions on his councilor's faces. He walked out followed closely by Tomo and the rest of the Pollen.

thirty-six

"**W**HAT IS THAT?" DEMANDED Fujin, her faceless voice echoed through the suffocating gloam of the chamber. She was pointing a long feminine finger toward a sack moist with a patina of black seepage from whatever was festering inside.

She'd given strict orders not to be disturbed. She had to get her head around of possibly both her sons now out in this decrepit metropolis. At least one of them was safely with her. She needed an hour or so to simply think. That frightened her the most. She was about to reprimand the Blue who disturbed her, but the growing death stench saved him from her wrath.

"We don't know," replied one of her Blues. "We found it at one of our hit shacks with a note addressed to you."

She didn't like the look or smell of the lumpy sac the two Blues had dropped on the floor in front of her. She had to hold her breath while she spoke "How long had it been sitting there rotting?"

The Blues look at each other hoping one would know the answer. Finally, one jittered up the nerve to speak "Don't know. Couple weeks or so?"

She mumbled under her breath, "Not surprising". There was a pastel pink envelope attached to the coagulating sack. She hesitantly peeled it from the bag. She read the contents in silence then folded it back up, stuffed it back into the envelope, and calmly put it into her pocket. "Get rid of it. It's beginning to spoil the air."

The two Blues grabbed a hold of it, sucking in deep breaths to ready themselves to haul it back out. Blood seeped out from the bottom leaving a glistening red-black trail behind.

She turned her back to the gore. "Get someone in here to clean it up."

"Yes Fujin-sama," replied an out-of-breath Blue.

Ogawa took the envelope out of her pocket and read the note again.

Your Blue envoy had suffered a rather decapitatingly severe Blue overdose—so severe that even my arch-idol could not stop it.

"An arch!?" She had never come up against one except the ever present but never here Mayor. The Mayor was an entirely unique entity; she had hoped one of a kind. It could not be destroyed without killing everyone in Hinodé. She crumpled up the letter, letting it fall into the gloppy blood smear.

She sprawled herself out on the soft sofa in her private office and allowed her eyes to close. She thought how easy it would be to retreat to a Wamono cloister. There was a nunnery just down the river in Akibi district. She lost count of how many times she seriously considered doing just that over the last twenty or so years of her miserable second life. She could finally hold onto the nerve and commit suicide. But vengeance was too strong of a life force.

With this latest news, it was becoming more difficult convincing herself to stay in the secular world and fight. She was no longer young. She hadn't been since that painful day of murder and violation. She put her hands against her head, trying to strangle the memories of that day. "I'm tired." She exhaled staring at the ceiling she could barely see in the dim room. "There's no end. Cannot see it anymore."

Tears began to stream back toward her ears. No one would dare barge in, but she couldn't take any chances. She wiped the offending emotion from her cheeks.

"Alliances!" she blurted out. "Those murderous gangs are forming an unholy alliance, and I stupidly tried one with an arch-idol or even god!." Her ways were too drastic for most organizations suffering under the daigunshyu to form alliances. She thought again of exposing herself to the Ue-No citizens' Council, but it—and she as head of it—had little power outside the districts it controlled. She could never convince the spineless advisors to actively take steps in ridding the city of the Tsudii-Suriidii-Dekora super plague.

She sat up wiping more of the stubborn self-sorry from her cheeks. Nothing seemed clear anymore. She saw no details to grasp onto and lead with.

In her quiet desperation for something tangible, she grabbed a pitcher and brought it closer. She scrunched her eyes to squeeze away the last puddle of tears. She felt its way around the piece of art, sensing every curve and relief as it worked its way around.

Her former community was the only group with any semblance of agency to counter the alleged combined forces of the Tsudii and Suriidii. She had to at least try and see if they would even consider a relationship; she refused to use 'alliance'. They despised her tactics, but it was time they talked. If they knew anything about what was happening between the Editor and that vain Suriidii leader, they would be less judgmental.

She killed the last tear running down her face and sat up straight, composing herself. "There's no longer the privilege of avoidance." She grazed her thumb along her ring. "Tell Kazunori and Shinya to come to my private quarters right away." Invigoration took hold of her. There was still hope.

Seconds after disconnecting, a discreet electronic beep sounded deep in her ear. She swiped her thumb the opposite way on her ring to answer the call. "Yes, Kazunori?" As she listened to the information given to her on the other line, a smile began to grow. "Is that so? Perfect. Bring in the request right away and prepare yourself and Shinya for Hana-cho immediately." She flicked her ring to off. "The timing could not have been more perfect."

"Azalea-sama, the representatives from the Fujin have arrived."

"Thank you, Tomo," responded Yuuki. "Please send them in." It was a ridiculous title the Pollen called him, but it was better than 'prophet', which he knew they called him amongst themselves.

"Be careful of her and her minions, Yuuki-Hana," vibrated Charm. "She has it out for us, you know that."

"She doesn't have it out for us, just Symbs. As far as anyone knows, we are not".

"Tell that to that Dekora and the Tsudii leader. They know."

"Mimi said she would keep our Symb secret."

"And the Editor?"

"I don't know!" shouted Yuuki. "Hopefully, we won't have to worry about him much longer if this alliance proves to be what we hope, Plus, who are they going to believe?"

"Azalea-sama," came the muffled voice of Tomo through the closed door.

"Come in." Yuuki was grateful for the interruption. He was glad he took a sip of his blood earlier. He would soon have to open another wound and let the old go to fallow and heal before festering.

For the first second, all Yuuki could see was the looming mass of Tomo with a couple of shadows emerging from his eclipse.

"Allow me to introduce you to the representatives of the Fujin," announced Tomo. "A major of the Blues, Kazunori, and his assistant."

The two negotiators passed out of the shade of the towering, reformed Character, coming into the full dusty light of the room.

"Shi—?" Yuuki stood up from his seat, mouth widening. "Shinya?" The second he stood up he had to sit back down.

Shinya released himself further from Tomo shadow. "Yuuki? Blessings of the Accolades!"

Shinya began to run over to his old cellmate and new love to embrace him. Tomo moved forward out of instinct to grab Shinya, but quickly realized Yuuki was not in danger. The two held each other for longer than was comfortable for the two onlookers.

The two interrupted lovers finally released and stood staring at each other. There was nothing else around them, and Yuuki wanted it to remain that way. Everything about the Editor, Ryudasu, and the impending conflict was, for a precious moment, exiled from his mind.

Yuuki motioned for Tomo to find a seat for his guests. He had too many questions to ask Shinya, but he could only utter one word, "How?"

"It is an involved story, and I would be very happy to tell you of it, which I am sure you want to do the same for me," said Shinya with that warming smile. He was afraid the memory of the last time he saw that smile would eventually fade into cobwebbed strands of a distant almost forgotten time. Yuuki could return only a more reticent smile.

Tomo brought over two heavy wooden chairs used for the elders during large Guild-wide events. The two representatives thanked Tomo with a slight bow and sat down.

"I'm sorry," interrupted Kazunori, "but I'm not sure what's going on here."

Yuuki looked at Shinya's almost equally handsome partner and felt a churn of jealousy, forcing himself to suppress it. He kept the smile for Shinya on his face for this major. "Pardon me. Shinya and I know each other from Aoheki. We lived together."

"You are a Wamono?" asked Kazunori.

"I was," said Yuuki. He looked at Shinya. "I don't think I would be too welcomed there now."

"He simply disappeared one day," Shinya started. He looked down to his feet. Yuuki followed the gaze of rejection. He had never seen Shinya's feet covered before. He drew in his own imprisoned feet under his modified kimono, embarrassed.

Shinya continued. "No one knew what happened to him. All we knew was that he probably escaped." He looked back up at Yuuki with a very thin film of hurt and sadness coating his eyes. "I had thought I would never see you again."

"I am so sorry, Shinya. I know it will take time to forgive me, if at all possible." responded Yuuki.

"Ehum." Tomo cleared his throat to wake the two from their increasingly private conversation.

"My apologies," said Yuuki, realizing where he was and who else was there. "Shinya and I can catch up later." He looked over to his brokenhearted day-old love hoping to get some kind of response in the affirmative. Shinya reached over and grabbed his hand and smiled. It was not the bright smile he had seen just a few moments ago or that day they kissed for the first time, but it was enough. "So, you two are the Fujin's representatives?"

"Yes," said Kazunori. "My name is Kazunori, her major. I see that I do not need to introduce my partner here."

"Quite the contrary," said Yuuki. "I know Shinya, or course, but not in his new role."

"He is the newest member in our army to fight the false prophets of this city."

Yuuki's heart plummeted into his abdomen. He remembered the Guild elders telling him the Fujin's 'army' were all addicted to some drug called Blue. *Is Shinya on the drug?* He looked into his eyes to see if he could see any blue oozing out of them.

"He is not on Illumination Blue, if that's what you are worried about," said Kazunori after seeing what Yuuki was looking for.

"I am sorry, I didn't mean to offend," responded Yuuki.

Shinya looked at him. "No offense taken."

"I'm assuming we are here to discuss forming a relationship between us to fight this growing threat of the unexpected thawing between the Editor and Ren," said Kazunori

"It is precisely why I contacted you, which was not easy."

"We make it a point not to have anyone know where we are headquartered. I'm sure you understand that."

"Completely," responded Yuuki. He didn't like this Kazunori. He was too harsh, unemotional. But what worried him more was that Shinya would eventually become the same if he continued being associated with this mechanical zealot.

"Something to drink?" Tomo asked the two guests.

"No thank you," Kazunori responded without much of a pause.

Shinya followed his superior's lead and shook his head and waving his hand in sync.

"Let us get down to business," responded Yuuki. He stood up to better adjust his kimono and sat back down, ready for a long discussion on the pros and cons of forming an alliance. He was sure there were reservations on the Fujin's side as well. He knew too well those on his. But he was confident that there would be some sort of agreement at the end of all this. There had to be. It was the only way out of this.

"Your body guard had mentioned you as a prophet when we arrived," said Kazunori.

Yuuki focused on the accusatory tone of the major's voice. "You heard correctly." He looked over to Shinya, who had moved back next to his superior, to see his reaction. There was something, but it was hard to tell if it was more positive or negative. He had no idea how indoctrinated he had become into the Fujin's fanaticism.

"What is the nature of your title?" Continued the Blue major. "I have to assume you have not succumbed to the abomination of Inanimate infestation."

"Insulting." Charm's vibrations became shooting pains crashing into each other inside Yuuki. He was using all his strength not to reveal his increasing discomfort to his guests.

"No, I am not one of those 'abominations'. I am not sure what an abomination would entail, but I can assure you that I am not in Symb with an Inanimate." The ease of the lie frightened him more than the possible and most likely eventuality of the truth becoming public.

"He is a true prophet," interrupted Tomo. Yuuki thought it wouldn't be possible for him to puff out his chest more than it already had. "He needs no help in his visions and leadership. He is the Azalea Prophet."

"Visions? Azalea Prophet?" Shinya looked at the person he left Aoheki for. Yuuki met those eyes, and his heart emptied. He was losing him and fast.

"Yes, I have seen what will happen if we allow the Editor and Ren go unchecked and form an alliance with that real abomination lurking, I'm assuming, freely within the sacred halls of Aoheki." The last part was more a question for Shinya to confirm.

"Are you referring to Ryudasu-sensei?" asked Shinya.

"Sensei? So, it is true then."

"Yes, she has been released as poor Kugai wished." Shinya looked at Yuuki again with those same stranger eyes. "How do you know about Ryudasu? You were long gone by the time she was revealed to the cloister."

"Who is this Ryudasu?" Interrupted Kazunori. His voice staccato with frustration.

"A true abomination," answered Yuuki. He returned his focus on Shinya, his stern leader expression relaxed. "I will be happy to fill you in on what I know later. We can fill each other in." His faced went back to rigid and looked at the major, a subtle polite smile concealed the gritting of his teeth. "Let us solidify our relationship first."

"Yes, agreed," responded Kazunori.

"I would like to make it official in front of the Fujin herself."

"That will not be possible, yet anyway," Kazunori said. "She does not meet others often. You must understand that she must keep a very low profile. Her identity must be kept secret."

"She must be someone of importance in the city then," vibrated Charm. "It would be a very good idea to find out who she really is in case things go wrong."

Agreed, thought-spoke Yuuki.

"I have the authority to speak in her name," said Kazunori. "I assume you are what you say considering the fact you have the Flower Guild behind you. They are a respected organization, perhaps the only one left in this city."

Yuuki felt suffocated by the constant influence, overt or implied, of the Wamono order. The Flower Guild is the worldly version of the order, and he was set on a collision course with Aoheki right in the middle.

"Thank you for your confidence, major Kazunori," said Yuuki. "I have just received word from one of our most recent converts that the Editor and Ren are planning something involving Aoheki."

Shinya's eyes widened at the news. "Aoheki?"

"Yes, I am afraid so. I hope you will forgive me in wanting to establish something between us rather quickly. I think you will agree, major." The information he had received was quite vague, but disturbing. *Ryudasu has to be behind it all.*

"Yes, of course. I don't need to hear anything else to convince me," said Kazunori. "In the name of Fujin, I declare our two organizations allied and friends."

Yuuki had to hold back a snicker at the absurd formality. "By the way, what is the name of your organization?"

"It is just Fujin. We have no name. Better that way." Are you still using the Flower Guild as yours?"

Yuuki hadn't thought of usurping the identity of the Guild. They were still the Flower Guild, and he was the Azalea prophet. They were separate but united. He had become one of its leaders. The Pollen would say the sole leader. "The Flower Guild is fine."

"The recent news has made everything a bit simpler," said Kazunori. "A Wamono cloister is in direct threat from these abom...false prophets. This cannot be tolerated."

Yuuki appreciated the fanatic's turn of phrase. "How is this simple?" He looked at the major trying to figure out the more than likely drug-rotted mind. *Is this what the drug does, turns people into religious loonies?* He looked over to Shinya and gave him a sad smile. *I need to get him away from him and Fujin.* Shinya returned the smile. Just the stretching of those warm lips made him almost forget the dilemma at hand.

"There's no grey area," answered Kazunori. "They are threatening the very base of our thinking, our cultures."

There it was. The Wamono commonality he would now never be free from. It didn't mean he had to embrace it. "I see," was all he could say.

"We will set up a line of communication with you," said Kazunori. "A dedicated human chain is the most secure way we have found. I'll send a map of the places to transmit messages and through whom."

"May I ask a favor before we end our most fruitful meeting?"

"Go ahead," responded the major.

"I would like it if Shinya could stay here with us, as a kind of ambassador. As you may have guessed, we have a lot to catch up on."

Kazunori looked at Shinya. His assistant's face was trying hard not to show his desire, but he wasn't fooling anyone. "I'm not sure if that is a good idea so early in our relationship."

"This relationship does not have the luxury of time. We have to trust each other. And that trust involves Shinya remaining here." He looked at Shinya with the slightest of smiles. "If he wishes, that is."

Shinya nodded and returned the pseudo-secret smile.

"Very well," said Kazunori. "A friendly gesture."

Yuuki closed his hand tight around the major's, knowing it would soon be snug into Shinya's.

thirty-seven

HÉGO AND OGUSHU WERE both nude in the Grand Atrium's waiting room preparing for the annual Gou Matsuri. The cloister-wide festival was the most anticipated yearly event celebrating how blessed the monks were to be safe and re-purified within these walls. The entire Atrium would soon become a massive Haiku-Bassbeat contemplative rave, a Wamono grand ball. Everyone would be adorned in their finest hair beads and freshly dyed locks.

"You have been spending quite a bit of time with that Aku," said Ogushu.

"I have to keep tabs on her." Hégo said in his usual cranky tone. "She confessed she caused a little bit of a raucous a couple weeks ago on visits to the lower walls."

The two remained silent while they had to burden themselves with wrapping their bodies in a much more elaborate kimono than even those for conclave. Ogushu's matsuri robe had to be quickly made since there had only ever been one for the traditional one Master of the Cloister. Hégo scowled toward the nude younger co-Master. He hated youth, even if only by a couple decades.

"Oh? What happened?"

Hégo didn't want to tell him the truth, but he needed an excuse to explain his increasing meetings with the Aku. Ogushu had made it clear that he only agreed with Kugai's original idea out of respect for the drooling vegetable still bedridden in the infirmary. Now that Hégo had taken it upon himself to go through with the idea, even embracing it, Ogushu was no longer quite as respectful.

"Nothing of great importance," Hégo said through heavy breaths from fighting the cumbersome robe. "Only some gawkers that grew into a small audience. Some apparently ran away screaming, but most stared dumbly with their mouths wide open like imbeciles."

He wanted the annoying bookish monk to cover his distracting nudity. He was getting tired of having to look at his unusually wrinkle- and spot-free body. He had much more important things to worry about. Ryudasu had told him that everything had gone to plan. The tunnel had been expanded and the two heretical prophets and their abomination armies were now waiting just on the other side. He had Ryudasu's word that the monks were not her or her cousins' real target. He knew her word probably didn't mean much, especially after hearing her refer to herself as Holy Spinner. He was in no position or the right species to force more information out of her.

He was so deep into the conspiracy that his only option was to put his future in her hands. It was the only way to reform the order, even if it meant sacrificing Aoheki to those disfigured heretics waiting like vultures outside. *It is all just dead skin that needs to be sloughed off*, he kept reminding himself.

He didn't care about their delusional plan to travel to what they thought was Yedo. He had never been a firm believer in a paradisiacal city to end the exhausting cycles of birth and death. It was too much silly hope in that. *The only reason those two "siblings" took to it so easily was because they are already too far gone on the far side of insanity.* He shrugged his shoulders to hoist up the heavy kimono. *They can have Aoheki and their figment of Yedo. When I am in control, I will have an even more glorious temple built. Ryudasu and her demented dynasty can have all these miserable outdated fortresses for all I care.* He had volunteered to go out into Keibu-yo, meet her contacts, and gather them into a 'force' to 'take back' Aoheki, looking the hero. With Ryudasu's infamy, he would then be unstoppable in his charge through every Wamono cloister until finally arriving at the High Cloister of Kyouseiheki.

Before the fraction of his mind convinced the plan was insane, Cane quickly put itself forward. "The plan will succeed, and you will be Dai-master."

Hégo smiled then quickly killed it when his eyes adjusted back onto Ogushu. "Are you ready yet?"

"Yes, almost," responded Ogushu. "It seems like everyone is already from the mumbling and laughing. It is always nice to hear monks laughing. It does not happen very often, does it?"

Hégo rolled his eyes but glad Ogushu was finally in full attire.

"Shall we go?" Said Ogushu. "I have a feeling this year's Gou Matsuri will be quite memorable."

"Yes, I will have to agree with you there."

The two Masters opened the old creaking doors. The drone the two heard from behind the closed doors was now a cacophony of hundreds of monks excited to start their revelation dancing to the bassbeats specially composed by Bassho-Jyon.

Before Hégo and Ogushu could step fully out into the festive almost raucous assembly, Toyo Jaibu-sensei ran up and blocked them.

"Masters-sama," the nervous doctor yelled even though he was now only a few centimeters from both their faces. He grabbed Hego's arm, but the old Master quickly jerked the doctor's grip off.

"What is it!" Hégo yelled back. The excited noise out in the Grand Atrium drowned out this localized agitation. "We are about to open the matsuri!"

"Yes, well, uh, I see," stuttered the doctor. "But it is, uh, uh, concerning Kugai-sam ... sensei," Toyo Jaibu corrected himself.

The Masters' faces slackened in mute resignation. Has he ...?" Hégo couldn't bring himself to finish his thought.

"No, no. Uh, nothing like that. He is, uh, fine physically."

"Then what?" Hégo immediately went back to his impatient insolent stance. "Get on with it or I will have Mashu-sensei physically remove you." Hégo was no longer looking at the distraught doctor, but for the Officer of Ceremony and Order.

"Kugai-sensei has been getting worse. He is screaming, uh, at the top of his, uh, lungs about something breaking through these walls very soon. It is becoming quite terrifying. I am, uh, afraid he will do serious harm to himself."

Hégo didn't hear the last part of what the doctor said. His mind focused on the invasion the lunatic was screaming about. *Does that crazy old man know what is about to happen?* Prickly sweat began to short every nerve ending.

"I am sure it is just the poor man's damaged mind playing tricks on him," said Ogushu in his signature sedated manner. "He is restrained, correct?"

"He was, but you can never, uh, underestimate how powerful the mind is when, uh, translated to physical power. That is why I am here. He went on a crazed, uh, rampage in the infirmary."

"Has he hurt any of the other patients?" asked Ogushu.

"Yes, but not seriously. Only, uh, a few, uh, punches and pulling of hair before my assistants, uh, could tackle him to the floor."

"So, he is back to being under control, then," said Hégo, finally coming out of his frozen paranoia.

"Yes, for now, but he, uh, will just have another episode after the, uh, sedative wears off, I am afraid."

"I am still confused as to why you are here, now," said Hégo.

"The room I put him in on your request, uh, is no longer secure enough. I came here to see if he can be moved somewhere else away from endangering any of the other monks while the room is made more secure. U..u..upon your permission of course."

"More secure!" Hégo glared at the doctor, forcing the fidgeting man to cower even more. "Are you saying that Kugai, who is not much younger than I, busted through a locked door?"

"Ye..ye.uh.yes, Master-sama. Again, the mind—"

"Yes, yes, I know," interrupted Hégo. "Very well. Bring him up to my cell. The door is quite thick and heavy. It should keep him in until I can think of another place to house him." This would give him an opportunity to see what the mind-mushed monk really knew of what was impending and his involvement in it. There was no telling how intelligent an insane mind could be. He had to quickly take care of this unruly variable. *The beloved former Master will simply have to be in the wrong place at the wrong time when the events waiting to happen finally manifest.*

"Go and do as I order," barked Hégo. "I have a matsuri to preside over."

"Yes, uh, Master-sama," said the doctor bowing his head to the left and backing away.

The thwomp thwomp of Mashu's staff followed, resounding through the Grand Atrium sharpening as the sound waves sped from their source and silencing the gathered mass of monks, novitiate, and Reincarnates. "Silence!" cried out the ever-unsmiling Officer of Ceremony and Order. "The three hundred twelfth Gou Matsuri on record is about to commence! The venerable Masters of the Cloister Daiso Hégo-sama and Goto Ogushu-sama!"

That was their cue to exit the waiting room in their full matsuri garb. The short but arduous climb up the steps went exactly as expected. Ogushu had to keep his hands steady on Hégo's back to make sure he did not fall backwards. Hégo tried to use Cane as much as possible, but the construction of the steps made the walking aid useless. He could feel Cane trying to keep the balance and appreciated it for that.

After the two Masters finally made it to the summit of the dais, Hégo lifted his hands to silence the crowed. He wanted to make sure it was he who was in control not Mashu and definitely not Ogushu.

"Today we outwardly celebrate the mysterious and unsentimental working of the Gou-Tairei," began Hégo. He kept his hands out and up, holding Cane in one and being careful not to lose his balance. "We should all be celebrating the Cyclic Force internally every day, but one day, and only one day, can we celebrate with each other. We are people, and people need celebration. Therefore, it is us who we celebrate, not the Gou-Tairei. We celebrate our devotion to the Cycle. Any of you who have the illusion, delusion, that the Gou-Tairei cares for any of this, that it cares at all, should have a hard think about why you are here."

Wamono heads undulated in silent confusion due to the overly serious tone of the opening address. *Now they know who is in charge and no more laxity.* He wouldn't change anything else. They will still have their specially composed Haiku-bassbeat sermon and their extra dose of Gouren in their budou-shu to get them more in 'the mood' for prolonged trance-worship. The air was full of the sweet spicy fragrance of the drug. He allowed a larger dose than in years past to be doled out by one of Jaibu's lackeys. He needed everyone to be nice and doped up when the invasion happened. *Means to a much more noble end; just a means,* he kept repeating to himself.

He signaled Basho Jyon to begin his composition. Within a few seconds, the entire hall vibrated with the heavy techno beats of the highly anticipated Haiku-bassbeat Jyon had kept secret for months. *Now, let us see what that old fool really knows.*

"What do you know?" Hégo hobbled over to Kugai, restrained in his former bed. "What is this about an attack?"

Kugai looked up but not at Hégo—at nothing—and stretched his sweaty lips into a wicked wide smile.

"Tell me!" Hégo didn't dare get any closer. Kugai's dementia had become dangerous. He was taking a risk by being in the same room.

Kugai remained silent except for a few crazed giggles under his breath. His bed soaked with a mixture of fresh and stale acrid sweat. The odor made Hégo woozy. He had reservations about leaving the matsuri. Ryudasu assured him there would be no bloodshed; that there was no need for it, but everyone had to be in their places. He was not.

"You've done it now," said Kugai. He kept on giggling.

The broken monk was not looking at him but straight up to the dark, almost invisible ceiling. There was only the light of Hego's gleamer sticks trying to keep back the greedy gloom. The dim light pasted Kugai's face with a lunatic yellow. His eyes fluttered, rolling back into his insanity-masticated mind.

Kugai continued. "You have brought this sacred place down. Down, down." He giggled. "Where down? Don't know. But down it shall go."

Hégo didn't know if the crazy bastard was aware he was in the room with him. They had yet to make any eye contact. He stood still listening to the schizophrenic one-man conversation hoping to glean any clues as to what his predecessor knew.

Kugai's giggles exploded into uncontrolled laughter followed by convulsing sobs. It was painful even for Hégo. Kugai didn't deserve what was happening to him. At first, it was a convenience, but now it was pathetic.

"I, me, the one who destroyed the Wamono," Kugai said in a bout of clarity that frightened Hégo even more than his insanity. "Why am I still here? Torn apart by the most terrible manifestations of Retributions the Gou-Tairei can control." The former Master began to laugh under his breath again. First it was a low rumble in his throat, morphing into yelling laughter that sent chills down Hego's neck and spine.

Hégo remained silent, waiting for another lucid window he could look through. *Come on you old fool*, he thought. *Tell me what I, and you, put into motion here. Am I going to be damned like you?* He didn't want to sit; it would be too complacent. He was leaning quite heavily on Cane, who had been uncharacteristically silent.

Just as the new Master was getting used to the shouting laughter tearing itself out of the shell of a man, the laughter stopped but just long enough for Hégo to hope for sustained silence. The noiselessness was soon ripped apart by an ear-piercing scream, no laughing mixed in. The horrible wailing unsettled Hégo's balance. He collapsed onto the cold stone floor. He looked up at Kugai who had twisted his neck to face him, eyes almost as wide as his screaming mouth. The terror of witnessing what Kugai had become, un-become, forced Hégo into a shivering velvety ball.

He knows I am here. Hégo wanted to cover both his ears, but his right hand was holding tightly onto Cane and couldn't let go. He felt something viscous coat the palm of the left hand that did make it to his ear. *Blood. He is slowly killing me.* Kugai didn't take breaths, just one long continuous high-pitched inhuman scream, his mouth never closing. His old friend and enemy had become Hégo's personal Retribution. A punishment for them both.

"You still have time, Daiso Hégo ... Master-sama," Kugai said through his scream, his words as clear as if they were talking face to face in the solitude of the cell. "You can stop all this. You can redeem yourself, if you really want to. It is your choice. I am to blame, not you—not yet."

"Do not listen to whatever he has become," said Cane. "This is only a ploy to interrupt your destiny."

"An Inanimate!" shouted Kugai. "You have been corrupted by an Inanimate!" the anger was increasing. Kugai's out-of-body voice changed from anger to disappointment, even sadness. His mouth still gaping, screaming, but his eyes watery with sorrow. "Then there is no hope for you, for anyone."

"You do not know what you are talking about!" Hégo shouted even though there was no need. Conversations and scream terror were on separate but coexisting sound dimensions. He kept his bloody palm over his ear, doing no good. "I am doing all this to save our order." It took all his strength to speak.

"Don't you see what he is trying to do?" said Cane. "Even in his insanity, he wants you to be less than what you should become. Don't listen to him."

But look at him! This is the Gou-Tairei. It is no longer Kugai!

"The Gou-Tairei does not care. It never cared, and it never will." The vibrations from Cane were adding to Hego's excruciating mental and physical pain.

"Obviously I cannot fight against a Symb. Just take this as your last chance, Daiso Hégo-sama," Kugai said while still emitting the same skin-peeling scream. "You, you alone, can change all this if you really want to, but you have to desire it, and it has to be you."

Kugai's mouth snapped shut as if by some mechanical spring system. The resulting silence caused a sharper pain than the scream deluge. All the physical pain from Hego's fall immediately shot through his entire body in full force. Now it was his turn to scream.

Kugai's head snapped back into alignment with his supine spine, his body rippling with tremors of fighting life. It all stopped. He was dead.

Hégo uncovered his ears, his shaking palm dripping with blood. He had been holding onto Cane this whole time. "How?" He tried to let go of it, but his fist and Cane's knobbed end had fused into a gnarled ball of old flesh and skin with a wooden core. The deformation hit him with a force more solid that the stone he was now flat against.

"Yes. Your anxious thinking is correct," said Cane. "We have finally entered Totality. We are one. The vibrations running through Hégo felt like a smile from the Inanimate.

"Hégo-sama!" shouted a voice he didn't quite recognize at first. He was turned facing away from the door. "Hégo-sama! Are you alright?" It was Ogushu. He had never heard him raise his voice before. "We need your help! We are being invaded!"

"Get me up!" Ogushu easily picked the frail Master up. Hégo took a few seconds to steady himself then began acting. "Invaded? By whom? How?"

"I do not know yet. They are unmistakenly from the outside."

"Any deaths?" Hégo wanted to know before he committed fully to this deception. It was too late to have that luxury of backing out.

"Not that I know of. The gruesome invaders just scream and run around with wild eyes and gnashing teeth and fangs. Seems like they just want to scare us, for now." Ogushu looked over to the lifeless former Master. "Is he?"

"Yes," Hégo answered, not even following Ogushu's gaze. "Come on, help me get out of here. We will deal with his body later."

"What are you going to do?" asked Ogushu. Voices of panicking monks rushed past. Some stopped hoping for some guidance or instruction from their Masters. "Go to your cells!" Commanded the junior Master every time a mumbling monk stopped.

Hégo grimaced. *I am supposed to be in control.*

"Then maybe your restriction on no deaths may have been too restrictive," responded Cane.

Ogushu gently wrapped his arm around the old man and slowly guided him out the door, Cane dragging behind.

"Take me to the invaders." Hégo demanded, hoping there was still chance to regain authority.

"Are you sure you are up to it?"

"How can anybody be up to this?" Hégo yelled forcing his helper to stop. Hégo didn't want anyone, especially this annoying parasite, to think he wasn't fit to lead. It was his whole point of the terribly risky charade. "I want you to make sure everyone is safe in their cells or at least out of the Atrium, understood? I can make it on my own to the invaders."

"But..."

"Understood?"

Ogushu reluctantly unwrapped his supportive arm from the cracker-frail man, keeping his muscles tensed and ready for any sign of collapse. "As you wish, but I insist on coming back when my task in complete."

"Yes, yes, just go. They need to see a Master in their state." Hégo didn't look back at his co-Master, only shooing him away with his boney shaking hand, his only free hand. He had to use all his strength to show Ogushu he was able to walk. He wasn't sure himself, but Cane would take over.

The corridor was black hazed with male wailing. He reached out to the side for a wall to guide him. The feel of the wall was different somehow. It no longer felt like the cloister he had lived within for most of his long life. *This will no longer be the same place.*?

"And that is good," responded Cane.

thirty-eight

THE PROCESSION OF GUILD viscersha along the grand boulevard of Ou Dori that carried the city's parasitic inhabitants across its east-west expanse of the city, forced the few pedestrians out this early to stop and gawk. Hundreds of fingers pointed at the ornate vehicles groaning and moaning from mechano-bio exhaustion. Yuuki wanted to open a sphincter-window to get a better look of the city that remained foreign to him. But the viscergas was even more foreign and still churned his stomach.

He had Shinya ride in another sha just behind. He badly wanted their arms around each other but couldn't afford the distraction of love, or whatever it was. He insisted on an aboveground route. He wanted the citizens of the city to see the grandeur and dedication of what would be his city; a want that frightened him. He wanted all this. He didn't want any of this. Did he have the agency to even want? He understood how these transport mechanical beasts must feel, forced to go with the flow—not wanting, just doing.

He was on his way to save what was left of the Wamono cloister of Aoheki, his home for all but the past several weeks of his life. *Can I save something I have loathed so much? Does it deserve to be saved?* It was his responsibility, put upon by whom? Righteous responsibility is just another guise of selfish power. Such constant moral contradictions and conflicts ticked-tocked in his mind's, running his psycho-clockwork to overdrive. One tick or tock that was louder than the others was that Aoheki and the entire Wamono Order was the means to more important ends. Those ends were this entire city he was now a part of and this other place that was not part of anyone but perhaps everyone was a part of it. *Yedo. Yedo.* Yuuki kept repeating the name out-loud and in-loud. *What really is it? Who is it?*

He stared out the flesh-lined window looking at the people along the sidewalks stopping and staring back. He felt the urge to wave but quickly admonished himself. *Ridiculous. No one knows who you are. I don't even know.* His name, title, would soon be on everyone's mind and coming out of everyone's mouths. He wished he could see less further in the future to just a day or two from now, but it didn't seem to work that way. Maybe that would be too much power. He tried to keep the Wamono notion that the Gou-Tairei is something more powerful than him and everyone, but it was becoming more difficult.

He pressed his face up to the glass trying to get a glimpse of the summits of some of the tallest scrapers he was passing. He still had so much of this city to explore, to learn. Most of the peaks were obscured by low-flowing clouds. *Who lives up there?* He wondered. *Only those who wanted to get away from the city would live up there.* He was curious if he would feel the same in a few years or even months. Would he return to the reclusive life he fought so hard to escape? Being so high and away from the fray appealed to him. He was conditioned to need seclusion, even though he didn't want it.

While looking at the passing scrapers cloaked in the early morning dark, he nibbled at the soft inner wall of his bottom lip. Gentle clamping at first just to make the flesh plump up with blood, then biting down hard, puncturing the traumatized tissue. The euphoria of his ink-blood sliding down his throat quickly overtook the pain. *Why didn't I think of this before?*

He released a sigh of satisfaction and turned his head away from the window. He scrutinized the interior of the viscersha. Except for just around the windows and doors, there was no sign of the fleshy body. The Guild members took great care in crafting an interior that would hide such strangeness they knew would put off someone like him, someone not used to this world. That's what he was, someone from another world. He had yet to figure out if he was just a long-term visitor or invader. How was he different from the Editor and Ren? He and Charm were invading this world. After today, this world and the Wamono world would be very different no matter the outcome. He would be at the center of the new hybrid; as its savior or conqueror, he didn't know—probably both.

"Your introspectiveness is becoming tedious," said Charm. "I'm not your self-conscience, so these little quiet outbursts of regret or second thoughts will not work on me."

Yuuki let his head drop backwards along the high head rest and tried not to say or think anything; an impossibility. He understood why people going through Communion into Totality went insane. The lack of one's own private space would do it alone. "My self-conscience is dead," he whispered.

Pardon me, my prophet?" The driver, a Pollen, thought his prophet was giving him some kind of cryptic orders.

"Nothing, just talking to myself. And please to not refer to me as your prophet."

"My apologies, Sensei." The driver smiled and went back to concentrating on maneuvering his charge through the usual congestion plaguing this part of the city. Yuuki didn't quite understand how a viscersha was driven. He couldn't see anything the driver was doing to operate the sort-of-beast.

"This is your chance to change these worlds of Wamono and Hinodé; to meld them into one with you as its leader," said Charm. The vibrations through Yuuki's body were becoming stronger.

You mean 'we'.

"Differentiation in pronouns is irrelevant at this point." said Charm. "No one cares what happens inside the Wamono walls. Why would they? But you have to make them care if what you have seen of the future is true."

That is the point. I do not know what it is or if it is. It all could be simply insanity.

"it is real. Insanity would not take hold so quickly," replied Charm.

How do you know? Communion wasn't supposed to happen so quickly, but it did. You said so yourself.

"We are almost there," said the driver. Yuuki was shaken out of his silent conversation and nodded to the driver.

The Aoheki walls came into his window view as the viscersha moaned and groaned along the immensity. The view was like a never-ending cyclopean loop; unchanging, forever. But it wasn't. that was why he was here.

He finally saw a change in the majestic monotony, it was the opening of the tunnel he had exited from that weird, wonderful day. The driver slowed the miserable viscerthing and pulled it over just beyond the gaping hole, which was much larger; ripped open to fit much more than just one person crawling on his belly.

He looked in front of his viscersha and saw a small group waiting for his arrival. He didn't recognize anyone except the Blue major, Kazunori. He saw a figure standing next to him cloaked in a black-brown hooded robe. He assumed it was the mysterious Fujin. The unlikely silhouette did have a slightly feminine stance.

Mimi had the overwhelming sense of being gargantuan. The sharp corners of the room were more like joints that could bend like those of her elbows or knees. The chairs, various side tables, and desk were the contours of her body, like unique cranial bumps and birthmarks.

We will soon be in control of the entire city," said Palace.

Mimi was barely but at the same time intently listening. She could almost predict what Palace was going to say. "This must be what it's like to be in the womb," she said as if there was no other conversation going on. *Something strange is happening here, but I'm just too at ease to care.*

"There's nothing strange happening, my dear. Our thoughts are continuing to mesh, that's all."

Mimi wanted to stand up and walk around, she also didn't want to. She kept her eyes closed; it was easier than trying to keep them open and seeing.

"Yes, that makes sense," she felt herself almost dreaming her response.

"I'm not sure if it was a good idea sending Viki to off that Fujin bitch."

"We had to take the opportunity when it presented itself," replied Palace.

Intelligence had been coming in fast and confused. Mimi's inherited network of spies and informants was working at full capacity. She had been receiving reports over the past couple weeks of Yuuki's increasing power over in Hana-cho. He was already being called some kind of flower prophet. She didn't remember what flower.

A morning report informed her that he was on the way with a force apparently made up of renegade Characters and Flower Guild members to Aoheki where there was a break-in or invasion happening by the combined forces of the Suriidii and Tsudii. *The world has fucked itself, turned upside down, then done a few flip-flops. What the fuck is going on?*

She was still trying to process the news when Hiroka rang in with the latest piece of the nonsensical puzzle. Fujin was on her way there as well. It seemed like the whole city was going nuts and she was shut in like an invalid not able to enjoy the insanity firsthand.

"She is a threat to all of us." Palace's tone was, as always, matter of fact. But Mimi sensed the slightest current of resentment in its vibrations. Or was it her resentment? "You're right. She needs to be stopped first. Plus, she would be the easiest," said Mimi.

"And you are the one to do it, my dear" added Palace.

"Don't you mean 'we'?"

"I, we, they're all the same now."

"What about the Mayor?" Mimi asked. She might as well add another actor in this bizarro play.

"Don't worry about the Mayor, not yet," said Palace.

Mimi never bothered to know about the Mayor. It didn't matter to her day-to-day life as a Dekora mercenary. Things have obviously changed. She needed to find out how much she the Mayor as she could.

"At this point the less we know the better," said Palace. "Such information would distract us from the more immediate problems of the more humankind."

Mimi sensed that the Mayor was of a similar ilk to Palace but different. It was her added humanity that was that difference.

Palace was right. They needed to focus on the knowns, and that included her new friend and newer enemy. "Yuuki and his Symb."

"Another future obstacle, my dear. We need to stay focused on what needs to be done now. Let's hope that Lolita remains focused as well."

"So, what do we do once that Fujin is no longer the immediate problem?" This was something new to Mimi—planning the future. She felt old and stodgy just like how she perceived her predecessor.

"We will then obtain more information on your friend, this Azalea Prophet. Is it what his minions are calling him?"

Azalea, that's the flower, thought Mimi. Her friend's new title did worry her, but she was no longer just Mimi. She was the Oné-chan. She snickered at the ridiculousness of the titles gunshyu leaders have given themselves over the centuries. Editor, queen, Oné-chan, even Fujin. *Why the fuck does she call herself 'lady'.*

"*It could also mean 'heartless' depending on what characters she uses*, added Palace.

"She should call herself 'crazy-ass bitch'." She exhaled, puffing out her cheeks in bored little girl fashion; that was what she felt herself doing. "All titles to hide who we really are, people; fucked up in a big way, but just people." She could comfort herself in the fact that she inherited her title. She never insisted on being called Oné-chan. It just happened. There is power in titles.

She imagined the streets and alleys she now controlled. She couldn't be bothered getting up to see their physicality. *Every street and alley will wear my pink and fear my power. The prophet business will be in my control.* She shook her head, or so she imagined, as if a tiny buzzing bug had mistakenly flown into her ear. "That wasn't just me thinking, was it?"

"No, my dear. It wasn't."

"Thank you for meeting me here." Yuuki looked at both Kazunori and the cloaked figure. "I know it was quite short notice, but I'm sure you understand considering the circumstances."

Before Yuuki could get a response from either, the robed figure went limp and fell to the ground as if whatever was inside suddenly disintegrated. Yuuki and Shinya instinctively lunged toward the fallen figure hoping in vain to break the fall. Kazunori blocked him.

"Stay where you are," ordered the Blue Major. Once he was sure he had stopped any threat to his vulnerable leader and mother, he bent down to see what had happened. He put his head near the still hidden face to see if there was any breath still coming out of her. His muscles relaxed. "She's alive." The Blues behind the two also relaxed and stood down from their defensive stance. Yuuki saw their eyes ignite into bright blue for the few seconds before their major confirmed the status of their leader.

"Let me through!" shouted Shinya. He pushed Yuuki out of the way but looked back with an apologetic stare. Yuuki nodded his acceptance. Shinya squatted next to Kazunori. "Yes, she is alive." Tears streamed down his face. He looked back at Yuuki smiling but still in emotional pain then looked at Kazunori. "What happened?" Yuuki couldn't quite determine if his tone was just a simple question or an accusation.

"I know just as much as you," Kazunori responded. "She just collapsed. Come on, hold her head up while I get this damn cowl off her so she can breathe easier." Shinya nodded and lifted the lifeless head of his mother. Yuuki and The Pollen closest to the scene craned their necks to get a glance at the infamous Fujin. Yuuki looked up at the Blues forming the opposite half of the human circle. Their fading blue eyes flashing back and forth between their concern for their leader and him and his massive guard.

When Yuuki looked back down to the three huddled together forming the nucleus of this highly unstable atom, his ability to breathe suddenly left him. *The woman from the station! It's her. My, my* "mother?"

All eyes snapped their stares to Yuuki wondering what he had said and for those who heard, why he said it. Shinya looked at Yuuki in confusion and answered. "Yes, my mother." Yuuki did not faint completely but crashed down onto his knees.

Tomo quickly rushed to his prophet's aid. He lifted him up from the ground and held on to him making sure he did not fall back down.

"Prophet-sama," whispered Tomo. "Are you alright?" The others behind scanned the vicinity for any signs of foul play. Most were looking accusingly at the Blues. The Blues, seeing this, readied their weapons, their eyes pulsating with the remnants of their latest hits.

"I am fine. You can let go of me." He wasn't alright. His mother was almost unconscious on the ground in front of him and Shinya was calling her mother. He looked up at the Blues and noticed their cold-burned eyes. "Stand down," he said looking back at his group. "I just lost my footing, that's all." His army of Guildsmen and Pollen was small, maybe twenty individuals at most. But the few Little Killers and hand-crafted knives and staffs of the Fighting Arts coterie would be enough to sustain an impromptu civil war within the wary confederacy.

He would have to force this discovery deep within him until the problem with the invaders was settled one way or the other, made easier with the presence of Charm.

Fujin, his mother, was starting to come out of her unconsciousness. He looked at Shinya who had thankfully forgotten their quick confusing exchange and went back to tending to his mother, their mother. *My brother.* This delayed revelation almost forced him back down to the ground.

Fujin's eyes slowly began to open and immediately stared at him. He knew she knew. He waited for any response from Charm. Nothing, not even a buzz of vibration.

Fujin was now on her feet. She looked at Yuuki with those cold knowing eyes but kept silent about it as expected. Yuuki's guts released the tension painfully constricting them. He let out a long sigh and walked over to his mother. "It is very nice to finally meet you, Fujin. But you understand if we forego the pleasantries until after." He wanted to hug and slap her at the same time.

"Yes, understood," responded Fujin. She brushed herself off and re-hooded herself.

Fujin and Yuuki's eyes shifted to beyond the small blue-eyed troop and saw another group heading toward them. They were all female and wearing the Dekora signature pink miniskirts and pigtails.

The Blues had formed a protective ring around their leader. "What are you doing here?" Yelled Kazunori and assumed both a defensive and offensive stance. Yuuki held up his hand wide open signaling to The Pollen to stay standing down if they were in a heightened alert.

"We've come to help," replied a young woman. She looked familiar to Yuuki. She was in Mimi's suite during their aborted reunion. She was dressed differently than the other girls. She was clad in frilly black lace with bright red lipstick painted on her. The look reminded him of a doll he remembered seeing in a store window on one of his several escapes through the city. He didn't understand what made him remember something so trivial.

"Come to help whom?" asked Fujin. "Us," she thrust her arm violently towards the nearby wall, "or them?"

"Our prophetess gave orders to help Yuuki-Hana," said the life-sized doll. Yuuki noticed his mother turn round to look at him. He wanted to believe he saw a smile after hearing his name. "She had heard what had happened here and sent us to help you defeat the invaders."

Fujin walked up to Yuuki, the first time they looked at each other eye to eye for longer than a fleeting moment. Yuuki saw the color of her eyes. They were the same as his, a winter-leaf brown. He was looking at himself. His heart raced, skipping the slightest of partial beats. "I don't trust them or that Oné-chan," she whispered. There was no sign of his mother or anyone's mother in those eyes and that hardened voice. She frightened him. *How can she be my mother?* He thought. *She's barely human as the prophets inside; any of us.* He closed his eyes to forget their shared blood. She had obviously done the same with him.

"Well, I do." He said as confidently as he could. "She is a friend and if she wants to help, then why not? We need as much as we can get. Who knows how many Tsudii and Suriidii are in there?" He looked out over his mother to the living doll. "Thank you. We appreciate any help you can give us." He did not look back down to his mother, who was a good half meter shorter than him. Instead, he kept his eyes looking forward and shouted, "Follow me and take Aoheki back for the Wamono, Hinodé, and Yedo!" He turned around and headed for the eviscerated tunnel. The Pollen and Dekora immediately followed. He glanced back, seeing his mother and her Blues looking at each other then following his lead.

Thirty-nine

"**C**ALM DOWN EVERYONE. CALM** down!" Hégo tried his best to shout over the nervous babbling crowd of monks below him. "I have negotiated a settlement to this despicable situation. He kept his hands waving up and down in front of him trying to silence his congregation. Mashu had given up his crowd-taming post and became one in the crowd.

"What kind of settlement would there be? We are prisoners in our own sanctuary!" An elderly monk shouted. Many nodded in agreement.

"I understand how you all feel." He finally let his exhausted arms fall. "The invaders have agreed to let us go about or lives. They have assured me they are not interested in our way of life and are not intent on destroying it." He wanted to sit his age-ravaged being down into the cathedra but needed to show his flock he was in control of an uncontrollable situation. "They agreed to remain down in in the old root cellar. I am not sure what they want, but they have promised me no harm will come to us. Ryudasu is with them making sure they fulfill that promise."

"And you believe them?" The voice sounded younger this time. "They are from Keibu-yo and rumors are that they are Symb prophets. They cannot be trusted!"

Shouts of agreement resounded through the stifling atrium. He raised his tiring sinewy arms to calm them down again. "I know who they are. I am no idiot!" The bizarre trio had told him he would be allowed to 'save the day' as long as they got what they wanted. They vaguely requested the squid Amedo. What they wanted with that flighty Reincarnate was beyond him, but he was expendable, supposed Founder-Same or not. The old Order was on its deathbed, and he is the one to resurrect it. *The Reincarnate's ink would no longer be required if events progressed as planned.* "They sounded sincere, and that is all I can rely on. Nothing but panic and over-reaction has injured some of you. You played your part exactly as they wanted."

"What is this settlement?" The same elderly monk asked. "Living with these invaders is hardly a settlement. They are still invaders."

"What is it they want?" This time Hégo knew who had spoken. It was that Haiku-Bassbeat cleric. He stared at him trying to intimidate him into shutting up. It wasn't working. "We need to know the whole story if we are to, what you say, live with them."

"First, I never said we were to 'live together'. I have no idea what they want. Some kind of relic I suppose, I do not know," he lied," but I think it is a sacrifice worth giving for our safety." He kept his eyes on the cleric the entire time.

Someone finally rose his hand before speaking. Hégo nodded to him to go ahead and speak. "So, once they get this relic, they will leave?"

"Yes. That is what they told me." Hégo looked out over the crowd of robed men and a few Reincarnates. He could hear the ones nearest the front debating what the relic could be. Aoheki was not known for its wealth of important Wamono relics from the order's murky past. He hoped his lie wouldn't die before at least growing for a bit. "I will have another meeting later and demand to know what specifically they want."

This seemed to quiet the agitated congregation. He would have to either tell them the truth about Amedo or choose some old forgotten chalice as a decoy.

"I say we fight back!" Yelled out the cleric.

"With what?" shouted another farther back in the crowd. The rest of the monks mumbled their agreement with the question.

"We are not trained to fight," another in the back shouted.

Hégo held out his hands again to calm the room. "They are correct Basho Jyon-sensei. We cannot fight them. Negotiation is the only means we have. I know it is not the ideal and we do not have much negotiation power, but I think we could have come out of this much worse. If they were lying, we would all probably be dead."

"The invasion is not over yet," cried out the cleric.

Hégo couldn't have someone like that causing panic, not now. "He would make a filling meal for Ryudasu," vibrated Cane. Hégo threw up his almost empty sleeves, let out a loud sigh, and sat heavily down into the oversized cathedra. He looked out into the atrium that had seen nothing but chaos since he took over. It used to be such a peaceful gathering place. He longed for the staleness of the meetings past.

Ogushu, who had remained sitting and silent, stood up and tried to calm the monks. "Please, everyone, calm down. We are doing our best to make this horrible incident as least painful as possible. I have all confidence in Hégo-sama's strategy in talking with the invaders.

"You are not part of the talks, Ogushu-sama?" one of the monks asked.

"No, I am not. They only wanted to talk to the most senior, eldest, of us."

Hégo lifted his head from resting on his branch-like hand. *They are getting suspicious.*

"Don't be paranoid," responded Cane. "He explained to them what you said to him, that's all."

They hate me. It will not take much for them to turn against me and make accusations of collusion.

"Don't give this cowering mass that much credit," said Cane. "They have only you saving them from annihilation; they know that. They may hate you, but they have to trust you."

Hégo worked his way out of the cathedra and eventually straightened himself into a standing posture. "Thank you, Ogushu-sama." He walked to the edge of the dais pretending to tightly hold onto Cane to keep his balance. "I will come back with a much better view of what they want in a day's time. Please have patience and be assured that I have your best interests in the forefront of my mind."

"But not your heart." mumbled the cleric.

Hégo didn't let on that he heard. Ogushu took hold of his cane-free arm and helped him along. He involuntarily shuddered but suppressed the urge to reject and let the younger Master guide him, twisting his neck slightly and smiling his thanks to his co-Master.

"Ahh, old friend Nonen Amedo." Ryudasu sounded almost sincere as she and her cousins entered the Yedo-seitai's cool wet cell. "Sorry, I have not gotten to talk with you since my release."

Amedo's gurgling voice echoed. "I was wondering when you would show your evil suffering face, Ryduasu." His agitated fluttering made small splashes throughout the pool, his tentacles flailing just under the water's service. The action made it difficult for him to be seen clearly, but more for him not to have to see those six small orbs of black nothing staring down at him.

"I went a little insane those centuries ago and slaughtered a few dozen monks or was it a few hundred? It happened." Ryudasu let out a nostalgic sigh. "That was a Gou Matsuri that should have never been forgotten." Her sickly green-yellow glow reflected off the water, forcing Amedo to glow along with her. The Editor and Ren peered over the pool's edge trying to get a better look at this strange water creature. The ripples still emanating from his body had the same effect on them as Ryudasu, but Amedo could still make out their surprise.

"Do not look like that, cousins," Ryudasu said, flicking her neck-less head as far as it could go without having to move her entire body. "Our squirming friend here is a delicacy in Yedo. You probably ate hundreds of his kind in that world."

Yedo? Amedo turned an almost pure white. *What does all this have to do with Yedo?*

Ryudasu snapped her bristly head back to focus her multiple eyes back onto the squid Reincarnate. "I have enjoyed it flayed and dried, oh and the innards fermented in a thick gelatinous spread - delicciousss." The rasping hiss lingered for seconds filling the small space with its echo.

Amedo imagined what that horrid creature would look like with the sinister human smile. "Them having been to Yedo is not possible. It is an end not a beginning."

"For some ... thing so wise, you are being quite foolish," said Ryudaus. She dipped one of her front pincers gently into the pool very near Amedo's arrowhead front. "I do not have time to explain away the religious detritus from your little mind. We require your assistance, old friend."

"I am not your friend and will not give any assistance to you, again," replied the fluttering Reincarnate. It was obvious by the looks on the other two's faces that they had only the faintest idea what the demented arachnid was talking about. Amedo scurried away from the pincer that was still piercing the surface of his home.

"You are quite wrong, Amedo," continued Ryudasu. "Your help is key in getting these two back to where they, we, belong." She took her pincer out of the cold water and pointed it at her cousins. They instinctively jumped back a step. Ryudasu put her two front pincers on the ledge as if she was about to plunge into the pool. She lowered her head to the water's edge and Amedo. "You are going to give us your ink."

Amedo was afraid of this. "What do you need my ink for?"

Ren interrupted. "What is all this about this thing's ink? How will that get us to this Yedo?"

It was clearly out in the open now. No hiding behind vagueness and nuance. They were really going to try to get into Yedo. "Impossible!" Amedo was more disbelieving than scared at this point. "No one can simply go to Yedo, not even abominations such as yourself with whatever twisted abilities you possess. He turned one of his oversized iridescent eyes on the spider.

"You are half correct. I cannot ... yet, but they can." Ryudasu purred her hisses and rasps.

"This is ridiculous. I'm tired of all this," said Ren. "Let's go Futoshi." She reached to grab her brother, but he refused to budge. It wouldn't have taken much effort to drag the stunted man with her, but Ryudasu swung her pincer and snapped the two claws together in front of Ren's face, halting her mid pace.

"I have been waiting centuries for this moment," hissed Ryudasu. The rest of her body was now in line with the pincer still only centimeters from the Suriidii queen's face. "I think you can wait a few minutes longer." Her pincer disappeared with only a puff of air. The void was replaced with her eyes. "Your scars show a lifetime of impatience." She lifted the same pincer and touched one of the healed wounds running along the back of her hands. "It is time to be done with all that."

The Editor took the opportunity of surprise to stand on the tip of his toes and whisper, "We are in a Wamono cloister talking to a giant spider woman and some water creature with no head. It might not be as ridiculous as you think."

"Now, where were we?" Ryudasu rasped as she turned her attention back on Amedo.

"Stealing my ink, like you did those centuries ago," responded the squid Reincarnate. He was defiant. He had absolutely no power to stop them taking what they wanted. It was the first time he was scared for his life. Murder never resulted in a harmonious transition to the next cycle, for both parties.

"Thanks to that little theft, I learned the real power of your disgusting secretions. Though, even after centuries of trial and error, I do not quite understand how. And that should satisfy the Gou-Tairei believer in us."

She pointed her pincer toward the Editor and shook it slightly. "Do you have the container?"

"Here," said the Editor. He thrust a jar out as far as he could just in case Ryudasu reached a bit too far or too hard and sliced his arm open or his hand clear off. Amedo watched the two. *Why do they want to go to Yedo? What is the connection?* He needed to know to placate his curiosity. *Cursed cephalopod brain!*

"Ryudasu-sensei," Amedo said as gently as he could. "Since I have no means of preventing you from depositing my ink or me in that jar, could you please tell me what all this is about. I think I at least deserve that." He immediately sank further under the water just in case the Aku decided that the ink would work from either a living or dead squid.

Ryudasu looked down at the water and laughed. "You are a curious creature. I suppose it cannot hurt. It is not a secret as far as I am concerned."

Amedo's mind hung on every word. *Who would it concern, then?* He re-surfaced, feeling it was safe to do so.

"Futoshi and Atsushi are brothers," she corrected herself, "siblings, and my cousins from a very long time ago when we were young acolytes at a temple in Yedo. Before our real lives were stolen from us and we ended up in this unreality."

Amedo felt the boom of her last few words. She was becoming angry. "Who spirited you here, then." He had to play along. She was even more than insane, which meant that she was capable of committing any kind of atrocity.

"I would hardly call it 'spirited', squid," Ryudasu almost roared but quickly calmed herself. "An incompetent superior of ours at the temple started what would soon be called the Great Furisodé Fire by attempting to burn an it-tan-momen yokai." She looked over to the siblings. "A particularly nasty textile idol to you, in the form of a furisodé kimono. The fire got out of control due to the spring winds and ended up destroying most of Yedo and over 100,000 lives. My cousins and I were unfortunate enough to witness the entire misguided deed, so this head priest had us killed to silence us. He was not about to be blamed for the deaths of so many. That damnable temple is probably still thriving. It is time for us to return home and address ... issues."

Amedo noticed the two siblings were listening as intently as he was. It seemed cathartic for the Aku to talk about, even though it made no sense to him. That horrid Aku, a victim? Places called temples? Retribution pets in Yedo?

Ryudasu continued. "I do not know how our why we ended up in this prison of the dead, but we should not be here. Ingesting your ink those centuries ago may have not been the most prudent thing to do, but it allowed me to see, to understand. Even understand what I still cannot. I still do not know, nor care, how I came to realizing that these two were my real cousins. It just came as part of the package of seeing the truth. I think you would agree, dear old friend, that the Gou-Tairei puts events into motion that are not logical, even to it."

Amedo thought he saw a softening of her eye cluster but knew it was wishful thinking on his part.

"Never mind about all this!" Ryudasu hissed causing ripples on the water. "Put him in the vessel. We need him alive."

Amedo was at least thankful for that clarification.

forty

"**KEEP AN EYE ON** them," Charm vibrated, agitating every filament of Yuuki's nerve endings. "They shouldn't be trusted."

Yuuki knew Charm was referring to Mimi's band of helpers, but he didn't not want to trust them. Charm advised Yuuki to fall back behind the pink squadron. He had given orders for Tomo and a couple other of the Pollen to lead the unlikely crew into the absolute unknown. Even though he had experienced the reverse journey, he had no idea what awaited them at the other end. It was no longer his home. It would be completely different, and he was a different person, being.

"Remain focused," said Charm.

Yuuki did as Charm said and kept an eye on the Moé contingent directly in front. Pig-tailed heads swished back and forth; the leader's full locks bouncing, conducting.

The tunnel also smelled differently. Instead of an overwhelming mineral odor, the walls exuded an inky stench. *The Tsudii*, Yuuki thought. *They must have spent weeks expanding this tunnel*. He didn't want to touch the walls.

His thoughts switched to the famously ill-tempered Shisa lions guarding the main gates. *Were they even aware what was happening behind their backs?* They never looked backwards, always forward. Their uselessness had become striking. *They're just for show.*

"Yuuki-Hana," Charm's vibrations made Yuuki shuddered in pain. "Focus."

The party continued almost silent through the eerie tunnel. It seemed much shorter than Yuuki remembered. *What is going on at the other end*? He imagined dead monks scattered everywhere, mutilated for mutilation's sake. Sticky webbing coating every stone wall, making the entire place a cushioned tomb. One little graze against one thin strand and that drooling behemoth would be on them in seconds if not sooner. Sweat began to break on his brow. Many were counting on him.

He tried to fight back the thoughts of his mother somewhere behind. He didn't want another scolding from Charm. But the thoughts were still there clawing their way through the still weak blockade of his will. *Would she be proud or still want nothing to do with me*?

"It doesn't matter," shocked in Charm. The interruption forced Yuuki to stop and grab hold of a sharp jagged outcrop of stone to keep his balance. "If she knew the truth, she wouldn't hesitate to kill us. You know that."

I am her son. But Charm was right. He hoped there would be some point at which he could hide at least the deepest of his thoughts from it.

"I am right," said Charm. Its vibrations were duller now. "She abandoned you. She's a fanatic. Any kind of reasoning capabilities died within her long ago. Don't let her get into your head by just the fact that she gave birth to you. You need to remember, Yuuki-Hana, that you never had a mother, unless you count that Master of the Cloister."

Would Shinya turn on him too if he found out the truth, both truths? He couldn't lose him as well. He tried to concentrate on what was happening at the very front. He could only see the Pollen hulk. Everything seemed to be proceeding smoothly. After a couple minutes their massive silhouettes were becoming sharper. The end was near. The light that leaked into the jagged passageway was only too familiar. It oozed a yellow-green hue.

"Ryudasu," whispered Yuuki.

"Send word up the line to be ready to fight. They would assume there would be light at the end of any tunnel," Charm said, almost commanding.

Yuuki did as Charm advised. He would have done it anyway. It didn't take long for the message to get to Tomo, who looked back nodding his understanding. "This is it," Yuuki spoke just loud enough so most could hear him. "Remember. Our targets are the Editor and Ren. Don't get distracted by the grotesqueness of the Suriidii flesh-and-clay golems. Try to avoid those Tsudii Characters that have not been truthed back to who they really are." He was now speaking directly to The Pollen. "They were colleagues of some of you and they can be again. Try to stay out of their way."

Not long after his short instructions, the sickening light intensified, distant shouting accompanied its fluorescence. It sounded like an argument. "Gou-Tairei, remain uncaring in this cycle for reward to fall upon of us in our next," whispered Yuuki.

Ryudasu slammed the root cellar door, breaking one of its hinges. "What do you mean she is no longer a Fujou?"

The Editor slowly backed away thinking that the tiny distance would make any difference if his grotesque cousin over-reacted to the news. "I personally went to her Fujou den to deliver your message, but she wasn't there. They said she defected to the Dekora."

"The what? Never mind," Ryudasu said without even an angry hiss. "There was bound to be a kink in the plan. She will fall back into my fold." She twitched her tiny head around the room looking at the Editor and Ren's hodgepodge army. "You had them swear to follow me, yes?"

"Yes, they will do as you command," responded the Editor.

"Only until I return," said Ren.

Ryudasu growled a sigh of boredom. "There will be no reason to return once you arrive into reality. She looked directly through the glass container filled with the squid Reincarnate. There was no room for Amedo to shrink away from the solid obsidian stare. "Let us begin making this disgusting wine."

"Everyone out! Only us three and that squid in here." Ryudasu looked back at Ren's ever-present assistant. "That means you too, little shadow."

"Masao stays!" Ren didn't care who she was talking to. The Editor noticed his new-found sibling shaking slightly.

Ryudasu grumbled a sigh and stared at her cousin for several long seconds "As you wish, cousin, as long as Futoshi has no objections."

"It doesn't matter."

"Very well." Ryudasu kept her ocular mass on Ren. "Now that little tantrum is over, Futoshi, empty the sack of grapes into that bowl." She stretched what little neck she had closer to Ren. "And Atsushi, be so kind as to take that squid out." She stooped to the imprisoned Reincarnate's level and tapped on the container. "Don't worry about hurting it."

The Editor, holding the sack to his chest as if it were full of precious treasure, struggled to extend his arms to place it in the bowl already placed on an even spot of the floor free of wall and ceiling crumbs. "Grapes?"

Ryudasu calmly click-clacked over to the Editor and growled a purr. "Precaution. Not completely sure the Wamono's blood rendered yours immune to the poison. You would not want to drop dead after a few minutes of sublime agony after only a few steps back home, would you?"

Ren began to cautiously stick her hand in the jar. "Does it bite?"

"Of course it does," answered Ryudasu. Ren's hand froze just above the water. "But not fatally." Ryudasu hissed a curt laugh that she murdered with a growl that vibrated through the stone and up through her conspirators. "Do it!"

Ren plunged her hand down into the jar and grabbed Amedo. The squid Reincarnate couldn't evade the grasping hand. She pulled Amedo out and held it far away from her body, tentacles dangling and dripping.

"Is it still alive?" asked the Editor.

Ryudasu leaned in close to the dropping mass of damp flesh. She stared into one of Amedo's large eyes, waiting for any kind of movement. It finally focused on her. The pupil expanded to take in as much light to better see the lightless mass that had taken up his entire view. "Yes. How much so, I do not know."

"How do we get the ink?" Asked Ren, still holding the squid at arm's length.

"Well," hissed Ryudasu, "if the squid cooperates and wants to remain unmurdered, he will volunteer the black substance." She was still looking directly into Amedo's unblinking eye. "If not, there are other ways to force it out of him."

Ren shook Amedo over the semi-iridescent berries. "Come on you weird little beast, puke or shit the ink out, come on." Her tone was of a little girl shaking a purloined bag hoping something valuable would eventually fall out.

"You cannot shake it out," said Ryudasu. She again crept close to Amedo's eye and growled in a low voice. "Do you really want to die, squid? Once they return to Yedo, who knows how that will affect yours or anyone else's cycles. Will you be able to end your cycling in your cherished Yedo, hmm? Do you really want to risk being stuck in limbo without life or death? I am sure your Gou-Tairei will not care one way or the other. In fact, I would not be surprised if it would be happy, if that is the right term, if no one reached the place where it had absolutely no power. Everyone, even the Gou-Tairei, is selfish."

"When did you become an unbeliever?" Amedo finally asked.

"Oh, you have decided to speak." Ryudasu feigned ecstatic surprise. "I believe. I simply do not give a damn. I am the one to be sincerely believed."

"You?" asked Amedo. Ren's arm was starting to tremble with fatigue from holding the slimy creature over the grapes.

"I, and eventually these two," she glanced at her cousins, "am the only one who knows the truth. Maybe ask yourself if you should even believe."

What if we all did die and remain where neither life nor death exist? Amedo thought. There was nothing in the teachings that addressed what would happen if the Gou-Tairei's universe of end-of-cycle cities were suddenly believed out of existence.

Ren interrupted the bizarre interspecies theological debate. "Are we going to do this?"

"Well, are we?" Asked Ryudasu, all eyes focused on Amedo.

Black viscous dribbled over Ren's hand. She had been holding Amedo the wrong end up. The Editor let a smile spread across his face. Ren turned the squid around, and ink began to slicken the grapes.

"Good, good," rasped Ryudasu. "Futoshi, reach in and start mashing."

The Editor looked at his spider cousin checking to see is she was serious. "If you haven't noticed, I'm not the best at working with my hands."

Ryudasu's glow intensified. "Atsushi, if you could be so kind. You can put that thing back in the jar."

Ren rolled her eyes at the Editor. "I can have Masao give you new ones."

"Focus!" hissed-growled Ryudasu.

Ren, relieved that she could finally put the slimy ink-slathered creature back into its jar, squatted near the bowl and started needing the slippery contents.

"Yes, good," Ryudasu growl whispered. "Almost ready, just a little bit more, and it will be ready to drink."

"How do you know the grapes will neutralize the ink?" Asked the Editor.

"As long as it is not in its pure form, anything should be fine."

"And what do we do when we get to Yedo?" Ren's hands turned black from the mashing. "I have a feeling it won't be the same place as when we left, died, were kidnapped." She was still not clear how their transfer between life and death dimensions worked.

"Questions. Always questions," growled Ryudasu. "Just do the same as you two did here. Take over the damn place. But play nice. We do not need the same kind of bickering between you two there."

The black gook in the bowl began to bubble, almost sizzle. Ren quickly re-tracted her hands. The mixture began to coalesce into a smooth thick colloid self-swirling in greens, purples, and reds.

"It is ready." Ryudasu hissed.

Amedo looked through the thick glass of his prison. *What have I done?*

"Both of you drink it. Drink as much as you can."

Ren picked up the bowl and began to drink. Amedo saw the look on the short one's face. He looked angry that his sibling began to drink first.

Ren didn't stop until half the concoction was down her throat. She lowered the bowl, still holding it and wiped her black lips with her free arm. She looked at her brother and gave him a sinister smile. "Masao, now!"

She thrust the bowl towards her chief modeler, keeping her smile and stare on the Editor. "Drink!"

Masao, not understanding what was going on, obediently took the bowl.

"What is this?" Roared Ryudasu.

"You bitch!" Shouted the Editor. He knocked over the jar filled with Amedo. The petit prison remained intact, but a small crack began creeping up from the base.

Ren began to shimmer in and out of existence. "Dink it, Masao! Now. I cannot be without y—" She sputtered out of existence.

Masao began drinking the strange brew.

"Damn her!" Ryudasu's roar turned into a piercing scream.

A soft sizzling pop came from the tunnel opening, hitting Masao somewhere in the back as he too faded out of existence. The bowl of inky wine crashed down onto the floor, the remaining drops of the concoction mixing with the dust.

The Editor quickly ducked behind his gruesome cousin. It took only a few seconds more for the Editor's Characters and Ren's golems to burst in to confront the ruckus. More sizzling pops claimed a few more victims before the room filled with human and mixi-matchi flesh occasionally illuminated by flashes of aiming Little Killers.

Yuuki's view was a chaos of living things in various stages of dying or killing. Some of the Pollen fell back and closed in tight around him forming an almost impenetrable wall. The Guildsmen did whatever they could, and the Blues emitted drug-induced screams, stopping even the most hardened killer in their tracks just long enough for the Dekora to invisibly come up and slit their necks or shoot them between the eyes.

Streaks of pink miniskirts, drug-induced blue eyes, and golden Guild tunics whizzed by him. It was all color and sound. Charm constantly vibrated orders/advice to Yuuki to stay out of the fray, that he needed to stay alive no matter what. *For the sake of Hinodé or for you*? Yuuki quickly thought. Every few seconds the solid black mass of Ryudasu came into view. She no longer glowed her repulsive yellow-green. There was no need, the lights on everyone's Little Killers lit the room. He heard deadly projectiles ricochet off stone walls and ceiling, dislodging more rubble. Soon the room was smothered with centuries-old dust. The Little-Killer lights were now beams of death. Everyone, including himself, began choking on the cloud. Ryudasu had disappeared into the mineral fog.

"Shinya!" he yelled, but his voice was useless through the solid mass of flesh engulfing him and over the sounds of battle. The pointlessness didn't deter him from repeatedly yelling his love's, his brother's, name. "Shinya!"

"Yuuki!"

He's still alive. His mother? He decided not to call out to her. What would he yell out?

He tripped over fleshy lifeless mounds as his protective cage moved around the room trying to find the safest place amongst the blind chaos. He regretted choosing to go barefoot to somehow show respect to his unexpected charge of the Wamono Order. He could feel from what faction the dead bodies belonged by the texture of their clothing or plasticine flesh. A faint waft of grape rose up and into his nostrils and the familiar almost non-existent saline fragrance. The tempting sludge was everywhere on the ground and blackening his feet. He had to fight the selfish urge to collapse onto his haunches and begin licking the precious substance from his toes and soles. It didn't matter why it was there. The only importance was that it was.

"It's ruined from the contamination of dust and grit." The zapping of Charm's warning was all that prevented Yuuki from obeying his addiction. "Do not succumb."

Before Yuuki, or the addict in him, could attempt to disobey, Ryudasu flashed before him in a break in the dust. She had been in the process of impaling what looked like a female. It had to be a Dekora from the drooping pig tails, the body convulsing on the poisonous spear. The slow-motion scene suddenly popped out of Yuuki's sight.

Yuuki's protective circle forced him to move and stumble over something smooth and hard. If felt out of place from the rough course debris and the lumps of the dead. He bent down to touch it. *Glass*. He picked up the object. The dust was so thick he had to put the object so close that it touched his nose. A giant eye stared back at him. "Amedo?" The Reincarnate was moving as much as he could in such a small prison. Yuuki held on tight to the jar. It wasn't going to be easy. Every few seconds his Pollen wall was struck by some sort of force. He was amazed that none had been shot dead.

There was another break in the dust. Shinya had grabbed a golem from behind and in the process of twisting its neck. His lover/brother's face looked terrified, like he had no idea what he was doing. The head he was twisting completely separated from its body. Shinya stood there holding the bodiless head. It's eyes still wide with both anger and fear, mouth silently screaming. The blinding dust bank swallowed him out of Yuuki's sight.

He was sure he and his entourage had traversed the entire perimeter of the room by now. Grunts, pre-death screams, and Little-Killer fizzes and sizzles filled his ears. The terror sounds seemed to become less frequent, slower. The dust was thinning, strangely only where he was looking. *Was it ending?* He saw silhouettes: all human, more or less. There was no spider shape to be found. His Pollen wall broke away, or was time slowing down, slowing him down? Whatever was happening, it allowed him to view the room in its entirety and the carnage that lay before him. Several Guildsmen lifeless on the ground, their gold tunics sullied with blood balled with grit. The pink of the Dekora, dull and lifeless as their wearers. He saw Shinya sitting on a large piece of rubble, his body heaving. He turned around to look for his mother. She was standing near the door looking at him. Was she smiling at him? The dying dust was still settling to its grave on the floor. He stood there staring at her.

That strange black Dekora stood to the left of his mother. She was not looking around like the others but intensely focused on his mother. Her eyes still showed that she still had a mission to accomplish. Before the clumps of synapses and dendrons in his brain could process and communicate the signs, the black Dekora had already grabbed his mother from the back with one arm and swiped her other hand across her throat. It took a slow-motion second more to see the blood slowly begin to ooze from the clean slice. Yuuki could not move, only watch the escaping blood flow faster until the black robe around her chest began to glisten. The assassin disappeared back through the tunnel. His mother fell backwards, the wall behind her breaking her fall.

The Editor had been nearby and was staring down at the dead woman, first in surprise then in what looked like deflation into mourning. Bodies and blood rushed into the vacuum of Yuuki's time bubble, throwing him back into the fast-forward of the battle.

forty-one

"**WHAT IS HAPPENING!" SHOUTED** Hégo. The strange thin creature assigned to 'protect' him earlier in the morning did not answer immediately. He was too busy frantically scratching on that equally strange orange glowing board. "Hey! You!" continued the Master. "I know something is awry. One minute you were casually drawing on that thing, now you look like you are trying to kill it with your scratches." He looked over at Ogushu who was also under 'protection' and lost in some archaic meditation. His co-Master's calmness irritated him more than the bizarre man-sheet making seizure-like love to his contraption.

The Illustrator finally spoke. "There is some sort of altercation down in the cellar."

"Altercation?" Hégo raised his arms and let them fall in frustration. "What, you people fighting amongst yourselves?"

"No," replied the Illustrator. There seems to be another group that had entered through the tunnel."

"Another group!" Hégo had to sit down. His plan was beginning to unravel. There was not supposed to be any 'altercation' and definitely no other outsiders. The inevitability of an open sore exposed to all the infection of the Scorned World had at the ready only now registered. He had lost all control.

The Illustrator remained looking at his control device but stopped scratching, "It's over now."

"So, I assume you won."

"No, the others," answered the Illustrator. His scratching slowed to an almost hypnotic rhythm.

Ryudasu burst through the door as if propelled by an explosion. Hégo found himself on the floor; a prickly sweat forcing its way out of his skin.

"You have to go." Hissed Ryudasu. She looked directly at Hégo.

"Why? What is going on. I need to know. I still run this place."

"No time."

Hégo looked over at Ogushu. His co-Master was backed up against the wall in terror at the sudden and violent appearance of the Aku.

"Not until we have your word that our needs will be met," interrupted Cane.

"There will not be anything to need unless you get out of the cloister now, Inanimate!" rasped the spider.

Hego's secret he had been keeping for decades was leaking out. He couldn't have it survive free. He needed to recapture it if he was to ever take over the entire Wamono order. He pointed over toward the confused co-Master. "Kill him first."

"I take no orders from you, monk," hissed Ryudasu. "There is no time. They are coming and only one of my cousins has made it to Yedo."

"You know he must die. He knows too much. He may not understand now, but he will."

Ogushu may not have completely grasped what was being revealed, but he showed he understood that Hégo wanted him dead. "No! Please. I can stay quiet. Murder will add horrific cycles to mine and your lives. Please!"

Before he could utter another string of pleas, Ryudasu had her fangs arching high over him. One of the poisoned spears slammed deep into the co-Master's head. The further it punctured, the less head remained. Hégo turned his head away. *Infinitely more cycles have just been added to my increasingly miserable existence.*

"The most important 'cycle' is the one you're in now," vibrated Cane. "We can still accomplish everything we wanted."

The old Master heard the spider sucking into her gullet the raw fluids of the dead Wamono. The accompaniment of panic further down the corridor added to the symphony grotesque.

"What are you doing to help the situation?" Hégo had to take his frustration out on someone or something. There was no point in keeping the conversations internal. "We are in Totality! We should be able to do something to defeat whatever is causing all this?"

"My, our, ability is much more subtle," said Cane. Its voice irritatingly calm. Though, the vibrations were a bit more painful to Hégo than usual.

"Subtle!" Yelled the ancient monk. "We do not need subtle!"

"How do you think you are now living beyond your normal years?"

"Immortal?" Hégo stared out at a wall trying to fathom the implications of this realization, almost forgetting what the chaos around him.

"Perhaps," said Cane. "But not invincible. We need to get out of here if that's what that spider thinks best."

"I needed that. Meagre juices, but no time for preparation." said Ryudasu. She came out of her feeding stupor and turned her attention to Hégo. "Go to a place called the Pink Palace. The Fujou Dame I have been in contact with seems to have joined another organization."

"The Dekora? Those murderous women? No!"

Ryudasu jumped toward the old man eclipsing him in her shadow. "Then die here and see your dream die with you. Go!"

"How?" Hégo screamed over the residual grumbling and hissing coming from the Aku.

"The tunnel. It should be abandoned soon. No one likes to stay around death for long. Stay hidden and sneak out. Remember to tell her or any of her followers who sent you.

"Yes, the Holy Spinner." Hégo narrowed his eyes in suspicion.

"Just say it!"

"What about the monks here? You promised me they would be safe."

"They will. No harm will come to them if they choose to follow me instead of the deceiver Gou-Tairei."

"There was nothing of this in our plan!"

"Plans change, monk!" Venom from her fangs began to pool around his feet. "If you want to reform your silly religion, then you will do as I say. You will have to abandon Aoheki now."

"Abandon it to you, you mean. Assure me that you will not abandon me. I need you."

"Assured. Leave!"

Hégo gingerly maneuvered himself around Ryudasu's legs and left the cell, making sure not to look at the hollow headless corpse of Ogushu. The strange thin man was still scratching away on his orange device, un-moved by the gore surrounding him.

I just sentenced the entire cloister to death.

"A necessity," responded Cane.

Yes. Necessity.

Everything was covered in a fine ash as if the battle had taken place centuries ago. Yuuki knelt beside his dead mother caressing her grimy forehead. He hovered his hand over her eyes to bring down her eyelids. They wouldn't close all the way. There was too much dust sticking to the glossless dead orbs. "I'm so sorry you had to die. It didn't need to happen." Yuuki felt another presence kneel next to him. Detecting a love's unique smell was as good as sight. He had to stop his tears from flowing. It would look strange to be crying for someone he supposedly had never known.

"I am so sorry, Shinya," Yuuki said as he rubbed Shinya's back. "She was your mother, right?"

"Yes, I have only re-connected with her, as you have probably guessed."

"I cannot imagine how you must feel right now." He could. "Please, take your time saying good-bye to her. It is not just us Wamono that go on living. It is everyone. They just do not know it." He was still using 'us' and was back inside the same walls he still hated.

Yuuki stood up and left Shinya to grieve alone. He ordered the Pollen to leave them be. *Amedo!* He was still carrying the glass container. There had been no connection between his mind and his tactile senses for the last several minutes. "Amedo?" He lifted the jar to his and looked to see if his old friend was alright or even still alive. There was slight movement. Yuuki let out a sigh of relief.

The water level inside the jar was dangerously low. Most of his tentacles were exposed to the stale air inside. They were above him, allowing his breathing parts to remain in the water. Yuuki saw the small crack causing the low water level.

He looked around trying to find someone to tell that he was going to find some water for his friend. He couldn't see any Guildsmen except those dead on the uneven floor. He saw Tomo looking for survivors among the fallen, particularly focusing on his former Tsudii colleagues.

"Tomo," Yuuki half yelled just to get his attention. "I am going to try to find water to save my friend."

"It is alright, friend," a voice gurgled from the container. "I can last a little while longer. It is best to make sure everything is settled here."

Yuuki smiled after hearing his friend's wise voice, even though it was weak, echoing pathetically off the grimy glass surface within. "There's not a lot of water left."

"Could you jiggle me around a bit so I can use one of my tentacles to seal off the crack?" That should do for a while. But do not forget me, Yuuki-Hana," the Yedo-setai bubbled a sage laugh.

Yuuki did as Amedo requested. It took a few shakes and jiggles, but eventually he got one of his suckered tentacles in the right position. During the jostling,

Yuuki turned himself around and saw Shinya collapsed over his mother's corpse, sobbing. Tears began to roll down his dirty cheeks at seeing the only person he had ever loved overtaken with despair. He wanted to cry with him, to tell him that she was his mother too. It wasn't the right time. He didn't know if there ever would be such a time.

"You cannot confess that." Charm's vibrations startled Yuuki. He almost dropped Amedo. "It would inject too many unknown variables into our plan. Maybe when we finally get rid of those other Symbs."

Nice of you to appear, said Yuuki. Frustrated at the inconsistency of his Symb.

"There was nothing I could or can do while another Symb was here," replied Charm.

Other Symb? Yuuki remembered the Editor and Ren. "Of course. Where are they?"

"Who?" Asked Tomo. He had walked up behind Yuuki. For a second Yuuki didn't know if the one-word question came from an Animate or Charm.

"The Editor and Ren."

"I don't know. I remember seeing the Editor, but I never saw the Suriidii queen."

You said 'Symb', Yuuki thought-spoke, hoping Charm hadn't tuned out already. *There was only one here*?

"Yes. Only one. Still is, but my sense is that the idol is quite weakened by an injury."

Which one?

"I don't know. I cannot determine individual idols. We can only sense another's presence.

"Tomo, get everyone to scan the bodies. The Editor or Ren is still here and alive."

"How do you know?" asked Tomo.

"I Just do, now go, please!" Ordered Yuuki. "I'll help." He looked towards his lover/brother and their mother. The heaving of Shinya's body slowed from grieving to sadness.

"You need to tell him who killed her, or more importantly, had her killed," advised Charm. "We need all the help we can when we will have to confront that arch Symb."

She has nothing to do with my nightmare visions.

"She had your mother killed," said Charm.

She was never my mother! It was getting more difficult to keep from yelling out loud at Charm. *She threw me away like a bin full of rotting compost. She would've done it again once she found out about us. I'm glad she's dead*! Yuuki regretted thinking those words.

"Good, good," calmly vibrated Charm. The vibrations up Yuuki's spine felt pleasant for a change. "But your Shinya probably thinks otherwise from the way he is behaving now. Would you want the murderer of his mother go unpunished?"

I don't want to have this conversation now. We need to ...

"Sensei!" The call from Tomo brought him back out from inside himself. "Over here. I found the Editor. He's wounded but still alive."

Yuuki watched a couple of the Pollen carry a mutilated corpse of a monk from the Master's cell now his temporary headquarters. It wasn't Hégo. The body was too young to be the old, rotted tree stump. There was no head, just a cavernous hole going deep down into the torso. It was so clean. *Ryudasu*. The room smelled of primal biology. *She was definitely here.*

"Sensei," said Tomo. His quiet respectful voice was in gross opposition to his form. "Here is the Reincarnate."

Tomo pushed a large flat cart with Amedo on top languid in a much larger container.

"Thank you, Tomo. Would it be possible for you to place him on the desk over there?" With a massive "issho", Tomo lifted the burdensome tank and gently placed it on the desk. Only a few splashes of water lopped over the rim. The desk creaked but held steady.

"Could you give us some time, Tomo?"

"Certainly. I will have a couple men stand guard outside. Tomo lumbered out the room and, again betraying his bulk, closed the door as if he was drawing a blanket over a sleeping child.

"Yuuki walked over to Amedo's tank. "I am so sorry for what you had to go through."

"Why should you apologize?" Amedo finally asked. You had nothing to do with this travesty."

"I think I have." Yuuki unconsciously fiddled with his bracelet. It was starting to stick to his skin; like it had been dropped in something gooey. It was more difficult to rub the charm between his thumb and forefinger. "I think I had a large role."

"I do not understand. How does that fit in with this invasion?"

"Unfortunately, I cannot explain it all to you now, but I do think I have something to do with them invading Aoheki." He brought around the sole chair in front of the tank and sat down. Everything suddenly seemed so fragile. The chair, desk, even his Reincarnate friend. He looked up at the walls encasing him in this cell and thought of the ominous barrier walls, imagining even those bastions of permanence crumbling into a long soft dyke of dust and dying grey moss. He looked back down at his friend. He wondered if the gentle Reincarnate was thinking of the same fragility around them. "Do you know what happened? I mean before we arrived? I heard yelling."

"Yes, I do," said Amedo. "There was betrayal."

"Yes. Ryudasu saw to that."

"No, Yuuki. Betrayal amongst them. The woman betrayed the other two by apparently stealing away to Yedo. By the reaction of the Editor and Ryudasu, that was not part of the plan."

"Yedo?" Yuuki's voice formed it as a question. In his mind, it was more of a disembodied realization. "It is true, then."

"What is true?" Asked Amedo. "What do you know?"

"I do not know what I know, only what I have seen but did not in actuality see," Yuuki replied. He stood up and walked to under the window high above, looking at the sliver of sky. He began to explain his visions of a ruined city. That he believed the destruction had something to do with the two insane prophets. He also confessed to ingesting his friend's ink but wasn't ready to confess the self-addiction.

"And you are feeling well?" Amedo swirled his tentacles in worry. "You feel as though you still have your wits, yourself, still?"

"Yes, sensei." I believe my so-called purity helped reduce the deadly affects."

"Very well." Responded Amedo. The response was not convincing. "Now we have the connection."

"Connection?" Yuuki stopped himself from sounding frustrated.

"My ink. It expands reality, so it makes sense that it would give you those visions."

Yuuki stared at his friend. "My visions were from your ink." He knew for a while that was the case, but it wasn't any easier getting confirmation. He dropped his head into his consoling palms.

"Yuuki-Hana," began Amedo. "My ink has a different effect depending on who ingests it and with what. The commonality is that is broadens one's perspective, one's universe so to speak. Thus, it was also due to you, not just the ink." He lifted and stretched out a tentacle toward his friend.

Yuuki felt the soft rubbery appendage gently touching his lowered head. He spoke without lifting his head. He was too embarrassed. "How do you know all this. Who else have you given your ink to?" His voice was muffled by his mask of hands.

"You were not the first, Yuuki-Hana." Replied Amedo. His tentacle still laying on Yuuki's head. "You know the other Masters take a special substance to communicate with each other?"

"Yes, Goushintei," replied Yuuki.

"One of the main ingredients is my ink. It is the only physical substance allowed to be transported among cloisters. Even when diluted, it can be quite dangerous, even deadly." Amedo tentacles drooped to the bottom of the tank. "Poor dear Kugai-sama."

"What do you mean?" Yuuki's stomach tightened then twisted from hearing those three words together."

"You do not see Kugai-sama here, do you?"

"No." Shame rouged Yuuki's cheeks for not having him in his mind this whole time. "Is he imprisoned someplace? Did Ryudasu do something to him?" Quick rage welled up. He wanted to scratch at the walls until they began to crumble away from his power or until his hands rubbed raw to stumps. It didn't matter which.

"No, he passed on to his next cycle shortly before all this happened. He had an unfortunate incident with the Goushintei. He went mad then eventually expired, here in this cell. Hégo-sama became Master." Amedo bubbled out a sigh. "I am afraid he had something to do with this invasion."

I just assumed he would be here. Yuuki thought. He had to shake himself out of the sudden onslaught of mourning. *Where is Hégo? Dead too. Escaped? Am I the new Master of the Cloister?* Yuuki slammed a fist down on the desk. *I do not want it!*

"You should. You need to act quickly and show yourself as this place's savior," said Charm.

Amedo shuddered away from the sudden reaction but continued. "Unfortunately, I only found out today that the ink has even more power than I could ever have known."

"What do you mean? What happened?"

"That was how that woman disappeared to Yedo. Or at least that is where they all thought they would go. They mixed my ink with the cloister's grapes."

"So, that horrible woman is now in Yedo?"

"I do not know if she made it to Yedo, or even it is even possible. I only know that was the intention. I can only hope it did not work. It goes against everything we stand for."

"What 'we' stand for does not matter. I saw what would happen if they made it there. It is more than just our beliefs coming into question." Yuuki couldn't help sounding angry. He knew his friend was simply trying to explain things.

"It did not go as planned, Yuuki-Hana," said Amedo. "Both or perhaps all three were planning to do so. So maybe—"

"No. It was supposed to be," Yuuki interrupted. He remembered the giants in his apocalyptic vision and connected her and her golems.

"We have to assume she did and that something bad will still come of it." He took in a deep breath. "The ink. I can drink more and try to find out more." All this talk about ink was making his addiction claw at the lining of his stomach.

"I am sorry, Yuuki,' said Amedo. "She squeezed me too hard in trying to get all the ink out of me. I am afraid my gland is damaged."

"Are you alright?" Asked Yuuki. He scolded himself for not making sure his friend wasn't seriously injured. *I need more fresh ink. I need to get more of it into my blood.*

"Yes, but I do not think I will be able to produce any more."

Yuuki felt the now all too familiar tingle of vibration run up his spine to his brain. "No need worrying about it now," interrupted Charm. "We need to concentrate on solidifying our power here before we can continue on this inky path of saving the two worlds."

"Shut up!" Yelled Yuuki. He couldn't control himself. He didn't want to hear what Charm had to say. He wanted more ink. He bit into the permanent wound inside his lip. He winced for just a second before relaxing into a barely noticeable stupor.

"Yuuki, I am sorry if I angered you in any way," said Amedo. He dipped back down farther below the water surface.

"No, Amedo. I was not talking to you. I was talking to myself. Sorry."

"What is tormenting you, Yuuki?" asked Amedo. "Your moods are swinging wildly."

"I just fought a battle where dozens were killed. I have had visions of mass destruction that apparently I can only see, and I am the only one who can change them. My moth ...." Yuuki stopped himself. Bringing up his mother's death was not something he wanted to talk about, even to his best friend.

"Of course. Who would not have such manic emotions," continued Amedo. "What happened to you out there? You seem a grown man with decades of experience."

"The outside will do that, I guess," responded Yuuki.

"We cannot stay here all day and talk to this chatty Reincarnate," interrupted Charm. "We should get on with taking back control of Aoheki."

"Take ..." He almost forgot to change his voice again. *Take it back? I never had control of it to begin with. I want to talk with my friend*! Yuuki wondered if this was what going insane meant—talking to two planes of existence simultaneously and the line blurring between the two.

"You know what I meant," said Charm. "Taking control wouldn't be the end of the world. It might save it."

"Are you sure you are alright?" Amedo asked.

"Yes, just all the stress from the last few days is trying to find its way out, that is all." Yuuki sat back down on the fragile chair and looked over the edge of the temporary pool trying to suppress his ink lust. "Did you see what happened to Ryudasu?"

"No, I did not. I can only assume she is still hiding out someplace inside the cloister. She is a Reincarnate, so she cannot physically step outside the cloister."

"That is not good, is it?"

"No, it is not. She is desperate. There is no telling what she will do next. If this is all true and there is some metaphysical means of being transported to Yedo, we cannot have her, especially her, going there.

"You are right," said Yuuki. "I have to take control of this cloister and seal off the root cellar and that damn tunnel.

"Will the Conclave go along with this?" Asked Amedo. "They do not like to go against convention."

"They gave up all power here when they lost the cloister to the insane prophets," said Yuuki. He was going to be the Master of the Cloister. The pride felt strange and not all his own.

"Very well, if that is what needs to be done, then I will support you. You seem to have found yourself in being a leader out there. No reason you cannot be one here." Amedo lowered himself deeper beneath the water surface after giving his blessing.

"Well, don't we all feel better that the creature agrees with us," said Charm.

Quiet! thought-spoke Yuuki. *You are getting what you want.*

"It's not just me, my prophet."

Charm's 'my' had a possessive tone that made Yuuki begin to sweat. He looked down smiling into the make-shift pool. Everything seemed to be settling down out in the wider cloister. The silence was welcome. "Dear friend, I am going to move you back to your original pool if that is O.K. with you. I will have our prisoner put up here instead of in the infirmary. It is too full and who knows what harm he could still do to others around him."

"Very well, Yuuki. I look forward to being back home."

Home, thought Yuuki. *Such an inconceivable concept.*

forty-two

"**W**HERE'S VIKI? IF SHE** failed, she'd better be dead." Any semblance of the human Mimi had disappeared days ago without her realizing. Her Mary-Janes were there only signs of her every existing.

"If she succeeded, she will be here soon." Palace was a comfortable hum through Mimi's consciousness. "I am receiving city motions and vibrations that whatever happened at Aoheki had happened and ended.

"Those two psychotics are too preoccupied with that ridiculous cloister." Mimi knew she should actively do something but couldn't bring herself to get up, even to the window.

"Let them have that pile of stone and moss under their control. I will never understand or care to understand the simplistic reasoning of lower idols.

"What do we need to concentrate on now, then?" *I'm so comfortable. Why? Things are falling apart all around us.*

"What about your monk?"

"Yuuki?" Mimi sensed the jitter of conflict in her bones. "You just said lesser idols are not much of a worry."

"It depends on the host as well. The Editor and Ren are not the most, let's say, radiant of the population. We could perhaps play nice with him or pretend to do so for the time being because, my dear, I think it time to concern ourselves with the Mayor."

"Already? Can't it wait to be a crisis until the others have been taken care of?" Mimi was no longer a woman, even human, but she kept her petulant attitude.

"I wish that were the case, my dear. "I'm feeling unsettling shakes from the direction of Juku. It is aware of a threat, of us." Palace's vibrations were progressively becoming less of an experience to Mimi and more abstract just like here own thoughts. Their communications were becoming of the same self, and Mimi preferred it. She had never been so relaxed and comfortable in her life. She didn't want it to end. Let Palace handle everything.

A ding sounded as the elevator doors opened. Viki walked through the opening out of breath. "I rushed here as fast as I could to tell ..." She stopped and looked around the suite and the empty couch and foot-less Mary-Janes. "Mimi? Mi?" The suite was completely empty. She walked over to an egg chair to catch her breath. She grabbed tight around her parasol ready for any attack, not from any intruder but by this building. "She's really gone." She sighed and leaned back into the egg hoping to disappear herself.

"I'm here."

"It is your voice, kind of. But it is not you" Viki didn't understand any of this Symb stuff. Her former gunshyu had always been Symb free. She stayed crouched inside the egg, knowing very well this thing had its no-eyes on her at all times from everywhere.

"I'm here, my dear. I've always been. Has the plan succeeded. Is she dead?"

"Yea. Dead." Viki felt weird talking to a building that was Mimi and was nothing of her. She did not want to converse with this all-together different entity.

Viki felt a slight rumble and her egg began to sway, almost imperceptible at first but slowly increased in intensity. She instinctively grabbed hold of the egg's edges and pressed her feet more firmly on the floor. "Is that you, Mimi?"

"No, it is not me."

The entire building began to shake. It began with a grumble from deep within the ground, then Viki was lifted from the egg for a split second then a crashing down, an invisible body slam. The ceiling support wire for the chair strained from the invisible attack. "Are you falling apart? What the fuck is happening!"

"I am perfectly fine, my dear. I can withstand a little grumbling tantrum." The Palace/Mimi voice remained calm as if nothing out of the ordinary was happening. "It seems I've gotten the attention of the Mayor."

"It looks like the storyboard has changed," said the Editor. His voice barely audible and his rogue hands too weak to add anything to the increasingly finite air drawing.

The prisoner's eyes were barely open. Yuuki wondered if they ever could close completely. *What a horrible existence to always be seeing.* There was no reason to restrain the Editor. His arms were useless and wounds too serious. Yuuki had him put in Hégo's former cell. A bed was already there, and it was secluded. He made sure to leave a good amount of distance between him and the dangerous casualty.

"It seems that way," replied Yuuki. He brought around the chair from the desk and placed in front of the bed. When he sat down, the chair sighed creaks.

"You've done well for yourself since your escape, naughty little exhibit," said the Editor. "How does it feel to be back home."

"This is not my home!" Yuuki shouted. There would be no way of going back to the old customs and rituals this place forced him to adhere to for two decades. He experienced the outside; there would no longer be any inside/outside.

"Very well, then," the Editor acquiesced with a sneer. "Just get on with whatever you came here for." He moaned in pain and touched the left side of his shirtless chest, wet with blood that seeped through carelessly applied bandaging. Yuuki studied the wound. The blood looked different, blacker than the redder-than-black oozing from other parts of his body.

"I came to get some answers," replied Yuuki. He stood with his arms crossed and hands hidden in the sleeves of his kimono. "Why did you and your enemy suddenly team up to invade Aoheki?"

"How about a bit of give and take, my fellow prophet?" The Editor turned the grimace of pain into a smirk of satisfaction.

"You are in no position to make deals," Yuuki barked, leaning forward a little hoping to still intimidate. "I am in no way a peer of yours."

"Oh, I don't know about that. I can die a silent man. It doesn't matter to me," replied the Editor.

A faint vibration shimmied up Yuuki's back. "Don't let him get into your head," said Charm, slightly weakened by the incapacitated Draw.

"You know. I see a lot of myself in you," continued the prisoner. "I was an outcast, just like you. Too small to be of any use to society. That's what they all thought, even my so-called mother."

Yuuki had a hard time believing he had a mother. But it piqued his curiosity. "I was never an outcast. I chose to leave on my own accord."

The Editor forced himself through the pain to sit up a bit. "You sure about that? How did you get there?"

"I am asking the questions," said Yuuki. "Why did you invade Aoheki?"

"Very well. There's no reason for me to keep it all within me. It's done. we failed." He scrunched his face in frustration then released a succumbing sigh. "Could you be a good lad and reach down into my pants pocket. I have something of yours."

"I'm not falling for your tricks!"

"No tricks. I'm in no position to carry out any. It's your little map. I have it."

"I don't want it. It's not mine. It's that Aku's useless map."

"Oh, I think you would want it after I tell you what it is really a map of." The Editor tried to smile, instead went into a coughing fit, spewing a fine bloody mist.

"You see, Atsushi ... Ren was my brother a very long time ago and in another world." With increasingly longer periods of labored breathing between explanations, the captive daigunshyu leader told the story, at least what he knew of it, of why he and his sibling invaded Aoheki with the help of Ryudasu. That something went wrong, or rather his sibling betrayed him and left for Yedo without him.

"Yedo is real," said Yuuki. He didn't know if he should be relieved or frightened. "So, the map— "

The Editor quietly laughed, coughing up just enough spittle to reinvigorate the dried blood crusting the corners of his mouth. "You're not as dumb as I thought."

"Apparently it is not just a Wamono myth," Charm almost whispered.

"You know we are quite alike, you and me," said the Editor. He pushed himself up a bit more.

"How's that?" Asked Yuuki. He didn't believe a word of it, but he was curious. At least he was talking.

"We both wanted to go home ... and failed."

How did he know so much about him? He had to start taking Charm's advice more seriously. The stunted creep was seeping into his head. But the Editor was right, he did fail. He was back where he started, surrounded by the same Gou-cursed walls that imprisoned him his whole life.

The Editor continued. "We both wasted our time on silly adventures that proved worthless." Yuuki noticed the annoying smirk the child-sized man constantly wore was beginning to fade. "I'm not the only prisoner here." The smirk came back, even more mocking. "Maybe we were never meant to go home." His black-egg eyes began to reveal something else to Yuuki.

"You and I were never a 'we'," Yuuki responded.

"Yes 'we' are. Much more than you think."

"Be careful Yuuki," said Charm. "He is trying to cause an imbalance within you. He and his idol are weak, but they can still do damage."

What does he mean? Should I take the bait or ignore it? The dichotomy of everything was afflicting him with psychic vertigo.

The Editor decided for him. There was no ignoring what he spoke. "You see, we are both victims of our environment." The disorientating facial expressions were still confusing Yuuki. Which one was really him? "And more importantly, our families."

"Families? You know nothing about my family." Yuuki clenched his fists the way he used to when being scolded by Kugai. He quickly spread his fingers out under his sleeves. *I'm no longer a child.*

The Editor snapped to attention as if he had never been wounded and stared at Yuuki with his large empty eyes weeping blood. "No! It is you who knows nothing!" His angry mouth quickly elongated back into its usual smirk, but longer than usual, his eyes squinted, as much as those huge unnatural orbs could, and made a futile attempt to shade them with his shriveled shaking hand. "I know all about yours." If his grey lips stretched any further both ends would end up touching his oversized earlobes. Yuuki knew that it was the Editor's Inanimate forcing him to calm down and compose himself. He was starting to learn the language of Totality insanity.

Yuuki leaned in close to try to intimidate the man not even half his size. He had no idea if it would work. "I barely know anything about them."

"This is what he wants," said Charm. "It's your choice if you want to go down this path. I helped you see what I could show you about your family. If you are desperate enough to know more, then listen to what this little terror has to say. But I warned you, Yuuki, and I will warn you again. Are you strong enough?"

The last few of Charm's words died away as if fleeing the scene. Yuuki sat there staring at his prisoner, watching the minute droplets of blood ooze out from the bottom arcs of his eyes. They were rapidly increasing in number and size. He was suffering and increasingly so. "I'm sure you would like your glasses back or dim the cell more by blocking out that window. We have your glasses; unfortunately, they are of no use, busted." He pointed to the small window high above burning brightness into the Editor's captive eyes. "But, putting something in front of the window should not be a problem."

"And what do I have to do, if I wanted to that is?" The Editor tried shutting his eyes, conscious of the show of weakness.

"Tell me what you know about my family, that is all. I know you want to tell me." Yuuki mirrored the smile of his interlocutor's. "Remember this, I know what you and your god are trying to do. You cannot play with a mind that is more than ready to play."

"Very well," said the Editor. "I do want to tell you. You dangling a lightless room in front of me is neither here nor there to me. You think I don't know suffering? This is nothing." He raised his hand to shield the light again, knowing that it was no use in hiding it any longer. "Thanks to my talent of recognizing family resemblances." He chuckled, coughing up phlegmy blood "It's the eyes; always the eyes."

Several of the viscous drops landed on Yuuki's hand. He didn't bother wiping them off. He let the Editor continue.

"After adding several other twos and twos together, I had my remaining Storyliner do a bit of back-storying. And you know what? I realized I am partly responsible for you being born. Fancy that." This time his chuckle was more cough. "I just shrugged it off since I thought I would never see you again. But here we are."

The pores all over Yuuki's skin burst open releasing the rapid buildup of heat his mind unleashed to deal with the onslaught. "What do you mean you were partly responsible?" He let out a condescending laugh and continued. "Do not tell me you are my father. I had enough family reunions today."

"Of course I'm not. Don't be ridiculous. I lost my reproductive abilities decades ago."

The image of this man participating in any sort of sexual act repulsed Yuuki. "Then, please do tell me, how are you responsible?" He tried to be flippant but was anxious to know.

"I've always had a thing for your mother," the Editor began. "I noticed her when we first started doing business with her and her husband, who by the way was not your father." His smirk transformed into a normal smile with real feeling. "She was beautiful. Those soft milk chocolate eyes always coyly hidden by the curtains of her black bangs. I never saw her smile. I didn't get to see her very often, I don't get out to personally conduct business. But when I did, I never saw her smile. Not that it was a negative thing. Quite the opposite. The quiet restrained beauty she exuded was perfection."

So far, nothing was said that would push Yuuki over the edge. He fully expected something and braced himself for it. *He's playing with me. Being soft until I'm exposed raw for the kill.* "So, you knew her from afar. I'm sure many have. What makes you so connected to me?"

"Like you, I'm a failure. There was no way to entice her away from her family to me. I know what I look like. This," he tried to wave his free hand over himself, "is a sacrifice." He smiled revealing bloody teeth. "You'll have to make a similar sacrifice soon enough."

"Get on with this farce." Yuuki needed to keep such sidetracks at bay. That was where the real danger lurked.

"Yes, of course. He leaned toward Yuuki and lifted one corner of his smirk as if they were both co-conspirators of an inside joke, "I had a mixi-matchi doc neuro re-wire one of my Storyliners to see if I could experience more … normal … life events through him. It was no easy task by the way."

Yuuki didn't want to know the inner workings of the bizarro world of the Tsudii. "And?"

The Editor continued. "I could feel the same sensations experienced by this Storyliner, though imperfectly. He didn't know about it. That would've been a bit too weird." Yuuki remained quiet. "Purely by coincidence, I sent him to, eh, address a minor issue with a manga shop concerning their sales policies. Things went a bit sideways, which happens quite often. The owners turned out to be your mother and her husband, not your father. I/the Storyliner confronted the husband, not your father, on his way back to the store from some errand. He was of course rather reluctant to resolve the issue and I/the Storyliner had to do a bit of an old-fashioned chase. We, me/Storyliner, and the husband, not your father, ended up at the store. Unfortunately, he didn't survive the consequences of not wanting to resolve this issue.

Yuuki kept his mouth shut thinking the cumbersome monologue would end shortly.

I saw his wife, your mother, being ever so bold and defending her now dead husband, not your father. It was her." The editor smiled. "It almost looked like a normal loving smile. This Storyliner had his own urges of course, and upon seeing your beautiful mother his angry lust took over. It was my chance to feel her the way I could never have any other way." He looked up toward the searing light to feel the pain. "She just disappeared."

Yuuki put his hand up to stop the Editor from continuing his gruesome story. "So, you raped my mother by proxy and your, whatever, puppet goon, is my father."

"Yes, you can put it like that, I suppose. He *was* your father. That bitch who's now the new Oné-chan assassinated him, along with any chance of ever reuniting with your mother." The Editor slumped back against the wall, his brow rough with mourning furrows.

Mimi? His head felt like a series of shorting lights flickering on and off depending on what the other did. The connections were there, but nothing was yet fully comprehensible.

The Editor continued. "Everything forgotten except for that annoying lingering sense of loss. That was until I saw here lifeless on the dirty floor below."

Rage at this horrific storyteller and Mimi's involvement in his mother's death contracted every muscle in his body to their shaking point. He swung his mass down to the Editor's shocked face. "You killed my mother long before today!"

The echoes from the outburst bounced chaotically around the small cell, each bounce warped the palimpsest voice further until it was no longer recognizable as human. He reached down toward the gasping invalid's heart and grabbed hold of the weakened god. "We are nothing alike!" He let gravity fight back and take control of the rest of the Editor's beaten body. Yuuki heard the flesh begin to tear around where his hand was grasping, his fingertips digging deeper as the flesh ripping progressed. Yuuki grinned at the powerless freak's whimpering turn to screams, tears drowning his eyes. *Am I doing this? This is you, not me!*

"It is all you, Yuuki-Hana, the Azalea Prophet. All us," answered Charm.

Yuuki felt the weight in his hand diminish greatly then heard a thud onto the bed. He squeezed his eyes shut to clear them of tears and opened them to look at what was still in his shaking hand. The utili-god Draw, a simple fountain pen, attached to a chunk of skin and flesh, felt cold. Yuuki inhaled a shuddery breath and looked under the umbrella of dripping frayed flesh. The Editor's heart, struggling to complete one last pump of non-existent blood, hung from the dead god.

Yuuki closed his eyes. The darkness was comforting. "I do not want to become this. But I must." He opened his eyes and focused on an outcropping of jagged stone making up the sweating wall on the other side of the Editor's bed and noticed a thin coating of bubbling orange-yellow fungus. He looked away, ashamed and let drop the one-time god, now just an unusable pen, and the Editor's still heart. He reached into the dead man's pocket and took out the supposed map of Yedo. It brought back memories of a person he no longer was. He wanted to rip it up and throw the confetti over the dead false prophet. But he put it into his kimono sleeve and quietly walked out the cell, inhaling the cool refreshing mineral humidity of the corridor.

A bracing wind screeched like long-suffering banshees outside the makeshift swaddle of webbing Ryudusu finished constructing. The constricting refuge dangled by a strong anchoring strand from the summit of the barrier wall; a sickly spidery yellow-green beacon within the soft opaque womb of the summit pall. The last few shivers from the biting wind ripped through her, forcing her abdomen to glow.

She peered through a semi-translucent section of webbing trying to make out anything through the suffocating cloud. There hadn't been a break in the ashy morass since she escaped the chaos far below, and there never would be this far up. Her nemesis in godliness had made sure that none of her pincers would be allowed to even tap onto the condemned ground of Hinodé.

She growled-hissed to herself. "Even a god must go through cumbersome trials." All forms of revenge fought for attention on the battleground of her sizzling synapses.

She dreamed focused into the grey nothing. "Cousin, I assume you had reasons for your betrayal. If you are there, and alive, there is still hope for the plan. I will choose to forgive you, and I will convince your bother to do the same. He must." A gust slammed against the cocoon, forcing her to adjust her weight to counter the assault. The silky bulb finally began to settle, but she had to remain tense. More gusts were inevitable. "You, monk. We will have to have another meeting soon, very soon. You still could be useful."

Strange movements began to sway then jolt her cocoon. They were not sky born but coming up to her from unknowable depths. She grumbled up a chuckle "Ahhh. My fellow disgraced god. Do not worry. I have not forgotten. I will not grant you second chances. You will have my pleasure of the most intense suffering within this web of hell you weaved." She struggled to caress her fangs with her restricted front legs and brought the sweet-tasting leftover monk gore to her frenzied mouthparts. "Hatred is inertia, forming a hard scabby prison. I have been its prisoner for too long. Vengeance will give me strength to break away. It is the providence I bestow upon myself."

Yuuki picked up the fragrance of another life as he stood in the middle of his old cell. The three beds were silent, the linen disheveled.

He quietly, he thought everything should be done quietly now, took a couple steps over to Shinya's old bed. He stroked the bed, feeling the subtle hills and valleys formed by the undisturbed blanket. He smiled. It seemed years ago when he studied, slept, and dreamed of a day he would be able to leave. Now it all seemed ridiculous.

He fought the desire to curl himself up on Shinya's cot. He walked the five steps over to his, again as quietly as possible, and sat down. He attempted to convince himself he had put the Editor out his misery, but it was murder. He fought back a smile he knew Charm was trying to make him express. His back arched forward, turning his upper body into a ball. *The Editor was right, we both failed.*

"I have to disagree," Charm interrupted. For the first time, the vibrations didn't jolt Yuuki. "Look at what you have accomplished in such a short time."

"What accomplishments haven't been followed by more intense failure?" Yuuki asked. He wasn't in the mood for a pep talk, especially from a selfish Inanimate. "Yes, I got out of here. But I followed Ryudasu's orders, big failure. I found where I came from thanks to you, but I was stupid enough to be imprisoned as one of the Editor's freak-show exhibits, another failure. I'm now some kind of neo-Wamono spiritual leader. I wanted to get away from everything Wamono, failure. I've come to terms with the fact that this is my home, but it still does not feel like much of an accomplishment. I found that I could see into a terrifying future and naïvely believed I could change that future, double failure. It was not me but Amedo's ink, and the future could still turn out just as horrible, perhaps even more so."

"There's no point dwelling on the failures along the way. You are still young in this life," said Charm. "Hasn't any of the old monks told you that success is built on a foundation of failure or some other similar drivel?" If Charm had the same kind of human feelings, he was sure it was not enjoying this little pep talk it was forced to give.

The thought forced a small convulsion of laughter to escape through Yuuki's nose. "Just let me get this out. You probably wouldn't understand." He continued his list of successes followed by painful failures. "I found my mother. But I still hated her, even now. But she's dead because of me. Despite the hate, I always hoped we could somehow work through that. That's no longer possible."

"I would put more blame on that friend of yours," said Charm.

Yuuki ignored his idol and continued to the one failure he most hated to admit. "Shinya. I'm failing Shinya right now." The urge to go over and wrap himself up in Shinya's thin blanket; to take in his essence, was strong. "I am lying to him. He is my brother, but I need him as my lover. I am as selfish as you."

A vibrational sigh crept through Yuuki. "You must keep it a lie. We need him. He can be your lover, brother, or both after we have settled things here."

"Settled?" Yuuki almost shouted. "When will all this end? Because I want it to end now!"

"Yuuki-Hana; the Azalea Prophet—"

"Do not call me that," Yuuki said as if he was whispering in someone's ear. It was useless to fight it. The name was going to stick. "Getting back on track. Is that what you are only concerned with?"

"What else is there to be of concern?" Replied Charm. "You are boring me and yourself with is pointless whining. Once we take control of our life and take care of whatever is threatening here and ... there," Yuuki knew it was referring flippantly to Yedo. "Then all this sniveling and pining will seem a bit embarrassing."

Yuuki's left hand involuntarily reached over and began to feel for the silver flower charm. He looked down to find the clasp holding the bracelet around his wrist. It was gone. He looked closer. The two meeting ends had burrowed into his skin. He wanted to rip out the ends from his wrist, but they wouldn't come out or he did not want them to come out. The skin around the injected string of metal stretched out into pale peaks, fighting with equal force to hold onto what it detected as part of itself.

"There's no use, Yuuki-Hana," said Charm. "It is an inevitable occurrence of us being in Totality. It is to ensure that we will never become separated. I don't understand why you are feigning fighting this. We have been working so well together."

Yuuki stopped the pulling. "We have? Then why am I here. Why am I not with my mother, still alive, trying to set things right with Shinya by my side as my brother instead of a lover lied to? Why am I back in this miserable dank fortress and not out in my real home?" There was no response coming from within. He was sure one of the Guildsmen would have a metal cutter he could use.

"I wouldn't attempt that," replied Charm. The vibrations were the most active they've been for days.

Yuuki, slouching further into himself. "And why is that?"

"Feel me."

"I feel you. Those shock waves you shoot through my body are evidence to that."

"No. I mean feel, touch, me."

Yuuki looked down to the bracelet, to the physical manifestation of the being that was living more in his head than anywhere else. "I've been touching you for the last few minutes."

"Touch, not pull. Touch and feel me."

Yuuki rolled his eyes and let his left hand rest over Charm. He waited for a few seconds but felt nothing. "I feel cold metal."

"Wait," said Charm.

Yuuki kept his hand on the now hated bracelet. A faint rhythmic pulse began to register with the nerves embedded in his hand. *Fumpwom, fumpwom, fumpwom.* It was almost soothing until he realized why. *Heartbeats.* He lifted the braceleted palm to his chest, while the other remained on Charm. Both hands sensed the same beating.

"If you cut me out, you will cut your life," explained Charm, not threatening but gently stating a factual warning.

The beating intensified, escaping into the stone floor then up the walls. Puddles of wall tears rippled, and dust rained down from the ceiling and formed grey cataracts down the walls. The entire cloister trembled.

"Is this us?" Yuuki tried to stand, but the shaking was too destabilizing. He had to sit back down on his cot. "Are we doing this?"

"I don't think so," responded Charm. "I believe it is something larger in the world."

"It is the Gou-Tairei. It has come out of its ambivalence to punish those of us who destroyed one of its cloisters." Yuuki crouch back rolled his body onto the cot curled into himself sobbing. "It is my fault, all of this. I am doomed to be like Ryudasu, probably worse."

"Don't be so arrogant. Not yet. This is not about us. It is simply a ground-shake."

Their Totality may be in its infancy, but Yuuki already knew when Charm was not telling the truth.

"Place your hands back on me and your chest. It will calm you."

Yuuki obeyed, but it was not entirely of his agency. The two beats as one did calm him. He felt the beats forming an invisible bubble around him, muting the rumbling and dampening the jolts. He stretched himself out of his ball of self-pity but kept his hands where they were, closed his eyes, and let the synchronized pulses sooth his tired mind. He felt Charm melt further into his wrist, with just the silver azalea dangling like a sole star of a hidden constellation. He kept rubbing it between his thumb and forefinger. "Bigman *has* arrived."

I The City tremble, roil. Not from fatuous emotion but against complacency. I The City exist for no reason than to be, to innervate the urban life force of decadence through perpetual creation and destruction, thus neither. I The City have no anger, no joy, no revenge, no pity, though they thrive as weeds to nourish the fauna within inflicting no disquiet but bestowing diversion. Their gluttony is the comedy performed upon the stage of savagery.

I The City am worlds; the sum of all, existing to be. I The City persist, amplify, escalate, inviting infinite choice and digression. I The City am the custodian; god-thing to all, savior to none.

Look for Book 2 in the Scorned World Series Coming soon!

For updates subscribe to the UrbanWeirdist newsletter https://urbanweird.com

Acknowledgment

I wish to thank my beta-readers Alex, Joy, and Michael; later beta reader/editor Nathan.

About the Author

Brian's creative work reflects his interest in the concept of The City as a living being both independent of and intimately connected to The Human. Because cities are beings, they have the same complexities as humans, e.g., changing moods from melancholia and broken to proud and whimsical; in other words, wonderfully weird. One goal with his writing is to give the reader/explorer an opportunity to simply contemplate their place, mentally or physically, in relation to the urban environment. How do they feel/fit in with the towering scrapers, littered alleys, masses of unimaginable diverse inhabitants, and crisscrossing orderly chaos of trains, subways, and cars? Is this all alien, a fantasy, or is it just too real?

Because of his upbringing in rural Pennsylvania in the US, The City has always been a fantastical world, something so different and wonderful; a place of hardened gritty acceptance where one can be who they really are. Even though he has been living in cities for a good part of his life, he still has that sense of living in a fantasy world where things are just weird enough to be interesting and many times disconcerting. The City is multi-dimensional, so limiting The City to just one would not do it justice.

The main influences in his creative expression are the writers and novelists of the New Weird who often set their stories and novels in outlandish decadent cities both imagined and real...ish. Thus, he constantly aspires to have his art to be 'Urban Weird'. The keywords he thinks of when being creative are "Decadence", "Banality" (making the weird mundane and the mundane weird), "Disorientating", the Japanese aesthetic concept of "Wabi-Sabi", and of course "City" and "Weird".

You can find more information about Brian and join his UrbanWeirdist newsletter at **www.urbanweird.com**

www.ingramcontent.com/pod-product-compliance
Lightning Source LLC
Chambersburg PA
CBHW030846030726
47495CB00005B/1399